SNUFF

Also by Terry Pratchett

The Carpet People

The Dark Side of the Sun

Strata

Good Omens
(WITH NEIL GAIMAN)

FOR YOUNG ADULTS

The Bromeliad Trilogy:
Truckers · Diggers · Wings

The Johnny Maxwell Trilogy:
Only You Can Save
Mankind · Johnny and the
Dead · Johnny and the Bomb

The Unadulterated Cat
(ILLUSTRATED BY GRAY JOLLIFE)

Nation

THE DISCWORLD® BOOKS

The Color of Magic

The Light Fantastic

Equal Rites

Mort

Sourcery

Wyrd Sisters

Pyramids

Guards! Guards!

Eric
(WITH JOSH KIRBY)

Moving Pictures

Reaper Man

Witches Abroad

Small Gods

Lords and Ladies

Men at Arms

Soul Music

Feet of Clay

Interesting Times

Maskerade

Hogfather

Jingo

The Last Continent

Carpe Jugulum

The Fifth Elephant

The Truth

Thief of Time

Night Watch

Monstrous Regiment

Going Postal

Thud!

SNUFF

A Novel of Discworld®

Terry Pratchett

HARPER

An Imprint of HarperCollinsPublishers
www.harpercollins.com

HarperCollins books may be purchased for educational, business, or sales promotional use. For information, please write: Special Markets Department, HarperCollins Publishers, 10 East 53rd Street, New York, NY 10022.

Published simultaneously in Great Britain by Doubleday, an imprint of Transworld Publishers, a division of the Random House Group, Ltd.

FIRST EDITION

Designed by William Ruoto

Frontispiece by Paul Kidby

Library of Congress Cataloging-in-Publication Data has been applied for.

ISBN: 978-0-06-201184-8

11 12 13 14 15   OV/QGF   10 9 8 7 6 5 4 3 2 1

For Rob . . . for in between his days off.

For Emma . . . for helping me understand goblins.

And for Lyn . . . for always.

SNUFF

The goblin experience of the world is the cult or perhaps religion of Unggue. In short, it is a remarkably complex resurrection-based religion founded on the sanctity of bodily secretions. Its central tenet runs as follows: everything that is expelled from a goblin's body was clearly once part of them and should, therefore, be treated with reverence and stored properly so that it can be entombed with its owner in the fullness of time. In the meantime the material is stored in unggue pots, remarkable creations of which I shall speak later.

A moment's distasteful thought will tell us that this could not be achieved by any creature, unless in possession of great wealth, considerable storage space and compliant neighbors.

Therefore, in reality, most goblins observe the Unggue Had—what one might term the common and lax form of Unggue—which encompasses earwax, finger- and toenail clippings, and snot. Water, generally speaking, is reckoned as not unggue, but something which goes through the body without ever being part of it: they reason that there is no apparent difference in the water before and after, as it were (which sadly shines a light on the freshness of the water they encounter in their underground lairs). Similarly feces are considered to be food that has merely undergone a change of state. Surprisingly, teeth are of no interest to the goblins, who look on them as a type of fungus, and they appear to attach no importance to hair, of which, it has to be said, they seldom have very much.

At this point, Lord Vetinari, Patrician of Ankh-Morpork, stopped reading and stared at nothing. After a few seconds, nothing was eclipsed by the form of Drumknott, his secretary (who, it must be said, had spent a career turning himself into something as much like nothing as anything).

Drumknott said, "You look pensive, my lord," to which observation he appended a most delicate question mark, which gradually evaporated.

"Awash with tears, Drumknott, awash with tears."

Drumknott stopped dusting the impeccably shiny black lacquered desk. "Pastor Oats is a very persuasive writer, isn't he, sir . . . ?"

"Indeed he is, Drumknott, but the basic problem remains and it is this: humanity may come to terms with the dwarf, the troll and even the orc, terrifying though all these may have proved to be at times, and you know why this is, Drumknott?"

The secretary carefully folded the duster he had been using and looked at the ceiling. "I would venture to suggest, my lord, that in their violence we recognize ourselves?"

"Oh, well done, Drumknott, I shall make a cynic of you yet! Predators respect other predators, do they not? They may perhaps even respect the prey: the lion may lie down with the lamb, even if only the lion is likely to get up again, but the lion will not lie down with the rat. Vermin, Drumknott, an entire race reduced to vermin!"

Lord Vetinari shook his head sadly, and the ever-attentive Drumknott noticed that his lordship's fingers had now gone back, for the third time that day, to the page headed "Unggue Pots" and he seemed, quite unusually, to be talking to himself as he did so. . .

"These are traditionally crafted by the goblin itself, out of anything from precious minerals to leather, wood or bone. Among the former are some of the finest eggshell-thin containers ever found in the world. The plundering

*of goblin settlements by treasure hunters in search of these, and the retalia-
tion by the goblins themselves, has colored human-goblin relationships even
to the present day."*

Lord Vetinari cleared his throat and continued, "I quote Pastor
Oats again, Drumknott: *'I must say that goblins live on the edge, often
because they have been driven there. When nothing else can survive, they
do. Their universal greeting is, apparently, "Hang" which means "Survive." I know dreadful crimes have been laid at their door, but the world
itself has never been kind to them. Let it be said here that those who live
their lives where life hangs by less than a thread understand the dreadful
algebra of necessity, which has no mercy and when necessity presses in ex-
tremis, well, that is when the women need to make the unggue pot called
"soul of tears," the most beautiful of all the pots, carved with little flowers
and washed with tears.'"*

Drumknott, with meticulous timing, put a cup of coffee in
front of his master just as Lord Vetinari finished the sentence and
looked up. "'The dreadful algebra of necessity,' Drumknott. Well,
we know about that, don't we?"

"Indeed we do, sir. Incidentally, sir, we have received a missive
from Diamond King of Trolls, thanking us for our firm stance on
the drugs issue. Well done, sir."

"Hardly a concession," Vetinari observed, waving it away. "You
know my position, Drumknott. I have no particular objection to
people taking substances that make them feel better, or more contented or, for that matter, see little dancing purple fairies—or even
their god if it comes to that. It's their brain, after all, and society
can have no claim on it, providing they're not operating heavy
machinery at the time. However, to sell drugs to trolls that actually make their heads explode is simply murder, the capital crime.
I am glad to say that Commander Vimes fully agrees with me on
this issue."

"Indeed, sir, and may I remind you that he will be leaving us very shortly. Do you intend to see him off, as it were?"

The Patrician shook his head. "I think not. The man must be in terrible turmoil, and I fear that my presence might make things worse."

Was there a hint of pity in Drumknott's voice when he said, "Don't blame yourself, my lord. After all, you and the commander are in the hands of a higher power."

H IS GRACE, THE DUKE of Ankh, Commander Sir Samuel Vimes of the Ankh-Morpork City Watch, was feverishly pushing a pencil down the side of his boot in order to stop the itching. It didn't work. It never did. All his socks made his feet itch. For the hundredth time he considered telling his wife that among her sterling qualities, and they were many, knitting did not feature. But he would rather have chopped his foot off than do so. It would break her heart.

They were dreadful socks, though, so thick, knotted and bulky that he had had to buy boots that were one and a half times bigger than his feet. And he did this because Samuel Vimes, who had never gone into a place of worship with religious aforethought, worshipped Lady Sybil, and not a day went past without his being amazed that she seemed to do the same to him. He had made her his wife and she had made him a millionaire; with her behind him the sad, desolate, penniless and cynical copper was a rich and powerful duke. He'd managed to hold on to the cynical, however, and a brace of oxen on steroids would not have been able to pull the copper out of Sam Vimes; the poison was in too deep, wrapped around the spine. And so Sam Vimes itched, and counted his blessings until he ran out of numbers.

Among his curses was doing the paperwork.

There was always paperwork. It is well known that any drive to reduce paperwork only results in extra paperwork.

Of course, he had people to do the paperwork, but sooner or later he had, at the very least, to sign it and, if no way of escape presented itself, even read it. There was no getting away from it: ultimately, in all police work, there was a definite possibility that the manure would hit the windmill. The initials of Sam Vimes were required to be on the paper to inform the world that it was *his* windmill, and therefore *his* manure.

But now he stopped to call through the open door to Sergeant Littlebottom, who was acting as his orderly.

"Anything yet, Cheery?" he said, hopefully.

"Not in the way I think you mean, sir, but I think you'll be pleased to hear that I've just had a clacks message from Acting Captain Haddock down in Quirm, sir. He says he's getting on fine, sir, and really enjoying the avec."*

Vimes sighed. "Anything else?"

"Dead as a doorknob, sir," said the dwarf, poking her head around the door. "It's the heat, sir, it's too hot to fight and too sticky to steal. Isn't that wonderful, sir?"

Vimes grunted. "Where there are policemen there's crime, sergeant, remember that."

"Yes, I do, sir, although I think it sounds better with a little reordering of the words."

"I suppose there's no chance at all that I'll be let off?"

Sergeant Littlebottom looked concerned. "I'm sorry, sir, I think

---

* The exchange scheme with the Quirm gendarmerie was working very well: they were getting instruction on policing à la Vimes, while the food in the Pseudopolis Yard canteen had been improved out of all recognition by Captain Emile, even though he used far too much avec.

there's no appeal. Officially Captain Carrot will relieve you of your badge at noon."

Vimes thumped his desk and exploded. "I don't deserve this treatment after a lifetime of dedication to the city!"

"Commander, if I may say so, you deserve a lot more."

Vimes leaned back in his chair and groaned. "You too, Cheery?"

"I really am very sorry, sir. I know this is hard for you."

"To be forced out after all this time! I begged, you know, and that doesn't come easy to a man like me, you can be sure. Begged!"

There was a sound of footsteps on the stairs. Cheery watched as Vimes pulled a brown envelope out of his desk drawer, inserted something into it, licked it ferociously, sealed it with a spit and dropped it on his desk, where it clanged. "There," he said, through gritted teeth. "My badge, just like Vetinari ordered. I put it down. It won't be said they took it off me!"

Captain Carrot stepped into the office, ducking briefly as he came through the door. He had a package in his hand and several grinning coppers were clustered behind him.

"Sorry about this, sir, higher authority and all that. If it's any help I think you've been lucky to be let off with two weeks. She was originally talking about a month."

He handed Vimes the package and coughed. "Me and the lads had a bit of a whip-round, commander," he said with a forced grin.

"You know, I prefer something sensible like Chief Constable," said Vimes, grabbing the package. "Do you know, I reckoned that if I let them give me enough titles I'd eventually get one I could live with."

Vimes tore open the package and pulled out a very small and colorful bucket and spade, to the general amusement of the sur- reptitious onlookers.

"We know you're not going to the seaside, sir," Carrot began, "but . . ."

"I wish it was the seaside," Vimes complained. "You get ship-wrecks at the seaside, you get smugglers at the seaside and you get drownings and crime at the flaming seaside! Something interest-ing!"

"Lady Sybil says you're bound to find lots to amuse yourself with, sir," said Carrot.

Vimes grunted. "The countryside! What's to amuse you in the countryside? Do you know why it's called the countryside, Carrot? Because there's bloody nothing there except damn trees, which we're supposed to make a fuss about, but really they're just stiff weeds! It's dull! It's nothing but a long Sunday! And I'm going to have to meet nobby people!"

"Sir, you'll enjoy it. I've never known you to take even a day off unless you were injured," said Carrot.

"And even then he worried and grumbled every moment," said a voice at the doorway. It belonged to Lady Sybil Vimes, and Vimes found himself resenting the way his men deferred to her. He loved Lady Sybil to distraction, of course, but he couldn't help noticing how, these days, his bacon, lettuce and tomato sandwich had be-come, not as it had been traditionally, a **bacon**, tomato and lettuce and had in fact become a **lettuce**, **tomato** and bacon sandwich. It was all about health, of course. It was a conspiracy. Why did they never find a vegetable that was bad for you, hey? And what was so wrong with onion gravy anyway? It had onions in it, didn't it? They made you fart, didn't they? That was good for you, wasn't it? He was sure he had read that somewhere.

Two weeks *holiday* with every meal overseen by his wife. It didn't bear thinking about, but he did anyway. And then there was Young Sam, growing up like a weed and into everything. A holiday in the fresh air would do him good, his mother said. Vimes hadn't ar-gued. There was no point in arguing with Sybil, because even if you thought that you'd won, it would turn out, by some magic unavailable to husbands, that you had, in fact, been totally misinformed.

At least he was allowed to leave the city wearing his armor. It was part of him, and just as battered as he was, except that, in the case of the armor the dents could be hammered out.

V IMES, WITH HIS SON on his knee, stared out at the departing city as the coach hurried him toward a fortnight of bucolic slumber. He felt like a man banished. But, to look on the bright side, there was bound to be some horrible murder or dreadful theft in the city which for the *very important* purposes of morale, if nothing else, would require the presence of the head of the Watch. He could but hope.

Sam Vimes had known ever since their marriage that his wife had a place out in the country. One of the reasons he knew this was because she had given it to him. In fact, she had transferred all the holdings of her family, said family consisting solely of her at that point, to him in the old fashioned but endearing belief that a husband should be the one doing the owning.* She had insisted.

Periodically, according to the season, a cart had come from the country house all the way to their home in Scoone Avenue, Ankh-Morpork, loaded with fruits and vegetables, cheeses and meats; all the produce of an estate that he'd never seen. He wasn't looking forward to seeing it now. One thing he knew about the country was that it squelched underfoot. Admittedly most of the streets of Ankh-Morpork squelched underfoot, but, well, that was the right

---

* And thenceforth would be glad to get a gentle second place in almost every domestic decision. Lady Sybil took the view that her darling husband's word was law for the City Watch while, in her own case, it was a polite suggestion to be graciously considered.

kind of squelch and a squelch that he had squelched ever since he could walk and, inevitably, slip.

The place was officially called Crundells, although it was always referred to as Ramkin Hall. Apparently it had a mile of trout stream and, Vimes seemed to recall from the deeds, a pub. Vimes knew how you could own a pub but he wondered how you could own a trout stream because, if *that* was your bit, it had already gurgled off downstream while you were watching it, yes? That meant somebody else was now fishing in *your* water, the bastard! And the bit in front of you now had recently belonged to the bloke upstream; that bloated plutocrat of a fat neighbor now probably considered you some kind of poacher, that other bastard! And the fish swam everywhere, didn't they? How did you know which ones were yours? Perhaps they were branded—that sounded *very* countryside to Vimes. To be in the countryside you had to be permanently on the defensive; quite the opposite of the city.

UNCHARACTERISTICALLY FOR HIM, LORD Vetinari laughed out loud. He very nearly gloated at the downfall of his enemy and slammed his copy of the *Ankh-Morpork Times*, open at the crossword page, on to his desk. "Cucumiform, shaped like a cucumber or a variety of squash! I thumb my nose at you, madam!"

Drumknott, who was carefully arranging paperwork, smiled and said, "Another triumph, my lord?" Vetinari's battle with the chief crossword compiler of the *Ankh-Morpork Times* was well known.

"I am sure she is losing her grip," said Vetinari, leaning back in his chair. "What is it that you have there, Drumknott?" He pointed at a bulky brown envelope.

"Commander Vimes's badge, sir, as delivered to me by Captain Carrot."

"Sealed?"

"Yes, sir."

"Then it doesn't have Vimes's badge in it."

"No, sir. A careful fingertip examination of the envelope suggests that it contains an empty tin of Double Thunder snuff. A conclusion confirmed by a casual sniff, my lord."

A still ebullient Vetinari said, "But the captain must have realized this, Drumknott."

"Yes, sir."

"Of course, that would be in the nature of the commander," said Vetinari, "and would we have him any other way? He has won a little battle and a man who can win little battles is well set up to win big ones."

Unusually, Drumknott hesitated a little before saying, "Yes, sir. Apropos of that, it *was* Lady Sybil who suggested the trip to the countryside, was it not?"

Vetinari raised an eyebrow. "Why yes, of course, Drumknott. I can't imagine who would propose otherwise. The brave commander is well known for his dedication to his work. Who else but his loving wife could possibly persuade him that a few weeks of jolly holiday in the countryside would be a good thing?"

"Who indeed, sir," said Drumknott, and left it at that, because there was no point in doing anything else. His master appeared to have sources of information unavailable even to Drumknott, however hard he tried, and only the heavens knew who all those were who scuttled in darkness up the long stairs. And thus life in the Oblong Office was a world of secrets and considerations and misdirections, where the nature of truth changed like the colors of the rainbow. He knew this because he played a not insignificant role in the spectrum. But to know what Lord Vetinari knew and *exactly* what Lord Vetinari thought would be a psychological impossibility, and a wise man would accept that and get on with his filing.

Vetinari stood up and stared out of the window. "This is a city of beggars and thieves, Drumknott, is it not? I pride myself that we have some of the most skilled. In fact, if there were such a thing as an inter-city thieving contest, Ankh-Morpork would bring home the trophy and probably everyone's wallets. Theft has a purpose, Drumknott, but one intrinsically feels that while there are things by nature unavailable to the common man, there are also things not to be allowed to the rich and powerful."

Drumknott's understanding of his master's thought processes would appear to an outsider to be magical, but it was amazing what could be gleaned by watching what Lord Vetinari was reading, listening to apparently pointless observations and integrating those, as only Drumknott could integrate, into current problems and concerns. He said, "Is this now about the smuggling, sir?"

"Quite so, quite so. I have no problem with smuggling. It involves the qualities of enterprise, stealth and original thinking. Attributes to be encouraged in the common man. In truth, it doesn't do that much harm and allows the man in the street a little *frisson* of enjoyment. Everyone should occasionally break the law in some small and delightful way, Drumknott. It's good for the hygiene of the brain."

Drumknott, whose cranial cleanness could never be in dispute, said, "Nevertheless, sir, taxes must be levied and paid. The city is growing. All of this must be paid for."

"Indeed," said Vetinari. "I could have taxed all kinds of things, but I have decided to tax something that you could eminently do without. It's hardly addictive, is it?"

"Some people tend to think so. There is a certain amount of grumbling, sir."

Vetinari did not look up from his paperwork. "Drumknott," he said. "Life is addictive. If people complain overmuch, I think I will have to draw that fact to their attention."

The Patrician smiled again and steepled his fingers. "In short, Drumknott, a certain amount of harmless banditry amongst the lower classes is to be smiled upon if not actively encouraged, for the health of the city, but what should we do when the highborn and wealthy take to crime? Indeed, if a poor man will spend a year in prison for stealing out of hunger, how high would the gallows need to be to hang the rich man who breaks the law out of greed?"

"I would like to reiterate, sir, that I buy all my own paper clips," said Drumknott urgently.

"Of course, but in your case I am pleased to say that you have a brain so pristine that it sparkles."

"I keep the receipts, sir," Drumknott inisted, "just in case you wish to see them." There was silence for a moment, then he continued. "Commander Vimes should be well on his way to the Hall by now, my lord. That might prove a fortunate circumstance."

Vetinari's face was blank. "Yes indeed, Drumknott, yes indeed."

THE HALL HAD BEEN a full day's journey, which in coaching terms really meant two, with a stay at an inn. Vimes spent the time listening for the sound of overtaking horsemen from the city bringing much-to-be-desired news of dire catastrophe. Usually Ankh-Morpork could supply this on an almost hourly basis but now it was singularly failing to deliver its desperate son in his hour of vegetation.

The *other* sun was setting on this particular son when the coach pulled up outside a pair of gates. After a second or two, an elderly man, an extremely elderly man, appeared from nowhere and made a great show of opening said gates, then stood to attention as the coach went through, beaming in the knowledge of a job well done. Once inside, the coach stopped.

Sybil, who had been reading, nudged her husband without looking up from her book and said, "It's customary to give Mr. Coffin a penny. In the old days my grandfather kept a little charcoal brazier in the coach, you know, in theory to keep warm but mostly to heat up pennies to red heat before picking them up in some tongs and tossing them out for the gatekeeper to catch. Apparently everybody enjoyed it, or so my grandfather said, but we don't do that anymore."

Vimes fumbled in his purse for some small change, opened the carriage door and stepped down, much to the shock of the aforesaid Mr. Coffin, who backed away into the thick undergrowth, watching Vimes like a cornered animal.

"Nice job, Mr. Coffin, very good lifting of the latch there, excellent work." Vimes proffered the coin and Mr. Coffin backed further away, his stance suggesting that he was going to bolt at any moment. Vimes flicked the coin in the air and the fearful man caught it, deftly spat on it and melted back into the scenery. Vimes got the impression that he resented the lack of hiss.

"How long ago did your family stop throwing hot money at the servants?" Vimes said, settling back into his seat as the coach progressed.

Sybil laid aside her book. "My father put a stop to it. My mother complained. So did the gatekeepers."

"I should think so!"

"No, Sam, they complained when the custom was stopped."

"But it's demeaning!"

Sybil sighed. "Yes, I know, Sam, but it was also free money, you see. In my great-grandfather's day, if things were busy, a man might make sixpence in a day. And since the old boy was almost permanently sozzled on rum and brandy he quite often threw out a dollar. One of the real old-fashioned solid-gold dollars, I mean. A man could live quite well for a year on one of those, especially out here."

"Yes, but—" Vimes began, but his wife silenced him with a smile. She had a special smile for these occasions; it was warm and friendly and carved out of rock. You had to stop discussing politics or you would run right into it, causing no damage to anything but yourself. Wisely, with a wisdom that had been well learned, Sam Vimes restricted himself to staring out of the window.

With the gate far behind he kept looking, in the fading light, to see the big house that was apparently at the center of all this, and couldn't find it until they had rattled along an avenue of trees, past what some wretched poet would have had to call "verdant pastures," dotted with almost certainly, Vimes considered, sheep, through manicured woodland, and then reached a bridge that would not have been out of place back in the city.* The bridge spanned what Vimes first thought was an ornamental lake but turned out to be a very wide river; even as they trundled over it, in dignified splendor, Vimes saw a large boat travelling along it by some means unknown, but which, to judge from the smell as it went past, must have something to do with cattle. At this point Young Sam said, "Those ladies haven't got any clothes on! Are they going to have a swim?"

Vimes nodded absently because the whole area of naked ladies

---

* Apart, that is, from the line of artistically naked ladies along its parapets. They were holding urns; urns is art.

was not something you wanted to discuss with a six-year-old boy. In any case, his attention was still on the boat; white water churned all around it and the seamen on the deck made what was possibly a nautical gesture to Lady Sybil or, quite possibly, one of the naked ladies.

"That *is* a river, isn't it?" said Vimes.

"It's the Quire," said Lady Sybil. "It drains most of the Octarine grass country and comes out in Quirm. If I recall correctly, however, most people call it 'Old Treachery.' It has moods, but I used to enjoy those little riverboats when I was a child. They really were rather jolly."

The coach rumbled down the far end of the bridge and up a long drive to, yes, the stately home, presumably so called, Vimes thought, because it was about the size of the average state. There was a herd of deer on the lawn, and a big herd of people clustered around what was obviously the front door. They were shuffling into two lines, as though they were a wedding party. They were, in fact, some kind of guard of honor, and there must have been more than three hundred there, from gardeners through to footmen, all trying to smile and not succeeding very well. It reminded Vimes of a Watch parade.

Two footmen collided while endeavoring to place a step by the coach, and Vimes totally spoiled the moment by getting out of the opposite door and swinging Lady Sybil down after him.

In the middle of the throng of nervous people was a friendly face, and it belonged to Willikins, Vimes's butler and general manservant from the city. Vimes had been adamant about that, at least. If he was going to the countryside, then he would have Willikins there. He pointed out to his wife that Willikins was definitely *not* a policeman, and so it was not the same as bringing your work home. And that was true. Willikins was definitely *not* a policeman, because most policemen don't know how to glass up some-body with a broken bottle without hurting their hands or how to make weapons of limited but specific destruction out of common kitchen utensils. Willikins had a history that showed up when he had to carve the turkey. And now Young Sam, seeing his scarred but familiar smile, ran up through the row of hesitant employees to cuddle the butler at the knees. For his part, Willikins turned Young Sam upside down and spun him around before gently put-ting him back on the gravel, the whole process being a matter of huge entertainment to a boy of six. Vimes trusted Willikins. He didn't trust many people. Too many years as a copper made you rather discriminating in that respect.

He leaned toward his wife. "What do I do now?" he whispered, because the ranks of worried half-smiles were unnerving him.

"Whatever you like, dear," she said. "You're the boss. You take Watch parade, don't you?"

"Yes, but I know who everyone is and their rank and, well, everything! It's never been like this in the city!"

"Yes, dear, that's because in Ankh-Morpork everybody knows Commander Vimes."

Well, how hard could it be? Vimes walked up to a man with a battered straw hat, a spade and, as Vimes neared, a state of subdued terror even worse than that of Sam Vimes himself. Vimes held out his hand. The man looked at it as if he had never seen a hand before. Vimes managed to say, "Hello, I'm Sam Vimes. Who are you?"

The man thus addressed looked around for help, support and guidance or escape, but there was none; the crowd was deathly silent. He said, "William Butler, your grace, if it's all the same to you."

"Pleased to meet you, William," said Vimes, and held out his

16

hand again, which William almost leaned away from before offering Vimes a palm the texture of an ancient leather glove.

Well, thought Vimes, this isn't too bad, and he ventured into unknown territory with, "And what's your job around here, William?"

"Gardener," William managed, and held up his spade between himself and Vimes, both as a protection and as exhibit "A," proof positive of his bona fides. Since Vimes himself was equally at sea, he settled for testing the blade with his finger and mumbling, "Properly maintained, I see. Well done, Mr. Butler."

He jumped when there was a tap on his shoulder and his wife said, "Well done, yourself, dear, but all you really needed to do is go up the steps and congratulate the butler and the housekeeper on the wonderful turnout of the staff. We'll be here all day if you want to chat to everybody." And with that, Lady Sybil took her husband firmly by the hand and led him up the steps between the rows of owlish stares.

"All right," he whispered, "I can see the footmen and the cooks and gardeners, but who are those blokes in the thick jackets and the bowler hats? Have we got the bailiffs in?"

"That is reasonably unlikely, dear. In fact, they are some of the gamekeepers."

"The hats look wrong on them."

"Do you think so? As a matter of fact they were designed by Lord Bowler to protect his gamekeepers from vicious attacks by poachers. Deceptively strong, I'm told, and much better than steel helmets because you don't get the nasty ringing in your ears."

Clearly unable to hide their displeasure that their new master had chosen to shake the hand of a gardener before addressing either of them, the butler and housekeeper, who shared the traditional girth and pinkness that Vimes had learned to expect on these occasions, were aware that their master had not come to them and, he noticed, were coming to him as fast as their little legs would carry them.

Vimes knew about life below stairs, hell, yes, he did! Not so long ago a policeman summoned to a big house would be sent around to the back door to be instructed to drag away some weeping chambermaid or not-very-bright boot boy accused without evidence of stealing some ring or silver-handled brush that the lady of the house would probably find later, perhaps when she had finished the gin. That wasn't supposed to be what coppers were for, although in reality, of course it was what coppers were for. It was about privilege, and young Vimes had hardly worn in his first pair of policeman's boots when his sergeant had explained what that meant. It meant private law. In those days an influential man could get away with quite a lot if he had the right accent, the right crest on his tie or the right chums, and a young policeman who objected might get away without a job and without a reference.

It wasn't like that now, not even close.

But in those days young Vimes had seen butlers as double-traitors to both sides and so the large man in the black tailcoat got a glare that skewered him. The fact that he gave Vimes a little nod did not help matters. Vimes lived in a world where people saluted.

"I am Silver, the butler, your grace," the man carefully intoned reprovingly.

Vimes immediately grabbed him by the hand and shook it warmly. "Pleased to meet you, Mr. Silver!"

The butler winced. "It's Silver, sir, not Mister."

"Sorry about that, *Mr.* Silver. So what's your first name?"

The butler's face was an entertainment. "*Silver*, sir! Always Silver!"

"Well, Mr. Silver," said Vimes, "it's an item of faith with me that once you get past the trousers all men are the same."

The butler's face was wooden as he said, "That is as maybe, sir, but I am and always will be, commander, Silver. Good evening, *your grace,* " the butler turned, "and good evening, Lady Sybil. It must be seven or eight years since anyone from the family came to stay. May we look forward to further visits? And might I please introduce to you my wife, Mrs. Silver, the housekeeper, whom I think you have not met before?"

Vimes could not stop his mind translating the little speech as: *I am annoyed that you ignored me to shake hands with the gardener . . .* which, to be fair, was not deliberate. Vimes had shaken the gardener's hand out of sheer, overpowering terror. The translation continued: *and now I am worried that we might not be having such an easy life in the near future.*

"Hold on a minute," said Vimes, "my wife is a Grace as well, you know, that's a bit more than a lady. Syb— Her Grace made me look at the score chart."

Lady Sybil knew her husband in the way people living next door to a volcano get to know the moods of their neighbor. The important thing is to avoid the bang.

"Sam, I have been Lady Sybil to all the servants in both our houses ever since I was a girl, and so I regard Lady Sybil as my name, at least among people I have come to look on as friends. You know that!" And, she added to herself, we all have our little quirks, Sam, even you.

And with that scented admonition floating in the air, Lady Sybil shook the housekeeper's hand, and then turned to her son. "Now it's bed for you, Young Sam, straight after supper. And no arguing."

Vimes looked around as the little party stepped into the entrance hall which was to all intents and purposes an armory. It would always be an armory in the eyes of any policeman although, undoubtedly, to the Ramkins who had put the swords, halberds, cutlasses, maces, pikes and shields on every wall, the assemblage was no more than a bit of historical furniture. In the middle of it all was the enormous

Ramkin coat of arms. Vimes already knew what the motto said, "What We Have We Keep." You could call it . . . a hint.

Soon afterward Lady Sybil was busily engaged in the huge laundry and ironing room with Purity the maid, whom Vimes had insisted she take on after the birth of Young Sam, and who, both he and his wife believed, had an understanding with Willikins, although exactly what it was they understood remained a speculation. The two women were engrossed in the feminine pastime of taking clothes out of some things, and putting them into other things. This could go on for a long time, and included the ceremony of holding some things up to the light and giving a sad little sigh.

In the absence of anything else to do, Vimes headed back out to the magnificent flight of steps, where he lit a cigar. Sybil was adamant about no smoking in the house. A voice behind him said, "You don't need to do that, sir. The Hall has a rather good smoking room, including a clockwork air extractor, which is very posh, sir, believe me, you don't often see them." Vimes let Willikins lead the way.

It *was* a pretty good smoking room, thought Vimes, although his first-hand experience of them was admittedly limited. The room included a large snooker table and, down below, a cellar with more alcohol than any reformed alcoholic should ever see.

"We did tell them I don't drink, didn't we, Willikins?"

"Oh yes, sir. Silver said that generally the Hall finds it appropriate—I think his words were—to keep the cellar full in case of arrivals."

"Well, it seems to me to be a shame to pass up the opportunity, Willikins, so be my guest and pour yourself a drink."

Willikins perceptibly recoiled. "Oh no, sir, I couldn't possibly do that, sir."

"Why not, man?"

"It's just not done, sir. I would be the laughingstock of the

League of Gentlemen's Gentlemen if I was so impertinent as to have a drink with my employer. It would be getting ideas above my station, sir."

This offended Vimes to his shakily egalitarian core,* who said, "I know your station, Willikins, and it's about the same station as mine when the chips are down and the wounds have healed."

"Look, sir," said Willikins, almost pleading. "Just occasionally we have to follow some rules. So, on this occasion I won't drink with you, it not being Hogswatch or the birth of an heir, which are accounted for under the rules, but instead I'll follow the acceptable alternative, which is to wait until you've gone to bed and drink half the bottle."

Well, thought Vimes, we all have our funny little ways, although some of Willikins' would not be funny if he was angry with you in a dark alley; but he brightened as he watched Willikins rummage through a well-stocked cocktail cabinet, meticulously dropping items into a glass shaker.†

It should not be possible to achieve the effect of alcohol in a drink without including alcohol, but among the skills that Willikins had learned, or possibly stolen, over the years was the ability to mix out of common household ingredients a totally soft drink that nevertheless had very nearly everything you wanted in alcohol. Tabasco, cucumber, ginger and chili were all in there somewhere and beyond that it was best not to ask too many questions.

Drink gloriously in hand, Vimes leaned back and said, "Staff okay, Willikins?"

---

* It was tricky; to Vimes all men were equal but, well, obviously a sergeant wasn't as equal as a captain and a captain wasn't as equal as a commander and as for corporal Nobby Nobbs . . . well, nobody . . . could be the equal of corporal Nobby Nobbs.

† Metal, in the circumstances, would not be appropriate . . . or safe.

Willikins lowered his voice. "Oh, they're skimming stuff off the top, sir, but nothing more than usual in my experience. Everyone sneaks something, it's the perk of the job and the way of the world."

Vimes smiled at Willikins' almost theatrically wooden expression and said loudly for the hidden listener, "A conscientious man, then, is he, Silver? I'm very glad to hear it."

"Seems like a steady one to me, sir," said the manservant, rolling his eyes toward heaven and pointing a finger to a small grille in the wall: the inlet to the fabled extractor, which no doubt needed a man behind the scenes to wind the clockwork, and would any butler worth his bulging stomach forgo an opportunity to keep tabs on what the new master was thinking? Would he hell.

It was perks, wasn't it? Of course people here would be on the take. You didn't need evidence. It was human nature. He had constantly suggested to Sybil—he wouldn't have dared insist—that the place be closed down and sold to somebody who really wanted to live in what he had heard was a creaking, freezing pile that could have housed a regiment. She would not hear of it. She had warm childhood memories of the place, she said, of climbing trees and swimming and fishing in the river, and picking flowers and helping the gardeners and similar jolly rural enterprises that were, to Vimes, as remote as the moon, given that *his* adolescent preoccupations had had everything to do with just staying alive. You *could* fish in the River Ankh, provided you took care not to catch anything. In fact it was amazing what you could catch by just letting one drop of the Ankh pass your lips. And as for picnicking, well, in Ankh-Morpork when you were a kid sometimes you nicked and sometimes you picked, mostly at scabs.

I T HAD BEEN A long day and last night's sleep in the inn had not been salubrious or restful, but before he got into the huge bed Vimes opened a window and stared out at the night. The wind was murmuring in the trees; Vimes mildly disapproved of trees, but Sybil liked them and that was that. Things that he didn't care to know about rustled, whooped, gibbered and went inexplicably crazy in the darkness outside. He didn't know what they were and hoped never to find out. What kind of noise was this for a man to go to sleep to?

He joined his wife in the bed, thrashing around for some time before he found her, and settled down. She had instructed him to leave the window open to get some allegedly glorious fresh air, and Vimes lay there miserably, straining his ears for the reassuring noises of a drunk going home, or arguing with the sedan-chair owner about the vomit on the cushions, and the occasional street fight, domestic disturbance or even piercing scream, all punctuated at intervals by the chiming of the city clocks, no two of which, famously, ever agreed; and the more subtle sounds, like the rumble of the honey wagons as Harry King's night-soil collectors went about the business of business. And best of all was the cry of the night watchman at the end of the street: *Twelve o'clock and all is well!* It wasn't so long ago that any man trying this would have had his bell, helmet and quite probably his boots stolen before the echoes had died away. But not anymore! No, indeedy! This was the modern Watch, Vimes's Watch, and anyone who challenged the watchman on his rounds with malice aforethought would hear the whistle blow and very quickly learn that if anybody was going to be kicked around on the street, it wasn't going to be a watchman. The duty watchmen always made a point of shouting the hour with theatrical clarity and amazing precision outside Number One Scoone Avenue, so that the commander would hear it. Now, Vimes stuck his head under an enormous pillow and tried not to hear the tremendous and disturbing lack of noise whose absence could wake a man up when he had learned to ignore a carefully timed sound every night for years.

But at five o'clock in the morning Mother Nature pressed a button and the world went mad: every blessed bird and animal and, by the sound of it, alligator vied with all the others to make itself heard. The cacophony took some time to get through to Vimes. The giant bed at least had an almost inexhaustible supply of pillows. Vimes was a great fan of pillows when away from his own bed. Not for him one or even two sad little bags of feathers as an afterthought to the bed—no! He liked pillows to burrow into and turn into some kind of soft fortress, leaving one hole for the oxygen supply.

The awful racket was dying down by the time he drifted up to the linen surface. Oh yes, he recalled, that was another bloody thing about the country. It started too damn early. The commander was, by custom, necessity and inclination a nighttime man, sometimes even an all-night man; alien to him was the concept of two seven o'clocks in one day. On the other hand, he could smell bacon, and a moment later two nervous young ladies entered the room carrying trays on complex metallic things which, unfolded, made it almost but not totally impossible to sit up and eat the breakfast they contained.

Vimes blinked. Things were looking up! Usually Sybil considered it her wifely duty to see to it that her husband lived forever, and was convinced that this happy state of affairs could be achieved by feeding him bowel-scouring nuts and grains and yogurt, which to Vimes's mind was a type of cheese that wasn't trying hard enough. Then there was the sad adulteration of his mid-morning bacon, lettuce and tomato snack. It was amazing but true that in this matter the watchmen were prepared to obey the boss's wife to the letter and, if the boss yelled and stamped, which was perfectly understandable, nay forgivable, when a man was forbidden his mid-morning lump of charred pig, would refer him to the instructions given to them by his wife, in the certain knowledge that all threats of sacking were hollow and if carried out would be immediately rescinded.

Now Sybil appeared among the pillows and said, "You're on holiday, dear." What you could eat on holiday also included two fried eggs, just as he liked them, and a sausage—but not, unfortunately, the fried slice, which even on holiday was apparently still a sin. The coffee, however, was thick, black and sweet.

"You slept very well," said Sybil, as Vimes stared at the unexpected largesse.

He said, "No, I didn't, dear, not a wink, I assure you."

"Sam, you were snoring all night. I heard you!"

Vimes's grasp of successful husbandry prevented him from making any further comment except, "Really? Was I, dear? Oh, I am sorry."

Sybil leafed through a small pile of pastel envelopes that had been inserted into her breakfast tray. "Well, the news has got around," she said. "The Duchess of Keepsake has invited us to a ball, Sir Henry and Lady Withering have invited us to a ball, and Lord and Lady Hangfinger have invited us to, yes, a ball!"

"Well," said Vimes, "that's a lot of—"

"Don't you dare, Sam!" his wife warned and Vimes finished lamely, " . . . invitations? You know I don't dance, dear, I just shuffle about and tread on your feet."

"Well, it's mainly for the young people, you see? People come for the therapeutic baths at Ham-on-Rye, just down the road. Really, it's all about getting the daughters married to suitable gentlemen, and that means balls, almost continuous balls."

"I can manage a waltz," said Vimes, "that's just a matter of counting, but you know I can't stand all those jumping-about ones like Strip the Widow and the Gay Gordon."

"Don't worry, Sam. Most of the older men find a place to sit and smoke or take snuff. The mothers do the work of finding the eligible bachelors for their daughters. I just hope that my friend Ariadne will find suitable husbands for her girls. She had sextuplets, very rare, you know. Of course, young Mavis is very devout, and there is invariably a young clergyman looking for a wife and, above all, a dowry. And Emily is petite, blonde, an excellent cook but rather conscious of her enormous bosom."

Vimes stared at the ceiling. "I suspect that not only will she find a husband," he forecast, "a husband will find her. Call it a man's intuition."

"And then there's Fleur," said Lady Sybil, not rising to the bait. "She makes quite nice little bonnets, so I understand." She thought for a moment and added, "oh, and then there's Jane. And, er, Amanda, I think. Apparently quite interested in frogs, although I fear I may have misheard her mother. Rather a strange girl, according to her mother, who doesn't seem to know what to make of her."

Vimes's lack of interest in other people's children was limitless, but he could count. "And the last one?"

"Oh, Hermione, she may be difficult as she has rather scandalized the family, at least in their opinion."

"How?"

"She's a lumberjack."

Vimes thought for a moment and said, "Well, dear, it is a truth universally acknowledged that a man with a lot of wood must be in want of a wife who can handle a great big—"

Lady Sybil interrupted sharply: "Sam Vimes, I believe that you intend to make an indelicate remark?"

"I think you got there before me," said Vimes, grinning. "You generally do, dear, admit it."

"You may be right, dear," she said, "but that is only to forestall *you* from saying it aloud. After all, you are the Duke of Ankh and widely regarded as Lord Vetinari's right-hand man, and that means a certain amount of decorum would be advisable, don't you think?"

To a bachelor this would have appeared to be gentle advice; to an experienced husband it was a command, all the more powerful because it was made delicately.

So, when Sir Samuel Vimes and Commander Vimes and His Grace the Duke of Ankh* walked out after breakfast, they were all on their best behavior. As it turned out, other people weren't.

There was a maid sweeping in the corridor outside the bedroom who took one frantic look at Vimes as he strolled toward her and turned her back on him, and remained staring fixedly at the wall. She appeared to be trembling with fear, and Vimes had learned that in these circumstances the last thing any man should do is ask a question or, above all, offer to lend a helping hand. Screaming could result. She was probably just shy, he told himself.

But it seemed that shyness was catching: there were maids carrying trays or dusting or sweeping as he walked down through the building, and every time he came near one she turned her back crisply and stood staring at the wall as if her life depended on it.

By the time he reached a long gallery lined with his wife's ancestors, Vimes had had enough, and when a young lady carrying a tea tray spun around like the dancer on the top of a musical box he said, "Excuse me, miss, am I as ugly as all that?" Well, that

---

* Not to mention Blackboard Monitor Vimes, a figure of note in dwarfish society.

was surely better than asking her why she was so rude, wasn't it? So why in the name of any three gods did she start to run away, crockery rattling as she headed down the hall? Among the various Vimeses it was the Commander who took over; the Duke would be too forbidding and the Blackboard Monitor just wouldn't do the trick. "Stop where you are! Put down your tray and turn around slowly!"

She skidded, she actually skidded and, turning with perfect grace while still clutching the tray, slowed gently to a stop, where she stood shaking with anxiety as Vimes caught up with her and said, "What's your name, miss?"

She answered while keeping her face turned away. "Hodges, your grace, I'm very sorry, your grace." The crockery was still rattling.

"Look," said Vimes, "I can't think with all that rattling going on! Just put it down carefully, will you? Nothing bad is going to happen to you, but I'd like to see who I'm talking to, thank you very much." The face turned reluctantly toward him.

"There," he said. "Miss, er, Hodges, what is the matter? You don't have to run away from me, surely?"

"Please, sir," and with that the girl headed for the nearest grezen baize door and vanished through it. It was at this point that Vimes realized there was another maid only a little way behind him, practically camouflaged by her dark uniform and facing the wall and, indeed, trembling. She was surely a witness to all that had happened, so he walked carefully toward her and said, "I don't want you to say anything. Just nod or shake your head when I ask you a question. Do you understand?" There was a barely perceptible nod. "Good, we make progress! Will you get into trouble if you say anything to me?"

Another microscopic nod.

"And is it likely that you'll get into trouble because I've talked to you?" The maid, rather inventively, gave a shrug.

"And the other girl?" Still with her back to him, the unseen girl stuck out her left hand with the thumb emphatically turned down.

"Thank you," said Vimes, to the invisible informant. "You've been very helpful."

He walked thoughtfully back upstairs, through an avenue of turned backs, and was thankful to encounter Willikins in the laundry on the way. The batman did not turn his back on Vimes, which was a relief.*

He was folding shirts with the care and attention he might otherwise have marshaled for the neat cutting off of a defeated opponent's ear. When the cuffs of his own spotlessly clean jacket slid up a little you could just see part of the tattoos on his arm but not, fortunately, spell out anything they said. Vimes said, "Willikins, what are the whirling housemaids all about?"

Willikins smiled. "Old custom, sir. A reason to it, of course— there often is if it sounds bloody stupid. No offense, commander, but knowing you I'd suggest that you let twirling housemaids spin until you have got the lie of the land, as it were. Besides, her ladyship and Young Sam are in the nursery."

A few minutes later Vimes, after a certain amount of trial and error, walked into what was, in a musty kind of way, a paradise.

Vimes had never had much in the way of relatives. Not many people are anxious to let it be known that their distant ancestor was a regicide. All that, of course, was history and it amazed the new

---

* Willikins was an excellent butler and/or gentleman's gentleman when the occasion required it, but in a long career he had also been an enthusiastic street fighter, and knew enough never to turn his back on anybody who could possibly have a weapon on them.

Duke of Ankh that the history books now lauded the memory of Old Stoneface, the watchman who executed the evil bastard on the throne and had suddenly struck a blow for freedom and law. History is what you make it, he had learned, and Lord Vetinari was a man with the access to and the keys of a whole range of persuasive mechanisms left over, as luck would have it, from the regicide days and currently still well oiled in the cellar. History is, indeed, what you make it and Lord Vetinari could make it . . . anything he wanted. And thus the dreadful killer of kings was miraculously gone—never been there, you must be mistaken, never heard of him, no such person—and replaced with the heroic, if tragically misunderstood, Slayer of Tyrants Stoneface Vimes, the famous ancestor of the highly respected His Grace the Duke of Ankh, Commander Sir Samuel Vimes. History was a wonderful thing, it moved like the sea and Vimes was taken at the flood.

Vimes's family had lived a generation at a time. There had never been heirlooms, family jewels, embroidered samplers stitched by a long-dead aunt, no interesting old urns found in granny's attic which you hoped that the bright young man who knew all about antiques would tell you was worth a thousand dollars so that you could burst with smugness. And there was absolutely no money, only a certain amount of unpaid debt. But here in the playroom, neatly stacked, were generations of toys and games, some of them a little worn from long usage, particularly the rocking horse, which was practically life-size and had a real leather saddle with trappings made from (Vimes discovered to his incredulity by rubbing them with a finger) genuine silver. There was also a fort, big enough for a kid to stand in and defend, and a variety of child-sized siege weapons to assault it, possibly with the help of boxes and boxes of lead soldiers, all painted in the correct regimental colors and in fine detail. For two pins Vimes would have got down on hands and knees and played with them there and then. There were model yachts, and a teddy bear so big that for one horrible moment Vimes wondered whether it was a real one, stuffed; there were catapults and boomerangs and gliders . . . and in the middle of all this, Young Sam stood paralysed, almost in tears with the knowledge that no matter how hard he tried he just couldn't play with everything all at once. It was a far cry from the Vimes childhood, and playing poo sticks with real poo.

While the apple of their eyes tentatively straddled the rocking horse, which had frighteningly big teeth, Vimes told his wife about the objectionable spinning housemaids. She simply shrugged, and said, "It's what they do, dear. It's what they're used to."

"How can you say that? It's so demeaning!"

Lady Sybil had developed a totally calm and understanding tone of voice when dealing with her husband. "That's because, technically speaking, they *are* demeaned. They spend a lot of time serving people who are a lot more important than they are. And you are right at the top of the list, dear."

"But I don't think I'm more important than them!" Vimes snapped.

"I think I know what you're saying, and it does you credit, it really does," said Sybil, "but what you actually said was nonsense. You are a Duke, a Commander of the City Watch and," she paused.

"A Blackboard Monitor," said Vimes automatically.

"Yes, Sam, the highest honor that the King of the Dwarfs can bestow." Sybil's eyes glittered. "Blackboard Monitor Vimes; one who can erase the writings, somebody who can rub out what is there. That's you, Sam and if you were killed the chanceries of the world would be in uproar and, Sam, regrettably they would not be perturbed at the death of a housemaid. She held up a hand because he'd opened his mouth and added, "I know *you* would be, Sam, but wonderful girls though I'm sure they are, I fear that if they were to die a family and, perhaps, a young man would be inconsolable, and the rest of the world would never know. And you, Sam, know that this is true. However, if you were ever murdered, dread the thought and indeed I do every time you go out on duty, not only Ankh-Morpork but the world would hear about it instantly. Wars might start and I suspect that Vetinari's position might become a little dangerous. You are more important than girls in service. You are more important than anybody else in the Watch. You are mistaking value for worth, I think." She gave his worried face a brief kiss. "Whatever you think you once were, Sam Vimes, you've risen, and you deserved to rise. You know the cream rises to the top!"

"So does the scum," said Vimes automatically, although he immediately regretted it.

"How dare you say that, Sam Vimes! You may have been a diamond in the rough, but you've polished yourself up! And however you cut it, husband of mine, although you are no longer a man of the people, it certainly seems to me that you are a man *for* the people, and I think the people are far better off for that, d'you hear?"

Young Sam looked up adoringly at his father, while the rocking horse rocked into a gallop. Between son and spouse, Vimes never had a chance. He looked so crestfallen that Lady Sybil, as wives do, tried a little consolation.

"After all, Sam, you expect your men to get on with their duties, don't you? Likewise the housekeeper expects the girls to get on with theirs."

"That's quite different, really it is. Coppers watch people, and I've never told them that they can't pass the time of day with somebody. After all, that somebody might provide useful information."

Vimes knew that this was technically true, but anybody who was seen giving anything more useful than the time of day to a policeman in most streets of the city would soon find a straw would be necessary to help him eat his meals. But the analogy was right, anyway, he thought, or would have thought, had he been a man to whom the word analogy came easily. Just because you were a member of somebody's staff didn't mean you had to act like some kind of clockwork toy . . .

"Shall I tell you the reason for the spinning housemaids, Sam?" said Sybil, as Young Sam cuddled the huge teddy bear, who frightened him by growling. "It was instituted in my grandfather's time at the behest of my grandmother. In those days we entertained all the time with scores of guests on some weekends. Of course, a number of these guests would be young men from very good families in the city, quite well educated and full of, shall I say, vim and vigor."

Sybil glanced down at Young Sam and was relieved to see he was now lining up some small soldiers. "The maids, on the other hand, in the very nature of things are not well educated and I'm ashamed to say might have been slightly too compliant in the face of people whom they had come to think of as their betters." She was starting to blush, and she pointed down at Young Sam, who she was glad to see was still paying no attention. "I'm sure you get the picture, Sam? Absolutely sure, and my grandmother, whom you would almost certainly have hated, had decent instincts, and therefore decreed that all the housemaids should not only refrain from talking to the male guests, but should not make eye contact with them either, on pain of dismissal. You might say she was being cruel to be kind, but not all that cruel, come to think of it. In the fullness of time, the housemaids would leave the Hall with good references and not be embarrassed about wearing a white dress on their wedding day."

"But I'm happily married," Vimes protested. "And I can't imagine Willikins risking the wrath of Purity, either."

"Yes, dear, and I'll have a word with Mrs. Silver. But this is the country, Sam. We do things a little more slowly here. Now, why don't you take Young Sam out to see the river? Take Willikins with you—he knows his way around."

Y OUNG SAM DID NOT need very much in the way of entertainment. In fact he made his own entertainment, manufacturing it in large quantities out of observations of the landscape, the stories that had lulled him to sleep at bedtime last night, some butterfly thought that had just sped across his mind and, increasingly, he'd talk about Mr. Whistle, who lived in a house in a tree but was sometimes a dragon. He also had a big boot and didn't like Wednesdays because they smell funny and he had a rainbrella.

Young Sam was thus totally unfazed by the countryside, and ran ahead of Vimes and Willikins, pointing out trees, sheep, flowers, birds, dragonflies, funny-shaped clouds and a human skull. He seemed quite impressed by the find and rushed to show it to his daddy, who stared at it as if he had seen, well, a human skull. It had clearly been a human skull for quite a long time, however, and appeared to have been looked after, to the point of being polished.

As Vimes turned it over in his hands, searching forensically for any sign of foul play, there was a flip-flop sound approaching through the shrubbery, accompanied by a vocal number on the subject of what a person unknown would do to people who stole skulls off him. When the bushes parted said person unknown turned out to be a man of uncertain age and teeth, a grubby brown robe and a beard longer than any Vimes had seen before, and Vimes was a man who had often been inside Unseen University, where wizards considered that wisdom was embodied in the growing of a beard that would keep the knees warm. This one tailed cometlike behind its owner. It caught up with him when his hugely sandaled feet slithered to a stop, but its momentum meant that it began to pile up on his head. Possibly it carried wisdom with it, because its owner was bright enough to stop dead when he saw the look in Vimes's eye. There was silence, apart from the chuckling of Young Sam as the endless beard, with a life of its own, settled on the man like the snows of winter.

Willikins cleared his throat, and said, "I think this is the hermit, commander."

"What's a hermit doing here? I thought they lived up poles in deserts!" Vimes glared at the raggedy man, who clearly felt that an explanation was called for and was going to deliver it whether it was called for or not.

"Yes, sir, I know, sir, that is a popular delusion, and personally I've never given it much credence, on account of the difficulty of dealing with what I might call the bathroom necessities and similar. I mean, that sort of thing might be all right in foreign parts, where there's sunshine and lots of sand, but it wouldn't do for me, sir, no indeed."

The apparition held out a grubby hand that was mostly fingernails and went on, proudly, "Stump, your grace, although I'm not often stumped, haha, my little joke."

"Yes, it is," said Vimes, keeping his eyes blank.

"Indeed it is, sir," said Stump. "The only one I've got. I've been following the noble profession of herming here for nigh on fifty-seven years, practicing piety, sobriety, celibacy and the pursuit of the true wisdom in the tradition of my father and grandfather and great-grandfather before me. That's my great-grandfather you are holding, there, sir," he added cheerfully. "Lovely sheen, hasn't he?" Vimes managed not to drop the skull he was holding. Stump went on, "I expect your little boy wandered into my grotto, sir, no offense meant, sir, but the village lads round here are a bit frolicsome sometimes and I had to get granddad out of the tree only two weeks ago."

It was Willikins who found the mental space to say, "You keep your great-grandfather's skull in a cave?"

"Oh yes, gentlemen, and my father's. Family tradition, see? And my grandfather's. Unbroken tradition of herming for nearly three hundred years, dispensing pious thinking and the knowledge that all paths lead but to the grave, and other somber considerations, to all those who seek us out—who are precious few these days, I might add. I hope my son will be able to step into my sandals when he's old enough. His mother says that he's turning out a very solemn young man, so I live in hopes that one day he might be giving me a right good polishin' up. There's plenty of room on the skull shelf back in the grotto, I'm pleased to say."

"Your son?" said Vimes. "You mentioned celibacy?"

"Very attentive of you, your grace. We get a week's holiday every year. A man cannot live by snails and herbs of the riverbank alone . . ."

Vimes delicately indicated that they had ground to cover, and left the hermit carefully carrying the family relic back to his grotto, wherever that was. When they seemed to be safely out of earshot he said, waving his hands in the air, "Why? I mean . . . why?"

"Oh, quite a few of the really old ancestral homes had a hermit on the strength, sir. It was considered romantic to have a grotto with a hermit in it."

"He was a bit whiffy on the nose," said Vimes.

"Not allowed to bathe, I believe, sir, and you should know, sir, that he gets an allowance consisting of two pounds of potatoes, three pints of small beer or cider, three loaves of bread and one pound of pork dripping per week. And presumably all the snails and herbs of the riverbank he can force down. I looked at the accounts, sir. Not a bad diet for an ornamental garden feature."

"Not too bad if you throw in some fruit and the occasional laxative, I suppose," said Vimes. "So Sybil's ancestors used to come along and talk to the hermit whenever they were faced with a philosophical conundrum, yes?"

Willikins looked puzzled. "Good heavens, no, sir, I can't imagine that any of them would ever dream of doing that. They never had any truck with philosophical conundra.* They were aristocrats, you see? Aristocrats don't notice philosophical conundra. They just ignore them. Philosophy includes contemplating the possibility that you might be wrong, sir, and a real aristocrat knows that he is *always* right. It's not vanity, you understand, it's built-in absolute certainty. They may sometimes be as mad as a hatful of spoons, but they are always *definitely* and *certainly* mad."

Vimes stared at him in admiration. "How the hell do you know all this, Willikins?"

"Watched them, sir. In the good old days when her ladyship's granddad was alive he made certain that the whole staff of Scoone Avenue came down here with the family in the summer. As you know, I'm not much of a scholar and, truth to tell, neither are you, but when you grow up on the street you learn fast because if you don't learn fast you're dead."

They were now walking across an ornamental bridge, over what was probably the trout stream and, Vimes assumed, a tributary of

---

* Later on Vimes pondered Willikins' accurate grasp of the plural noun in the circumstances, but there you were; if someone hung around in houses with lots of books in it, some of it rubbed off just as, come to think of it, it had on Vimes.

Old Treachery, a name whose origin he had yet to comprehend. Two men and one little boy, walking over a bridge that might be carrying crowds, and carts and horses. The world seemed unbalanced.

"You see, sir," said Willikins, "being definite is what gave them all this money and land. Sometimes lost it for them as well, of course. One of Lady Sybil's great-uncles once lost a villa and two thousand acres of prime farmland by being definite in believing that a cloakroom ticket could beat three aces. He was killed in the duel that followed, but at least he was *definitely* dead."

"It's snobbishness and I don't like it," Vimes said.

Willikins rubbed the side of his nose. "Well, commander, it ain't snobbishness. You don't get much of that from the real Mc-Coy, in my experience. The certain ones, I mean . . . they don't worry about what the neighbors think or walking around in old clothes. They're confident, see? When Lady Sybil was younger the family would come down here for the sheep-shearing, and her father would muck in with everybody else, with his sleeves rolled up and everything, and he'd see to it that there was a round of beer for all the lads afterward, and he'd drink with them, flagon for flagon. Of course, he was a brandy man mostly, so a bit of beer wouldn't have him on the floor. He never worried about who he was. He was a decent old boy, her father—and her granddad, too. Certain, you see, never worried."

They walked along an avenue of chestnut trees for a while and then Vimes said, morosely, "Are you saying that I don't know who I am?"

Willikins looked up into the trees and replied, thoughtfully, "It looks as though there'll be a lot of conkers this year, commander, and if you don't mind me suggesting it, you might think of bringing this young lad down here when they start falling. I was the dead-rat conkers champion for years when I was a kid, until I found out that the real things grew on trees and didn't squish so easily. As for your question," he went on, "I think Sam Vimes is at his best when he's confident that he's Sam Vimes. Good grief, and they are fruiting early this year!"

The avenue of chestnut trees ended at this point and before them lay an apple orchard. "Not the best of fruit, as apples go," said Willikins as Vimes and Young Sam crossed over to it, raising the dust on the chalky road. The comment seemed inconsequential to Vimes, but Willikins appeared to consider the orchard very important.

"The little boy will want to see this," Willikins said enthusiastically. "Saw it myself when I was the boot boy. Totally changed the way I thought about the world. The third earl, 'Mad' Jack Ramkin, had a brother called Woolsthorpe, probably for his sins. He was something of a scholar and would have been sent to the university to become a wizard were it not for the fact that his brother let it be known that any male sibling of his who took up a profession that involved wearing a dress would be disinherited with a cleaver.

"Nevertheless, young Woolsthorpe persevered in his studies of natural philosophy in the way a gentleman should, by digging into any suspicious-looking burial mounds he could find in the neighborhood, filling up his lizard press with as many rare species as he could collect, and drying samples of any flowers he could find before they became extinct. The story runs that, on one warm summer day, he dozed off under an apple tree and was awakened when an apple fell on his head. A lesser man, as his biographer put it, would have seen nothing untoward about this, but Woolsthorpe surmised that, since apples and practically everything else always fell down, then the world would eventually become dangerously unbalanced . . . unless there was another agency involved that natural philosophy had yet to discover. He lost no time in dragging one of the footmen to the orchard and ordering him, on pain of dismissal, to lie under the tree until an apple hit him on the head! The possibility of this happening was increased by another footman who had been told by Woolsthorpe to shake the tree vigorously until the required apple fell. Woolsthorpe was ready to observe this from a distance.

"Who can imagine his joy when the inevitable apple fell and a second apple was seen rising from the tree and disappearing at speed into the vaults of heaven, proving the hypothesis that what goes up must come down, provided that what goes down must come up, thus safeguarding the equilibrium of the Universe. Regrettably, this only works with apples and, amazingly, only the apples on this one tree, *Malus equilibria*! I hear someone has worked out that the apples at the top of the tree fill with gas and fly up when the tree is disturbed so that it can set its seeds some way off. Wonderful thing, nature, shame the fruit tastes like dog's business," Willikins added as Young Sam spat some out. "To tell you the truth, commander, I wouldn't give you tuppence for a lot of the upper classes I've met, especially in the city, but some of them in these old country houses changed the world for the better. Like Turnip Ramkin, who revolutionized agriculture . . ."

"I think I've heard of him," said Vimes. "Wasn't he something to do with planting root crops? Wasn't that how he got his nickname?"

"Very nearly right, sir," said Willikins. "In fact, he invented the seed drill, which meant more reliable crops and a great saving in seed corn. He only looked like a turnip. People can be so cruel sometimes, sir. There was also his brother, 'Rubber Ramkin,' who devised not only rubber boots but also rubberized fabric, even before the dwarfs did. Very interested indeed in rubber, so I heard, but it takes all sorts to make a world and it would be a funny old place if we were all the same, and especially if we were all like him. Dry feet and dry shoulders, sir, what every farmworker prays for! I did a spell cutting cabbages one winter, sir, weather as cold as charity and rain coming down so fast it had to queue up to hit the ground. I blessed his name then, so I did, even if it was true what they said about the young ladies, who I heard actually enjoyed the experience . . ."

"This is all very well," said Vimes, "but it doesn't make up for all the stupid, arrogant—"

This time it was Willikins who interrupted his master. "And then there was the flying machine, of course. Her ladyship's late brother put a lot of work into the project, but it never got off the ground. Flying without a broomstick or a magic spell was his goal, but regrettably he fell victim to the outbreak of crisms, poor lad. There's a model of it in the nursery, as a matter of fact. It runs on rubber bands."

"I expect there was plenty of material around the place, unless Rubber Ramkin tidied up after himself," said Vimes.

The tour continued, across meadows of what Vimes decided to call cows and around fields of standing corn. They navigated their way around a ha-ha, kept their distance from the ho-ho and completely ignored the he-he, then climbed a gentle path up a hill on which was planted a grove of beech trees and from which you could see practically everywhere, and certainly to the end of the universe, but that probably involved looking straight up with no beech trees in the way. It was even possible to make out the tall cloud of smoke and fumes that rose from the city of Ankh-Morpork.

"This is Hangman's Hill," said Willikins, as Vimes got his breath back. "And you might not want to go any further," he said as they neared the summit, "unless, that is, you want to explain to your young lad what a gibbet is."

Vimes looked questioningly at his servant. "Really?"

"Well, as I say, this is Hangman's Hill. Why do you think they named it that, sir? 'Black Jack' Ramkin was regrettably mistaken when he made an enormous drunken wager with one of his equally drunk drinking pals that he could see the smoke of the city from his estate. He was told by a surveyor, who had tested the hypothesis, that the hill was thirty feet too short. Pausing only to attempt to bribe the surveyor and when unsuccessful to subsequently horsewhip the same, he rallied all the working men from this estate and all the others round here and set them to raise the hill by the aforesaid thirty feet, a most ambitious project. It cost a fortune, of course, but every family in the district probably got warm winter clothes and new boots out of it. It made him very popular, and of course he won his bet."

Vimes sighed. "Somehow I think I know the answer to this, but I'm going to ask anyway: how much was the bet?"

"Two gallons of brandy," said Willikins triumphantly, "which he drank in one go while standing on this very spot, to the cheers of the assembled workforce, and then, according to legend, rolled all the way down to the bottom, to more cheers."

"Even when I was a boozer I don't think I could have taken two gallons of brandy," said Vimes. "That's twelve bottles!"

"Well, toward the end I expect a lot of it went down his trousers, one way or the other. There were plenty like him, even so . . ."

"All down his trousers," Young Sam piped up, and dissolved into that curious hoarse laughter of a six-year-old who thinks he has heard something naughty. And by the sound of it the workmen who had cheered the old drunk had thought the same way. Cheering a man drinking a year's wages in one go? What was the point?

Willikins must have read his thoughts. "The country isn't as subtle as the city, commander. They like big and straightforward things here, and Black Jack was as big and as straight as you could hope for. That's why they liked him, because they knew where they stood, even if he was about to fall down. I bet they boasted about him all over the Shires. I can just imagine it. *Our drunken old lord can outdrink your drunken old lord any day of the week*, and they would be proud of it. I'm sure you thought you were doing the right thing when you shook hands with the gardener, but you puzzled people. They don't know what to make of you. Are you a man or a master? Are you a nob or one of them? Because, commander, from where they sit no man can be both. It would be against nature. And the countryside doesn't like puzzles, either."

"Big puzzled trousers!" said Young Sam and fell on the grass, overwhelmed with humor.

"I don't know what to make of me either," said Vimes, picking up his son and following Willikins down the slope. "But Sybil does. She's got me marked down for balls, dances, dinners, and, oh yes, soirées," he finished, in the tones of a man genetically programmed to distrust any word with an acute accent in it. "I mean, that sort of thing in the city I've come to terms with. If I reckon that it's going to be too bloody dreadful I make certain I get called out in an emergency halfway through—at least I used to, before Sybil twigged on. It's a terrible thing when a man's employees take their orders from his wife, you know?"

"Yes, commander. She has given the kitchen staff orders that no bacon sandwiches are to be prepared without her express permission."

Vimes winced. "You brought the little cookery kit, didn't you?"

"Unfortunately, her ladyship knows about our little cookery kit, commander. She has forbidden the kitchen to give me bacon unless the order comes directly from her."

"Honestly, she's as bad as Vetinari! How does she find out all this stuff?"

"As a matter of fact, commander, I don't think she does, at least as an actual fact. She just *knows* you. Perhaps you should think of it as amiable suspicion. We should be getting along, commander. I'm told there is chicken salad for lunch."

"Do I like chicken salad?"

"Yes, commander, her ladyship tells me that you do."

Vimes gave in. "Then I do."

Back in Scoone Avenue, Vimes and Sybil generally took only one meal a day together, in the kitchen, which was always pleasantly snug by then. They sat facing one another at the table, which was long enough to carry Vimes's huge collection of sauce bottles, mustard pots, pickles and, of course, chutneys, Vimes being of the popular persuasion that no jar of pickles is ever truly empty if you rattle the spoon around inside it long enough.

Things were different at the Hall. For one thing there was far too much food. Vimes had not been born yesterday, or even the day before, and refrained from commenting.

Willikins served Vimes and Lady Sybil. Strictly speaking it wasn't his job while they were away from home, but strictly speaking most gentlemen's gentlemen didn't carry a set of brass knuckles in their well-cut jacket either.

"And what did you boys do this morning?" said Sybil cheerfully, as the plates were emptied.

"We saw the stinky bone man!" said Young Sam. "He was like all beard, but stinky! And we found the smelly apple tree which is like poo!"

Lady Sybil's placid expression did not change. "And then you came down the roly-poly hill, didn't you? And what about the ha-ha, the ho-ho and the he-he?"

"Yes, but there's all cow poo! I treaded in it!" Young Sam waited for an adult response, and his mother said, "Well, you've got your new country boots, haven't you? Treading in cow poo is what they're for."

Sam Vimes watched his son's face glow with impossible pleasure as his mother went on. "Your grandfather always told me that if I saw a big pile of muck in a field I should kick it around a bit so as to spread it evenly, because that way *all* the grass will grow properly." She smiled at Vimes's expression and said, "Well, it's true, dear. A lot of farming is about manure."

"Just so long as he understands that he doesn't start kicking up the gutters when he gets back to the city," Vimes said. "Some of that stuff will kick back."

"He should learn about the countryside. He should know where food comes from and how we get it. This is important, Sam!"

"Of course, dear."

Lady Sybil gave her husband a look only a wife can give. "That was your put-upon-but-dutiful voice, Sam."

"Yes, but I don't see—"

Sybil interrupted him. "Young Sam will own all this one day and I'd like him to have some idea about it all, just as I'd like you to relax and enjoy your holiday. I'm taking Young Sam over to Home Farm later on, to see the cows being milked, and to collect some eggs." She stood up. "But first I'm going to take him down to the crypt, to see his ancestors." She noted her husband's look of panic and added, quickly, "It's all right, Sam, they aren't walking around; they are, in fact, in very expensive boxes. Why don't you come too?"

S AM VIMES WAS NO stranger to death, and vice versa. It was
the suicides that got him down. They were mostly hangings,
because you would have to be extremely suicidal to jump into the
River Ankh, not least because you would bounce several times
before you broke through the crust. And they all had to be investigated, just in case it was a murder in disguise,* and whereas Mr.
Trooper, the current city hangman, could drop someone into eter-
nity so quickly and smoothly that they probably didn't notice, too
often Vimes had seen what amateurs managed to do.

The Ramkin family crypt reminded him of the city morgue
after hours. It was crowded; some coffins were stacked edgewise,
as though they were on shelves in the mortuary, but, it was to be
hoped, they didn't slide out. Vimes watched warily as his wife carefully took their son from plaque to plaque reading out the names
and explaining a little about every occupant, and he felt the cold,
bottomless depths of time around him, somehow breathing from
the walls. How could it feel for Young Sam to know the names
of all those grandfathers and grandmothers down the centuries?
Vimes had never known his father. His mum told him that the
man had been run over by a cart, but Vimes suspected that if this
was true at all, then it was probably a brewer's cart, which had "run
him over" a bit at a time for years. Oh, of course there was Old
Stoneface, the regicide, now rehabilitated and with his own statue
in the city which was never graffitied because Vimes had made it
clear what would happen to the perpetrator.

But Old Stoneface was just a point in time, a kind of true myth.

---

* More than once watchmen had found handwritten suicide notes which on
careful examination weren't in the right handwriting.

There wasn't a line between him and Sam Vimes, only an aching gulf.

Still, Young Sam would be a duke one day, and that was a thought worth hanging on to. He wouldn't grow up worrying about what he was, because he would *know*, and the influence of his mother might just outweigh the enormous drag factor of having Samuel Vimes as a father. Young Sam would be able to shake up the world the right way. You need confidence to do that, and having a bunch of (apparently) loony but interesting ancestors could only impress the man in the street, and Vimes knew a lot of streets, and a lot of men.

Willikins hadn't entirely told the truth. Even city people liked a character, especially a black-hearted one or one interesting enough to materially add to the endless crazy circus show which was the street life of Ankh-Morpork, and while having a drunkard for a father was a social faux pas, having a great-great-great-grandfather who could drink so much brandy that his urine must surely have been inflammable, and then, according to Willikins, proceeded to go home to a meal of turbot followed by roast goose (with appropriate wines) and then played a hand of saddle pork* with his cronies until dawn, winning back his earlier losses . . . Well, people loved that sort of thing, and that sort of person, who kicked the world in the arse and shouted at it. That was an ancestor to be proud of, surely?

"I think . . . I'd like to go for a walk by myself," said Vimes. "You know, have a look round, poke about a bit, get the hang of this countryside business at my own pace."

---

* Saddle pork was invented some time around the Year of the Stoat by Reverend Joseph "Causality" Robinson, rector of All Saints and Three Sinners in the parish of Lower Overhang. As far as can be determined from notes made by his contemporaries, the game may be considered an amalgam of spillikins, halma and brandy. No known rules exist, if, indeed, there ever really were any.

47

"Willikins ought to accompany you, dear," said Lady Sybil, "just in case."

"In case of what, my dear? I walk around the streets of the city every night, don't I? I don't think I need a chaperone for a stroll in the country, do I? I'm trying to get into the spirit of things. I'll look at daffodils to see if they fill me with joy, or whatever it is they're supposed to do, and keep an eye open for the very rare grebe warbler and watch the moles take flight. I've been reading the nature notes in the paper for weeks. I think I know how to do this by myself, dear. The commander of the Watch is not afraid to spot the spotted flycatcher!"

Lady Sybil had learned from experience when it was wise not to argue, and contented herself with saying, "Don't upset anybody, at least, will you, dear?"

AFTER TEN MINUTES OF walking, Vimes was lost. Not physically lost but metaphorically, spiritually and peripatetically lost. The fragrances of the hedgerows were somehow without body compared with the robust stinks of the city, and he had not the faintest idea what was rustling in the undergrowth. He recognized heifers and bullocks, because he often walked through the slaughterhouse district, but the ones out here weren't bewildered by fear and stared at him carefully as he walked past as if they were calmly taking notes. Yes—that was it! The world was back to front! He was a copper, he had always been a copper, and he would die a copper. You never stopped being a copper, on the whole, and as a copper he walked around the city more or less invisible, except to those people who make it their business to spot coppers, and whose livelihood depends upon their spotting coppers before coppers spot them. Mostly you were part of the scenery, until the scream, the tinkle of broken glass and the sound of felonious footsteps brought you into focus.

But here *everything* was watching him. Things darted away behind a hedge, flew up in panic or just rustled suspiciously in the undergrowth. He was the stranger, the interloper, not wanted here.

He turned another corner, and there was the village. He had seen the chimneys some way off, but the lanes and footpaths criss-crossed one another in a tangle, repeated in the overflowing hedgerows and trees, that made tunnels of shade—which were welcome—and played merry hells with his sense of direction, which was not.

He had lost all his bearings and was hot and bothered by the time he came out into a long dusty lane with thatched cottages on either side and halfway down a large building which had "pub" written all over it, particularly by the three old men who were sitting on the bench outside it eyeing the approaching Vimes hopefully in case he was the kind of man who would buy another man a pint. They wore clothes that looked as if they had been nailed on. Then, when he got closer, one said something to the other two and they stood up as he passed, index fingers touching their hat brims. One of them said, "Garternoon, yer grace," a phrase which Vimes interpreted after a little thought. There was also a slight and meaningful tip of the empty tankards to indicate that they were, in fact, empty tankards and therefore an anomaly in need of rectification.

Vimes knew what was expected of him. There wasn't a pub in Ankh-Morpork which didn't have the equivalent three old men sunning themselves outside and ever ready to talk to strangers about the good old days, i.e., when the tankards they were nursing still had beer in them. And the form was that you filled them up with cheap ale and got a "Well, thank you, kind sir," and quite possibly little bubbles of information about who had been seen where doing what and with whom and when, all grist to the copper's mill.

But the expressions on these three changed when another of them whispered hurriedly to his cronies. They pushed themselves back on the wooden seat as if trying to make themselves inconspicuous while still clasping the empty flagons because, well, you never knew. A sign over the door proclaimed that this was the Goblin's Head.

Opposite the pub was a large open space laid, as they say, to grass. A few sheep grazed on it and toward the far end was a large stack of wood licker wicker wood hurdles, the purpose of which Vimes could not guess. He was, however, familiar with the term "village green," although he had never seen one. Ankh-Morpork wasn't very big on greens.

The pub smelled of stale beer. This helped as a bulwark against temptation, although Vimes had been clean for years, and could face the occasional sherry at official events, because he hated the taste of it anyway. The smell of antique beer had the same effect. By the pitiful light of the tiny windows Vimes made out an elderly man industriously polishing a tankard. The man looked up at Vimes and gave him a nod, the basic nod which is understood everywhere as meaning "I see you, you see me, it's up to you what happens next," although some publicans can put an inflection on a nod which also manages to convey the information that there might just be a two-foot length of lead piping under the counter should the party of the second part want to start anything, as it were.

Vimes said, "Do you serve anything that isn't alcoholic?"

The barman very carefully hung the tankard on a hook over the bar and then looked directly at Vimes and said, without rancor, "Well, you see, sir, this is what we call a pub. People gets stuffy about it if I leaves out the alcohol." He drummed his fingers on the bar for a moment and went on, uncertainly, "My wife makes root beer, if that takes your fancy?"

"What kind of root?"

"Beetroot, as it happens, sir. It's good for keeping you regular."

"Well, I've always thought of myself as a regular kind of person," said Vimes. "Give me a pint—no, make that half a pint, thanks." There was another nod and the man disappeared briefly behind the scenes and came back with a large glass overflowing with red foam. "There you go," he said, putting it carefully on the bar. "We don't put it in pewter because it does something to the metal. This one is on the house, sir. My name is Jiminy, landlord of the Goblin's Head. I dare say I know yours. My daughter is a maid at the big house, and I treat every man alike, the reason being that the publican is a friend to any man with money in his pockets and also, if the whim takes him, perhaps even to those who temporarily find themselves stony broke, which does not, at the moment, include them three herberts outside. The publican sees all men after a couple of pints, and sees no reason to discriminate."

Jiminy winked at Vimes, who held out his hand and said, "Then I'll happily shake the hand of a republican!"

Vimes was familiar with the ridiculous litany. Every man who served behind a bar thought of himself as one of the world's great thinkers and it was wise to treat him as such. After the handshake he added, "This juice is pretty good. Rather tangy."

"Yes, sir, my wife puts chilli peppers in it, and celery seed to make a man think that he's drinking something with bones in."

Vimes leaned on the bar, inexplicably at peace. The wall over the bar was hung with the heads of dead animals, particularly those possessed of antlers and fangs, but it came as a shock to spot, in the grubby light, a goblin's head. I'm on holiday, he thought, and that probably happened a long time ago, ancient history, and he left it at that.

Mr. Jiminy busied himself with the dozens of little tasks that a barman can always find to do, while occasionally glancing at his single customer. Vimes thought for a moment and said, "Can you take a pint to those gentlemen outside, Mr. Jiminy, and put a brandy in each one so that a man knows he's drinking something?"

"That would be Long Tom, Short Tom and Tom Tom," said Jiminy, reaching for some mugs. "Decent lads—triplets, as it happens. They earn their keep but, as you might say, they shared one brain out between all three of them and it wasn't that good a brain to start with. Very good when it comes to scaring crows, though."

"And were all named Tom?" said Vimes.

"That's right. It's by way of being a family name, see, their dad being called Tom also. Maybe it saves confusion, them being easily confused. They're getting on a bit now, of course, but if you give them a job they can do then they'll do it well, and won't stop until you tell them to. No beggars in the countryside, see? There's always little jobs that need doing. By your leave, sir, I'll give them short measure on the brandy. They don't need too much confusing, if you get my drift."

The publican put the mugs on a tray and disappeared out into the bright sunshine. Vimes moved swiftly behind the bar and back again without stopping. A few seconds later he was leaning nonchalantly on the bar as three faces peeped in through the open door. With a look of some apprehension three thumbs-up salutes were aimed at Vimes and the faces were hauled back out of sight again, presumably in case he exploded or developed horns.

Jiminy came back with the empty tray, and gave Vimes a cheerful smile. "Well, you've made some friends there, sir, but don't let me keep you. I'm sure you've got a lot to do."

A copper, thought Vimes. I recognize a police truncheon when I see one. That's the copper's dream, isn't it—to leave the streets behind and run a little pub somewhere, and because you're a copper and because being a copper never leaves you, you will know what is going on. I know you and you don't know that I do. And from where I'm sitting I call that a result. You wait, Mr. Jiminy. I know where you live.

Now Vimes could hear slow and heavy footsteps in the distance, getting closer. He saw the local men as they arrived in their working clothes and carrying what most people would call agricultural implements, but which Vimes mentally noted as offensive weapons. The troupe stopped outside the door and now he heard whispering. The three Toms were imparting today's news, apparently, and it seemed to be received with either incredulity or scorn. Some sort of conclusion was being reached, not happily.

And then the men lurched in, and Vimes's mind clocked them for ready reference. Exhibit one was an elderly man with a long white beard and, good heavens, a smock. Did they really still wear those? Whatever his name the others probably called him "Granddad." He shyly touched his forefinger to his forehead in salute and headed for the bar, job safely done. He had been carrying a big hook, not a nice weapon. Exhibit two carried a shovel, which could be an ax or a club if a man knew what he was doing. He was smocked up too, didn't catch Vimes's eye, and his salute had been more like a begrudged wave. Exhibit three, who was holding a toolbox (terrific weapon if swung accurately) scurried past with speed and barely glanced in Vimes's direction. He looked young and rather weedy, but nevertheless you can get a good momentum on one of those boxes. Then there was another elderly man, wearing a blacksmith's apron, but the wrong build, so Vimes marked him down as a farrier. Yes, that would be it, short and wiry, would easily be able to get under a horse. The man presented a reasonable attempt at a forelock salute, and Vimes was unable to make out any dangerous bulges concealed by the apron. He couldn't help this algebra; it was what you did when you did the job. Even if you didn't expect trouble, you, well, expected trouble.

And then the room froze.

There had been some desultory conversation in the vicinity of Jiminy but it stopped now as the real blacksmith came in. Bugger. All Vimes's warning bells rang at once, and they weren't tinkly bells. They clanged. After a brief glower round the room the man headed for the bar on the course that would take him past, or probably over, or even through Sam Vimes. As it was, Vimes carefully pulled his mug out of harm's way so that the man's undisguised attempt to "accidentally" spill it failed.

"Mr. Jiminy," Vimes called out, "a round of drinks for these gentlemen, all right?"

This caused a certain amount of cheerfulness among the other newcomers, but the smith slammed a hand like a shovel down on the wood so that glasses jumped.

"I don't care to drink with them as grinds the faces of the poor!"

Vimes held his gaze, and said, "Sorry, I didn't bring my grinder with me today." It was silly, because a couple of sniggers from hopeful drinkers at the bar merely stoked whatever fires the blacksmith had neglected to leave at work, and made him angry.

"Who are you to think you're a better man than me?"

Vimes shrugged, and said, "I don't know if I am a better man than you." But he was thinking: you look to me like a big man in a small community, and you think you're tough because you're strong and metal doesn't sneak up behind you and try to kick you in the goolies. Good grief, you don't even know how to stand right! Even Corporal Nobbs could get you down and be kicking you industriously in the fork before you knew what was happening.

Like any man fearing that something expensive could get broken, Jiminy came bustling across the floor and grabbed the smith by one arm, saying, "Come on, Jethro, let's have no trouble. His grace is just having a drink the like of which any man is entitled to . . ."

This appeared to work, although aggression smouldered on Jethro's face and indeed in the surrounding air. By the look on the faces of the other men, this was a performance they were familiar with.It was a poor copper who couldn't read a pub crowd, and Vimes could probably write a history, with footnotes. Every community has its firebrand, or madman, or self-taught politician. Usually they are tolerated because they add to the gaiety of nations, as it were, and people say things like "It's just his way," and the air clears and life goes on. But Jethro, now sitting in the far corner of the bar nursing his pint like a lion huddled over his gazelle, well, Jethro, in the Vimes lexicon of risk, was a man likely to explode. Of course the world sometimes needed blowing up, just so long as it didn't happen where Vimes was drinking.

Vimes was becoming aware that the pub was filling up, mostly with other sons of the soil, but also with people who, whether they were gentlemen or not, would expect to be called so. They wore colorful caps and white trousers and spoke continuously.

There was also further activity outside; horses and carriages were filling the lane. Hammering was going on somewhere and Jiminy's wife was now manning or, more correctly, womaning the bar while her husband ran back and forth with his tray. Jethro remained in his corner like a man biding his time, occasionally glaring daggers, and probably fists as well with an option on boots, if Vimes so much as looked at him.

Vimes decided to take a look out of the grubby pub window. Regrettably, the pub was that most terrifying of things, picturesque, which meant that the window consisted of small round panes fixed in place with lead. They were for letting the light in, not for looking out of, since they bent light so erratically that it nearly broke. One pane showed what was probably a sheep but which looked like a white whale, until it moved, when it became a mushroom. A man walked past with no head until he reached another pane and then had one enormous eyeball. Young Sam would have loved it, but his father decided to give eventual blindness a miss and stepped out into the sunshine.

Ah, he thought, some kind of game.

Oh well.

Vimes wasn't keen on games because they led to crowds, and crowds led to work for coppers. But here in fact he wasn't a copper, was he? It was a strange feeling, so he left the pub and became an innocent bystander. He couldn't remember when he had been one before. It felt . . . vulnerable. He strolled over to the nearest man, who was hammering some stakes into the ground, and asked, "What's going on here, then?" Realizing that he had spoken in copper rather than in ordinary citizen, he added quickly, "If you don't mind me asking?"

The man straightened up. He was one of the ones with the colorful caps. "Haven't you ever seen a game of crockett, sir? It's the game of games!"

Mr. Civilian Vimes did his best to look like a man eager for more delicious information. Judging by his informant's enthusiastic grin, he was about to learn the rules of crockett, whether he wanted to or not. Well, he thought, I did ask . . .

"At first sight, sir, Crockett might seem like just another ball game wherein two sides strive against one another by endeavoring to propel the ball by hand or bat or other device into the opponents' goal of some sort. Crockett, however, was invented during a game of croquet at St. Onan's Theological College in Ham-on-

Rye, when the novice priest Jackson Fieldfair, now the Bishop of Quirm, took his mallet in both hands, and instead of giving the ball a gentle tap . . ."

After that Vimes gave up, not only because the rules of the game were incomprehensible in their own right, but also because the extremely enthusiastic young man allowed his enthusiasm to overtake any consideration of the need to explain things in some sensible order, which meant that the flood of information was continually punctuated by apologetic comments on the lines of "I'm sorry, I should have explained earlier that a second cone is not allowed more than once per exchange, and in normal play there is only one tump, unless, of course, you're talking about royal crockett . . ."

Vimes died . . . The sun dropped out of the sky, giant lizards took over the world, the stars exploded and went out and all hope vanished with a gurgle into the sink-trap of oblivion, and gas filled the firmament and combusted and behold there was a new heaven, one careful owner, and a new disc, and lo, and possibly verily, life crawled out of the sea, or possibly didn't because it had been made by the gods—that was really up to the bystander—and lizards turned into less scaly lizards, or possibly did not, and lizards turned into birds, and worms turned into butterflies, and a species of apple turned into bananas, and possibly a kind of monkey fell out of a tree and realized that life was better when you didn't have to spend your time hanging onto something, and, in only a few million years, evolved trousers and ornamental stripy hats and lastly the game of crockett and there, magically reincarnated, was Vimes, a little dizzy, standing on the village green looking into the smiling countenance of an enthusiast.

He managed to say, "Well, that's amazing, thank you so very much. I look forward to enjoying the game." At which point, he thought, a brisk walk home might be in order, only to be foiled by a regrettably familiar voice behind him saying, "You, I say you, yes, you! Aren't you Vimes?"

It was Lord Rust, usually of Ankh-Morpork, and a fierce old warhorse, without whose unique grasp of strategy and tactics several wars would not have been so bloodily won. Now he was in a wheelchair, a newfangled variety pushed by a man, whose life was, knowing his lordship, quite probably unbearable.

But hatred tends not to have a long half-life and in recent years Vimes had regarded the man as now no more than a titled idiot, rendered helpless by age, yet still possessed of an annoying horsy voice that, suitably harnessed, might be used to saw down trees. Lord Rust was not a problem anymore. There were surely only a few more years to go before he would rust in peace. And somewhere in his knobbly heart Vimes still retained a slight admiration for the cantankerous old butcher, with his evergreen self-esteem and absolute readiness not to change his mind about anything at all. The old boy had reacted to the fact that Vimes, the hated policeman, was now a duke, and therefore a lot more nobby than he was, by simply assuming that this could not possibly be true, and therefore totally ignoring it. Lord Rust, in Vimes's book, was a dangerous buffoon but, and here was the difficult bit, an incredibly, if suicidally, brave one. This would have been absolutely tickety-boo were it not for the suicides of those poor fools who followed him into battle.

Witnesses had said that it was uncanny: Rust would gallop into the jaws of death at the head of his men and was never seen to flinch, yet arrows and morningstars always missed him while invariably hitting the men right behind him. Bystanders—or rather people peering at the battle from behind comfortably large rocks—had testified to this. Perhaps he was capable of ignoring, too, the arrows meant for him. But age could not be so easily upstaged, and the old man, while no less arrogant, had a sunken look.

Rust, most unusually, smiled at Vimes and said, "First time I've ever seen you down here, Vimes. Is Sybil going back to her roots, what?"

"She wants Young Sam to get some mud on his boots, Rust."

"Well done, her, what! It'll do the boy good and make a man of him, what!"

Vimes never understood where the explosive *what*s came from. After all, he thought, what's the point of just barking out "What!" for absolutely no discernible reason? And as for, "What what!" well, what was that all about? Why what? *What*s seemed to be tent-pegs hammered into the conversation, but what the hells for, what?

"So not down here on any official business, then, what?"

Vimes's mind spun so quickly that Rust should have heard the wheels go round. It analyzed the tone of voice, the look of the man, that slight, ever so slight but nevertheless perceptible hint of a hope that the answer would be "no," and presented him with a sugges-tion that it might not be a bad idea to drop a tiny kitten among the pigeons.

He laughed. "Well, Rust, Sybil has been banging on about coming down here since Young Sam was born, and this year she put her foot down and I suppose an order from his wife must be considered official, when!" Vimes saw the man who pushed the enormous wheelchair trying to conceal a smile, especially when Rust responded with a baffled "What?"

Vimes decided not to go with "Where" and instead said, in an offhand way, "Well, you know how it is, Lord Rust. A policeman will find a crime anywhere if he decides to look hard enough."

Lord Rust's smile remained, but it had congealed slightly as he said, "I should listen to the advice of your good lady, Vimes. I

don't think you'll find anything worth your mettle down here!"
There was no "what" to follow, and the lack of it was somehow an
emphasis.

IT WAS OFTEN A good idea, Vimes had always found, to give
the silly bits of the brain something to do, so that they did not
interfere with the important ones which had a proper job to fulfil.
So he watched his first game of crockett for a full half-hour before
an internal alarm told him that shortly he should be back at the
Hall in time to read to Young Sam—something that with any luck
did not have poo mentioned on every page—and tuck him into
bed before dinner.

His prompt arrival got a nod of approval from Sybil, who gingerly handed him a new book to read to Young Sam.

Vimes looked at the cover. The title was *The World of Poo*. When
his wife was out of eyeshot he carefully leafed through it. Well,
okay, you had to accept that the world had moved on and these
days fairy stories were probably not going to be about twinkly
little things with wings. As he turned page after page, it dawned on
him that whoever had written this book, they certainly knew what
would make kids like Young Sam laugh until they were nearly
sick. The bit about sailing down the river almost made *him* smile.
But interspersed with the scatology was actually quite interesting
stuff about septic tanks and dunnakin divers and gongfermors and
how dog muck helped make the very best leather, and other things
that you never thought you would need to know, but once heard
somehow lodged in your mind.

Apparently it was by the author of *Wee* and if Young Sam had
one vote for the best book ever written, then it would go to *Wee*.
His enthusiasm was perhaps fanned all the more because a rare

imp of mischief in Vimes led him to do all the necessary straining noises.

Later, over dinner, Sybil quizzed him about his afternoon. She was particularly interested when he mentioned stopping by to watch the crockett.

"Oh they still play it? That's wonderful! How did it go?"

Vimes put down his knife and fork and stared thoughtfully at the ceiling for a moment or two, then said, "Well, I was talking to Lord Rust for some of the time, and I had to leave, of course, because of Young Sam, but fortune favored the priests, when their striker managed to tump a couple of the farmers by a crafty use of the hamper. There were several appeals to the hat man about this, because he broke his mallet in so doing, and in my opinion the hat man's decision was entirely correct, especially since the farmers had played a hawk maneuver." He took a deep breath. "When play recommenced, the farmers still had not found their stride but got a breathing space when a sheep wandered onto the pitch and the priests, assuming that this would stop play, relaxed too soon, and Higgins J. fired a magnificent handsaw under the offending ruminant . . ."

Sybil finally stopped him when she realized that the meal was growing very cold, and said, "Sam! How did you become an expert on the noble game of crockett?"

Vimes picked up his knife and fork. "Please don't ask me again," he sighed. In his head meanwhile a little voice said, *Lord Rust tells me there is nothing here for me. Oh dear, I'd better find out what it is, what?*

He cleared his throat and said, "Sybil, did you actually look at that book I'm reading to Young Sam?"

"Yes, dear. Felicity Beedle is the most famous children's writer in the world. She's been at it for years. She wrote *Melvin and the*

Enormous Boil, Geoffrey and the Magic Pillow Case, The Little Duckling Who Thought He Was an Elephant . . ."

"Did she write one about an elephant who thought he was a duckling?"

"No, Sam, because that would be silly. Oh, she also wrote *Daphne and the Nose Pickers* and *Gaston's Enormous Problem* won for her the Gladys H. J. Ferguson award—the fifth time she's been given it. She gets children interested in reading, you see?"

"Yes," said Vimes, "but they're reading about poo and brain-dead ducklings!"

"Sam, that's part of the commonality of mankind, so don't be so prudish. Young Sam's a country boy now, and I'm very proud of him, and he likes books. That's the whole point! Miss Beedle also finances scholarships for the Quirm College for Young Ladies. She must be quite wealthy now, but I hear she's taken Apple Tree Cottage—you can practically see it from here, it's on the side of the hill—and I think it right, if you don't mind, of course, that we invite her here to the Hall."

"Of course," said Vimes, though his dontmindedness was entirely due to the way his wife's question had been phrased and the subtle resonances that Miss Beedle's attendance was a done deal.

V IMES SLEPT A LOT better that night, partly because he could feel that somewhere in the universe nearby there was a clue waiting for him to pull. That made his fingers itch already.

In the morning, as he had promised, he took Young Sam horse riding. Vimes could ride, but hated doing so. Nevertheless, falling off the back of a pony onto one's head was a skill that every young man should learn if only so that he resolved never to do it again.

The rest of the day, however, did not work out well. Vimes, suspicions filling his mind, was metaphorically and only just short of literally dragged by Sybil to see her friend Ariadne, the lady blessed with the six daughters. In actual fact there were only five visible in the chintzy drawing room when Sybil and he were ushered in. He was feted as "the Dear Brave Commander Vimes"—he hated that shit, but under Sybil's benign but careful gaze he was wise enough not to say so, at least not in those precise words. And so he grinned and bore it while they fluttered around him like large moths, and he waved away yet more teacakes, and cups of tea that would have been welcome were it not that they looked and tasted like what proper tea turns into shortly after you drink it. As far as Sam Vimes was concerned, he liked tea, but tea was not tea if, even before drinking, you could see the bottom of the cup.

Still worse than the stuff he was being offered was the conversation, which inclined toward bonnets, a subject on which his ignorance was not just treasured but venerated. And besides, his breeches were chafing: wretched things, but Sybil had insisted, saying that he looked very smart in them, just like a country gentleman. Vimes had to suppose that country gentleman had different arrangements in the groinal department.

There was, besides himself and Lady Sybil, a young Omnian curate, wisely dressed in a voluminous black robe, which presumably presented no groinal problems. Vimes had no idea why the young man was there, but presumably the young ladies needed somebody to fill with weak tea, suspect scones and mindless twittering conversation when someone like Vimes wasn't there. And it seemed that when the subject of bonnets lost its fascination the only other topics were legacies and the prospects for forthcoming balls. And so, inevitably, given his restlessness in female company, a growing disaffection for urine-colored tea, and small talk that would barely be visible under a microscope, Vimes said, "Excuse me asking, ladies, but what is it that you actually, I mean actually *do* . . . For a living, I mean?"

This question elicited five genuinely blank looks. Vimes couldn't tell the daughters one from the other, except the one called Emily, who certainly lodged in the mind and possibly also in doorways, and who now said, in the tones of one slightly out of her depth, "I do beg your pardon, commander, but I don't think we understand what you just vouchsafed?"

"I meant, well, how do you make a living? Are any of you in employment? How do you make your daily crust? What work do you do?" Vimes could pick up nothing from Sybil, because he couldn't see her face, but the girl's mother was staring at him with gleeful fascination. Oh well, if he was going to get it in the neck he might as well get it all the way down. "I mean, ladies," he said, "how do you make your way in the world? How do you earn your keep? Apart from bonnets, do you have any skills—like cookery, for example?"

Another daughter, quite possibly Mavis, but Vimes was guessing, cleared her throat and said, "Fortunately, commander, we have servants for that sort of thing. We're gentlewomen, you see? It would be quite, quite unthinkable for us to go into trade or commerce. The scandal! It's just not done."

By now there appeared to be a competition to see who could terminally baffle who, or possibly whom, first. But Vimes managed to say, "Don't you have a sister in the timber business?"

It was amazing, he thought, that neither their mother nor Sybil was as yet adding anything to the conversation. And now another sister (possibly Amanda?) looked about to speak. Why in the world did they all wear those silly diaphanous dresses? You couldn't hope to do a day's work in something as skimpy as that. Amanda (possibly) said carefully, "I'm afraid our sister is a bit of an embarrassment to the family, your grace."

"What, for getting a job! Why?"

Another one of the girls, and Vimes was in fact getting really confused at this point, said, "Well, commander, she has no hope of making a good marriage now . . . er, not to a gentleman."

This was becoming a tangle and so Vimes said, "Tell me, ladies, what is a gentleman?"

After some whispered conversation a sacrificial daughter said, very nervously, "We understand the gentleman is a man who does not have to sully his hands by working."

Adamantium is said to be the strongest of all metals, but it would have bent around the patience of Sam Vimes as he said, with every syllable carefully smelted, "Oh, a layabout. And how do you go about snagging such a gentleman, pray?"

Now the girls looked as if they were indeed praying. One of them managed to say, "You see, commander, our dear late father was unlucky in the money market, and I'm afraid that until the death of Great-aunt Marigold, of whom we have expectations, there is, alas, no money for a dowry for any of us."

The heavens held their breath while the concept of a dowry was explained to Sam Vimes, and ice formed on the windows as he sat in strangulated thought.

At last, he cleared his throat and said, "Ladies, the solution to your problem, in my opinion, would be to get off your quite attractive backsides, go out there in the world and make your own way! A dowry? You mean some man has to be *paid* to marry you? What century do you think you're living in? Is it just me, or is it the most bloody stupid thing you could ever imagine?" He glanced at the beautiful Emily and thought, good grief, men would line up on the lawn to fight one another, my dear. How come no one's ever told you? Gentility is all very well, but practicality has its uses. Get out in the world and let the world see you and it might find a new word in its vocabulary such as, perhaps, "wow!" Aloud he continued, "Honestly, there are lots of jobs out there for a young lady with her wits about her. The Lady Sybil Free Hospital is always on the lookout for sharp girls to train as nurses, for example. Good pay, very fetching uniforms, and a fine chance of snagging a skilled young physician who is on the way to the top, especially if you get your boot behind him. Plus, of course, as a nurse you inherit an amazingly large amount of amusing and embarrassing stories about things which people put . . . Perhaps this is not the time, but anyway, there is also the possibility of becoming matron if you reach the specified weight. A *very* responsible job, of use to the community at large and giving you at the end of a long day the satisfaction that you have done some good in the world."

Vimes looked around at the pink and white faces contemplating a jump into the unknown and continued. "Of course, if you really want to stick with bonnets, then Sybil and I own a decent property in Old Cobblers, in the big city, which is standing empty. Used to be a tough area, but the upwardly mobile trolls and vampires are moving in right now, and the heavy dollar and the dark dollar are not to be sneezed at, especially because they'll pay top dollar for what they want. Quite a sophisticated area, too. People actually put tables and chairs out on the pavement and they *don't always all get stolen*. We could let you have it rent free for three months to see how you do and then maybe you'd have to learn the concept of rent, if only for your self-respect. Trust me, ladies, self-respect is what you get when you don't have to spend your life waiting for some rich old lady to pop her clogs. Any takers?"

Vimes took as an optimistic sign the fact that the girls were staring at one another with what could only be called a wild surmise at the prospect of not being totally useless ornaments, and so he added, "And whatever you do, stop reading bloody silly romantic novels!"

There was, however, a pocket—or possibly purse—of resistance to the revolution. One girl was standing by the curate as if she owned him. She looked at Vimes defiantly and said, "Please don't think me forward, commander, but I'd rather like to marry Jeremy and help him in his ministry."

"Very good, very good," said Vimes. "And you love him and he loves you? Speak up, the pair of you." They both nodded, red with embarrassment, each with one eye on the girl's mother, whose wide grin suggested that would be a definite plus. "Well then, I suggest you get yourselves sorted out, and you, young man, would be advised to find a better-paying job. Can't help you with that, but there are loads of religions these days, and if I were you I'd impress some bishop somewhere with my common sense, which is what a clergyman needs above everything else . . . Well, nearly everything else, and remember there's room at the top . . . Although in the case of religion, not right at the top, eh?" Vimes thought for a moment and added, "But maybe the best idea, ladies, might be to take a look around a bit until you find some lad that's got the makings of a successful man, noble or not, and if he suits then get behind him, support him as necessary, help him up when he's down, and generally be around when he looks for you, and make certain that he'll be around when you look for him. Well, if both of you put your backs into it then it might turn out to be something good. It has certainly worked once before, didn't it, Sybil?"

Sybil burst out laughing and the overwhelmed girls nodded dutifully as if they actually understood, but Vimes was gratified to feel a gentle little prod from Lady Sybil that offered hope that he was not going to pay too high a price from his wife for speaking his mind to these precious flowers.

He looked around as if seeking to tidy things up. "Well, that seems to be that, yes?"

"Excuse me, commander?" It took Vimes some time to see where the voice had come from; this daughter hadn't spoken a word all afternoon, but had occasionally scribbled in a notebook. Now she gazed at him with a look somewhat brighter than those of her sisters.

"Can I help you, miss? And perhaps you'll tell me your name?"

"Jane, commander. I am endeavoring to be a writer, may I ask if you have any views on that as an acceptable career for a young lady?"

Jane, thought Vimes, the strange one. And she was. She was just as demure as the other sisters, but somehow as he looked at her he got the impression that she was seeing right through him, thoughts and all.

Vimes leaned back in his chair, a little defensively and said, "Well, it can't be a difficult job, given that all the words have probably been invented already, so there's a saving in time right there, considering that you simply have to put them together in a different order." That was about the limit of his expertise in the literary arts, but he added, "What sort of thing were you thinking of writing, Jane?"

The girl looked embarrassed. "Well, commander, at the moment I'm working on what might be considered a novel about the complexities of personal relationships, with all their hopes and dreams and misunderstandings." She coughed nervously, as if apologizing.

Vimes pursed his lips. "Yes. Sounds basically like a good idea, miss, but I can't really help you on that—though if I was you, and this is me talking off the top of my head, I'd be putting in a lot of fighting, and dead bodies falling out of wardrobes . . . and maybe a war, perhaps, as a bit of background?"

Jane nodded uneasily. "A remarkable suggestion, commander, with much to recommend it, but possibly the relationships would be somewhat neglected?"

Vimes considered this input and said, "Well, you might be right." Then, out of nowhere, possibly some deep hole, a thought struck him, just as it had many times before, sometimes in nightmares. "I wonder if any author has thought about the relationship between the hunter and the hunted, the policeman and the mysterious killer, the lawman who must think like a criminal sometimes in order to do his job, and may be unpleasantly surprised at how good he is at such thinking, perhaps. Just an idea, you understand," he said lamely, and wondered where the hell it had come from. Maybe the strange Jane had pulled it out of him and even, perhaps, could resolve it.

"Would anybody like some more tea?" said Ariadne brightly.

L ADY SYBIL WAS VERY quiet as their coach drove away, and so Vimes decided to bite the bullet now and get it over with. She was looking thoughtful, which was always worrying.

"Am I in trouble, Sybil?"

His wife looked at him blankly for a moment and then said, "You mean for telling that bunch of precious blooms to stop yearning for a life and to get out there and make one? Good heavens, no! You did everything I would have expected of you, Sam. You always do. I told Ariadne that you wouldn't let her down. She doesn't have much of an income, and if you hadn't given them the righteous word I think she would have eventually driven them out with a shovel. No, Sam, I just wonder what goes on in your head, that's all. I mean, I'm sure some people think being a policeman is just a job, but you don't, do you? I'm very proud of you, Sam, and wouldn't have you any other way, but I do worry sometimes. Anyway, well done! I'll look forward with interest to see what young Jane writes."

N EXT DAY, VIMES TOOK his little boy fishing, hampered somewhat by a total lack of knowledge of the art. Young Sam didn't seem to mind. He had located a shrimping net among the largesse of the nursery and messed about in the shallows, chasing crayfish and sometimes going almost rigid in order to stare at things. Once he got over the shock, Vimes noticed that Young Sam did this quite happily, and on one occasion pointed out to his doting father things in the stream "like insects in the water with a coat made of little pebbles," which Vimes had to investigate, to find that this was entirely true. This amazed Sam Vimes even more than it did his son, who in fact, he told his father as they strolled back for lunch, had been really looking to see if fish did a poo, a question that had never exercised Sam Vimes in his life, but which appeared to be of great importance to his son. So much so that on the way home he had to be restrained from doubling back to the stream to see if they got out to do it because otherwise, er, yuck!

Sybil had promised Young Sam another trip around Home Farm in the afternoon, which left Sam Vimes to his own devices, or such devices as the policeman could find in the quiet lanes. Vimes was streetwise; he didn't know what lanewise might entail, but possibly it would deal with things like throttling stoats and knowing whether whatever it was that had just said "moo" was a cow or a bull without having to bend down to find out.

And as he walked around his rolling acres on his aching feet, wishing that there were cobblestones under him, once again he could feel the tingle; the tingle that raises little hairs on a copper's neck when his well-honed senses tell him that there was something happening around here that shouldn't be, and was crying out to have something done about it.

But there was another copper here, wasn't there, a real old flat-foot let out to grass, but being a copper stained you to the bone; you never got rid of it. He smiled. Time perhaps to go for a convivial drink with Mr. Jiminy.

The Goblin's Head was bare of customers at this time of day except the ever-present trio on the bench outside. Vimes settled himself at the bar with a glass of Mrs. Jiminy's root beer and leaned confidentially toward the barman. "So, Mr. Jiminy, what's of interest here to an old copper?"

Jiminy opened his mouth, but Vimes went on, "Rosewood truncheon, Pseudopolis City Watch? I know I'm right. It's no crime. That's the copper's dream, and you take your trusty truncheon with you to have a little friend you can depend on if the customer can't hold his liquor and won't take a hint." Vimes was now settled with one elbow on the bar and doodling on a small puddle of spilt beer. "But the job follows you, doesn't it? And if you run a pub, well that goes double, because you hear all sorts of things, things you don't do anything about because you aren't a copper anymore, except you know you are. And it must worry you, somewhere in your soul, that there are things going wrong in these parts. Even I can tell. It's the copper's nose. I can smell it in the air. It comes up through my boots. Secrets and lies, Mr. Jiminy, secrets and lies."

Mr. Jiminy made a point of wiping his cloth over the spilt beer and said, as if absent-mindedly, "You know, Commander Vimes, things are different in the country. People think that the country is where you can go to hide out. It ain't so. In the city you're a face in the crowd. In the country people will stare at you until you're out of sight, just for the entertainment value. Like you say, I'm not a copper anymore: I ain't got a warrant card, and I ain't got the inclination. And now, if you don't mind, I have some work to do. There'll be more customers soon. Watch where you tread, your grace."

Vimes didn't let him off the hook. "Interesting thing, Mr. Jiminy: I know you have the lease on this pub but, amazingly enough, I'm still your landlord. I'm sorry about that, but before we came down here I looked at a map and saw a pub on our land, and what a waste, I thought, but that makes me your landlord. Not very republican of me, I know, but I just wonder, Mr. Jiminy, if it may be that not everyone in these parts is not that keen on having the Commander of the City Watch down here in this quiet little hideaway, hmm?" An image of poor old Lord Rust artlessly telling him that there was nothing here of interest passed across Vimes's inner vision.

Jiminy's expression was frozen, but Vimes, who knew this game, saw that tiny twitch which, when decoded, meant, "Yes, but I didn't say anything and no one can prove I did. Not even you, my friend."

Further discussion on the point was interrupted when the sons of the soil began to come in, one by one, to celebrate the ending of the working day. This time there was less suspicion in their eyes as they nodded to Vimes en route to the bar, and so he sat nursing his pint of spiced-up beetroot juice and just enjoyed the moment. It was a very short moment, at the end of which the blacksmith swaggered into the bar and walked straight up to him.

"You are sitting in my seat!"

Vimes looked around. He was sitting on a bench that was indistinguishable from all the others in the room, but he accepted the possibility that there was something mystic about the one he was occupying, picked up his glass and strolled over to an unoccupied one, where he sat down just in time to hear the blacksmith say, "That one's my seat too, understand?"

Oh dear, here was the overture and beginners to a brawl, and Vimes was no beginner, right enough, and the blacksmith's eyes held the look of a man who wanted to punch somebody and very likely thought that Vimes would make the ideal candidate.

He felt the gentle pressure of his own brass knuckles in his trouser pocket. Vimes had been economical with the truth when he promised his wife that he would not take any weapons on holiday with him. However, he'd reasoned that a knuckleduster was not so much a weapon as a way of making certain that he stayed alive. It could be called a defensive instrument, a kind of shield, as it were, especially if you needed to get your defense in before you were attacked.

He stood up. "Mr. Jethro, I'd be grateful if you'd be so kind as to choose which chair is yours for the evening, thank you very much, after which I intend to enjoy my drink in *peace*."

Whoever said that a soft answer turneth away wrath had never worked in a bar. The blacksmith glowered at about the same temperature as his forge. "I ain't Jethro to you, not by a long way. You can call me Mr. Jefferson, do you hear?"

"And you can call me Sam Vimes." He watched Jefferson very deliberately place his drink on the bar before he strode toward Vimes.

"I know what I can call *you*, mister . . ."

Vimes felt the smooth brass of the surrogate knuckles, polished as they had been by years of abrasion from his pants and, needless to say, the occasional chin. As he dug down, they almost leapt to his grasp.

"Sorry about this, your grace," said Jiminy as he pushed him gently out of the way and said to the smith. "Well now, Jethro, what's this all about, then?"

"Your grace?" sneered Jethro. "I ain't going to call you that! I ain't going to lick your boots like all the others do! Coming back here, lording it over us, ordering us about as if you owned the place! And that's it, isn't it? You do own the place! One man with all this country! That's not right! You tell me, how did that happen? Go on, you tell me!"

Vimes shrugged. "Well, I'm not an expert, but as I understand it my wife's ancestors fought somebody for it."

The blacksmith's face bloomed with an evil pleasure as he threw off his leather apron. "Well, okay. No problem. That's how it's done, is it? Fair enough. Tell you what I'll do, I'll fight *you* for it, here and now, and, tell you what I'll do, I'll fight you with one hand strapped behind my back, on account of you being a bit shorter than me."

Vimes heard a slight wooden sound behind him: it was the sound of a barman stealthily pulling a two-foot-long rosewood truncheon from its accustomed place under the bar.

Jethro must have heard it too, because he called out, "And don't you try anything with that, Jim. You know I'll have it out of your hands before you know what's happening, and this time I'll shove it where the sun doesn't shine."

Vimes took a look at the rest of the clientele, who were doing remarkable impersonations of stone statues. "Look," he said, "you really don't want to fight me."

"I do, indeed I do! You said it yourself. Some ancestor got all of this by fighting for it, yeah? Who said it's the time to stop fighting?"

"Burleigh and Stronginthearm, sir," said a polite yet chilly voice behind the big man. To Vimes's shock it was Willikins. "I'm not cruel, sir, I won't shoot you in the guts, but I will make you realize how much you took your toes for granted. No, please do not make any sudden movements. Burleigh and Stronginthearm crossbows have notoriously responsive triggers."

Vimes resumed breathing again when Jethro raised his hands. Somewhere in all that rage there must have been a halfpennyworth of self-preservation. Nevertheless the blacksmith glared at him and said, "You need to be protected by a hired killer, do you?"

"In point of fact, sir," said Willikins smoothly, "I am employed by Commander Vimes as a gentleman's gentleman, and I require this crossbow because sometimes his socks fight back." He looked at Vimes. "Do you have any instructions, commander? and then he shouted, "Don't move, mister, because as far as I know a blacksmith needs two hands to work with." He turned back to Vimes. "Do excuse that interjection, commander, but I know his sort."

"Willikins, I rather think you *are* his sort."

"Yes, sir, thank you, sir, and I wouldn't trust me one little inch, sir. I knows a bad one when I sees them. I have a mirror."

"Now, I want you to put that bloody thing down, Willikins. People could get hurt!" Vimes said in his formal voice.

"Yes, sir, that would have been my intention. I could not face her ladyship if anything had happened to you."

Vimes looked from Willikins to Jethro. Here was a boil that needed lancing. But you couldn't blame the lad. It wasn't as if he hadn't thought the same way himself, many times. "Willikins," he said, "please put that wretched thing down carefully and get out your notebook. *Thank you*. Now please write down as follows: "I, Samuel Vimes, somewhat reluctantly the Duke of Ankh, do intend to Duke it out, haha, with my friend Jethro . . . What's your full name again, Jethro?"

"Now look here, mister, I didn't—"

"I asked you your damn name, mister! Jiminy, what's his surname?"

"Jefferson," said the landlord, holding his truncheon like a security blanket. "But look, your grace, you don't want to go . . ."

Vimes ignored him and went on, "Now where was I? Oh, yes:

'my friend Jethro Jefferson, in a friendly fight for the ownership of the Manor and environs, whatever the hell they are, which will go to the which of us that does not first cry "uncle," and should it be myself that utters the same, there will be no repercussions of any sort upon my friend Jethro, or on my man Willikins, who pleaded with me not to engage in this friendly bout of fisticuffs.' Got that, Willikins? I'll even give you a get-out-of-jail-free card to show to her ladyship if I get bruised. Now give it to me to sign."

Willikins handed over the notebook with reluctance. "I don't think it'll work on her ladyship, sir. Look, dukes aren't expected to go around—" His voice faltered in the face of Vimes's smile.

"You were going to say that dukes shouldn't fight, weren't you, Willikins? And if you had, I would have said that the word 'duke' absolutely means that you do fight."

"Oh, very well, sir," said Willikins, "but perhaps you ought to warn him . . . ?"

Willikins was interrupted by the pub's customers pushing their way out at speed and running through the village, leaving Jethro standing alone and bewildered. Halfway toward the man, Vimes turned to look back at Willikins and said, "You may think you see me lighting a cigar, Willikins, but on this occasion, I think, your eyes may turn out to be at fault, do you understand?"

"Yes, and in fact I am deaf as well, commander."

"Good lad. Now let's get outside where there's less glass and a better view."

Jethro looked like a man who had had the ground cut from under his feet but didn't know how to fall down.

Vimes lit his cigar and savored, just for a moment, the forbidden fruit. Then he offered the packet to the blacksmith, who waved it away without a word.

"Very sensible," said Vimes. "Now then, I'd better tell you that at least once a week, even these days, I have to fight people who're trying to kill me with everything from swords to chairs and in one case a very large salmon. They probably don't actually want to kill me, but they'll try to stop me arresting them. Look," he waved a hand at the landscape in general, "all this . . . stuff, just happened, whether I wanted it to or not. By trade I'm just a copper."

"Yeah," said Jethro, glaring at him. "Stamping on the faces of the struggling masses!"

Vimes was used to this sort of thing, and put it mildly. "Can't tread on their faces these days, my grinder gets in the way. All right, not very funny, I admit." Vimes was aware that people were coming back down the lane. They included women and children. It looked as though the pub's clientele had roused the neighborhood. He turned to Jethro. "Are we going to do this by the Marquis of Fantailer's Rules?"

"What are they?" said the blacksmith, waving at the oncoming horde.

"Rules of sparring by the Marquis of Fantailer," said Vimes.

"If they was written by a marquis I don't want no truck with them!"

Vimes nodded. "Willikins?"

"I heard that, commander, and have recorded it in my notebook: 'refused Fantailer.'"

"Well then, Mr. Jefferson," said Vimes. "I suggest we ask Mr. Jiminy to start the proceedings?"

"I want your lackey to write down in that book of his that my mum won't get put out of her cottage, whatever happens, right?"

"It's a deal," said Vimes. "Willikins, please make a memorandum that Mr. Jefferson's old mum should not be thrown out of her cottage, hit with sticks, put in the stocks, or otherwise manhandled in any way, understand?"

Willikins, trying ineffectually to hide a smile, licked his pencil and wrote industriously. Vimes, less noisily, made a mental note and the note said: "The ferocity is draining out of this lad. He is wondering if he actually might get killed. I haven't thrown a punch, not one little punch, and he is already preparing for the worst. Of course, the right way about it is to prepare for the best."

The crowd was growing by the second. Even as Vimes looked on, people came down the lane carrying a very old man on a mattress, their progress accelerated by his delight in hitting them on the back of the legs with his walking stick. Mothers toward the back of the crowd were holding up their children for a better look and, all unknown, every man had a weapon. It was like a peasants' revolt, without the revolt and with a very polite class of peasant. Men touched their forelocks when Vimes looked in their direction, women curtsied, or at least bobbed up and down a bit, disturbingly out of sequence, like organ pedals trembling.

Jiminy approached Vimes and the blacksmith cautiously and, to judge by the glistening of his face, very apprehensively. "Now then, gents, I'm choosing to consider this a little demonstration of fisticuffs, a jolly trial of strength and prowess such as may be found on any summer evening, all friends under the skin, okay?" There was a pleading look in his eyes as he went on. "And when you've got it out of your systems there'll be a pint waiting for each of you on the bar. Please don't break anything." He produced an overused handkerchief from a waistcoat pocket and held it in the air. "When this touches the ground, gentlemen . . ." he said, backing away very quickly.

The slip of linen seemed to defy gravity for a while, but the moment it touched the ground Vimes caught the blacksmith's boot in both hands as it swung toward him and said very quietly to the struggling man, "A bit previous, weren't you? And what good has it done you? Hear them all sniggering? I'll let you off, this time."

Vimes gave a push as he loosened his grip on the foot, causing Jethro to stagger backward. Vimes felt a certain pleasure in seeing the man losing it this early, but the blacksmith pulled himself together and rushed at him, and paused, possibly because Vimes was grinning.

"That's the ticket, my lad," said Vimes, "you just saved yourself a dreadful pain in the unmentionables." He made fists and beckoned suggestively to his bewildered adversary over the top of his left fist. The man came swinging and got a kick on the kneecap, which floored him, and he was picked up by Vimes, which metaphorically floored him again.

"Whyever did you think I was going to box? That's what we professionals call *misdirection*. You want to go for the hug? I would if I were a big bloke like you, but you ain't going to get the chance." Vimes shook his head sorrowfully. "Should have gone for the Marquis of Fantailer. I believe that has been carved on many a gravestone." He took a generous pull of his cigar; the ash had yet to be disturbed.

Enraged beyond belief, Jethro threw himself at Vimes and caught a glancing blow to his head, receiving at almost the same time a knee in the stomach which knocked all the breath out of him. They went down together with Vimes as the conductor of this orchestra. He made certain he ended on top, where he leaned down and hissed into Jethro's ear, "Let's see how smart you are, shall we? Are you a man who can control his temper? 'Cos if you aren't, then I'll give you a nose so wide that you'll have to hold your handkerchief on the end of a stick. Don't you, for one moment, think I'm not capable of it. But I reckon a blacksmith knows when to cool the metal, and I'm giving you a chance to say that at least you got the duke on the floor in front of all your friends, and we'll stand up and shake hands like the gentlemen neither of us is, and the crowd will cheer and go into the pub to get happily ratted on the beer that I shall pay for. Are we men of one accord?"

There was a muffled "Yes," and Vimes stood up, took the blacksmith's hand in his hand and raised it up high, which caused some slight puzzlement, but when he then said, "Sam Vimes invites you all to take a drink with him in Mr. Jiminy's establishment!" everybody shrugged bewilderment aside to make room for the beer. The crowd surged into the pub, leaving the blacksmith and Vimes on their own—plus Willikins, who could be remarkably self-effacing when he wanted.

"Blacksmiths should know about temper, too," said Vimes, as the crowd dispersed pubward. "Sometimes cool is better than hot. I don't know anything much about you, Mr. Jefferson, but the City Watch needs people who learn fast and I reckon you would soon make it to sergeant. We could use you as a smith, too. It's amazing how dented the old armor can get when you're standing on the faces of the poor."

Jethro stared down at his boots. "All right, you can beat me in a fight, but that doesn't mean it's right, all right? You don't know the half of it!"

There were sounds of merriment coming from the pub. Vimes wondered how embroidered that little scuffle would turn out to be. He turned back to the smith, who hadn't moved. "Listen to me, you stupid young fool, I wasn't born with a silver spoon in my mouth! When I was a kid the only spoons I ever saw were made of wood and you were lucky if there was some edible food on the end of them. I was a street kid, understand? If I had been dumped out here I would have thought it was paradise, what with food jumping out on you from every hedge. But I became a copper because they paid you and I was taught how to be a copper by decent coppers, because believe me, mister, I wake every night knowing that I could have been something else. Then I found a good lady and if I were you, kid, I'd hope that I'd find one of them, too. So I smartened myself up and then one day Lord Vetinari—you have heard of him, haven't you, kid? Well, he needed a man to get things done, and the title opens doors so that I don't actually have to kick them open myself, and do you know what? I reckon my boots have seen so much crime down the years that they walk me toward it of their own accord, and I know there's something that needs kicking. So do you, I can smell it on you. Tell me what it is."

Jethro still stared at his own boots and said nothing.

Willikins cleared his throat. "I wonder, commander, if it might help if I had a little talk with the young man, from what you might call a less elevated position? Why don't you take a look at the beauties of the local countryside?"

Vimes nodded. "By all means, if you think it'll do some good." And he went away and examined a honeysuckle hedge with considerable interest, while Willikins, with his shiny gentleman's gentleman shoes and his immaculate jacket, strolled over to Jethro, put an arm around him and said, "This is a stiletto I'm holding to your throat and it ain't no ladies' shoe, this is the real thing, the cutting edge, as it were. You are a little twit, and I ain't the commander and I will slice you to the bone if you make a move. Got that? *Now don't nod your head!* Good, we are learning, aren't we? Now, my lad, the commander here is trusted by the Diamond King of Trolls and the Low King of the Dwarfs, who would only have to utter a word for your measly carcass to come under the caress of a large number of versatile axes, and by Lady Margolotta of Uberwald, who trusts very few people, and by Lord Vetinari of Ankh-Morpork, who doesn't trust anybody at all. Got that? *Don't nod!* And you, my little man, have the damn nerve to doubt his word. I'm an easygoing sort of fellow, but that sort of thing leaves me right out of sorts, I don't mind telling you. You understand? I said, do you understand? Oh, all right, you can nod now. Incidentally, young man, be careful who you call a lackey, all right? Some people might take violent exception to that sort of thing. A word to the wise, lad: I know the commander, and you thought about your old mum and what might happen to her and I reckon that is why I won't be seeing you in lavender, because he is a sensitive soul at heart."

Willikins' knife disappeared as quickly as it had come, and with the other hand the gentleman's gentleman produced a small brush and tidied the blacksmith's collar.

"Willikins," said Vimes from the distance. "Will you go for a little walk now, please?"

When his manservant was loitering under a tree a little way further up the lane, Vimes said, "Sorry about that, but every man has his pride. I bear that in mind. So should you. I'm a copper, a policeman, and something here is calling to me. It seems to me that you have something you'd like me to know and it's not just about who sits in the high castle, am I right? Something bad has happened, you are practically sweating it. Well?"

Jethro leaned toward him and said, "Dead Man's Copse on the hill. Midnight. I won't wait."

The blacksmith then turned round and walked away without a glance behind.

V IMES LIT A FRESH cigar and strolled toward the tree where Willikins was appearing to enjoy the landscape. He straightened up when he saw Vimes. "We'd better get a move on, sir. Dinner is at eight o'clock and her ladyship would like you to be smart. She sets a lot of store by your being smartly turned out, sir."

Vimes groaned. "Not the official tights?"

"Happily not, sir, not in the country, but her ladyship was very specific about my bringing the plum-colored evening dress, sir."

"She says it makes me look dashing," said Vimes morosely. "Do you think it makes me look dashing? Am I a dashing kind of person, would you say?" The birds started singing from a low branch of the tree.

"I'd put you down as more the sprinting sort, sir," said Willikins.

They set off home, in silence for a while, which is to say that neither man spoke while wildlife sang, buzzed and screeched, eventually causing Vimes to say, "I wish I knew what the hell all those things are."

Willikins put his head on one side for a moment, then said, "Parkinson's warbler, the deep-throated frog-eater and the common creed-waggler, sir."

"You know?"

"Oh, yes, sir. I frequent the music halls, sir, and there's always a bird or animal impersonator on the bill. It tends to stick. I also know seventy-three farmyard noises, my favorite of which is the sound of a farmer who has had one boot sucked from his foot by the muck he's trying to avoid and has nowhere else to put his stockinged foot but in the said muck. Hugely amusing, sir."

They had reached the long drive to the Hall now, and gravel crunched beneath their boots. Under his breath, Vimes said, "I've arranged to meet young Mr. Jefferson at midnight in the copse on Hangman's Hill. He wishes to tell me something important. Remind me, Willikins, what *is* a copse, exactly?"

"Anything between a clump of trees and a small wood. Technically, sir, the one at the top of Hangman's Hill is a beech hanger. That just means, well, a small beech wood on top of a hill. You remember Mad Jack Ramkin? The bloke that got it made thirty feet higher at great expense? He had the beech trees planted on the top."

Vimes liked the crunching of the gravel; it would mask the sound of their conversation. "I talked to the blacksmith with, I would swear, no one else in earshot. But this is the country, yes, Willikins?"

"There was a man setting rabbit snares in the hedge behind you," said Willikins. "Perfectly normal activity, although to my mind he took too long over it."

They crunched onward for a while, and Vimes said, "Tell me, Willikins. If a man had arranged to meet another man at midnight in a place with a name like Dead Man's Copse, on Hangman's Hill, what would you consider to be his most sensible course of action, given that his wife had forbidden him to bring weapons to his country house?"

Willikins nodded. "Why, sir, given your maxim that everything is a weapon if you choose to think of it as such, I would advise said man to see whether he has a compatriot what has, for example, acquired the keys to a cabinet that contains a number of superbly made carving knives, ideal for close fighting; and I personally would include a side order of cheesewire, sir, in conformance with my belief that the only important thing in a fight to the death is that the death should not be yours."

"Can't carry cheesewire, man! Not the Commander of the Watch!"

"Quite so, commander, and may I therefore advise your brass knuckles—the gentleman's alternative? I know you never travel without them, sir. There's some vicious people around and I know you have to be among them."

"Look, Willikins, I don't like to involve you in all this. It's only a hunch, after all."

Willikins waved this away. "You wouldn't keep me out of it for a big clock, sir, because all this is tickling my fancy as well. I shall lay out a selection of cutting edges for you in your dressing room, sir, and I myself will go up to the copse half an hour before you're due to be there, with my trusty bow and an assortment of favorite playthings. It's nearly a full moon, clear skies, there'll be shadows everywhere, and I'll be standing in the darkest one of them."

Vimes looked at him for a moment and said, "Could I please amend that suggestion? Could you not be there in the second darkest shadow one hour before midnight, to see who steps into the darkest shadow?"

"Ah yes, that's why you command the watch, sir," said Willikins, and to Vimes's shock there was a hint of a tear in the man's voice. "You're listening to the street, aren't you, sir, yes?"

Vimes shrugged. "No streets here, Willikins!"

Willikins shook his head. "Once a street boy always a street boy, sir. It comes with us, in the pinch. Mothers go, fathers go—if we ever knew who they were—but the Street, well, the Street looks after us. In the pinch it keeps us alive."

Willikins darted ahead of Vimes and rang the doorbell, so that the footman had the door open by the time Vimes came up the steps. "You've got just enough time to listen to Young Sam read to you, sir," Willikins added, making his way up the stairs. "Wonderful thing, reading, I wish I'd learned it when I was a kid. Her ladyship will be in her dressing room and guests will be arriving in about half an hour. Must go, sir. I've got to teach that fat toad of a butler his manners, sir."

Vimes winced. "You're not allowed to strangle butlers, Willikins. I'm sure I read it in a book of etiquette."

Willikins gave him a look of mock offense. "No garrotting will be involved, sir, Willikins went on, opening the door to Vimes's dressing room, "but he is a snob of the first water. Never did meet a butler who wasn't. I just have to give him an orientation lesson."

"Well, he is the butler, and this is his house," said Vimes.

"No, sir, it's *your* house, and since I am your personal manservant I, by the irrevocable laws of the servants' hall, outrank every one of the lazy buggers! I'll show them how we do things in the real world, sir, don't you worry—"

He was interrupted by a heavy knock at the door, followed by a determined rattling of the doorknob. Willikins opened the door and Young Sam stomped in and announced, "Reading!"

Vimes picked up his son and sat him on a chair. "How was your afternoon, my lad?"

"Do you know," said Young Sam, as if imparting the results of strict research, "cows do really big floppy poos, but sheep do small poos, like chocolates."

Vimes tried not to look at Willikins, who was shaking with suppressed laughter. He managed to keep his own expression solemn and said, "Well, of course, sheep are smaller."

Young Sam considered this. "Cow poos go flop," he said. "It never said that in *Where's My Cow?*" Young Sam's voice betrayed a certain annoyance that this important information had been withheld. "Miss Felicity Beedle wouldn't have left it out."

Vimes sighed. "I just bet she wouldn't."

Willikins opened the door. "I'll leave you gentlemen to it, then, and see you later, sir."

"Willikins?" said Vimes, just as the man had his hand on the doorknob. "You appear to think that my brass knuckles are inferior to yours. Is that so?"

Willikins smiled. "You've never really *agreed* with the idea of the spiked ones, have you, sir?" He carefully shut the door behind him.

YOUNG SAM WAS ALREADY reading by himself these days, which was a great relief. Fortunately the works of Miss Felicity Beedle did not consist solely of exciting references to poo, in all its manifestations, but her output of small volumes for young children was both regular and highly popular, at least among the children. This was because she had researched her audience with care, and Young Sam had laughed his way through *The Wee Wee Men, The War with the Snot Goblins,* and *Geoffrey and the Land of Poo.* For boys of a certain age, they hit the squashy spot. At the moment he was giggling and choking his way through *The Boy Who Didn't Know How to Pick His Own Scabs,* an absolute hoot for a boy just turned six. Sybil pointed out that the books were building Young Sam's vocabulary, and not just about lavatorial matters, and it was indeed true that he was beginning, with encouragement, to read books in which nobody had a bowel movement at all. Which, when you came to think about it, was a mystery all by itself.

Vimes carried his son to bed after ten minutes of enjoyable listening, and had managed to shave and get into the feared evening clothes a few moments before his wife knocked on the door. Separate dressing rooms and bathrooms, Vimes thought . . . if you had the money, there was no better way to keep a happy marriage happy. And in order to keep a happy marriage happy he allowed Sybil to bustle in, wearing, in fact, a bustle,* to adjust his shirt, tweak his collar and make him fit for company.

---

* Sybil had explained to Vimes that in the country one dresses at least a decade earlier than in the city, hence the bustle, and, for Vimes, a pair of breeches: the ancient ones with trap doors front and rear and a slightly distressing smell all over.

And then she said, "I understand you gave the blacksmith a short lesson in unarmed combat, my dear . . ." The pause hung in the air like a silken noose.

Vimes managed, "There's something wrong here, I know it."

"I think so, too," said Sybil.

"You do?"

"Yes, Sam, but this is not the time. We have guests arriving at any minute. If you could refrain from throwing any of them over your shoulder in between courses I would be grateful." This was a terrific scolding by Sybil's normally placid standards. Vimes did what any prudent husband would do, which was dynamically nothing. Suddenly all downstairs was full of voices and the noise of carriages crunching over the gravel. Sybil trimmed her sails and headed down to be the gracious hostess.

Despite what his wife liked to imply, Vimes was rather good at dinners, having sat through innumerable civic affairs in Ankh-Morpork. The trick was to let the other diners do the talking while agreeing with them occasionally, giving himself time to think about other things.

Sybil had made certain that this evening's dinner was a light occasion. The guests were mostly people of a certain class who lived in the country but were not, as it were, of it. Retired warriors; a priest of Om; Miss Pickings, a spinster, together with her companion, a strict-looking lady with short hair and a man's shirt and pocket watch; and, yes, Miss Felicity Beedle. Vimes thought he had put his foot in it when he said, "Oh yes, the poo lady," but she burst out laughing and shook his hand, saying, "Don't worry, your grace, I wash mine thoroughly after writing!" And it was a big laugh. She was a small woman with the strange aspect that you see in some people that causes them to appear to be subtly vibrating even when standing perfectly still. You felt that if some interior restraint suddenly broke, the pent-up energy released would catapult her through the nearest window.

Miss Beedle prodded him in the stomach. "And *you* are the famous Commander Vimes. Come to arrest us all, have you?" Of course, you got this all the time if you didn't stop Sybil accepting the invitation to yet another posh society do. But while Miss Beedle laughed, silence fell on the other guests like a cast-iron safe. They were scowling at Miss Beedle, and Miss Beedle was staring intently at Vimes, and Vimes *knew* that expression. It was the expression of somebody with a story to tell. Certainly this was no time to broach the subject, and so Vimes filed it under "interesting."

Whatever Vimes's misgivings, Ramkin Hall did a damn good dinner and—and this was the important thing—the dictates of popular social intercourse decreed that Sybil had to allow a menu full of things that would not be permitted at home if Vimes had asked for them. It's one thing to act as arbiter of your own husband's tastes, but it is frowned on to do the same to your guests.

Across the table from him a retired military man was being assured by his wife that he did not, contrary to what he himself believed, like potted shrimps. In vain the man protested weakly that he thought he did like potted shrimps, to get the gentle response, "You may like potted shrimps, Charles, but they do not like you."

Vimes felt for the man, who seemed puzzled at having developed enemies among the lower crustacea. "Well, er, does lobster like me, dear?" he said, in a voice that did not express much hope.

"No, dear, it does not get on with you at all. Remember what happened at the Parsleys' whist evening."

The man looked at the groaning sideboard and tried: "Do you think the scallops could get on with me for five minutes or so?"

"Good heavens no, Charles."

He cast a glance at the sideboard again. "I expect the green salad is my bosom friend, though, isn't it?"

"Absolutely, dear!"

"Yes, I thought so."

The man looked across at Vimes and gave him a hopeless grin followed by, "I am given to believe that you are a policeman, your grace. That right?"

Vimes took proper stock of him for the first time: a whiskery old warrior, now out to grass—and that was probably all his wife was going to let him eat without an argument. He had burn scars on his face and hands and the accent of Pseudopolis. Easy. "You were with the Light Dragons, weren't you, sir?"

The old man looked pleased. "Well done, that man! Not many people remember us. Alas, I'm the only one left. Colonel Charles Augustus Makepeace—strange name for a military man, or perhaps not, I don't know." He sniffed. "We're just a scorched page in the history of warfare. I dare say you haven't read my memoirs, *Twenty-four Years Without Eyebrows*? No? Well, you are not alone in that, I have to say. Met your missus in those days. She told us it would be totally impossible to breed dragons stable enough for use in warfare. She was right, and no mistake. Of course, we went on trying, because that's the military way!"

"You mean, pile dreadful failure on top of failure?" said Vimes.

The colonel laughed. "Well, it works sometimes! I still keep a few dragons, though. Wouldn't be without 'em. A day without a singe is a day without sunshine. They're a great saving in matches, and, of course, they keep undesirables away, too."

Vimes reacted like an angler who, after some time dozing by the water's edge, felt that the fish were rising.

"Oh, you don't get many of them around here, surely?"

"You think so? You don't know the half of it, young man.

I can tell you a few stories—" He stopped talking abruptly, and Vimes's experience of husbandry told him that the man had just been kicked under the table by his wife, who did not look happy and, to judge by the lines on her face, probably never had. She leaned past her husband, who was now accepting another brandy from the waiter, and said, icily, "As a policeman, your grace, does your jurisdiction extend to the Shires?"

Another ring in the water, thought the angler inside Vimes's head. He said, "No, madam, my beat is Ankh-Morpork and some of the surrounding area. Traditionally, however, the policeman drags his jurisdiction with him if he is in hot pursuit in connection with crime committed within his domain. But, of course, Ankh-Morpork is a long way from here, and I doubt if I'd be able to run that far." This got a laugh from the table in general and a thin-lipped smile from Mrs. Colonel.

Play the fish, play the fish . . . "Nevertheless," Vimes continued, "if I was to witness an arrestable offense here and now, I'd have the authority to make an arrest. Like a citizen's arrest, but somewhat more professional, and after that I'd be required to turn the suspect over to the local force or other suitable authority, as I deemed fit."

The clergyman, whom Vimes had noticed out of the corner of his eye, was taking an interest in this conversation and leaned forward to say, "As you deem fit, your grace?"

"My grace would not come into it, sir. As a sworn member of the Ankh-Morpork City Watch it would be my bounden duty to ensure the safety of my suspect. Ideally I'd look for a lockup. We don't have them in the city anymore, but I understand most rural areas still do, even if they only hold drunks and escaped pigs."

There was laughter, and Miss Beedle said, "We do have a village constable, your grace, and he keeps pigs in the lockup down by the old bridge!"

She looked brightly at Vimes, whose expression was stony. He said, "Does he ever put people in there? Does he have a warrant card? Does he have a badge?"

"Well, he puts the occasional drunk in there to sober up, and he says the pigs don't seem to mind, but I have no idea what a warrant card is."

There was more laughter at this but it faded quickly, sucked into nowhere by Vimes's implacable silence.

Then he said, "I would not consider him to be a policeman, and until I found that he was working within a framework of proper law enforcement I would regard him not as a policeman by my standards but as a slightly bossy street cleaner. Of some use, but not a policeman."

"By your standards, your grace?" said the clergyman.

"Yes, sir, by my standards. My decision. My responsibility. My experience. My arse if things go wrong."

"But, your grace, as you say, you are outside your jurisdiction here," said Mrs. Colonel gently.

Vimes could sense her husband's nervousness, and it was certainly not to do with the food. The man was wishing heartily that he wasn't there. It was funny how people always wanted to talk to policemen about crime, and never realize what strange little signals their anxieties betrayed.

He turned to the man's wife, smiled and said, "But as I've said, madam, if a copper comes across a flagrant crime his jurisdiction reaches out to him like an old friend. And do you mind if we change the subject? No offense meant to any of you ladies and gentlemen, but over the years I've noticed that bankers and military men and merchants all get a chance to eat their dinners at their leisure at affairs like this, while the poor old copper has to talk about police work, which is most of the time rather dull." He smiled again to keep everything friendly, and went on, "Exceedingly dull around here, I would imagine. From my point of view, this place is as quiet as the . . . grave." Score: one wince from the dear old colonel, and the priest looking down at his plate, although the latter shouldn't be taken too seriously, he thought, because you seldom saw a clergyman who couldn't strike sparks with his knife and fork.

Sybil, using her hostess voice, shattered the silence like an icebreaker. "I think it's time for the main course," she said, "which will be superb mutton avec no talking about police work at all. Honestly, if you get Sam going he'll quote the laws and ordinances of Ankh-Morpork and force standing orders until you throw a cushion at him!"

Well done, Vimes thought, at least I can now eat my dinner in peace. He relaxed as the conversation around him became less fraught and once again replete with the everyday gossip and grumblings about other people living in the area, the difficulties with servants, the prospects for the harvest and, oh yes, the trouble with goblins.

Vimes paid attention then. Goblins. The City Watch appeared to contain at least one member of every known bipedal sapient species plus one Nobby Nobbs. It had become a tradition: if you could make it as a copper, then you could make it as a species. But nobody had ever once suggested that Vimes should employ a goblin, the simple reason being that they were universally known to be stinking, cannibalistic, vicious, untrustworthy bastards.

Of course, *everybody* knew that dwarfs were a chiselling bunch who would swindle you if they could, and that trolls were little more than thugs, and the city's one resident medusa would never look you in the face, and the vampires couldn't be trusted, however much they smiled, and werewolves were only vampires who couldn't fly, when you got right down to it, and the man next door was a real bastard who threw his rubbish over your wall and his wife was no better than she should be. But then again it took all sorts to make a world. It was not as if you were prejudiced because, after all, there had been an orc working at the university, but he liked his football, didn't he just, and you could forgive *anyone* who could score from the center spot and, well, you took as you found . . . But not bloody goblins, thank you very much. People hounded them out if they came into the city and they tended to end up downriver, working for the likes of Harry King in the bone-grinding, leather-tanning and scrap-metal industries. A fair walk outside the city gates and so outside the law.

And now there were some in the vicinity of the Hall, as evidenced by chickens and cats disappearing, and so on. Well, probably, but Vimes remembered when people said that trolls stole chickens; there was nothing of interest to a troll in a chicken. It would be like humans eating plaster. He certainly did not mention any of this.

Yes, no one had a good word to say about goblins, but Miss Beedle had no word to say at all. Her gaze remained firmly fixed on Vimes's face. You could read a dining table if you learned the knack and if you were a policeman then you could build a clear picture of what each diner thought about the others; it was all in the looks. The things said or not said. The people who were in the magic circle and the people who weren't. Miss Beedle was an outsider, tolerated, because obviously there is such a thing as good manners, but not exactly included. What was the phrase? *Not one of us.*

Vimes realized that he was staring at Miss Beedle just as she was staring at him. They both smiled, and he thought that an inquisitive man would go and see the nice lady who had written the books that his little boy enjoyed so much and not because she looked like somebody prepared to blow so many whistles that it would sound like a pipe band.

Miss Beedle frowned a lot when the talk was about goblins, and occasionally people, especially the people he had tagged as Mrs. Colonel, would cast a look at her as one might glance at a child who was doing something wrong.

And so he maintained a nice exterior air of attention while at the same time sifting through the affairs of the day. The process was interrupted by Mrs. Colonel saying, "By the way, your grace, we were very pleased to hear that you gave Jefferson a drubbing this afternoon. The man is insufferable! He upsets people!"

"Well, I noticed that he's not afraid to air his views," said Vimes, "but nor are we, are we?"

"But surely you of all people, your grace," said the clergyman, looking up earnestly, "cannot possibly believe that Jack is as good as his master?"

"Depends on Jack. Depends on the master. Depends what you mean by good," said Vimes. "I suppose I was a Jack, but when it comes to the Ankh-Morpork City Watch, I am the Master."

Mrs. Colonel was about to answer when Lady Sybil said brightly, "Talking of which, Sam, I had a letter from a Mrs. Wainwright commending you highly. Remind me to show it to you."

All long-term couples have their code. Classically there is one that the wife uses in polite conversation to warn her husband that, because of hasty dressing, or absent-mindedness, he is becoming exposed in the crotch department.[*]

In the case of Vimes and Lady Sybil, any mention of Mrs.

---

[*] See Dr. Bentley Purchase, *The Vicar Is Coming to Tea and One Hundred and Twenty-seven Other Warnings of Social Embarrassment* (Unseen University Press).

Wainwright was a code that meant, "If you don't stop annoying people, Sam Vimes, then there will be a certain amount of marital discord later this evening."

But this time Sam Vimes wanted the last word, and said, "In fact, come to think of it, I know quite a few risen Jacks in various places, and let me tell you, they often make better masters than their erstwhile masters ever did. All they needed was a chance."

"Do remind me to show you the letter, Sam!"

Vimes gave in, and the arrival of the ice-cream pudding lowered the temperature somewhat, especially since her ladyship made certain that everybody's glasses remained filled—and in the case of the colonel this meant an extremely regular top-up. Vimes would have liked to talk to him further, but he too was under wifely orders. The man had definitely had something important on his mind that caused the presence of a policeman to make him very nervous indeed. And the nervousness was apparently catching.

This wasn't a posh affair, by any means. Sybil had organized this little party before building up to anything more lavish, and some fairly amicable goodbyes were being said long before eleven. Vimes listened intently to the colonel and his wife as they walked, in his case unsteadily, to their carriage. All he heard, however, was a hissed, "You had the stable door open all evening!"

Followed by a growled, "But the horse was fast asleep, my dear."

WHEN THE LAST CARRIAGE had been waved away and the big front door firmly shut, Sybil said, "Well, Sam, I understand, I really do, but they were our guests."

"I know, and I'm sorry, but it's as if they don't think. I just wanted to shake their ideas up a bit."

Lady Sybil examined a sherry bottle and topped up her glass.

"Surely you don't think that the blacksmith really had the right to fight you for this house?"

Sam wished that he could drink, right now. "No, of course not. I mean, there wouldn't be an end to it. People have been winning and losing on the old roulette wheel of fate for thousands of years. I know that, but you know that I think that if you're going to stop the wheel then you have to spare some thought for the poor buggers who're sitting on zero."

His wife gently took his hand. "But we endowed the hospital, Sam. You know how expensive that is. Dr. Lawn will train up anyone who shows an aptitude for medicine, even if they, in his words, turn up with the arse hanging out of their trousers. He's even letting girls train! As *doctors*! He even employs Igorinas! We're changing things, Sam, a bit at a time, by helping people help themselves. And look at the Watch! These days a kid is proud to say that his father or even his mother is a watchman. And people need pride."

Vimes grasped her hand. He said, "Thank you for being kind to the boy from Cockbill Street."

She laughed this away. "I waited a long time for you to turn up, Samuel Vimes, and I don't intend to let you go to waste!"

This seemed to Sam Vimes a good time to say, "You don't mind if Willikins and I take a little stroll to Dead Man's Copse before I go to bed?"

Lady Sybil gave him the smile women give to husbands and small boys. "Well, I can hardly say no, and there is a strange atmosphere. I'm glad Willikins is involved. And it's very pleasant up there. Perhaps you'll hear the nightingale."

Vimes gave her a little kiss before going up to change and said, "Actually, dear, I'm hoping to hear a canary."

Probably no duke or even commander of the City Watch had found in their dressing room anything like that which lay on the bed of Sam Vimes right now. Pride of place was for a billhook, which was a useful agricultural implement. He had seen a couple of them being carried earlier in the day. He reminded himself that "agricultural implement" did not mean "not a weapon." They turned up sometimes among the street gangs and were almost as much to be feared as a troll with a headache.

Then there was a truncheon. Vimes's own truncheon, which his manservant had thoughtfully brought along. Of course, it had silverwork on it because it was the ceremonial truncheon of the Commander of the Watch, and wasn't a weapon at all, oh dear me, no. On the other hand, Vimes knew himself not to be a cheesemonger and therefore it would be somewhat difficult to explain why he had a foot of cheesewire about his person. That was going to stay here, but he'd take the billhook. It was a pretty poor lookout if a man walking on his own land couldn't take the opportunity to trim a branch or two. But what to make of the pile of bamboo which resolved itself into a breastplate of articulated sections and a most unfetching bamboo helmet? There was a small note on the bed. It said, in Willikins' handwriting, *The gamekeeper's friend, commander. Yours too!!!*

Vimes grunted and hit the breastplate with his truncheon. It flexed like a living thing and the truncheon bounced across the room.

Well, we live and learn, Vimes thought, or perhaps more importantly, we learn and live. He crept downstairs and let himself out into the night . . . which was a checkerboard of black and white. He'd forgotten that outside the city, where the smogs, smokes and steams rendered the world into a thousand shades of gray, out in places like this there was black and white, and, if you were looking for a metaphor, there was one, right there.

He knew the way to the hill, you couldn't miss it. The moon

illuminated the way as if it had wanted to make things easier for him. Actual agriculture ran out around here. The fields gave way to furze, and to turf nibbled by rabbits into something resembling the baize of a snooker table . . . although given that rabbits did other things than just eat grass, he would play snooker with a lot of very small balls. Bunnies scattered as he climbed and he worried that he was making too much noise, but it was his land and therefore this *was* just a walk in the park. So he walked a little more jauntily, following what seemed to be the only path, and saw, in the moonlight, the gibbet.

Well, he thought, it says Dead Man's Copse on the map, doesn't it? They used to do a lot of things like this in the old days, didn't they? And the metal cage was just there to keep the corpses upright so that the ravens didn't have to kneel. Good old-fashioned policing, you could call it, if you wanted to chill a spine or two. A pile of crumbling ancient bones at the foot of the gibbet testified to the old-fashioned policing at work.

Vimes felt the stealthy movement of a knife on the hairs of his neck.

A moment later Willikins got up off the ground and fastidiously brushed dirt from his clothing. "Oh, well done, sir!" he said, wheezing a little, owing to the shortness of breath. "I can see that I can't put anything across you, commander." He stopped, held his hand up to his nose and sniffed. "Blow me down, commander! There's blood all over my clothes! You didn't stick me, did you, sir? You just spun round and kicked me in the nuts, which I may say, sir, was done most expertly."

Vimes sniffed. You learned to smell blood. It smelled like metal. Now, people would say that metal doesn't smell, it does, but it smells like blood.

"You got up here on time?" said Vimes.

"Yes, sir. Didn't see a living soul." Willikins knelt down. "Didn't see a thing. Wouldn't have seen the blood if you hadn't kicked me into a puddle of it. It's all over the place."

I wish I had Igor here, thought Vimes. These days he handed over the forensic to the experts. On the other hand, you acquired a forensics skill of your own and beyond the smell of blood he could smell butchery and unbelievable coincidence. Everybody sees everything in the countryside. Jefferson was going to meet Vimes, but here there was a definite shortage of Jefferson and no shortage whatsoever of blood while, at the same time, a noticeable absence of corpse. Vimes' brain worked through things methodically. Of course, you took it for granted that if a citizen was surreptitiously going to tell a policeman a secret it was likely that somebody did not wish said citizen to say said thing. And if said citizen was found dead then said policeman, who had been seen to have a scrap with him earlier, might just be considered to be a tiny bit guilty when all is said and done, and while all was being said and all was being done, someone really intent on getting Vimes into difficulties would have left the corpse of the blacksmith there, wouldn't they?

"Found something, sir," said Willikins, straightening up.

"You what?"

"Found something, sir, felt along the ground, as you might say."

"But it's soaked with blood, man!"

This didn't seem to worry Willikins. "Never minded blood, commander, leastways when it wasn't mine." There was some scrabbling, then light appeared: Willikins had shifted the trap door of a dark lantern. He handed it to Vimes and then held something small to the glow. "It's a ring, sir. Looks like it's been made of stone."

"What? You mean it's a stone with a hole in it?"

He heard Willikins sigh. "No, sir, it's polished smooth. And there's a claw in it. Looks like goblin to me."

Vimes thought, all that blood. Severed claw. Goblins aren't that big. Somebody bothered to come up here to kill a goblin. Where's the rest of it?

In theory, moonlight should help the search, but moonlight is deceptive, creating shadows where shadows should not be, and the wind was getting up. Dark lantern or not, there was little he could do here.

T HE CURTAINS WERE DRAWN and a few lights still burned in the Goblin's Head. Apparently, there were licensing laws. A good copper should always be ready to test the strength of them. He led the way round to the back of the pub and knocked on the little wooden sliding panel set into the building's back door. After a few moments Jiminy pulled the sliding panel aside and Vimes stuck his hand in the hole before the man could close it again.

"Not you, please, your grace, the magistrates would have my guts for garters!"

"And I'm sure they'll be very decorative," said Vimes, "but it won't happen, because I'll warrant that about a third of your regular customers are still imbibing intoxicating liquors at this hour, and probably at least one magistrate is among them . . . No, I take back that last remark. Magistrates do their drinking at home, where there are no licensing laws. I won't say a word, but it'll be a bad old day for the job if a thirsty copper can't mump a nighttime beverage from a former colleague." He slapped some coins on the tiny shelf inside the little panel and added, "That should buy a double brandy for my man here, and for me the address of Mr. Jefferson, the smith."

"You can't treat me like this, you know."

Vimes looked at Willikins. "Can I?"

The gentleman's gentleman cleared his throat. "We are now in the world of feudal law, commander. You own the ground this public house stands on, but he has rights as strong as your own. If he has paid his rent, then you can't even go into the property without his permission."

"How do you know all this stuff?"

"Well, commander, as you know, I've had one or two holidays in the Tanty in my time, and one thing about prison is there are always a lot of books about the law lying around, criminals being very keen on going through the old legal smallprint, just in case it turns out that giving a rival gang member some cement boots and dropping him in the river might be legal after all. That kind of learning sticks."

"But I'm investigating a mysterious disappearance now. The blacksmith was very keen to see me up the hill, but when I got up there there was nothing but a load of blood all over the place. Jefferson wanted to tell me something and you must know what that smells like to a copper." *Even though I'm not sure*, said Vimes to himself. "Definitely something iffy, that's for sure."

The landlord shrugged. "Not my business, squire."

Vimes's hand gripped the landlord's wrist before the man could pull it away and tugged him so hard that his face was up against the woodwork.

"Don't you squire me. There's something going down here, something wrong; I can feel it in my boots and, believe me, they are the most sensitive boots that ever were. The man who runs the village pub knows everything—I know that and so do you. If you're not on my side you're in my way and you know something, I can see it in your eyes. If it turns out you knew something of importance about the blacksmith you'll have invited yourself to be an accessory after the fact, with a free option, if I can get the bit between my teeth, of before the fact, which leaves you right in the middle, and that's a fact."

Jiminy wriggled, but Vimes's grip was steely. "Your badge doesn't work here, Mr. Vimes, you know that!"

Vimes heard the tiny whine of fear in the man's voice, but old coppers were tough. If you weren't tough, you never became an old copper. "I'm going to let go, *sir*," said Vimes, which is policeman's code for "trembling arsehole." "You think that legally around here I don't have a leg to stand on. This may or may not be true, but my man here is not a policeman and is not accustomed to doing things nicely like we in the job do, and you might end up without a leg to stand on as well. I'm telling you this as a friend. We both know this game, eh? I expect you were working in the bar when the goblin was killed, yes?"

"I didn't know a bloody goblin was killed, did I? So how would I know when it may or may not have happened? My advice, *sir*," said Jiminy, with the same coded inflection that Vimes had used, "would be to report the matter to the authorities in the morning. That would be young Feeney, calls himself a copper. Look, I came here to retire, Vimes, and staying alive is part of that. I do not poke my nose into that which does not concern me. And I know there's a lot of things that you could do and I know you ain't going to do them, but just so's you don't go home empty-handed, Jethro lives where all blacksmiths live, right in the center of the village overlooking the green. He lives with his old mum, so I wouldn't disturb her at this time of night. And now, gents, I'd better shut the pub. Don't want to break the law."

The panel slid back, and there was the sound of a bolt slotting into place. A moment later, to the time-honored cry of "Ain't you lot got no homes to go to?" they heard the front door open and the lane filled with men trying to get their brains to go in the direction of their feet, or vice versa.

In the shadows of the pub's back yard, which smelled of old barrels, Willikins said, "Would you like to take a bet on whether your blacksmith is tucked up in his bed tonight, sir?"

"No," said Vimes, "but this stinks to me. I think I've got a murder, but I haven't got a corpse, not all of it anyway," he said, as Willikins opened his mouth. Vimes grunted. "For it to be definitely murder, Willikins, you need to be missing an important bit of you that you really need to stay alive, like your head. Okay, or like your blood, but it's difficult to collect that in the dark, isn't it?"

They set off, and Vimes said, "The one thing you can say about the dead is that they stay dead, well, generally speaking, and so . . . it's been a long day, and that's a long walk and old age is creeping on, okay?"

"Not very noticeably from the outside, commander," said Willikins loyally.

T HE DOOR WAS OPENED to them by a yawning night footman and as soon as he had retired Willikins produced from the pocket of his coat the reeking and severed goblin claw and placed it on the hall table.

"Not much to a goblin once you get past the head, or so they say. See, there's the ring on the finger. Definitely looks like stone, pretty good workmanship for a goblin."

"Animals don't wear jewelry," said Vimes. "You know, Willikins, I've said it before, you'd make a bloody good copper if it wasn't for the fact that you'd make a bloody good assassin."

Willikins grinned. "I did think about the assassins when I was a lad, sir, but unfortunately I was not of the right social class and, besides, they have rules." He helped Vimes out of his jacket and went on, "The street don't have rules, commander, except one, which is

'Survive' and my dear old dad would probably turn in his grave if I even thought of being a copper."

"But I thought you never knew who your father was?"

"Indeed, sir, that is the case, but one must consider the fact of heredity." Willikins produced a small brush and whisked a speck of dirt off the coat before putting it on a hanger, then went on, "I do feel the absence of a parent sometimes and I have wondered whether it might be a sensible idea to go along to the cemetery at Small Gods and shout out 'Dad, I'm going to be a copper,' and then see which gravestone revolved, sir."

The man was still grinning. Vimes reflected, and not for the first time, that he had quite an unusual gentleman to be a gentleman's gentleman, especially given that neither of them was a gentleman in the first place. "Willikins, and I mean this most sincerely, if I were you I'd go instead down to the Tanty and shout it out into the lime pit next to the gallows."

Willikins' grin widened. "Thank you, sir. I don't have to tell you that that means a lot to me. If you would excuse me, sir, I'll go and put my jacket in the incinerator before retiring."

SYBIL TURNED OVER AND made a big warm noise when Vimes got into bed next to her. It had been a long day, and he dropped into that pink semiconscious stupor that is even better than sleep, waking up slightly every hour when nobody rang a bell in the street below to say that all was well.

And he woke up again to hear the sound of heavy cart wheels rumbling over stones. Half asleep as Vimes was, suspicion woke him the rest of the way. Stones? It was all bloody gravel around the Hall. He opened a window and stared out into the moonlight. It was an echo bouncing off the hills. A few brain cells doing the night shift wondered what kind of agriculture had to be done at night. Did they grow mushrooms? Did turnips have to be brought in from the cold? Was that what they called crop rotation? These thoughts melted into his somnolent brain like little grains of sugar in a cup of tea, slithering and dripping from cell to synapse to neurotransmitter until it arrived in the receptor marked "suspicion," which if you saw a medical diagram of a policeman's brain would probably be quite a visible lump, slightly larger than the lump marked *"ability to understand long words."* He thought, *Ah yes, contraband!* and, feeling cheerful, and hopeful for the future, he gently closed the window and went back to bed.

THE FOOD AT THE Hall was copious and sumptuous and quite probably very nearly everything else ending in *us*. Vimes was old enough to know that the senior staff got to eat the leftovers and therefore made certain there would *be* leftovers. With this in mind he had a very large helping of haddock kedgeree and ate all four rashers of bacon on his plate. Sybil tut-tutted about this, and Vimes pointed out that he was on holiday, after all, and on holiday you did not do the things you did on other days, causing Sybil, with forensic accuracy, to point out that this should therefore include police work, should it not, but Vimes was ready, and said that of course he understood this, which was why he was going to take Young Sam for a walk down to the center of the village to put his suspicions in the hands of the local policeman. Sybil said, "All right, then," in deliberate tones of disbelief, and he was to be sure to take Willikins with him.

This was another aspect of his wife that puzzled Vimes to the core. In the same way that Sybil thought that Nobby Nobbs, although a rough diamond, was a good watchman, she thought that

Vimes was safer in the company of a man who never moved abroad without the weaponry of the street about his person, and who had once opened a beer bottle with somebody else's teeth. This was true, but in some ways very disconcerting.

He heard the doorbell ring, heard the footman open the front door, heard a muffled conversation followed by somebody walking on the gravel path round to the back of the Hall. It wasn't important, it was just ambience, and the sound of a footman coming into the room and whispering to Sybil fell into the same category.

He heard her say, "What? Oh well, I suppose you'd better show him in," then snapped to attention when she addressed him. "It's the local policeman. Can you see him in the study? Policemen never wipe their feet properly, especially you, Sam."

Vimes hadn't seen the study yet. The Hall seemed never to run out of rooms. By dint of being pointed the way by a swiveling maid, he arrived in the study a few seconds before the local copper was shown in by a footman, who was making a face like a man having to handle a dead rat. At least, it was presumably the local copper; he looked like the local copper's son. Seventeen years old, Vimes reckoned, and he smelled of pigs. He stood where the footman had deposited him, and stared.

After a while Vimes said, "Can I help you, officer?"

The young man blinked. "Er, am I addressing Sir Samuel Vimes?"

"Who are you?"

This query appeared to take the young man by surprise, and after a while Vimes took pity on him and said, "Look, son, the correct drill is to say who you are and then ask me if I am me, so to speak. After all, I don't know who you are. You're not wearing a uniform I recognize, you have shown me no warrant card or badge and you don't have a helmet. I assume, nevertheless, and for the purposes of concluding this interview before lunchtime, that you are the chief constable in this vicinity? What's your name?"

"Er, Upshot, sir, Feeney Upshot . . . er, Chief Constable Up-shot?"

Vimes felt ashamed of himself, but this kid was representing himself as a police officer and even Nobby Nobbs would have laughed.

Aloud, he said, "Well, Chief Constable Upshot, I am Sir Samuel Vimes, amongst other things, and I was thinking only just now that I should talk to you."

"Er, that's good, sir, because I was thinking only just now that it was about time I should arrest you on suspicion of causing the death of Jethro Jefferson, the smith."

Vimes's expression did not change. So, what do I do now? Nothing, that's what. You have the right to remain silent, I've said that to hundreds of people, knowing it for the rubbish that it is, and I'm absolutely certain of one other thing, that I certainly haven't laid anything more than an educational hand on that damned blacksmith and therefore it's going to be very interesting to find out why this little twerp thinks he can feel my collar for doing so.

A copper should always be willing to learn, and Vimes had learned from Lord Vetinari that you should never react to any comment or situation until you had decided exactly what you were going to do. This had the dual attraction of preventing you from saying or doing the wrong thing while at the same time making other people extremely nervous.

"Sorry about that, sir, but it took me an hour to get the pigs out and make the lockup comfortable, sir, it still smells a bit of disinfectant, sir, and pig, if it comes to that, but I whitewashed the walls and there's a chair and a bed you can curl up on. Oh, and so you don't get bored I found the magazine." He looked hopefully at Vimes, whose expression had not changed, merely calcified, but after a suitably long stare Vimes said, "Which magazine?"

"Sir? I didn't know there was more than one. We've always had it. It's about pigs. It's a bit worn now, but pigs is always pigs."

Vimes stood up. "I'm going to go for a walk, chief constable. You can follow me if you like."

"Sorry, sir, but I've arrested you!"

"No, son, you haven't," said Vimes, heading toward the front door.

"But I definitely told you that you were arrested, sir!" It was almost a wail.

Vimes opened the front door and started down the steps with Feeney trotting along behind him. A couple of gardeners who would otherwise have turned away leaned on their brooms at the sight, suspecting a cabaret.

"What in the world have you got on you that tells me you are an official policeman?" enquired Vimes over his shoulder.

"I have the official truncheon, sir. It's a family heirloom!"

Sam Vimes stopped walking and turned. "Well, my lad, if it's official then you'd better let me look at it, hadn't you? Come on, hand it over." Feeney did so.

It was just an oversized blackjack, with the word "law" inexpertly burnt into it with maybe a poker. Good weight, though. Vimes tapped it in his palm and said, "You've given me to understand that you believe that I'm potentially a murderer and you've handed your weapon to me! Don't you think that's unwise?"

VIMES SAW THE LANDSCAPE drift past as he floated over the terrace and landed on his back in a flower bed, staring at the sky. Feeney's concerned face, somewhat overlarge, appeared in his vision. "Sorry about that, commander. Personally I wouldn't hurt you for anything, but I didn't want to give you the wrong impression. That move translates as *One Man He Up Down Very Sorry*."

Vimes watched the patch of sky above him in a state of inexplicable peace as the boy said, "You see, my granddad worked on the tall ships when he was a lad, sailing over to Bhangbhangduc and all them places where folk is so strange, and when he came back he brought my granny, Ming Chang, and she taught that to my dad and to me." He sniffed. "She died a few months ago, but at least she taught my mum cookery, too. Bung Ming Suck Dog is still a favorite in these parts and, of course, it's not too difficult to get the ingredients, being so close to the sea. Bong Can Bang Keng doesn't grow very well around here, although Packed Shop Chop Muck Dick grows pretty well. Oh, the color is coming back to your face, sir, I'm very pleased to say."

Aching at every joint, Vimes pulled himself upright. "Don't do that again, d'you hear?"

"I'll try not to do so, sir, but you are under arrest, sir."

"I told you, young man, you have not properly arrested me." Vimes got to his feet, wheezing a little. "In order to effect a legal arrest, the arresting officer must be physically touching the suspect while clearly uttering the words 'I arrest you,' like this, although at that time you need not specify the crime of which your suspect is suspected. While so doing . . ." and here Vimes punched the boy so hard in the solar plexus that he curled up, " . . . it pays to take care, which you are going to need to do, my lad, if you intend to arrest me, which I may point out you still have not done, which is a shame because if you had you would now have a clear case against me for resisting arrest as well as assaulting a policeman in the execution of his duty. With the proviso that nothing about you so far leads me to believe that you truly are a policeman."

Vimes sat down on a handy stone and watched as Feeney began to unfold. "I'm Sam Vimes, young man, so don't try that chop sally stuff on me, understand?"

Now Feeney's voice was a sort of attenuated wheeze: "And one day someone will say to you, 'Do you know who I am, constable?' to which you will reply, 'Yes, sir, or, as it may be, madam, you are the person I am interviewing in connection with the aforesaid crime,' or similar appropriate wording, which should not include such phrases as 'You are going down, chummy,' or 'I've got you bang to rights and no mistake.' Ignore, but remember, all threats made. The law is one and immutable. It does not care who anybody is and at that moment you, in a very real way, are it, and therefore nor do you."

Vimes stood with his mouth open as Feeney continued. "We don't often get *The Times* over here, but I bought a load of pig medicine a year ago and it was wrapped in *The Times* and I saw your name when you spoke about being a policeman. It made me feel very proud, sir."

Vimes remembered that speech. He'd had to write it for the passing-out parade of some newly trained officers from the Watch School. He had spent hours trying to get it down, hampered by the fact that for him any form of literature was in every sense a closed book.

He had shown it to Sybil and asked her whether she thought he should get somebody to help him with it, and she had patted him on the head and said, "No, dear, because then it would look like something written by somebody for somebody else, whereas right now the pure Vimes shows through, like a radiant beacon." That had quite cheered him up, because he had never been a radiant beacon before.

But now his heart sank as his train of thought was interrupted by a very polite cough and the voice of Willikins, who said, "Excuse me, commander, I thought it right at this time to introduce the young gentleman to my friends Mr. Burleigh and Mr. Stronginthearm. Lady Sybil would not be happy to see you arrested, commander. I fear that you would find her a bit . . . acerbic, sir."

Vimes found his voice. "You're a bloody fool, man! Put that damn thing down! You keep it on a hair trigger! Put it down right now!"

Willikins wordlessly set down the shining crossbow on the parapet of the staircase like a mother putting her baby to bed. There was a twang, and seventeen yards away a geranium was decapitated. This passed without notice, except by the geranium and a raggedy figure hiding in the rhododendrons, that said "Snack!" to itself, but resolutely carried on staring at Vimes.

The tableau of shock on the steps was interrupted by Lady Sybil, who could walk very quietly for a large woman. "Gentlemen, what is going on here?"

"This young man, allegedly the local policeman, wishes to take me into custody on a charge of suspicion of murder, my dear."

There passed between husband and wife a look that deserved the status of telepathy. Sybil stared at Feeney. "Ah, you would be young Upshot, I suppose. I was sorry to hear about the death of your grandmother, and I do trust that your mother continues well. I used to visit her when I was a girl. And you want to arrest my husband, do you?"

Feeney, goggle-eyed, managed an unprofessional "Yes, ma'am."

Sybil sighed and said sternly, "Well, then, can I hope that at least this can be done without further vegetable carnage?" She looked at Vimes. "Is he taking you to prison?"

She turned her attention back to Feeney, a man now confronted by a cannon loaded with a thousand years of upper-class self-assurance. "He'll need fresh clothing, constable. If you tell me where you're taking him, and you *will* tell me where you're taking him, I'll personally bring down suitable garments. Will I need to sew the stripes on them, or does that happen automatically? And I would be grateful if you had him back here by teatime, because we're expecting visitors."

Lady Sybil took a step forward and Feeney took a step backward to escape the wrath of the impending bosom. She said, "May I wish you the best of luck in your undertaking, young man. You'll need it. Now please excuse me. I have to go and talk to the cook."

She swept away, leaving the incredulous Feeney staring after her. Then the doors that had just closed behind her opened again, and she said, "Are you still a bachelor, young man?"

Feeney managed a "Yes."

"Then you are invited to tea," she said cheerfully. "There are some very eligible young ladies coming, and I'm sure that they will be most excited to see a young man who is prepared to dance on the very *edge* of hell. Do wear your helmet, Sam, in case there is any police brutality. Willikins, come with me. I want to have a talk to you!"

Vimes let the silence curdle. After too much of it, Feeney said, "Your wife is a very remarkable woman, sir."

Vimes nodded. "You have no idea. What do you want to do now, chief constable?"

The boy hesitated. That was Sybil for you. Just by speaking calmly and confidently she could leave you believing that the world had turned upside down and dropped on to your head.

"Well, sir, I believe I must take you before the magistrates?"

Vimes noted the little question mark. "Who is your boss, Feeney?"

"The aforesaid bench of magistrates, sir."

Vimes began to walk down the steps, and Feeney hurried after him. Vimes waited until the boy was racing, and then stopped dead so that he ran into Vimes. "Your boss is the law, chief constable, and don't you forget it. In fact, one of the jobs of the magistrates is to make certain that you do not! Did you ever take an oath? What did it say? Who was it to?"

"Oh, I remember that all right, sir. It was to the bench of magistrates, sir."

"It . . . was . . . what?! You made an oath to obey the magistrates? They can't make you do that!" He stopped. Remember, in the country there is always somebody watching you, he thought, and probably listening too.

Feeney looked shocked, so Vimes said, "Get me down to your lockup, kid, and lock me in. And while you're about it, lock yourself in with me. Don't rush, don't ask questions, and keep your voice down, apart from possibly saying things like 'I have you bang to rights, you miscreant,' and other rubbish of that general nature, because, young man, I believe somebody is in real difficulties here and I believe that person is you. If you have any sense, you'll keep quiet and take me to your lockup, okay?"

Eyes wide, Feeney nodded.

I T WAS A PLEASANT walk down to the lockup, which turned out to be on a small quay by the river. The area had all the semi-nautical detritus that a man might expect and there was a swing bridge, presumably to allow the bigger boats to pass. The sun shone and nothing was happening, in a slow sort of way. And then there was the much spoken of lockup. It looked like a giant pepperpot built of stone. A flowering creeper grew up it, and, next to the door and restrained by a chain, there was an enormous pig.

When it saw their approach it got on its hind legs, and, tottering somewhat, begged.

"This is Masher," said Feeney. "His father was a wild boar, his mother was surprised. See those fangs? No one gives me much trouble when I threaten to let Masher off his lead, do they, Masher?" He disappeared behind the lockup and returned immediately with a bucket of swill, into which Masher tried to bury himself, with hugely contented noises—as huge, in fact, as his fangs. Vimes was staring at them when a friendly looking woman wearing an apron bustled out of a thatched cottage, stopped when she saw Vimes and dropped a curtsy. She looked hopefully at Feeney. "Who would this fine gentleman be, son?"

"It's Commander Vimes, Mum . . . You know, the duke."

There was a pause while the woman clearly wished that she had been wearing a better dress, hairdo, and shoes, and had cleaned the privy, the kitchen, the scullery, and had tidied up the garden, painted the front door and cleaned the inside of the roof.

Vimes prevented her spin from making a hole in the ground by holding out his hand, and saying, "Sam Vimes, madam, pleased to make your acquaintance," but this only caused her to run indoors in a panic.

"My mum is very keen on the aristocracy," Feeney confided as he unlocked the door of the lockup with an unfeasibly large key.

"Why?" said Vimes, mystified. It was reasonably comfortable in the lockup. Granted, the pigs had left a fragrant memory behind them, but for a boy from Ankh-Morpork this counted as fresh air. Feeney sat down beside him on a well-scrubbed bench. "Well, sir, when my granddad was young, Lord Ramkin gave him a whole half-dollar for opening a gate, just to let the hunt go by. According to my dad, he said, 'no canting hypocrite going on about the rights of man ever gave me as much as a quarter-farthing so I say here's to Lord Ramkin, who gave me a whole half-dollar when he was as pissed as a fart, and never asked for it back when he were sober. That's what I call a gentleman.' "

Vimes squirmed inside, knowing that the supposedly generous old drunkard would have had more money than you could ever imagine, and here was a working man pathetically grateful for a handout from the old piss-artist. He snarled in his soul to a man long dead. But the part of him that had been married to Sybil for years whispered, *But he didn't have to give the man anything, and in those days a whole half-dollar was probably more money than the old man could imagine!* Once Sybil, in one of their very infrequent arguments, had surprised him by blurting out, "Well, Sam, my family got its start in life, its grub stake if you like, by piracy. You should like that, Sam! Good honest manual labor! And look what it led to! The trouble with you, Sam Vimes, is that you're determined to be your very own class enemy."

"Is there something wrong, commander?" said Feeney.

"Everything," said Vimes. "For one thing, no policeman swears allegiance to the civil power, he swears allegiance to the law. Oh, politicians can change the law, and if the copper doesn't like it then he can quit, but while he is in the job it's up to him to act in accordance with the law as laid down." He leaned his back against the stone wall. "You do not swear to obey magistrates! I'd like to see what it was that you signed—" Vimes stopped talking because the little metal plate in the lockup door slid open to reveal Feeney's mother, looking very nervous.

"I've made Bang Suck Duck, Feeney, with swede and chips, and there's enough for the duke as well, if he would be so condescending as to accept it?"

Vimes leaned forward and whispered, "Does she know you've arrested me?"

Feeney shuddered. "No, and, sir, please, please don't tell her, because I think she'd never let me into the house ever again."

Vimes walked over to the door and said to the slot, "I shall be honored by your hospitality, Mistress Upshot."

There was a nervous giggle from the other side of the slot, and Feeney's mother managed to say, "I'm sorry to say we have no silver plates, your highness!"

At home Vimes and Sybil ate off serviceable earthenware, cheap, practical and easy to keep clean. He said aloud, "I'm sorry you don't have any silver plates, too, Mistress Upshot, and I'll have a set sent to you directly."

There was something like a scuffle from the other side of the slot, at the same time as Feeney said, "I beg your pardon? Have you gone mad, sir?"

Well, that *would* help, Vimes thought. "We've got hundreds of damn silver plates up at the Hall, my lad. Bloody useless, they make the food cold and they turn black as soon as your back is turned. We appear to be overrun with silver spoons, too. I'll see what we've got."

"You can't do that, sir! She gets scared of having valuables in the house!"

"Do you have much theft hereabouts, chief constable?" said Vimes, emphasizing the last two words.

Mr. Feeney opened the door of the lockup and picked up his mother, who had apparently been stunned by the possibility of owning silver plates, brushed her down and said over her shoulder, "No, sir, the reason being no one has anything to steal. My mum always told me money can't buy you happiness, sir."

Yes, Vimes thought, so did my ma, but she was glad enough when I gave her my first wages, because it meant we could have a meal with meat in it, even if we didn't know what kind of meat it was. That's happiness, isn't it? Blimey, the lies we tell ourselves . . .

When a blushing Mistress Upshot had gone to fetch the meal, Vimes said, "Between ourselves, chief constable, do you believe that I'm guilty of murder?"

"No, sir!" said Feeney instantly.

"You said that very quickly, young man. Are you going to say that it's copper's instinct? Because I get the impression you ain't been a copper long and haven't had much to do. I'm no expert, but I don't reckon pigs try lying to you very much either."

Feeney took a deep breath. "Well, sir," he said calmly, "my granddad was a wily old bird and he could read people like books. He used to walk me around the area introducing me to people, sir, and then as they strolled along he'd tell me their stories, like the one about the man who'd been caught in *flagrante delicto* with a common barnyard fowl . . ."

Vimes listened openmouthed as the pink, well-scrubbed face talked about the gentle, fragrant landscape as if it was populated by devils from the most insidious pit. He unrolled a crime sheet that badly needed the laundry: no major murders, just nastiness, silliness and all the crimes of human ignorance and stupidity. Of course, where there were people there was crime. It just seemed out of place in the slow world of big spaces and singing birds. And yet he'd smelled it as soon as he was here and now he was in the middle of it.

"You get a tingle," said Feeney. "That's what my dad told me. He said watch, listen and keep your eye on every man. There never was a good policeman who didn't have a slice of villain somewhere in him, and this will call to you. It will say 'This man has something to hide,' or 'This man is far more frightened than he should be' or 'This man is acting too cocky by half because underneath he's a bag of nerves.' It *will* call to you."

Vimes opted for admiration rather than shock, but not too

much admiration. "Well, Mr. Feeney, I reckon your grandfather and your dad got it right. So I'm sending the right signals, am I?"

"No, sir, none at all, sir. My granddad and my dad could go like that sometimes. Totally blank. It makes people nervous." Feeney cocked his head on one side and said, "Just a moment, sir, I think we have a little problem . . ."

The door to the lockup clanged open as Chief Constable Upshot skidded around to the rear of the squat little building. Something yelped and squealed and then Vimes, sitting peacefully inside, suddenly had goblins on his lap. In fact it was only one goblin, but one goblin is more than sufficient at close quarters. There was the smell, to begin with, and not to end with either, because it appeared to permeate the world. Yet it wasn't the stink—although heavens knew that they stank with all the stinks an organic creature could generate—no, anyone who walked the streets of Ankh-Morpork was more or less immune to stinks, and indeed there was now a flourishing, if that was the word, hobby of stink-collecting,* and Dave, of Dave's Pin and Stamp Emporium, was extending the sign over his shop again. You couldn't bottle (or whatever it was the collectors did) the intrinsic smell of a goblin because it wasn't so much a stink as a sensation, the sensation in fact that your dental enamel was being evaporated and any armor you might have was rusting at some speed. Vimes punched at the thing but it hung on with arms and legs together, screaming in what was theoretically a voice, that sounded like a bag of walnuts being jumped on. And yet it wasn't attacking—unless you considered the biological

---

* It was all a mystery to Vimes, who was absolutely sure that it was impossible to tell the difference between a chicken fart and a turkey fart, but there were those who professed to be able to do so, and he was glad that such people had chosen this outlet for their puzzling inclinations rather than, for example, fill their sink with human skulls, collected in the high street.

warfare. It clung with its legs and waved its arms, and Vimes just managed to stop Feeney braining it with his official truncheon, because, once you paid attention, the goblin was using words, and the words were: *Ice! Ice! We want just ice! Demand! Demand just ice! Right? Just ice!*

Feeney, on the other hand, was shouting, "Stinky, you little devil, I told you what I'd do to you if ever I saw you stealing the pigswill again!" He looked at Vimes as if for support. "They can give you horrible diseases, sir!"

"Will you stop dancing around with that damn weapon, boy!" Vimes looked down at the goblin now struggling in his grasp, and said, "As for you, you little bugger, stop your racket!"

The little room went silent, apart from the dying strains of "They eat their own babies!" from Feeney and "Just ice!" from the goblin, simply and accurately named as "Stinky."

Not panicking now, the goblin pointed a claw at Vimes's left wrist, looked him in the face, and said, "Just ice?" It was a plea. The claw tugged at his leg. "Just ice?" The creature hobbled to the door and looked up at the glowering chief constable and then turned to Vimes with an expression that bored into the man's face and said very deliberately, "Just ice? Mr. Po-leess-maan?"

Vimes pulled out his snuffbox. You could say this for the brown stuff: all that ceremony you went through before you took a pinch gave you rather more thinking time than lighting a cigar. It also got people's attention. He said, "Well now, chief constable, here is somebody asking you for justice. What are you going to do about it?"

Feeney looked uncertain, and took refuge in a certainty. "It's a stinking goblin!"

"Do you often see them around the lockup?" said Vimes, keeping his tone mild.

"Only Stinky," said Feeney, glowering at the goblin, who stuck out his worm-like tongue. "He's always hanging around. The rest of them know what happens if they're caught thieving around here!"

Vimes glanced down at the goblin and recognized a badly set broken leg when he saw one. He turned the snuffbox over and over in his hands, and did not look at the young man. "But surely a policeman wonders what has happened for a wretched thing like this to walk right up to the law and risk being maimed . . . *again*?"

It was a leap in the dark, but, hell, he had leapt so often that the dark was a trampoline.

His arm itched. He tried to ignore it, but just for a moment there was a dripping cave in front of him, and no other thought except of terrible endless vengeance. He blinked and the goblin was tugging at his sleeve again and Feeney was getting angry.

"I didn't do that! I didn't see it done!"

"But you know it happens, yes?" And again Vimes remembered the darkness and the thirst for vengeance, in fact vengeance itself made sapient and hungry. And the little bugger had touched him on that arm. It all came back, and he wished that it hadn't, because while all coppers must have a bit of villain in them, no copper should walk around with a piece of demon as a tattoo.

Feeney had lost his anger now, because he was frightened. "Bishop Scour says they're demonic and insolent creations made as a mockery of mankind," he said.

"I don't know about any bishops," said Vimes, "but something is going on here and I can feel the tingle, felt it on the day I came here, and it's tingling on *my* land. Listen to me, chief constable. When you apprehend the suspect you should take the trouble to ask them if they did it, and if they say no you must ask them if they can prove their innocence. Got it? You're supposed to ask. Understand? And my answers are, in order, hell no and hell yes!"

The little clawed hand scratched at Vimes's shirt again. "Just ice?"

Vimes thought, Oh well, I thought I'd been gentle with the lad up until now. "Chief constable, something is wrong, and you know that something is wrong, and you are all alone, so you'd better enlist the help of anyone you know that can be trusted. Such as me, for example, in which case I'll be the suspect who, having been bailed on my own recognizance of one penny," and here Vimes handed a partly corroded small copper disc to the astonished Feeney, "has been requested to help you with your inquiries, such as they are, and that will be all fine and dandy and in accordance with the standard work on police procedure, which, my lad, was written by me, and you had better believe it. I'm not the law, no policeman is the law. A policeman is just a man, but when he wakes up in the morning it is the law that is his alarm clock. I've been nice and kind to you up until now, but did you really think I was going to be spending the night in a pig pen? Time to be a real copper, lad. Do the right thing and fudge the paperwork afterward, like I do."

Vimes looked down at the persistent little goblin. "Okay, Stinky, lead the way."

"But my old mum is just coming out with your dinner, commander!" Feeney's voice was a wail, and Vimes hesitated. It didn't do to upset an old mum.

It was time to let the duke out. Vimes never normally bowed to anybody, but he bowed to Mistress Upshot, who almost dropped her tray in ecstatic confusion. "I am mortified, my dear Mistress Upshot, to have to ask you to keep your Man Dog Suck Po warm for us for a little while, because your son here, a credit to his uniform and to his parents, has asked me to assist him in an errand of considerable importance, which can only be entrusted to a young man with integrity, as your lad here."

As the woman very nearly melted in pride and happiness Vimes pulled the young man away.

"Sir, the dish was Bang Suck Duck, we only have Man Dog Suck Po on Sundays. With mashed carrots."

Vimes shook Mrs. Upshot warmly by the hand and said, "I look forward to tasting it later, my dear Mistress Upshot, but if you'll excuse me, your son is a stickler for his police work, as I'm sure you know."

COLONEL CHARLES AUGUSTUS MAKEPEACE had long ago, with the expertise of a lifelong strategist, decided to let Letitia have her way in all things. It saved so much trouble and left him able to potter around in his garden, take care of his dragons and to occasionally go trout fishing, a pastime that he loved. He rented half a mile of stream, but was sadly now finding it difficult to keep running fast enough. Nowadays he spent a lot of time in his library, working on the second volume of his memoirs, keeping from under his wife's feet and not getting involved.

Until this moment he had been quite happy that she had the role of chairman of the magistrates because it kept her away from home for hours at a time. He had never been very much of a one for thinking in terms of good or bad and guilty or not guilty. He had learned to think in terms of us and them and dead and not dead.

And therefore he wasn't exactly listening to the group sitting around the long table at the other end of the library, talking in worried voices, but nevertheless he couldn't help overhearing.

She had signed that damned document! He ought to have tried to talk her out of it, but he knew where that would have ended. Commander Vimes! Okay, by all accounts the man was the sort to rush in, and maybe he *did* have a scrap with what'shisname the blacksmith, who wasn't too bad a cove in his way, bit of a hothead of course but he'd made a damn good dragon prod only the other day at quite a reasonable price. Vimes? Not a killer, surely. That's one thing you learned in the military. You don't last long if you're a killer. Killing as duty called was another thing entirely. Letitia had listened to that unspeakable lawyer and they had all agreed that it be signed simply because that wretched Rust fella wanted it.

He opened this month's edition of *Fang and Fire*. Occasionally somebody lowered their voice, which you couldn't help thinking was damn insulting, given that they were sitting in a chap's library and especially when the chap hadn't been consulted. But he didn't protest. He had long ago learned not to protest, and so he kept his eyes focused on the pullout feature on flame-retardant incubators, holding it in front of him as if to ward off evil.

However, among the words he *didn't* hear were, "Of course, he only married her for her money, you know." That was his wife's voice. Then, "*I* heard she was desperate to find a husband." The curiously sharp tone of that voice identified its owner as Miss Pickings, who, the colonel couldn't help noting, as he stared grimly at a full-page advertisement for asbestos kennels, had clearly been in no hurry to find a husband herself.

The colonel was, by inclination, a live-and-let-live personality and, frankly, if a gel wanted to go around with another gel who wears a shirt and tie, trains horses and has a face like a bulldog licking vinegar off a thistle, then it was entirely *her* business. After all, he told himself, what about old "Beefy" Jackson, eh? Wore a dress every night in the mess and rather flowery aftershave for a chap, but when the call to arms came he could fight like a bloody demon. Funny old world.

He tried to find his place on the page again, but was interrupted by the Very Reverend Mouser. He never could get on with padres, couldn't see the point. "I find it very suspicious that the Ramkin family have turned up here after so many years, don't you? I keep reading about Vimes in the newspaper, not the kind of person you can imagine as simply taking a holiday."

"According to Gravid, he is known as Vetinari's terrier," said Letitia.

At the other end of the room her husband thrust his head even deeper into his magazine so as not to snigger. Gravid! Who would call their child Gravid? No one who had ever kept dragons or fish, that was certain. Of course, there was such a thing as a dictionary, but then the old Lord Rust had never been the kind of man to open a book if he could help it. The colonel tried to contemplate an article on the treatment of Zig-Zag Throat in older males and the wife of his heart continued, "Well, we don't want any of Vetinari's nonsense here. *Apparently*, his lordship rather enjoys allowing Vimes to break wind in the halls of the mighty. *Apparently*, Vimes is no respecter of rank. Indeed, quite the reverse. And indeed, it would seem that he is prepared to ambush a decent working man."

Funny, thought the colonel, first time I ever heard her call the smith anything other than a blasted nuisance. It seemed to him that the gossip around the table was trite, artificial, like the conversation of raw recruits on the eve of their first battle. He thought, there's a warrant out for Commander Vimes, hero of Koom Valley (Bloody good show! Wonderful execution. Peace in our time between brother troll and brother dwarf and that sort of thing. Just the job! I've seen too much killing in my time) and now you are going to put him out of a job and a reputation, just because that greasy lad with a name like a pregnant frog has charmed you into doing so.

"I understand he has a very violent nature," said, oh, what was his name? Bit of a bad hat in the colonel's opinion. Bought a big villa up near Overhang, one of Rust's cronies. Never seemed to do any work. What was his name, ah yes, Edgehill, not a man that you would trust behind you or in front of you, but they'd sworn him in even so.

"And he was just a street kid *and* a drunkard!" said Letitia. "What do you think of that?"

The colonel paid careful attention to his magazine while his unspoken thoughts said, Sounds jolly good to me, my dear. All I got when I married you was the promise of a half-share in your dad's fish and chip shop when I left the service, and I never even got that.

"Everybody knows that his ancestor killed a king, so I can't imagine a Vimes would jib at killing a blacksmith," said the Honorable Ambrose. Bit of a mystery, this one. Something to do with shipping. Sent out from the city to lie low here because of something to do with a girl. And the colonel, who spent a lot of time thinking,* had some time ago wondered to himself how, in these modern days, you got banished from the city because of a girl, and instinct had told him that possibly it had something to do with the age of the girl. After incubating that thought for a while, the colonel had written to his old chum "Jankers" Robinson, who always knew a thing or two about this and that and one thing and another and who was now some political wallah in the palace. He had made an enquiry, as one might, of his friend whom he had once dragged to safety over the pommel of his saddle before a Klatchian scimitar got him, and had received a little note with nothing more than "Yes indeed, under-age, hushed up at great expense," and after that the colonel had taken great care never to shake the bastard's hand again.

Blithely unaware of the thoughts of the colonel, the Honorable Ambrose, who always seemed to be slightly bigger than his

---

* Because he wasn't allowed much time talking.

clothes—said clothes being of a fashion more suited to somebody twenty years his junior—sneered, "Frankly, I think we're doing the world a service. They say that he favors dwarfs and all kinds of low-life. You might expect anything of a man like that!"

Yes, you might, thought the colonel.

And Miss Pickings said, "But we haven't done anything wrong . . . Have we?"

The colonel turned a page and smoothed it down with military exactitude. He thought, Well, you all condone smuggling when the right people are doing it because they're chums, and when they aren't they're heavily fined. You apply one law for the poor and none for the rich, my dear, because the poor are such a nuisance.

He felt eyes suddenly upon him because marital telepathy is a terrible thing. His wife said, "It doesn't do any harm, everybody does it." Her head swung round again as her husband turned the page, his eyes fixedly on the type as he thought, as noiselessly as his brain could contrive: and of course there was the . . . incident, a few years ago. Not good, that. Not good. Not good when little babies of any sort are taken away from mothers. Not good at all. And you all know it and it worries you, and well it should.

The room was silent for a moment and then Mrs. Colonel continued. "There will not be any problems. Young Lord Rust has promised me. We have rights, after all."

"I blame that wretched blacksmith," said Miss Pickings. "He keeps bringing it back into people's memories, him and that damn writing woman."

Mrs. Colonel bridled at this. "I have no idea what you're talking about, Miss Pickings. Legally nothing wrong has happened here." Her head swiveled toward her husband. "Are you all right, dear?" she demanded.

For a moment he looked as though he wasn't and then the colonel said, "Oh, yes, dear. Right as rain. Right as rain." But his thoughts continued: you have partaken in what is, I strongly suggest, a cynical attempt to ruin the career of a very good man.

"I heard you coughing." It sounded like an accusation.

"Oh, just a bit of dust or something, dear, right as rain. Right as rain." And then he slammed his magazine on to the table. Standing up, he said, "When I was nothing but a subaltern, dear, one of the first things I learned was that you never give away your position by frantic firing. I think I know the type of your Commander Vimes. Young Lord Rust may be safe, with his money and contacts, but I doubt very much that you all will be. Who knows what would have happened if you hadn't been so hasty? What's a bit of smuggling? You've just pulled the dragon's tail and made him angry!"

When his wife regained control of her tongue, she said, "How dare you, Charles!"

"Oh, quite easily, as it turns out, dear," said the colonel, smiling happily. "A bit of smuggling might be considered a peccadillo, but not when you're supposed to be upholding the law. It baffles me that none of you seems to realize that. If you have any sense, ladies and gentlemen, you will explain that whole unfortunate goblin event to his grace right now. After all, your chum Gravid organized it. The only little problem is that you allowed him to do it, as I recall, without so much as a murmur."

"But it was not illegal," said his wife icily.

Her husband didn't move, but in some ineffable sense he was suddenly taller. "I think things got a bit tangled: you see, you thought about things as being legal or illegal. Well, I'm just a soldier and never was a very good one, but it's my opinion you were so worried about legal and illegal that you never stopped to think about whether it was right or wrong. And now, if you will excuse me, I'm going down to the pub."

Automatically, his wife said, "No, dear, you know drink doesn't agree with you."

The colonel was all smiles. "This evening I intend to settle my differences with drink and make it my friend."

The rest of the magistrates looked at Mrs. Colonel, who glared at her husband. "I'll talk to you about this later, Charles," she growled.

To her surprise, his smile did not change. "Yes, dear, I suspect you will, but I think you'll find that I won't be listening. Good evening to you all." There was a click as the door shut behind him. There should have been a slam, but some doors never quite understand the situation.

T HE GOBLIN WAS ALREADY moving quite fast with a dot-and-carry-one gait that was deceptively speedy. Vimes was surprised to find that Feeney made heavy weather of the little jog toward—he was not surprised—Hangman's Hill. He could hear the boy wheezing slightly. Perhaps you didn't need to be all that fast to overtake a wayward pig, but you needed to be *very* fast indeed to catch up with a young troll blizzarded to the eyeballs with Slice and you needed lots of stamina to overtake him and slap the cuffs on him before he came down enough to try to twist your head off. Policing was obviously very different in the country.

In the country, there is always somebody watching you, he thought as they sped along. Well, there was always somebody watching you in the city, too, but that was generally in the hope that you might drop dead and they could run off with your wallet. They were never *interested*. But here he thought he could feel many eyes on him. Maybe they belonged to squirrels or badgers, or whatever the damn things were that Vimes heard at night; gorillas, possibly.

He had no idea what he was going to see, but certainly didn't expect to find the top of the hill bright with lines of rope, painted yellow. He gave it only a second's glance, however. With their backs to one of the trees, and looking very apprehensive, were three goblins. One of them stood up, thus bringing its head and therefore its eyes to a level in the vicinity of Vimes's groin, not a good position to find himself. It held up a wrinkled hand and said, "Vimes? Hang!"

Vimes stared down at it and then at Feeney. "What does he mean, 'Hang'?"

"Never been quite sure," said Feeney. "Something like, have a nice day, I think, but only in goblin."

"Vimes!" the old goblin continued. "It said be, you be po-leess-maan. It be big po-leess-maan! If po-leess-maan, then just ice! But just ice it be no! And when dark inside dark! Dark moving! Dark must come, Vimes! Dark rises! Just ice!"

Vimes had no idea of the sex of the speaker, or even its age. Dress wasn't a clue: goblins apparently wore anything that could be tied on. Its companions were watching him unblinkingly. They had stone axes, flint, vicious stuff, but it lost its edge after a couple of blows, which was no consolation when you were bleeding from the neck. He had heard that they were berserk fighters, too. Oh, and what was the other thing people said? Ah yes, whatever you do, don't let them scratch you. . .

"You want justice, do you? Justice for what?"

The goblin speaker stared at him and said, "Come with me po-leess-maan," the words rolling out like a curse, or, at least, a threat. The speaker turned and began to walk solemnly down the far side of the hill. The other three goblins, including the one known to Vimes as Stinky, did not move.

Feeney whispered, "This could be a trap, sir."

Vimes rolled his eyes and sneered, "You think so, do you? I thought it was probably an invitation to a magical show featuring the Amazing Bonko and Doris and the Collapsing Unicycle Brothers with Fido the Cat. What's this yellow rope all about, Mr. Upshot?"

"Police cordon, sir. My mum knitted it for me."

"Oh yes, I can see she's managed to work the word PLICE in black in there several times, too."

"Yes, sir, sorry about the spelling, sir," said Feeney, clearly spooked by the stares. He went on, "There was blood all over the ground, sir, so I scraped some into a clean jam jar, just in case."

Vimes paid that no attention, because the two goblin guards had unfolded and were standing up. Stinky beckoned Vimes to walk ahead of them. Vimes shook his head, folded his arms and turned to Feeney.

"Let me tell you what you thought, Mr. Upshot. You acted on information received, didn't you? And you heard that the blacksmith and I indulged in a bout of fisticuffs outside the pub the other night, and that is true. No doubt you were also told that at some time later someone heard a conversation in which he arranged to meet me up at this place, yes? Don't bother to answer, I can see it in your face—you haven't quite got the copper's deadpan yet. Has Mr. Jefferson gone missing?"

Feeney gave up. "Yes, Mr. Vimes."

He didn't deserve or perhaps he *did* deserve, the force with which Vimes turned on him.

"You will not call me Mr. Vimes, lad, you ain't earned the right. *You* call me 'Sir' or 'Commander,' or even 'Your grace' if you're dumb enough to do so, understand? I could have sent the blacksmith home walking very strangely if I'd had a mind to do so the other night. He's a big man but no street hero. But I let him get the steam out of his tubes and calm down without losing face. Yes, he did say he wanted to meet me up here last night. When I came up here, with a witness, there was blood on the ground which I will warrant is goblin blood, and certainly no sign of any black-smith. You had a bloody stupid case against me when you came up to my house and it's still a bloody stupid case. Any questions?"

Feeney looked down at his feet. "No, sir, sorry, sir."

"Good, I'm glad. Think of this as a training experience, my lad, and it won't cost you a penny. Now, these goblins seem to want us to follow them and I intend to do so, and I also intend that you will come with me, understood?"

Vimes looked at the two goblin guards. An ax was waved in a half-hearted sort of way, indicating that they should indeed be traveling. They set off and he could hear sorrowful Feeney trying to be brave, but broadcasting anxiety.

"They're not going to touch us, kid, first because if they had intended to do that they'd have done it already, and second, they want something from me."

Feeney moved a little closer. "And what would that be, sir?"

"Justice," said Vimes. "And I think I have a premonition about what that is going to mean . . ."

SOMETIMES PEOPLE ASKED COMMANDER Vimes why Ser-geant Colon and Corporal Nobbs were still on the strength, such as it was, of the modern Ankh-Morpork City Watch, given that Nobby occasionally had to be held upside down and shaken to reclaim small items belonging to other people, while Fred Colon had actually cultivated the ability to walk his beat with his eyes closed, and end up, still snoring, back at Pseudopolis Yard, some-times with graffiti on his breastplate.

To Lord Vetinari, Commander Vimes had put forward three defenses. The first was that both of them had an enviable knowledge of the city and its inhabitants, official and otherwise, that rivaled Vimes's own.

The second was the traditional urinary argument. It was better to have them inside pissing out than outside pissing in. It was at least easy to keep an eye on them.

And not least, oh my word not least, they were lucky. Many a crime had been solved because of things that had fallen on them, tried to kill them, tripped one of them up, been found floating in their lunch, and in one case had tried to lay its eggs up Nobby's nose.

And so it was that, today, whatever god or other force it might be that regarded them as its playthings directed their steps to the corner of Cheapside and Rhyme Street, and the fragrant Emporium of Bewilderforce Gumption.*

Sergeant Colon and Corporal Nobbs, as is the way with policemen, entered the building by the back door and were greeted by Mr. Gumption with that happy but somewhat glassy smile with which a trader greets an old acquaintance who he knows will end up getting merchandise with a discount of one hundred per cent.

"Why, Fred, how nice to see you again!" he said, while awakening the mystic third eye developed by all small shopkeepers, especially those who see Nobby Nobbs coming into the shop.

"We were patrolling in the area, Bewilderforce, and I thought

---

* The fourth Gumption to run the tobacco house and snuff mill felt that his surname lacked prestige, and for some reason chose the name "Bewilderforce"— which did indeed become prestigious owing to the success of his tobacco enterprise, which was extremely well thought of by the gentry and others. And thereafter there was at least one Bewilderforce in every generation of the line (although girls were generally named Bewildred).

I'd drop in to get my tobacco and see how you were managing, with all this fuss about the tax and everything?"

The sergeant had to speak up to be heard above the rumbling of the snuff mill, and the carts that were moving across the factory floor in a stream. Rows of women at tables were packing snuff and—here, he leaned sideways to get a better view—the cigarette production line was also a-bustle.

Sergeant Colon looked around. Policemen always look, on the basis that there is always something to see. Of course, sometimes they may find it sensible to forget that they have seen anything, at least officially. Mr. Gumption had a new tie pin, in which a diamond flashed. His shoes were also clearly new—bespoke, if Fred Colon was any judge—and a barely noticeable sniff suggested the wearing of, let's see now, oh yes, Cedar Fragrance Pour Hommes, from Quirm at $15 a pop.

He said, "How's business doing? Is the new tax hitting you at all?"

Mr. Gumption's visage flew into the expression of a hard-working man sorely pressed by the machinations of politics and fate. He shook his head sadly. "We're barely making ends meet, Fred. Lucky to break even at the end of the day."

Oh, and a gold tooth, too, thought Sergeant Colon. I nearly missed that. Out loud he said, "I'm very sorry to hear that, Bewilderforce, I really am. Allow me to raise your profits by expending two dollars in the purchase of my usual three ounces of twist tobacco."

Fred Colon proffered his wallet and Mr. Gumption, with a scolding noise, waved it away. It was a ritual as old as merchants and policemen, and it allowed the world to keep on turning. He cut a length of tobacco from the coil on the marble counter, wrapped it quickly and expertly, and as an afterthought reached down and came up with a large cigar, which he handed to the sergeant.

"Try one of these handsome smokes, Fred, just in, not local, made on the plantation for our valued customers. No no, my pleasure, I insist," he added, as Fred made grateful noises. "Always nice to see the Watch in here, you know that."

Actually, Mr. Gumption thought, as he watched the departing policemen, that was pretty mild: all that the Nobbs creature had done was stare around.

"They must be coining it," said Nobby Nobbs as they ambled onward. "Did you see the 'staff wanted' note in their window? And he was writing out a list of prices on the counter. He's lowering them! He must have a good deal going on with the plantation people, that's all I can say."

Sergeant Colon sniffed the big fat cigar, the fattest he had ever seen, which smelled so good it was probably illegal, and he felt the tingle, the feeling that he had walked into something that was a lot bigger than it seemed, the feeling that if you pulled a thread something large would unravel. He rolled the cigar between his fingers the way he had seen connoisseurs do. In truth, Sergeant Colon was, when it came to tobacco products, something of a bottom-feeder, cheapness being the overriding consideration, and the protocol of cigars was unfamiliar to a man who very much enjoyed a good length of chewing tobacco. What was the other thing he had seen posh types do? Oh yes, you had to roll it in your fingers and hold it up to your ear. He had no idea why this had to be done, but he did it anyway.

And swore.

And dropped it on the ground . . .

THE TRACK FROM THE top of Hangman's Hill went beyond the trees and down, mostly through furze bushes and rocky outcrops, with the occasional patch of raw and useless soil, all sub-stance eroded away. Wild land, wasteland, home to skinny rabbits, hopeless mice, the occasional concussed rat, and goblins.

And there among the bushes was the entrance to a cave. A human would have to bend double to get into that fetid hole and would be an easy target. But Vimes knew, as he ducked through, that he was safe. He knew that. He had suspected it out in the daylight, and down in the darkness he *knew*. The knowledge was almost physical as wings of darkness spread over him, and he heard the sounds of the cave, every sound.

He suddenly *knew* the cave, all the way down to the place where water could be found, the fungus and mushroom gardens, the pathetically empty storerooms, and the kitchen. These were human translations, of course. Goblins generally ate where they could and slept where they fell asleep; they had no real concept of a room with one particular purpose. He knew this now as if he had known it all his life, and he had never before been in any place that a goblin would call home.

But this was the dark, and Vimes and the dark had an . . . un-derstanding, didn't they? At least, that's what the dark thought. What Vimes thought, unprosaically, was *Damn, here we go again.*

He was prodded in the small of his back, and he heard Feeney gasp. Vimes turned to a grinning goblin and said, "Try that one more time, sunshine, and I'll give you a smack around the head, understand?" And that was what he said, and that was what he heard himself say . . . Except that something, not exactly another voice, climbed along his words like a snake coiling itself around a tree, and both his guards dropped their weapons and bolted back into the daylight. It was instant. They didn't yelp or shout. They wanted to save their breath for running.

"Great hells, Commander Vimes! That was bloody magical!"

said Feeney, as he bent to grope for the fallen axes. Vimes watched in the thick darkness as he saw the boy's hands scrabbling and, by luck, find them.

"Drop them! I said drop them right now!"

"But we're unarmed!"

"Don't you bloody argue with me, boy!" There were a couple of thumps as the axes hit the ground.

Vimes breathed again. "Now, we're going to see that nice senior goblin, you understand, and we walk without fear because we *are* the law, you understand? And the law can go everywhere in pursuit of its inquiries."

The headroom increased as they walked onward, until Vimes was able to stand fully upright. Feeney, on the other hand, was having difficulties. Behind Vimes there was a chorus of thumps, scrapes and words that dear old mums should not know about, let alone hear. Vimes had to stop and wait for the boy to catch up, stubbing his feet on easily avoidable outcrops and banging his head where the ceiling dipped briefly.

"Come on, chief constable!" Vimes shouted. "A copper should have good night vision! You should eat more carrots with your Bang Sung Suck Dog or whatever!"

"It's pitch black, sir! I can't see my hand in front of my face—Ouch!" Feeney had walked directly into Vimes. Light dawned, although not on Feeney.

Vimes looked around the meandering cave. It was lit as if by daylight. There were no torches, no candles, just a pervading, moderately bright light—the light he had seen before, years ago now, in a cave, a big cave, far away, and he knew what it meant: he was seeing darkness, probably better than the goblins did. The dark had become incredibly light on that day when Vimes underground, had fought creatures—walking, speaking creatures—that made their home away from the light, and had hatched dark plans. But Vimes had fought them, and he had won, and because of that, the Koom Valley Accord had been written and signed, and the oldest war in the world had ended in, if not peace, then a place where the seeds of peace could hopefully be planted. It was good to know that, because out of the darkness Vimes had acquired . . . a companion. The dwarfs had one name for it: the Summoning Dark. And they had any amount of explanations for what it was: a demon, a lost god, a curse, a blessing, vengeance made flesh, except that it had no flesh other than the flesh it borrowed, a law unto itself, a killer but sometimes a protector, or something that no one could find the right words for. It could travel through rock, water, air and flesh and, for all Vimes knew, through time. After all, what limits can you put on a creature made of nothing? Yes, he had met it and when they parted, for amusement, playfulness, mischief or simply reward the Summoning Dark had put its mark on him, drifting through him and leaving that little glowing tattoo.

Vimes pulled up his shirt sleeve and there it was, and it seemed to be brighter. Sometimes he met it in dreams, where they nodded at one another in respect and then went their separate ways. Months, even years might pass between meetings and he might think it had gone for good, but its mark was on his forearm. Sometimes it itched. All in all, it was like having a nightmare on a leash. And now it was giving him sight in the darkness. But hold on, this was a goblin burrow, not a dwarf cave! And his own thoughts came right back at him with that slight overtone, as if they were a duet: "Yes, but goblins steal *everything*, commander."

Right here and now, it appeared that goblins had stolen away. The floor of the cave was covered with debris, rubbish and things that presumably goblins thought were important, which would probably mean everything, bearing in mind they religiously collected their own snot. He could see the old goblin beckoning him to follow before disappearing. There was a door ahead of him, of goblin manufacture, as was borne out by its look of rottenness and the fact that it was hanging by one hinge, which broke when Vimes gave the door a push. Behind him Feeney said, "What was that? Please, sir, I can't see a thing!"

Vimes walked across to the boy and tapped him on the shoulder, causing him to jump.

"Mr. Upshot, I'll take you up to the entrance so that you can go home, okay?"

He felt the boy shudder. "No, sir! I'd rather stay with you, if it's all the same to you . . . Please?"

"But you can't see in the dark, lad!"

"I know, sir. I've got some string in my pocket. My granddad said a good copper should always have a piece of string." His voice was trembling.

"It *is* generally useful, yes," said Vimes, carefully picking it out of the boy's pocket. "It's amazing how helpless a suspect can be with his thumbs tied together. Are you sure you wouldn't feel better up in the fresh air?"

"Sorry, sir, but if it's all the same to you I think the safest place to be right now is behind you, sir."

"You really can't see a thing, lad?"

"Not a blessed thing, sir. It's like I've gone blind, sir."

In Vimes's opinion the young man was about to go postal, and maybe tethering him to Vimes was better than hearing him knock himself out in an attempt to flee.

"You're not blind, lad, it's just that all that night duty I've done . . . well, it looks as if I'm better than I thought at seeing in the dark."

Feeney shuddered again at Vimes's touch, but together they

succeeded in linking Chief Constable Upshot to Vimes with about
six feet of hairy string, which smelled of pig.

There were no goblins behind the broken door, but a fire was
smouldering fitfully, with a piece of blessedly unrecognizable meat
on a spit above it. A man might think that a goblin had found a
reason to leave his tea behind in a hurry. And talking of tea, there
was a pot, which was to say a rusty tin can, bubbling in the embers
of the fire. Vimes sniffed at it, and was surprised that it smelled of
bergamot, and somehow the idea of a goblin drinking posh tea
with his pinkie extended managed, temporarily, to overwhelm his
incongruity functions. Well, it grew, didn't it? And goblins probably got thirsty, didn't they? Nothing to worry about. Although if
he found a plate of delicate biscuits he would definitely have to sit
down and rest.

He walked on, the light never failing, goblins never appearing.
The cave complex certainly sloped downward, and there were still
signs of goblins everywhere, but of goblins themselves no sign,
which in theory should be a good thing, given that generally the
first sign of a goblin would be one landing on your head and trying
to turn it into a bowling ball. And then there was a flash of color in
this drab subterranean landscape of ices and browns: it was a bunch
of flowers, or what had been a bunch before it had been dropped.
Vimes wasn't an expert on flowers, and when he bought them for
Sybil, at maritally advisable intervals, he generally stuck to a bunch
of roses, or its seemingly acceptable equivalent, one single orchid.
He was vaguely aware of the existence of other flowers, of course,
which brightened up the place, to be sure, but he had never been
one for the names.

There were no roses here, no orchids either. These flowers had
been plucked from hedgerows and meadows and even included the
scrawny plants that managed to hang on and flower in the wilder-

ness up above. Someone had carried them. Someone had dropped them. Someone had been in a hurry. Vimes could read it in the flowers. They had fallen from somebody's open hand, so that they spread back along their path like a comet tail. And then more than one person had trampled them underfoot, but probably not because they were chasing the aforesaid bouquet carrier, but by the look of it because they wanted to go the way that he or she had run, and even faster than he or she did.

There had been a stampede, in fact. Scared people running away. But running away from what?

"You, Commander Vimes, you, the majesty of the law. See how I help you, commander?" The familiarity of the voice annoyed him; it sounded too much like his own voice. "But I'm here because they wanted me to come!" he said to the cave in general. "I wasn't intending to fight anybody!" And in his head his own voice told him, "Oh my little ragtag, rubbish people, who do not trust and are not trusted! Tread with care, Mr. Policeman; the hated have no reason to love! Oh, the strange and secret people, last and worst, born of rubbish, hopeless, bereft of god. The best of luck to you, my brother . . . my brother in darkness . . . Do what you can for them, Mr. Po-leess-maan."

On Vimes's wrist the sigil of the Summoning Dark glowed for a moment.

"I'm not your brother!" Vimes shouted. *"I'm not a killer!"* The words echoed around the caves, but under them Vimes thought he felt something slithering away. Could something with no body slither? Gods damn the dwarfs and their subterranean folklore!

"Are you, er, all right, sir?" came the nervous voice of Feeney behind him. "Er, you were shouting, sir."

"I was just cussing because I banged my head on the ceiling, lad," Vimes lied. He had to deliver reassurance quickly before

Feeney got so unnerved that he might try to make a break for the exit out of panic. "You're doing very well, chief constable!"

"Only, I don't like the dark, sir, never have . . . Er, do you think anyone'll worry if I have a wee up against the wall?"

"I should go ahead if I was you, lad. I don't think anything could make this place smell worse."

Vimes heard some vague sounds behind him, and then Feeney said, in a damp little voice, "Er, nature has taken its course, sir. Sorry, sir."

Vimes smiled to himself. "Don't worry, lad, you won't be the first copper to have to wring out his socks, and you won't be the last, either. I remember the first time I had to arrest a troll. Big fellow, he was, a very nasty character. I was a bit damp around the socks that day, and I don't mind admitting it. Think of it as a kind of baptism!" Keep it jolly, he thought, make a joke of it. Don't let him dwell on the fact that we're walking into the scene of a crime that he can't see. "Funny thing—that troll is now my best sergeant, and I've relied on him for my life quite a few times. That just goes to show that you never know, although what it is we never know I suspect we'll never know."

Vimes turned a corner and there were the goblins. He was glad that young Feeney couldn't see them. Strictly speaking, Vimes wished he couldn't see them either. There must have been a hundred of them, many of them holding weapons. They were crude weapons, to be sure, but a flint ax hitting your head does not need a degree in physics.

"Have we got somewhere, sir?" said Feeney behind him. "You've stopped walking."

They're just standing there, Vimes thought, as if they're on parade. Just watching in silence, waiting for that silence to break.

"There are a few *goblins* in this cave, lad, and they're watching us."

After a few seconds of silence Feeney said, "Could you tell me exactly what a 'few' means, sir?"

Dozens and dozens of owlish faces stared at Vimes without expression. If the silence was going to be broken by the word "charge" then he and Feeney would be smears on the floor, which was pretty smeared as it was. Why did I come in here? Why did I think it was a good thing to do? Oh well, the lad is a policeman, after all, and it isn't as if he doesn't already have a clothing problem. He said, "I would say there are about a hundred, lad, all heavily armed, as far as I can see, except for a couple of broken-down ones right at the front; could be chieftains, I suppose. Beards you could keep a rabbit in, and, by the look of it, may have. It looks as if they are waiting for something."

There was a pause before Feeney said, "It's been an education, working with you, sir."

"Look," said Vimes, "if I have to turn and run, just hang on, okay? Running is another skill a policeman sometimes needs."

He turned to the crowd of impassive goblins and said, "I am Commander Vimes of the Ankh-Morpork City Watch! How can I help you?"

"Just ice!" The cry caused things to drop from the ceiling. It echoed around the cave and echoed again, as cavern after cavern picked up the shout, spun it around, and sent it back. Light rose as torches were kindled. It took Vimes a few moments to realize this, because the light he had seen, some curious artificial light that was probably in his head, had been brighter, and mixed strangely with the smoky orange that was now filling the cave.

"Well, sir, it looks as though they're pleased to see us, yes?"

Feeney's relief and hope should have been bottled and sold to despairing people everywhere. Vimes just nodded, because the ranks were pulling apart, leaving a pathway of sorts, at the end of which there was, inarguably, a corpse. It was a mild relief to see that it was a goblin corpse, but no corpse is good news, particularly when seen in a grimy low light and especially for the corpse. And yet something inside him exulted and cried *Hallelujah!*, because here was a corpse and he was a copper and this was a crime and this place was smoky and dirty and full of suspicious-looking goblins and here was a *crime*. His world. Yes, here was *his* world.

I N THE ANKH-MORPORK CITY Watch forensic laboratory Igor was brewing coffee, to the accompaniment of distant rumblings, strange flashes of light and the smell of electricity. At last he pulled the big red lever and frothing brown liquid gurgled into a pot, to be subsequently delivered into two mugs, one of which carried the slogan "Igorth htitch you up," while the other was emblazoned with "Dwarfs do it slightly lower down." He handed that one to Sergeant Cheery Littlebottom, whose previous experience as an alchemist meant that she sometimes did duty in the lab. But at this point the cosiness of morning coffee was interrupted by Nobby Nobbs, towing Sergeant Colon behind him. "The sergeant has had a bit of a shock, Igor, so I thought you might be able to help him."

"Well, I could give him another one," Igor volunteered, as Fred Colon slumped into a chair, which creaked ominously under his weight. The chair had straps on it.

"Look," said Nobby, "I'm not mucking about! You've heard of the tobacco that counts? Well, he just had a cigar that cries. I've put it in this 'ere evidence bag, as per standing instructions."

Cheery took the bag and peered inside. "It's got egg sandwiches in it! Honestly, Nobby, has anyone explained to you what forensic means?" On the basis that she probably couldn't make things actually worse, Cheery emptied the sandwiches on to the table, where they were joined by one cigar with mayonnaise. She wiped this down with some care and looked at it. "Well, Nobby? I don't smoke and I don't know much about cigars, but this one appears to be quite happy at the moment."

"You have to hold it to your ear," said Nobby helpfully.

Cheery did so, and said, "All I can hear is the crinkling of the tobacco, which I suspect hasn't been properly kept." The dwarf held the cigar away from her face and looked at it suspiciously, and then wordlessly she handed it to Igor, who put it to his ear, or at least the one that he was currently using, because you never know with Igors. They looked at one another and Igor broke the silence. "There are such things, I believe, as tobacco weevils?"

"I'm sure there are," said Cheery, "but I doubt very much if they . . . chuckle?"

"Chuckle? It sounded to me like somebody crying," said Igor, as he squinted at the bulging cigar, and added, "We should wash down the table and clean a scalpel and use the number-two tweezers and two, no, make that four sterilized surgical masks and gloves. It may be some kind of unusual insect in there."

"I held that cigar up to my ear," said Nobby. "What kind of insect are we talking about?"

"I'm not sure," said Igor, "but generally the places in the world where tobacco is cultivated are known for some remarkably dangerous ones. For example, the yellow grass weevil of Howondaland has been known to enter the skull via the ears, lay its eggs in the victim's brain and leave the poor victim hallucinating continuously until it has exited via the nostrils. Death inevitably ensues. My cousin Igor has a tank full of them. They're very good at getting skulls scrupulously clean." Igor paused. "So I'm told, that is, although I personally cannot confirm that." He paused again, then added, "Of course."

Nobby Nobbs headed for the door, but, unusually, Sergeant Colon did not follow his friend. Instead, he said, "I'll just stay with my fingers in my ears, if it's all the same to you?"

He craned his head to watch as Igor carefully pulled the cigar apart, and said conversationally, "They say that the cigars made in foreign parts are rolled on the thighs of young women. Personally I call that disgusting."

There was a tinkle and a glint* and something dropped onto the table. Cheery leaned cautiously forward. It looked like a small expensive vial for the most delicate alchemical experiments and yet, she thought later, it seemed to have movement in it, movement while staying still. Igor looked over her shoulder and said, "Oh."

They looked at the vial in silence, silence that was soon broken by Sergeant Colon. "That looks shiny," he said. "Is it worth anything?"

Cheery Littlebottom raised her eyebrows at Igor, who shrugged. He said, "Priceless, I should think, if you could find a buyer with enough money and the, how shall I put it, right taste in ornamentation."

"It's an unggue pot," Cheery said carefully. "A goblin ceremonial pot, sarge."

The dawn of understanding began to flow across Sergeant Colon's gas giant of a face. "Ain't they the things they make to store all their piss and shit in?" he said, backing away.

Igor cleared his throat and looked at Cheery as he said, icily, "Not this type, if I'm right, and at least not down here on the Plains. Those that feel themselves protected in the high mountains make pots, and also use the unggue brushes and, of course, the unggue masks." He looked expectantly, but without any real hope,

---

* A glint is, in fact, a visual tinkle.

at the sergeant. Cheery, who had known him for longer, said, "I understand, sarge, that the goblins on the Plains think the ones in the mountains are rather strange. As for this pot," she hesitated, "I rather fear that this is a particularly special one."

"Well, it looks like the little buggers got that right," said Fred cheerfully, and, to Cheery's horror, he snatched up the tiny pot. "It's mine, that's why, far too good for a stinking goblin, but how come it makes a noise?"

Sergeant Littlebottom looked at Igor's expression, and, to prevent trouble in the Forensic Department, she grabbed the sergeant's arm and dragged him out of the door, slamming it behind them.

"Sorry about this, sergeant, but I could see that Igor was becoming a little bit agitated."

Sergeant Colon brushed himself down with as much dignity as he could muster, and said, "If it's valuable, then I want it, thank you so very much. After all, it was given to me in good faith. Right?"

"Well, of course that is so, sergeant, but you see, it already belongs to a goblin."

Sergeant Colon burst out laughing. "Them? What have they got to own apart from big piles of crap?"

Cheery hesitated. Lazy and bombastic as Fred Colon was, the record showed that, against all apparent evidence, he had been a helpful and useful officer. She needed to be tactful.

"Sergeant, can I say right now that I appreciate all the help you have given to me since I arrived in Pseudopolis Yard? I'll always remember you pointing out to me all those places where a watchman could stand out of the wind and the worst of the rain, and I definitely committed to memory the list of public houses who would be generous to a thirsty copper after hours. And indeed I remember you telling me that a copper should never take a bribe, and why a meal was not a bribe. I cherish your approval, sergeant, since I know that by upbringing you are not particularly happy about women in the Watch, and especially when one of those women is of the dwarf persuasion. I realize that in the course of your long career you have had to adapt your thinking to meet the new circumstances. Therefore, I'm proud to be a colleague of yours, Sergeant Colon, and I hope you'll forgive me when I tell you that there are times when you should shut up and get some new ideas in that big fat head of yours rather than constantly reheating the old ones. You picked up a little trinket, sergeant, and now it really is yours, more yours than I think you can possibly imagine. I wish I could tell you more, but I only know what the average dwarf knows about goblins; and I don't know too much about this type of unggue pot but I think, given the floral decoration and its small size, that it is the one they call the *soul of tears*, sergeant, and I think you have made your life suddenly *very* interesting because— Can I ask you to put it down for just one moment, please? I promise most sincerely that I won't take it away from you."

Colon's somewhat piggy eyes looked at Cheery suspiciously, but he said, "Well, if it gives you any satisfaction." He went to put the pot on the nearby windowsill and she saw him shake his hand. "Seems to be stuck on."

Cheery thought to herself, *so it's true.* Out loud she said, "I'm very sorry to hear that, sergeant, but you see, in that pot is the living soul of a goblin child and it belongs to you. Congratulations!" she said, trying to keep the rising sarcasm out of her voice.

T HAT NIGHT SERGEANT COLON dreamed he was in a cave with monsters chattering away at him in their dreadful lingo. He put it down to the beer, but it was funny the way he couldn't let the little glittering thing go. His fingers never quite managed it, however hard he tried.

THE MOTHER OF SAM Vimes had managed, heavens know how, to scrape up the penny a day necessary for him to be educated at the Dame School run by Mistress Slightly.

Mistress Slightly was everything a dame should be. She was fat, and gave the impression of being made of marshmallows, had a gentle understanding of the fact that the bladders of small boys are almost as treacherous as the bladders of old men, and, in general, taught the basics of the alphabet with a minimum of cruelty and a maximum of marshmallow.

She kept geese, as any self-respecting dame should do. Later in life the older Vimes had wondered if, underneath the endless layers of petticoats, Mistress Slightly wore red-and-white spotted drawers. She certainly had a mob cap and a laugh like rainwater going down a drain. Invariably, while she gave lessons, she was peeling potatoes or plucking geese.

There was still a place in his heart for old Mistress Slightly, who occasionally had a mint in her pocket for a boy who knew his alphabet and could say it backward. And you had to be grateful to someone who taught you how not to be afraid.

She had one book in her tiny sitting room, and the first time she had given it to young Sam Vimes to read he had got as far as page seven when he froze. The page showed a goblin: the jolly goblin, according to the text. Was it laughing, was it scowling, was it hungry, was it about to bite your head off? Young Sam Vimes hadn't waited to find out and had spent the rest of the morning under a chair. These days he excused himself by remembering that most of the other kids felt the same way. When it came to the innocence of childhood, adults often got it wrong. In any case, she had sat him on her always slightly damp knee after class and made him really look at the goblin. It was made of lots of dots! Tiny dots, if you looked closely. The closer you looked at the goblin the more it wasn't there. Stare it down and it lost all its power to frighten. "I hear that they are wretched, badly made mortals," the dame had said sadly. "Half-finished folk, or so I hear. It's only a blessing this one had something to be jolly about."

Later on, because he had been a good boy, she had made him blackboard monitor, the first time anyone had entrusted him with *anything*. Good old Mistress Slightly, Vimes thought, as he stood in this gloomy cave surrounded by ranks of silent, solemn goblins. I'll have a bag of peppermints on your grave if I get out of this alive. He cleared his throat. "Well now, lad, what we appear to have here is a goblin who has been in a fight." He looked down at the corpse, and then to Feeney. "Perhaps you would care to tell me what you see?"

Feeney was one step away from trembling. "Well, sir, I surmise that it is dead, sir."

"And how do you deduce this, please?"

"Er, its head isn't attached to its body, sir?"

"Yes, we generally recognize that as a clue that the corpse is indeed dead. Incidentally, lad, you may as well take the string off. I wouldn't say this is the best light I've ever seen by, but it'll do. Do you notice anything else, chief constable?" Vimes tried to keep his tone level.

"Well, sir, it's pretty cut about, sir."

Vimes smiled encouragingly. "Notice anything about that, lad?" Feeney was making heavy weather of it, but recruits often did at the start, doing so much looking that they forgot to *see*. "You're doing well, chief constable. Would you care to extrapolate?"

"Sir? Extrapolate, sir?"

"Why would somebody be all cut about on their arms? Think about that."

Feeney's lips actually moved as he thought, and then he grinned. "He was defending himself with his hands, sir?"

"Well done, lad, and people who are defending themselves with their hands are doing so because they don't have a shield or a weapon. I would wager, too, that his head was cut off while he was on the ground. Can't exactly put my finger on it, but that looks to me like deliberate butchering rather than a hasty slice. Everything is messy, but you can see that the belly has been sliced open, yet there is hardly any blood around it. He was taken by surprise. And because of the belly would I know something else about him that I wish I didn't know," he said.

"What's that, sir?"

"He is a she, and she was ambushed, or maybe trapped." And, he thought, there's a claw missing.

After a while it becomes a puzzle, not a corpse, said Vimes to himself as he knelt down, but never soon enough, and never for long enough. Aloud he said, "Look at the marks on this leg, lad. I reckon she stepped in a rabbit snare, probably because she was running away from . . . somebody."

Vimes stood up so fast that the watching goblins backed away. "Good grief, boy, we shouldn't do that, not even in the country! Isn't there some kind of code? You kill the bucks, not the does, isn't that right? And this isn't some spur-of-the-moment thing! Someone wanted to get a lot of blood out of this lady! You tell me why!"

Vimes wasn't certain what Feeney would have replied had they not been surrounded by solemn-faced goblins, which was just as well.

"This is murder, lad, the capital crime! And do you know

why it was done? I'll wager anything that it was so that Constable Upshot, acting on information received, would find a lot of blood in Dead Man's Copse, where Commander Vimes was apparently going to have a meeting with an annoying blacksmith, and so, given that both of them were men of quick temper, quite possibly foul play could have been involved, yes?"

"It's a legitimate deduction, sir, you must admit that."

"Of course I do, and now it's a total bastard of a deduction, and now *you* must admit that."

"Yes, sir, I do, sir, and apologize. However, I'd like to search the premises for any sign of Mr. Jefferson." Feeney looked half ashamed, half defiant.

"And why do you want to do that, chief constable?"

Feeney stuck out his chin. "Because I've been shown to be a bloody fool once, and I don't intend to be one again. Besides, sir, you might be wrong. This poor lady might have been in a fight with the blacksmith, perhaps, I don't know, but I do know that if I don't make a search here in the circumstances, somebody important is bound to ask me why I didn't. And that person would be you, wouldn't it, commander?"

"Good answer, young man! And I have to admit that I've been a bloody fool more times than I can count, so I can sympathize."

Vimes looked down again at the corpse and it was suddenly urgent to try to find out what Willikins had done with the claw, complete with ring, that they had found the previous night. Awkwardly, he said to the assembled goblins, "I believe that I have found some jewelry belonging to this young lady and, of course, I shall bring it to you."

There was not so much as an acknowledgment from the impassive horde. Vimes considered that thought. Hordes come in killing and stealing. This lot look like a bunch of worried people. He walked over to a grizzled old goblin who might have been the one he had seen up on the surface a thousand years ago, and said, "I'd like to see more of this place, sir. I'm sorry for the death of the lady. I'll bring the killers to justice."

"Just ice!" Once again it echoed around the cave. The old goblin stepped forward very gently and touched Vimes's sleeve. "The dark is your friend, Mr. Po-leess-maan. I hear you, you hear me. In the dark you may go where you wish. Mr. Po-leess-maan, please do not kill us."

Vimes looked past the goblin to the ranks behind, most of them as skinny as rakes, and this, well, chieftain probably, who looked as though he was decomposing while standing up, didn't want him to hurt them? He remembered the scattered flowers. The orphaned bergamot tea. The uneaten meal. *They were trying to hide away from me?* He nodded and said, "I do not attack anyone who isn't attacking me, sir, and I will not start today. Can you tell me how this lady came to be . . . killed?"

"She was thrown into our cave last night, Mr. Po-leess-maan. She had gone out to check the rabbit snares. Thrown down like old bones, Mr. Po-leess-maan, like old bones. No blood in her. Like old bones."

"What was her name?"

The old goblin looked at Vimes as if shocked, and after a moment said, "Her name was *The Pleasant Contrast of the Orange and Yellow Petals in the Flower of the Gorse.* Thank you, Mr. Po-leess-maan of the dark."

"I'm afraid I'm only just starting to investigate this crime," said Vimes, feeling unusually embarrassed.

"I meant, Mr. Po-leess-maan, thank you for believing that goblins have names. My name is *Sound of the Rain on Hard Ground.* She was my second wife."

Vimes stared at the rugged face that only a mother could toler-
ate and perhaps love, searching for any sign of anger or grief. There
was just a sense of sorrow and hopeless resignation at the fact that
the world was as it was and always would be and there was nothing
that could be done. The goblin was a sigh on legs. In dejection he
looked up at Vimes and said, "They used to send hungry dogs into
the cave, Mr. Po–leess–maan. Those were good days; we ate well."

"This is *my* land," said Vimes, "and I think I can see to it that
you're not disturbed here."

Something like a chuckle found its way through the old goblin's
ragged beard. "We know what the law is, Mr. Po–leess–maan. The
law is the land. You say " 'This is my land,' but you did not make
the land. You did not make your sheep, you did not make the rabbits on which we live, you did not make the cows, or the horses,
but you say, 'These things are mine.' This cannot be a truth. I make
my ax, my pots, and these are mine. What I wear is mine. Some
love was mine. Now it has gone. I think you are a good man, Mr.
Po–leess–maan, but we see the turning of the times. Maybe a hundred, or two hundred years ago there was in the world what people
called 'the wilderness,' or 'no man's land,' or 'wasteland,' and we
lived in such places, we are waste people. There was the troll race,
the dwarf race, the human race and I am sorry for the goblin race
that we cannot run so fast."

Somebody pulled at Vimes's shirt. This time it was Feeney.
"You'd best be going now, sir."

Vimes turned. "Why?"

"Sorry, sir, but her ladyship did instruct you to be back for tea."

"We're conducting a murder investigation, chief constable! I
don't mean to be rude, but I'm sure Mr. Rain on Hard Ground
here will understand. We must see for ourselves that the missing
blacksmith is not here."

Feeney fidgeted. "I couldn't help noticing that her Ladyship was very expressive on the subject, sir."

Vimes nodded to the old goblin. "I'll find out who killed your wife, sir, and I'll bring them to justice." He paused on cue as another chorus of "Just ice!" echoed around the caves. "But first I must, for police reasons, inspect the rest of this . . . establishment, if you have no objection."

The goblin looked at him bright-eyed. "And if I object, Mr. Po-leess-maan?"

Vimes matched his stare. "An interesting question," he said "and if you threatened us with violence I would leave. Indeed, if you forbade me to search then I would leave, and, sir, the worst part is that I would not come back. Sir, I respectfully ask that I may in the pursuit of my inquiries be shown around the rest of these premises."

Was that a smile on the old goblin's face? "Of course, Mr. Po-leess-maan."

Behind the old goblin the rest of the crowd began to move away, presumably to either make pots or fill them. Rain on Hard Ground, who, it had to be assumed, because nothing had been said to the contrary, was either a chieftain (as Vimes would understand it) or simply a goblin tasked with talking to stupid humans, said, "You are seeking the blacksmith? He visits us sometimes. There is iron down here, not much, but he finds it useful. Of course it is no good for pots, but we trade it for food. I don't think I have seen him for several days. However, by all means look for him without hindrance. The dark is in you. I would not *dare* to stand in your way, Mr. Po-leess-maan. Such as it is, this place is yours."

With that the old goblin beckoned to some juvenile goblins to pick up all that was left of his wife and drifted away toward another cave mouth.

"Have you seen a lot of dead bodies, commander?" said Feeney, in a voice that almost managed not to shake.

"Oh yes, lad, and some of them I helped to make."

"You've killed people?"

Vimes looked at the ceiling so as not to have to look at Feeney's face. "I like to think I did my best not to," he said, "and on the whole I've been good at that, but sooner or later there's always going to be somebody who is determined to finish you off and you end up having to take him down the wrong way because he's just too damn stupid to surrender. It doesn't get any better, and I've never seen a corpse that looked good."

The funeral group had disappeared into the other cave now, and the two policemen were left alone, but feeling, however, that around them people were going about their business.

The old goblin had just stood there and mentioned that the woman was his wife almost as an afterthought. He hadn't even raised his voice! Vimes couldn't have stood there like that if it had been Sybil's body on the ground in front of him, and as sure as hell he would not be polite to any goblins who were in front of him either. How can you get like that? How can life so beat you down?

The Street was always with you, just as Willikins had said. And Vimes remembered the ladies who scrubbed. Cockbill Street got scrubbed so often that it was surprising it wasn't now at a lower level than the ground around it. The doorstep was scrubbed, and then whitened; the red tiles on the floor inside were scrubbed and then polished with red lead; and the black cooking stove was blackened even further by being rubbed ferociously with black lead. Women in those days had elbows that moved like pistons. And it was all about survival, and survival was all about pride. You didn't have much control over your life but by Jimmy you could keep it clean and show the world you were poor but respectable. That was the dread: the dread of falling back, losing standards, becoming no better than those people who bred and fought and stole in that ferocious turmoil of a rookery known as the Shades.

The goblins had succumbed, had they? Going through the motions now, while the world gently expelled them, they were giving up, letting go . . . but murder was murder in any jurisdiction or none at all. He tied his thoughts in a knot under his chin, snatched a couple of smouldering torches and said, "Come on, chief constable, let's go and fight crime."

"Yes, sir," said Feeney, "but can I ask you another question?"

"Of course," said Vimes, heading toward a tunnel that was perceptibly sloping downward.

"What's going on here, sir, if you don't mind me asking? I mean, I know that there's been a murder and maybe some bugger wanted me to think it was you as done it, but how come, sir, that you understand that heathen lingo of theirs? I mean, I hear you talking to them, and they must understand you, 'cos they talk back, sir, but they talk like somebody cracking walnuts under their foot, sir, and I can't understand a damn word of it, sir, if you'll excuse my Klatchian, not a damn word. I want an answer, sir, because I feel enough of a bloody fool as it is; I don't want to be even more foolish than I feel now."

Vimes, in the privacy of his own head, tried out the statement, "Well, since you ask, I have a deadly demon sharing my mind, which seems to be helping me for reasons of its own. It lets me see in this gloom and somehow allows me and goblins to communicate. It's called the Summoning Dark. I don't know what its interest in goblins is but the dwarfs think it brings down wrath on the unrighteous. If there has been a murder I'll use any help I can get." He did not in fact articulate this, on the basis that most people would have left very quickly by the time he had finished, so he settled for saying, "I have the support of a higher power, chief constable. Now, let's check out this place." This didn't satisfy Feeney, but he appeared to understand that this was all he was going to get.

I T WAS AN EERIE journey. The hill was honeycombed with passages natural and, occasionally, by the look of it, artificial. It was a small city. There were middens, crude cages now empty of whatever had been in them, and here and there quite large beds of fungus, in some cases being harvested very, very slowly, by goblins who barely glanced at the policemen. At one point they passed an opening which appeared to lead to a crèche, by the sound of it, in which case baby goblins twittered like birds. Vimes couldn't bring himself to look further inside.

As they went lower down they came across a very small rivulet that trickled out of one wall. The goblins in a rough and ready way had made a culvert, so that their journey onward was to the sound of running water. And everywhere there were goblins, and the goblins were making pots. Vimes was prepared for this, but badly prepared. He had expected something like the dwarf workshops he had seen in Uberwald—noisy, busy and full of purposeful activity. But that wasn't the goblin way. It appeared that if a goblin wanted to start on a pot, all it needed to do was find a place to hunker down, rummage through whatever it was it had in its pockets and get to work, so slowly that it was hard to tell that anything was going on. Several times Vimes thought he heard the chip of stone on stone, or the sound of scratching, or what might be sawing, but whenever he came close to a squatting goblin it politely edged around and leaned over the work like a child trying to keep a secret. How much snot, he thought, how many fingernail clippings, how much earwax did a goblin accumulate in one year? Would an annual pot of snot be something like a lady's delicate snuffbox, or would it be a sloshing great bucketful?

And why not, yes, why not teeth? Even humans were careful when it came to the escaped teeth, and, come to that, there were people, especially wizards, who made a point of ensuring that their toenails were put beyond use. He smiled to himself. Maybe the goblins weren't all that stupid, only more stupid than humans were, which, when you came to think about it, took some effort.

And then, as they crept past a cross-legged goblin, it sat back on its haunches and held up . . . light. Vimes had seen plenty of jewels: generations of rings, brooches, necklaces and tiaras had funneled down the centuries and into Lady Sybil's lap, although these days most of them were kept in a vault. That always amused him.

Sparkle though Sybil's jewels might, he would have sworn that none of them could have filled the air with light as much as the little pot did when its creator held it up for a critical appraisal. The goblin turned it this way and that, inspecting it like a man thinking of buying a horse from somebody called Honest Harry. White and yellow beams of light shimmered as it moved, filling the drab cave with what Vimes could only think of as echoes of light. Feeney was staring as a child might stare at his first party. The goblin, however, appeared to sneer at its creation and tossed it dismissively behind him, where it smashed on the wall.

"Why did you do that?" Vimes shouted, so loudly that the goblin he was addressing cowered and looked as if it expected to be struck. It managed to say, "Bad pot! Bad work! For to be ashamed! Make much better one time more! Will start now!" It took another terrified look at Vimes and hurried into the darkness of the cave.

"He smashed it! He actually smashed it!" Feeney stared at Vimes. "He took one look at it and smashed it! And it was wonder-

ful! That was criminal! You can't just destroy something as wonderful as that, can you?"

Vimes put a hand on Feeney's shoulder. "I think you can if
you've just made it and think you could have done it better. After
all, even the best craftsmen sometimes make mistakes, yes?"

"You think that was a mistake?" Feeney rushed over to where
the debris of the late pot had hit the floor, and picked up a handful
of glittering remains. "Sir, he did throw these away, sir?"

Vimes opened his mouth to reply, but there was a faint noise
from Feeney's hand: dust was falling between his fingers like the
sands of time. Feeney grinned nervously at Vimes and said, "Maybe
it was a bit shoddy after all, sir!"

Vimes squatted down and ran his fingers through the pile of
dust. And it was just dust, stone dust, no more color or sparkle to it
than you would find in a pebble by the road. There was no trace of
the scintillating rainbow that they had just seen. But on the other
side of this cave another goblin was trying to look inconspicuous as
it worked on what was probably another pot. Vimes stepped over
to it with care, because it was holding its pot as if prepared to use
it to defend itself.

Casually, to show that he meant no harm, Vimes put his arms
behind his back and said in tones learned from his wife, "My word!
That looks like a very good pot. Tell me, how do you make a pot,
sir? Can you tell me?"

The potter looked down at the thing in its hands, or the thing
in its claws if you wanted to be nasty, and perhaps slightly more
accurate, and said, "I make the pot." It raised the work in progress.

Vimes wasn't that good at stone which wasn't part of masonry,
but this one was slightly yellow and shiny. He said, "Yes, I can see
that, but how do you actually make the pot?" Once again, the potter sought enlightenment from the universe, looking up and down

and everywhere that Vimes wasn't. At last inspiration dawned. "I make pot."

Vimes nodded gravely. "Thank you for sharing the secrets of your success," he said and turned to Feeney. "Come on, let's keep going."

It seemed that a goblin cave—or lair or burrow, depending on what effect you wanted to give—was not quite the hellhole that you might have thought. Instead it was just, well, a hole, stuffy with the smoke of the innumerable small fires goblins appeared to need, along with the associated small pile of rotted kindling, and not forgetting the personal midden.

Goblins old and young watched them carefully as they passed, as if expecting them to put on a program of entertainment. There were certainly juvenile goblins. Vimes had to admit that alone among the talking species, goblin babies were plug ugly, merely small versions of their parents who themselves were no oil paintings, and not even a watercolor. Vimes told himself that they could not help it, that some incompetent god had found a lot of bits left over, and decided that the world needed a creature that looked like a cross between a wolf and an ape, and gave them what was surely one of the most unhelpful pieces of religious dogma, even by the standards of celestial idiocy. They *looked* like the bad guys and, without the intervention of the Summoning Dark, they sounded like them, too. If walnuts could shriek when they were being cracked, then people would say, "Doesn't that remind you of a goblin?" And it appeared that, not content with all this, the laughing god had apparently given them that worst of gifts, self-knowledge, leaving them so certain that they were irrevocably walking rubbish that metaphorically they couldn't even find the energy to clean the step.

"Oh, blast! I'm treading on something . . . in something," said

Feeney. "You seem to be able to see much better than me down here, sir."

"Good clean living, lad, carrots and whatnot."

"Jefferson could be in here somewhere. I'm sure there are caves that we're missing."

"I know he's not in here, lad, only don't ask me how I know because I would have to lie to you. I'm going through the motions to help myself think. It's an old copper trick."

"Yes, sir, treading in every motion, I should think!"

Vimes smiled in the gloom. "Well done, lad. A sense of humor is the copper's friend. I always say the day isn't complete without a little chuckle—" He paused because something had clanged against his helmet. "We've reached Jefferson's iron workings, my lad. I just found an oil lamp; I certainly haven't seen those higher up." He felt in his pocket and soon a match flame bloomed.

Well, Vimes thought, it's not that much of a mine, but I bet it works out better than paying dwarf prices.

"I can't see any way out," Feeney volunteered. "I suppose he drags the ore out through the main entrance."

"I don't think that the goblins are stupid enough to live in a set of caves that have just one entrance. There's probably one that doesn't even show up on the outside. Look, you can see where somebody's been lugging heavy weights across the stone—" Vimes stopped. There was another human in the cave. Well, thank you, darkness, he thought. I suppose asking who it is might be in order?

"Sir, I don't think it's just mining that goes on here. Take a look at these," said Feeney, behind Vimes.

Feeney held out some books, children's books, by the look of it. They were grubby—this was, after all, the home of goblins—but Vimes turned to the first page of the first book and was not surprised to see an unfeasibly large red apple, currently somewhat soiled by the pressure of many dirty hands.

A voice in the gloom, a female voice, said, "Not all questions are answered, commander, but fortunately some answers are questioned. I'm attempting to teach the goblin children. Of course, I had to bring in an apple for the young ones to see," the woman in the shadows added. "Not many knew what one was, and certainly not what they were called. Troll language is unbelievably complex compared with what these poor devils have got. "Good day to you too, Mr. Upshot. Not cowering away from the truth in your lockup?"

Vimes had spun round when he first heard that voice, and was now staring with his mouth open. "You? Aren't you the, er . . ."

"The poo lady, yes, Commander Vimes. It's amazing, isn't it, how people remember?"

"Well, you must admit that it does—how can I put it?—stick in the mind, Miss Felicity Beedle."

"Very well done, commander, considering that we've met only once!"

And now Vimes noticed that with her there was a goblin, a young one by the size of it, but more noticeable because it was staring directly at him with a keen and interested gaze, quite uncharacteristic of the goblins that he had seen so far, apart from the wretched Stinky. Feeney, on the other hand, was taking great care not to catch the lady's eye, Vimes noticed.

Vimes smiled at Miss Beedle. "Madam, I reckon I see your name at least once every day. When I was putting my lad to bed yesterday, do you know what he said? He said 'Dad, do you know why cows do big wet sloppy poos and horses do them all nice and soft and smelling of grass? Because it's weird, isn't it? That you get two different kinds of poo when they're both about the same size

and it's the same grass, isn't it, Dad? Well, the poo lady says it's because cows have room in ants, and the ants help them get, sort of,
more food out of their food, but because horses don't have room in
ants, they don't sort of chew all that much, so that their poo is still
very much like grass and doesn't smell too bad.'"

Vimes saw that the woman was grinning, and went on, "I believe that tomorrow he is going to ask his mother if he may chew
his dinner very hard one day, and the next day not do it very
much, and see if he gets different smells. What do you think of
that, madam?"

Miss Beedle laughed. It was a very enjoyable laugh. "Well,
commander, it would seem that your son combines your analytical
thinking with the inherited Ramkin talent for experimentation.
You must be very proud? I certainly hope you are."

"You can bet on that, madam." The child standing in Miss
Beedle's shadow was smiling too, the first smile he'd seen on a
goblin. But before he could say anything, Miss Beedle directed a
disapproving look at Feeney and went on, "I only wish I could find
you in better company, commander. I wonder if you know where
my friend Jethro is, officer?"

Even in the lamplight, Feeney looked furious, but if you read
people, and Vimes was a ferocious reader, it was clear the fury was
spiced with shame and dread. Then Vimes looked down at the
little bench, where there were a few tools and some more brightly
covered books. It was the streets that had taught Vimes that there
were times when you would find it best to let a nervous person get
really nervous, and so he picked up a book as if the previous dreadful exchange had not taken place, and said, "Oh, here's *Where's
My Cow?*! Young Sam loves it. Are you teaching it to the goblins,
Miss?"

With her eyes still on the agitated Feeney, Miss Beedle said,

"Yes, for what it's worth. It's hard work. Incidentally, technically I'm *Mrs.* Beedle. My husband was killed in the Klatchian war. I went back to 'Miss' because, well, it's more authory, and besides, it wasn't as though I'd had much time to get accustomed to 'Mrs.'"

"I'm sorry about that, madam, Had I known I'd have been a lot less flippant," said Vimes.

Miss Beedle gave him a wan smile. "Don't worry, flippant sometimes does the trick." Beside the teacher the little goblin said, "Flip-ant? The ant is turned over?"

"Tears of the Mushroom is my star pupil. You're wonderful, aren't you, Tears of the Mushroom?"

"Wonderful is good," said the goblin girl, as though tasting every word. "Gentle is good, the mushroom is good. Tears are soft. I am Tears of the Mushroom, this much is now said."

It was a strange little speech: the girl spoke as if she were pulling words out of a rack and then tidily putting them back in their places as soon as they had been said. It sounded very solemn and it came from an odd, flat, pale face. In a way, Tears of the Mushroom looked handsome, if not exactly pretty, in what looked like a wraparound apron, and Vimes wondered how old she was. Thirteen? Fourteen, maybe? And he wondered if they would all look as smart as this if they got their hands on some decent clothing and did something about their godawful hair. The girl's hair was long and braided and pure white. Amazingly, in this place, she looked like a piece of fragile porcelain.

Not knowing what to say, he said it anyway: "Pleased to meet you, Tears of the Mushroom." Vimes held out his hand. The goblin girl looked at it, then looked at him, and then turned to Miss Beedle, who said, "They don't shake hands, commander. For people who seem so simple they're astoundingly complicated."

She turned to Vimes. "It would seem, commander, that providence has brought you here in time to solve the murder of the goblin girl, who was an excellent pupil. I came up here as soon as I heard, but the goblins are used to undeserved and casual death. I'll walk with you to the entrance, and then I've got a class to teach."

Vimes tugged at Feeney to make him keep up as they followed Miss Beedle and her charge toward the surface and blessed fresh air. He wondered what had become of the corpse. What did they do with their dead? Bury them, eat them, throw them on the midden? Or was he just not thinking right, a thought which itself had been knocking at his brain for some time. Without thinking, he said, "What else do you teach them, Miss Beedle? To be better citizens?"

The slap caught him on the chin, probably because even in her anger Miss Beedle realized that he still had his steel helmet on. It was a corker, nonetheless, and out of the corner of his stinging gaze he saw Feeney take a step back. At least the boy had some sense.

"You are the gods' own fool, Commander Vimes! No, I'm not teaching them to be fake humans, I'm teaching them how to be goblins, clever goblins! Do you know that they have only five names for colors? Even trolls have around sixty, and a lot more than that if they find a paint salesman! Does this mean goblins are stupid? No, they have a vast number of names for things that even poets haven't come up with, for things like the way colors shift and change, the melting of one hue into another. They have single words for the most complicated of feelings; I know about two hundred of them, I think, and I'm sure there are a lot more! What you may think are grunts and growls and snarls are in fact carrying vast amounts of information! They're like an iceberg, commander: most of them is where you can't see or understand, and I'm teaching Tears of the Mushroom and some of her friends so that they may be able to speak to people like you, who think they are dumb. And do you know what, commander? There isn't much time! They're being slaughtered! It's not called that, of course, but slaughter is how it ends, because they're just dumb nuisances, you see. Why don't you ask Mr. Upshot what happened to the rest of the goblins three years ago, Commander Vimes?"

And with that Miss Beedle turned on her heel and disappeared down into the darkness of the cave with Tears of the Mushroom bobbing along behind her, leaving Vimes to walk the last few yards out into the glorious sunlight.

THE FEELING THAT HIT Samuel Vimes when he stepped into the vivid light of day was as if somebody had pushed an iron wire through his body and then, in one moment, pulled it out again. It was all he could do to keep his balance and the boy grabbed him by the arm. Full marks, Vimes thought, for being either smart enough to see how the land lay, or at least smart enough not to make a run for it just now.

He sat down on the turf, relishing the breeze through the gorse bushes and sucking in pure fresh air. Whatever you thought about goblins, their cave had the kind of atmosphere about which people say, "I should wait two minutes before going in there, if I was you."

"I'd like to talk with you, chief constable," he said now. "Copper to copper. About the past and maybe about the shape of things to come."

"Actually, I meant to thank you, commander, for thinking that I'm a policeman."

"Your father was policeman down here three years ago, yes?"

Feeney stared straight ahead. "Yes, sir."

"So, what happened with the goblins, Feeney?"

Feeney cleared his throat. "Well, Dad told me and Mum to stay indoors. He said we was not to look, but he couldn't tell us not to listen, and there was a lot of shouting and I don't know what, and it upset my old mum no end. I heard later that a load of goblins had been taken out of the hill, but Dad never spoke about it until much later. I think it broke him, sir, it really did. He said he watched while a bunch of men, gamekeepers and roughs mostly, came down from the cave dragging goblins behind them, sir. Lots of them. He said what was so dreadful was that the goblins were all sort of meek, you know? Like they didn't know what to do."

Vimes relented a little at the sight of Feeney's face. "Go on, lad."

"Well, sir, he told me people came out of their houses and there was a lot of running about and he started to ask questions and, well, the magistrates said it was all right because they were nothing more than vermin, and they were going to be taken down to the docks where they could earn their living for a change and not bother other people. It was all right, Dad said. They were going somewhere sunny, a long way away from here."

"Just out of interest, Mr. Feeney, how could he know that?"

"Dad said the magistrates were very firm about it, sir. They were just to be put to work for their living. He said that it was doing them a favor. It wasn't as if they were going to be killed."

Vimes kept his expression deliberately blank. He sighed. "If it was without their consent, then that would be slavery, and if a slave doesn't work for his living he's dead. Do you understand?"

Feeney looked at his boots. If eyeballs had polish on them his boots would have been gleaming. "After he told me this, my dad told me that I was a copper now and I was to look after Mum, and he gave me the truncheon and his badge. And then his hands started shaking, sir, and a few days later he was dead, sir. I reckon something snuck up on him, sir, in his head, like. It overcame him."

"Have you heard about Lord Vetinari, Feeney? I can't say I like him all that much but sometimes he's bang on the money. Well, there was a bit of a fracas, as we say, and it turned out that a man had a dog, a half-dead thing, according to bystanders, and he was trying to get it to stop pulling at its leash, and when it growled at him he grabbed an ax from the butcher's stall beside him, threw the dog to the ground and cut off its back legs, just like that. I suppose people would say 'Nasty bugger, but it was his dog,' and so on, but Lord Vetinari called me in and he said to me, 'A man who would do something like that to a dog is a man to whom the law should pay close attention. Search his house immediately.' The man was hanged a week later, not for the dog, although for my part I wouldn't have shed a tear if he had been, but for what we found in his cellar. The contents of which I will not burden you with. And bloody Vetinari got away with it again, because he was right: where there are little crimes, large crimes are not far behind."

Vimes stared at the rolling acres stretching out below: his fields, his trees, his fields of yellow corn . . . All his, even though he'd never planted a seed in his life, except for the time when he was a kid and he tried to grow mustard and cress on a flannel, which he'd then thrown up because no one had told him he should have washed the flannel first to get all the soap out. Not a good background for a landowner. But . . . His land, right? And he was sure that neither he nor Sybil had ever said yes to turning a lot of sad-looking goblins out of the mess they were pleased to call a home and taking them to who knew where.

"Nobody told us!"

Feeney leaned back to escape that particular ball of wrath. "I wouldn't know about that, sir."

Vimes stood up and stretched his arms. "I've heard enough, lad, and I've had enough too! It's time to report to a higher authority!"

"I think it'd take at least a day and a half to get a galloper to the city, sir, and you'd have to be lucky with horses."

Sam Vimes began to walk smartly down the hill. "I was talking about Lady Sybil, lad."

Sᴄʏʙɪʟ ᴡᴀs ɪɴ ᴀ drawing room full of teacups and ladies when Vimes arrived at the Hall in a run, with Feeney lagging behind. She took one look at him and said, rather more brightly than warranted, "Oh, I see you have something to discuss with me." She turned to the ladies, smiled and said, "Please do excuse me, ladies. I must just have a brief word with my husband." And with that she grabbed Vimes and pulled him none too gently back into the hallway. She opened her mouth to deliver a wifely sermon on the importance of punctuality, sniffed and recoiled. "Sam Vimes, you stink! Did you fall into something rural? I've hardly seen you since breakfast! And why are you still dragging that young policeman behind you? I'm sure he's got something more important to do. Didn't he want to arrest you? Is he coming to tea? I hope he washes first." This was said to Vimes but aimed at Feeney, who was keeping his distance and looked ready to run.

"That was a misunderstanding," said Vimes hastily, "and I'm sure that if I ever find out where my escutcheon is there won't be a stain on it, but Mr. Feeney here has been generously and of his own free will imparting information to me."

And by the time the husband and wife conversation was in full swing, containing shouted whispers on the lines of "Surely not!" and "I think he's telling the truth," Feeney looked ready to sprint.

"And they didn't put up a fight?" said Sybil. The young policeman tried to avoid her gaze, but she had the kind of gaze that came around to find you wherever you stood.

"No, your ladyship," was all he managed.

Lady Sybil looked at her husband and shrugged. "There would be one hell of a fight with someone who wanted to take *me* off to a place I didn't want to go to," she said, "and I thought goblins had weapons? Pretty nasty fighters, so I've heard. I'd have thought there'd have been a war! We would have heard about it! From the way you talk about it, it sounds as if they were sleepwalking. Or perhaps they were starving? I haven't noticed very many rabbits around here, compared with when I was a little girl. And why leave some behind? It's all a bit of a puzzle, Sam. Nearly everyone around here is a family friend—" She held up a hand quickly. "I wouldn't dream of asking you to fail in your duty, Sam, you must understand that, but be careful and be sure of every step. And please, Sam— and I know you, Sam—don't go at it like a bull at a gate. People round here might get the wrong idea."

Sam Vimes was certain that he did have the wrong idea and his brow wrinkled as he said, "I don't know, Sybil, how does a bull go at a gate? Does it just stop and look puzzled?"

"No, dear, it smashes everything to pieces."

Lady Sybil gave a warning smile and brushed herself down. "I don't think we need detain you any longer, Mr. Upshot," she said to the grateful Feeney. "Do remember me to your dear mother. If she doesn't mind, I'd like to meet her while I'm down here again to talk about old times. In the meantime I suggest you leave via the kitchen, no matter what my husband thinks about a policeman using the servants' entrance, and tell Cook to supply you with, well, anything your mother would like."

She turned to her husband. "Why don't you escort him down there, Sam? And since you're enjoying the fresh air, why not go and find Young Sam? I think he's back in the barnyard, with Willikins."

Feeney was silent as they went down the long corridors, but Vimes sensed the boy's mind working its way through a problem, which came out when he said, "Lady Sybil is a very nice kind lady, isn't she, sir?"

"I do not need to be reminded of that," said Vimes, "and I'd like you to understand that she stands in vivid contrast to me. I get edgy when I think there's a crime unsolved. A crime unsolved is against nature."

"I keep thinking of the goblin girl, sir. She looked like a statue, and the way she spoke, well, I don't know what to say. I mean, they can be a bloody nuisance—they'll have the laces out of your boots if you don't move quick enough—but when you see them in their cave you realize there's, well, kids, old granddad goblins and—"

"Old mum goblins?" Vimes suggested quietly.

Once again, Mrs. Upshot's little boy struggled in the unfamiliar and terrifying grip of philosophy and fetched up with, "Well, sir, I dare say cows make good mothers, but at the end of the day a calf is veal on the hoof, yes?"

"Maybe, but what would you say if the calf walked up to you and said, 'Hello, my name is Tears of the Mushroom?'"

Feeney's face once again frowned in the effort of novel cogitation. "I think I'd have the salad, sir."

Vimes smiled. "You were in a difficult position, lad, and I'll tell you something: so am I. It's called being a copper. That's why I like it when they run. That makes it all so simple. They run and I chase. I don't know if it's metaphysical, or something like that. But there *was* a corpse. You saw it, so did I and so did Miss Beedle. Keep that in mind."

YOUNG SAM WAS SITTING on a hay bale in the farmyard, watching the horses come in. He ran to his dad, looking very pleased with himself, and said, "Dad, you know chickens?"

Vimes picked up his son and said, "Yes, I have heard of them, Sam."

Young Sam wriggled out of his father's grasp as if being picked up and swung around was inappropriate activity for a serious researcher in scatological studies, and looked solemn. "Do you know, Dad, that when a chicken does a poo, there's a white bit on top which is the wee? Sometimes it's like the icing on a bun, Dad!"

"Thank you for letting me know," said Vimes. "I'll remember that next time I eat a bun." And every time after that, he added to himself. "I suppose you know everything about poo now, Sam?" Vimes said hopefully, and he saw Willikins smile.

Young Sam, now staring at a pile of chicken droppings through a little magnifying glass, shook his head without looking up. "Oh no, Dad, Mr. . . ." Here, Young Sam stopped and looked at Willikins hopefully.

Willikins cleared his throat and said, "Mr. Trout, one of the gamekeepers, was around half an hour ago, and of course your lad will strike up a conversation with anybody, and the upshot is that young Sam, it would appear, sir, would like to amass a collection of the droppings of a number of woodland creatures."

Gamekeepers, thought Vimes. He ran that across his brain and thought about who had actually rounded the goblins up three years ago. And then he thought, how important is that compared with the question *who told them to?* I think I've got the smell of this place: people do what they're told because they've always done what they're told. But gamekeepers are a canny lot; it's not just human beings they have to outsmart. And remember, this is the countryside, where everybody knows everybody else, and notices everybody else. I don't think Feeney is lying, so other people know what happened here one night three years ago. I mustn't be a bull at a gate, said Sybil, and she's right. I need to know where I'm treading. What happened happened three years ago? I can afford to take my time over this one. Aloud he said, "How far can I take this?"

"It seems you've had a busy day, sir," said Willikins. "This morning you went down to the lockup with a little tit who thinks he is a copper, and then, in company with a goblin, you and said little tit went up to Dead Man's Copse, where you remained for quite some time, until you and the aforesaid little tit came out and you arrived here, minus one tit just now." Willikins grinned at Vimes. "There's people coming and going down in the kitchens all the time, sir, and gossip is a kind of currency when you get beyond the green door. You've got to remember, sir, that, despite Mr. Silver's dirty looks, I am the top nob below stairs and I can go where I like and do what I like and they can *choke* on it if they like. The whole of the hill is visible from some window or other in this house, and maids are very cooperative, sir. It seems that all the girls are busting for a job in the Scoone Avenue establishment. Very keen they are for the city lights, sir. Very cooperative. Also, I found quite a good telescope in the study. Remarkable view of Hangman's Hill, you know. I could practically read your lips. Young Sam quite enjoyed the game of searching for Dad."

Vimes felt a pang of guilt at those words. This was supposed to be a family holiday, wasn't it? But . . . "Someone killed a goblin girl up at Dead Man's Copse," he said, his voice dull. "They made sure there was a lot of blood to give our keen young copper something that he could think of as a case. He's floundering; I don't think he's ever seen a corpse before."

Willikins looked genuinely taken aback. "What, never? Maybe I'll retire down here, except I'd die of boredom."

A thought struck Vimes and he said, "When you were looking through the telescope, did you see anyone else go up the hill?"

Willikins shook his head. "No, sir, just you."

They both turned to watch Young Sam, who was carefully drawing chicken poo in his notebook, and Willikins said quietly, "You've got a good lad there, very bright. Make the most of the time, sir."

Vimes shook his head. "Gods know you're right, but, well, she was cut about, and with steel, definitely steel. *They* only have stone weapons. They cut her about to make certain there was enough blood that even a stupid flatfoot would spot it. And she was named after the colors of a flower."

There was a disapproving noise from Willikins. "Coppers shouldn't get sentimental, it's bad for the judgement. You said it yourself. You find yourself in some bloody awful domestic scene and you think things could be improved by kicking the shit out of somebody, only how do you know when to stop? That's what you said. You said whacking a bloke in a fight is one thing, but when he's been cuffed, it ain't right."

To Vimes's surprise Willikins tapped him on the shoulder in a kindly way (you'd know it instantly if Willikins tapped you in an unfriendly way).

"Take my advice, commander, and have tomorrow off, too. There's a boating house on the lake, and later you could take the little lad out in the woods, which are, by all accounts, knee-deep in poo of all sorts. He'll be in poo heaven! Oh, and he also told me that he wants to go and see the smelly skull man again. I'll tell you what, I reckon with a mind like his, he'll be Archchancellor of Unseen University by the time he's sixty!"

Willikins must have seen the grimace on Vimes's face, be-cause he went on, "Why so surprised sir? He might want to be an alchemist, right? Don't say you'd want him to be a copper: you wouldn't, would you? At least when you're a wizard people don't try to kick you in the fork, right? Of course you do have to go up against dreadful creatures from hellish dimensions, but they don't carry knives, and you get training. Worth thinking about, commander, 'cos he's growing like a weed and you should be putting him on the right track through life. And now, if you'll excuse me, commander, I'm off to annoy the servants."

Willikins took a few steps then stopped, looked at Vimes and said, "Look at it like this, sir, if you take some time off, the guilty will be no less guilty, and the dead won't get any less dead, and her ladyship will not try to behead you with a coat hanger."

T HE GUESTS AT LADY Sybil's tea party were leaving when Vimes got back to the Hall. He scraped the countryside off his boots and headed to the Hall's master bathroom.

Of course, there were plenty of bathrooms around the place— probably more than there were in a street in most of the city, where a tin bath, a jug and basin, or nothing at all were the ablutions of choice or necessity . . . but this bathroom had been built to a design by Mad Jack Ramkin and resembled the famous bathroom at Unseen University, although, had Mad Jack designed *that* one, it would have been called the Obscene University, since Mad Jack had a healthy (or possibly unhealthy) liking for the ladies, and in his bathroom it showed, oh dear, it showed. Of course, the white marble lovelies were dignified with urns, bunches of marble grapes, and the ever-popular length of gauze which had, happily, landed in just the right place to stop art becoming pornography. It was also, in all probability, the only bath that had taps marked *hot, cold, brandy.*

And then there were the frescoes, such that if you were a man easily persuaded then it was a good job there was a cold tap, because not to put too fine a point on it, as it were, there were a large number of fine points all over them, yes indeed, and the ladies were only the start of the problem. There were marble gentlemen, as well, definitely gentlemen, even the ones with goat's feet. It was surprising that the water in the bath didn't boil of its own accord. He had asked Sybil about it, and she said that it was an important feature of the Hall, and gentlemen collectors of antiquities would often visit in order to inspect it. Vimes had said that he expected that they did, oh yes indeed. Sybil had said that there was no need for that tone of voice, because she had occasionally taken a bath there from the time she had been twelve and had seen no harm in it. It had, she said, stopped her from being surprised later on.

And now Vimes lay in the luxurious tub, feeling as if he was trying to fit all the bits of his brain together. He was only vaguely aware of the bathroom door opening, and of hearing Sybil say, "I've put Young Sam to bed, and he's sleeping soundly, although I can't imagine what he might be dreaming about."

Then Vimes floated again in the warm steamy atmosphere and was only just aware of the swish of cloth hitting the floor. Lady Sybil slid in beside him. The water rose, and so, in accordance with the physics of this business, did the spirits of Sam Vimes.

A FEW HOURS LATER, ALMOST drowning in the pillows on the huge bed and floating just above unconsciousness in a warm pink glow, Sam Vimes was certain that he heard his own voice whispering to him. And it said, "Think of the things that don't fit. Wonder why the nice lady of the nobby classes wanders down into a goblin cave as if it's a natural thing to do." He replied, "Well, Sybil spends half her time at home covered in heavy protective gear and a flameproof helmet because she likes dragons. It's the sort of thing that nobby ladies tend to do."

He considered what he had to say, and responded to himself, "Yes, but dragons are what you might call socially acceptable. Goblins, on the other hand, definitely aren't. No one has got a good word to say for goblins, except Miss Beedle. Why not take Young Sam along to see her tomorrow? After all, she is the one that got him on to this poo business, and she is a writer, so I expect she'll be quite glad of the interruption. Yes, that'd be a good idea, and it'd be educational for Young Sam and not an investigation at all . . ." Thus satisfied, he waited for the onset of sleep, against a chorus of howls, shrieks, mysterious distant bangs, surreptitious rustlings, screeches, disconcerting ticking noises, dreadful scratching sounds, terrible flappings of wings very close, and all the rest of the unholy orchestra that is known as the peace of the countryside.

He had enjoyed a late-night game of snooker with Willikins, just to keep his hand in, and Vimes, half listening now to the outlandish cacophony, wondered whether the solving of a complex crime, one that needed a certain amount of care, could be compared to a game of snooker. Sure, there were a lot of red balls and they got in the way, so you had to knock them down, but your target, your ultimate target, was going to be the black.

Powerful people lived in the Shires and so he would tread with care. Metaphorically, Sam Vimes, somewhere in his head, picked up his cue.

Vimes lay back in the bed, enjoying the wonderful sensation of gradually being eaten by the pillows, and said to Sybil, "Do the Rust family have a place down here?"

Too late he reflected that this might be a bad move because she might well have told him all about it on one of those occasions when, so unusually for a married man, he was not paying much attention to what his wife was saying, and therefore he might be the cause of grumpiness in those precious, warm minutes before sleep.

All he could see of her right now was the very tip of her nose, as the pillows claimed her, but she mumbled, drowsily, "Oh, they bought Hangnail Manor ten years or so ago, after the Marquis of Fantailer murdered his wife with a pruning knife in the pineapple house. Don't you remember? You spent weeks searching the city for him. In the end everybody seemed to think he'd gone off to Fourecks and disguised himself by not calling himself the Marquis of Fantailer."

"Oh yes," said Vimes, "and I remember that a lot of his chums were quite indignant about the investigation! They said that he'd only done one murder, and it was his wife's fault for having the bad taste to die after just one little stab!"

Lady Sybil turned over, which meant that—since she was a woman happily rich in gravitational attraction—as she turned, the pillow closest to Sam, acting like a gear in a chain, spun softly in the opposite direction so that Sam Vimes found himself now lying on his face. He struck out for the surface again and said, "And Rust bought it, did he? It's unusual for the old fart to spend a penny more than he needs to."

"It wasn't him, dear, it was Gravid."

Vimes woke a little more. "The son? The criminal?"

"I believe, Sam, that the word is *entrepreneur*, and I'd like to go to sleep now, if it's all the same to you."

Sam Vimes knew that the best thing he could say was nothing, and he sank back into the depths, thinking words like, *fiddler, sharp dealer, inserter of a crafty crowbar between what is right and wrong*, and *mine and thine, wide boy, financier* and *untouchable* . . .

Gently drifting into a nightmare world where the good guys and bad guys so often changed hats without warning, Vimes wrestled sleeplessness to the ground and made certain that it got eight hours.

NEXT MORNING VIMES, HAND in hand with his son, walked toward the house of Miss Beedle thoughtfully, not knowing what to expect. He had little experience of the literary world, much preferring the literal one, and he had heard that writers spent all day in their dressing gowns drinking champagne.* On the other hand, as he approached the place up another little lane, some reconsideration began to take place. For one thing, the "cottage" had a garden that would do credit to a farm. When he looked over the fence he saw lines of vegetables and soft fruit, and there was an orchard and what was probably a pigsty and, over there, a proper outdoor privy, very professionally done, with the very-nearly compulsory crescent-moon shape fretsawed into the door, and the log pile close at hand so that the most efficient use could be made of every trip down the path. The whole place had a sensible and serious air, and certainly wasn't what you would expect of somebody who just mucked about with words every day.

Miss Beedle opened the door a fraction of a second after he had knocked. She didn't look surprised.

"I was rather expecting you, your grace," she said, "or is it Mr. Policeman today? From what I hear, it's always Mr. Policeman one way or the other." Then she looked down. "And this must be Young Sam." She glanced up at his father and said, "They tend to get rather tongue-tied, don't they?"

"You know, I've got lots of poo," said Young Sam proudly. "I keep it in jam jars and I've got a laboratory in the lavatory. Have you got any elephant poo? It goes"—and here he paused for effect—"*dung!*"

For a moment Miss Beedle had that slightly glazed sheen often

---

* This is, of course, absolutely true.

seen on the face of someone meeting Young Sam for the first time. She looked at Vimes. "You must be very proud of him."

The proud father said, "It's very hard to keep up—I know that."

Miss Beedle led the way out of the hall and into a room in which chintz played a major part, and drew young Sam over to a large bureau. She opened a drawer and handed the boy what looked like a small book. "This is a bound proof of *The Joy of Earwax*, and I shall sign it for you if you like."

Young Sam took it like one receiving a holy object, and his father, temporarily becoming his mum, said, "What do you say?" To which Young Sam responded with a beam and a thank you and a, "Please don't scribble on it. I'm not allowed to scribble in books."

While Young Sam was happily turning the pages of his new book, his father was introduced to an overstuffed chair. Miss Beedle gave him a smile and hurried off toward the kitchen, leaving Vimes with not much to look at except for a room full of bookcases, more overstuffed furniture, a full-size concert harp, and a wall clock made to look like an owl, whose eyes swung backward and forward hypnotically in time with the tick—presumably to the point where you either committed suicide or picked up the poker in the hearth nearby and beat the damn thing until the springs broke.

While Vimes was warmly contemplating this he realized that he was being watched, and he looked round into the worried face and prognathous jaw of the goblin called Tears of the Mushroom.

Instinctively he looked at Young Sam, and suddenly the biggest raisin in his cake of apprehension was: what will Young Sam do? How many books has he read? They haven't told him nasty tales about goblins, have they, or read him too many of those innocent, colorful fairytale books which contained nightmares ready to leap out and some needless fear that would cause trouble one day?

And what Young Sam did was march across the floor, stop dead in front of the girl and say, "I know a lot about poo. It's very interesting!"

Tears of the Mushroom looked frantically for Miss Beedle while Young Sam, totally at ease, began a brief dissertation on sheep poo. In response, with words slapping together like little bricks, she said, "What . . . is . . . *poo* . . . for?"

Young Sam frowned at this as if somebody was questioning his life's work. Then he looked up brightly and said, "Without poo, you would go off bang!" And he stood there beaming, the meaning of life completely solved.

And Tears of the Mushroom laughed. It was a rather staccato laugh, reminding Vimes of the laughter of certain kinds of women, after certain kinds of too much gin. But it was laughter—straight, genuine and unaffected—and Young Sam bathed in it, giggling, and so did Sam Vimes, with sweat beginning to cool on his neck.

Then Young Sam said, "I wish I had big hands like you. What's your name?"

In that clipped way Vimes was learning to recognize, the goblin girl said, "I am the Tears of the Mushroom."

Instantly Young Sam threw his arms around as much of her as he could encompass and shouted, "Mushrooms shouldn't cry!"

The look that the goblin girl gave Vimes was one that he had seen many times before on the face of someone in receipt of Young Sam's hugs: a mixture of surprise and what Vimes had to call nonplussedness.

At this point Miss Beedle came back into the room holding a plate which she passed to Tears of the Mushroom. "Please be so good as to serve our guests, my dear."

Tears of the Mushroom picked up the plate and tentatively pushed it toward Vimes, and said something that sounded like half a dozen coconuts rolling downstairs, but somehow managed to include the syllables *you* and *eat* and *I make*. There seemed to be a pleading in her expression, as if trying to make him understand.

Vimes stared at her face a while and then thought, Well, I could understand, couldn't I? It has to be worth a try, and closed his eyes, an errand of some dubiousness when you were face-to-longer-face with a jaw like that. With eyes firmly shut, and one hand over them to cut out the last vestige of light, he said, "Will you say that again, young . . . lady?" And in the darkness of his skull he heard, quite clearly, "I have baked biscuits today Mr. Po-lecce-man. I washed my hands," she added nervously. "They are clean and tasty. This I have said and it is a thing exact."

Baked by a goblin, thought Vimes as he opened his eyes and took a knobbly but appetizing-looking biscuit from the plate in front of him, then shut his eyes again and asked, "Why does the mushroom cry?"

In the dark he heard the goblin girl gasp, and then say, "It cries so that there are many more mushrooms. This is a certain thing."

Vimes heard the faint chink of crockery behind him, but as he took his hands away from his eyes Miss Beedle said, "No, stay in darkness, commander. So it's true what the dwarfs say about you."

"I wouldn't know. What do the dwarfs say about me, Miss Beedle?"

Vimes opened his eyes. Miss Beedle sat down on a chair almost opposite, while Tears of the Mushroom waited for more biscuit activity with the air of someone who would probably wait forever or until told not to. She looked imploringly at Vimes and then at Young Sam, who was studying Tears of the Mushroom with interest, although, knowing Young Sam, most of the interest had to do with the plate of biscuits. So he said, "Okay, lad, you may ask the lady for a biscuit, but mind your manners."

"They say that the dark is in you, commander, but you keep it in a cage. A present from Koom Valley, they say."

Vimes blinked in the light. "A dwarf superstition in a goblin cave? You know a lot about dwarfs?"

"Quite a lot," said Miss Beedle, "but far more about goblins, and they believe in the Summoning Dark, just like the dwarfs, after all, they are both creatures of the caves and the Summoning Dark is *real*. It's not all in your head, commander: no matter what you hear, I sometimes hear it too. Oh dear, you of all people must recognize a substition when you're possessed by it? It's the opposite of a superstition: it's real even if you don't believe in it. My mother taught me that; she was a goblin."

Vimes looked at the pleasant brown-haired woman in front of him and said, politely, "No."

"All right, perhaps you'll allow me a little theatricality and mis-direction for effect? Truthfully, my mother was found as a child when she was three and raised by goblins in Uberwald. Until she was about eleven—and I say *about* because she was never quite cer-tain about the passage of time—she pretty much thought and acted like a goblin and picked up their language, which is insanely dif-ficult to learn if you're not brought up to it. She ate with them, had her own plot in the mushroom farm and was very highly thought of among them for the way she looked after the rat farm. She once told me that until she met my father, all her best recollections were of those years in the goblin cave."

Miss Beedle stirred her coffee and continued. "And she also told me her worst recollections, the ones that haunted her night-mares and, I might say, haunt mine now: of one day after some nearby humans had found out that there was a golden-haired, pink-cheeked human girl running around underground with evil, treacherous brutes who, as everybody knows, eat babies. Well, she screamed and fought as they tried to take her away, especially since people who she had thought of as family were being slaughtered around her."

There was a pause. And Vimes glanced somewhat fearfully at Young Sam, who, thankfully, had returned to *The Joy of Earwax* and was therefore oblivious of all else.

"You haven't touched your coffee, commander. You're just holding it in your hand and looking at me."

Vimes took a deep draft of very hot coffee, which at the moment suited him just fine. He said, "This is true? I'm sorry, I don't know what to say."

Tears of the Mushroom was watching him carefully, ready should he feel a biscuit attack coming on. They were in fact pretty good, and to hide his confusion he thanked her and took another one.

"Best not to say anything, then," said Miss Beedle. "All slaughtered, for no reason. It happens. Everybody knows they're a worthless people, don't they? I tell you, commander, it's true that some of the most terrible things in the world are done by people who think, genuinely think, that they're doing it for the best, especially if there is some god involved. Well, it took a lot of those things, and quite a lot of time, to convince a little girl that she wasn't one of the nasty goblins anymore and was really one of the human beings who were not nasty at all, because one day they were certain she would understand that all this terrible business with the bucket of cold water and the beatings every time she spoke in the goblin tongue, or started absentmindedly to sing a goblin song, was in her best interest. Fortunately, although she probably didn't think so at the time, she was strong and clever and she learned: learned to be a good girl, learned to wear proper dresses and eat with a knife and fork and kneel down to pray her thanks for all that she was receiving, including the beatings. And she learned not to be a goblin so successfully that they allowed her to work in the garden, where she vaulted over the wall. They never broke her, and she said to me that there would always be some goblin in her. I never met my father. According to my mother he was a decent and hardworking man, and a considerate and understanding one too, I suspect."

Miss Beedle stood up and brushed at her dress, as if trying to remove the crumbs of history. Standing there, in the chintzy room with the harp in it, she said, "I don't know who those people were who killed the goblins and beat my mother, but if I ever found out I would slaughter them without a thought, because good people have no business being so bad. Goodness is about what you do. Not what you pray to. And that's how it went," she said. "My father was a jeweler, and he soon found out that my mother was absolutely gifted in that respect, probably because of her goblin background that led her to have a feel for stones. I'm sure that made up for having a wife who would swear in goblin when she was annoyed—and let me tell you a good goblin swear can go on for at least a quarter of an hour. She wasn't one for the books, as you might expect, but my dad had been, and one day I thought, "How hard can writing be? After all, most of the words are going to be *and*, *the* and *I* and *it*, and so on, and there's a huge number to choose from, so a lot of the work has already been done for you. That was fifty-seven books ago. It seems to have worked."

Miss Beedle sat back down in her chair and leaned forward. "They have the most complex language you could possibly imagine, commander. The meaning of every word is contingent on the words around it, the speaker, the listener, the time of year, the weather, oh, and so many other things. They have something equivalent to what we think of as poetry; they use and control

fire . . . And about three years ago nearly all of them in this countryside were rounded up and carted away, because they were a
nuisance. Isn't that why you're here?"

Vimes took a deep breath. "Actually, Miss Beedle, I came here
to see my wife's family estate and let my lad learn about the countryside. In the process of which I've already been arrested on suspicion of killing a blacksmith and have seen the brutally slaughtered
body of a goblin woman. On top of this I have no knowledge of
the whereabouts of said blacksmith and, Miss Beedle, would like
somebody to enlighten me, preferably yourself."

"Yes, I saw the poor thing, and I'm sorry that I can't tell you
where Jethro is."

Vimes stared at her and thought, she's probably telling the truth.
"He's not hiding in some part of the mine, is he?"

"No, I've looked. I've looked everywhere. No note, nothing.
And his parents have no idea either. He's a bit of a free spirit, but
he's not the sort of person to go away without telling me." She
looked down, clearly embarrassed.

The silence said a lot. Vimes broke it by saying, "The murder
of that poor girl on the hill will not go unpunished while I live.
I'm taking it personally, you might say. I think someone was trying
to set me up and mud sticks." He paused. "Tell me—these pots the
goblins make. Do they carry them around all the time?"

"Well, yes, of course, but only the ones they're filling at the
moment, obviously," said Miss Beedle, with a trace of annoyance.
"Is this relevant?"

"Well, a policeman, you might say, thinks in goblin language:
everything is contingent on everything else. Incidentally, how
many other people know that you have a tunnel into the hill?"

"What makes you think I have a tunnel going into the hill?"

"Let me see now. This place is practically at the foot of the hill, and if I lived here I'd have dug out a decent wine cellar for myself. That's one reason, and the other is because I saw the flash in your eyes when I asked you the question. Would you like me to ask you the question again?"

The woman opened her mouth to speak, and Vimes raised a finger. "Not finished yet. What isn't as simple is the fact that the other day you arrived in the cave without anybody seeing you walk up the hill. Everyone tells me that there are eyes watching you everywhere in the country and, as luck would have it, I had a few working for me yesterday. Please don't waste my time. You've committed no crime that I know of—you understand being kind to goblins is not a crime?" He thought about that and added, "Although perhaps some people round here might think it is. But I don't and I'm not stupid, Miss Beedle. I saw that goblin head in the pub. It looked as if it's been there for years. Now, I just want to go back up to the cave without anybody seeing me, if you don't mind, because I have a few questions to ask."

Miss Beedle said, "You want to interrogate the goblins?"

"No, that word suggests that I mean to bully them. I simply have to obtain the information I need to know before I start to investigate the murder of the girl. If you don't want to help me, I'm afraid that will be your choice."

THE NEXT DAY SERGEANT Colon did not turn up for work. Mrs. Colon sent a note around by a boy as soon as she got back from work herself.*

★ The Colons had survived a long and happy marriage by having as little to do with the other partner as possible. This was achieved by the expedient of his working the night shift when she was working days and vice versa. This was agreed on the basis that anything else would spoil the romance.

There was nothing romantic about Fred Colon when she got home, and so after sweeping the floor, doing the washing-up, wiping all the surfaces and spending some time teasing out the lumps of mud that had got caught on the doormat, she made haste to Pseudopolis Yard—after visiting her friend Mildred who had a rather nice porcelain jug and basin set she wanted to sell. When she eventually got to the Watch House she explained that Fred was terribly poorly, and sweating cobs and gabbling about rabbits.

Sergeant Littlebottom was sent to investigate, and returned looking solemn as she climbed the steps to Vimes's office, now occupied by Captain Carrot. You could tell he was the occupant now not simply because he was sitting in the chair, which was a persuasive hint, but also because all the paperwork was done and aligned, a trait which always impressed Inspector A. E. Pessimal, a small man who had the heart of a lion and the physical strength of a kitten and the face, disposition and general demeanor that would make even hardened accountants say, "Just look at him. Doesn't he look like a typical accountant to you?"

But this didn't worry the lion heart of A. E. Pessimal. He was the Watch's secret weapon. There wasn't a bookkeeper in the city who would like to see a visit from A. E. Pessimal unless, of course, he was perfectly innocent—although generally that could be ruled out, because Mr. and Mrs. Pessimal's little boy could track an error all the way through the ledger and down into the cellar where the *real* books had been hidden. And all Inspector A. E. Pessimal wanted for his genius was a meticulously calculated wage and a chance, every now and again, to go out on the streets with a real policeman, swinging his truncheon and glaring at trolls.

Carrot leaned back. "So how's Fred getting on, Cheery?"

"Nothing much that I can see, really, um . . ."

"That was a big um, Cheery."

The trouble was that Captain Carrot had a friendly, honest and open face, that made you *want* to tell him things. It didn't help that Sergeant Littlebottom held a small torch for the captain, even though he was well and truly spoken for—he was also a dwarf, well, technically, and you can't help how you dream. "Well . . ." she began reluctantly.

Carrot leaned forward. "Yes, Cheery?"

She gave in. "Well, sir, it's unggue. You come from Copperhead . . . Did you run into many goblins up there?"

"No, but I know that unggue is their religion, if you can call it that."

Cheery Littlebottom shook her head, trying to get out of her mind some speculation about the part a reasonably high stool might play in a relationship, and telling herself that Sergeant Hammer-of-Gold, over in the Dolly Sisters Watch House, caught her eye every time she was busily catching his eye when they happened to meet on patrol, and was probably a really good catch if she could pluck up the courage to ask him if he was actually male.[*] She said, "Onggue is not a religion, it's a superstition. The goblins don't believe in Tak,[†] sir, they're savages, scavengers, but . . ." She hesitated again. "There's something I was told once, and it's unbelievable, but sometimes they eat their babies, sir, or at least, the mother will eat her child, her *newborn* child, if there's famine. Can you *believe* that?"

---

[*] Strictly speaking, the sexuality of any given dwarf remained a secret between him or, as it might be, her, and his, or, as it might be, her mother, until they decided to tell someone else about it, although generally you could work it out by observing dwarfs closely and spotting the ones that were drinking sherry or light white wine. Regrettably, this didn't always work with dwarf policemen, because like all policemen everywhere they would drink anything strong enough to help them forget what they'd to deal with that day.

[†] According to dwarf lore the universe was written into being by Tak, who also wrote its lores. All writing is sacred to the dwarfs.

Carrot's mouth dropped open for a moment, and then a small voice said, "Yes, I think I can, sergeant, if you would excuse my saying so."

A. E. Pessimal looked defiantly at their expressions and tried to stand a little straighter. "It's a matter of logic, you see? No food? But the mother may survive by reconsuming the child, as it were, whereas, if all other food has been exhausted, then the child will die. In fact the child is dead as soon as the conundrum is postulated. The mother, on the other hand, might, by so doing, survive for long enough for more food to be found and become available, and in the course of time may bear another child."

"You know, that is a very *accountancy* thing to say!" said Cheery.

A. E. Pessimal remained calm. "Thank you, Sergeant Littlebottom, I shall take that as a compliment because the logic is impeccable. It's what is known as the dreadful logic of necessity. I'm well versed in the logistics of survival situations."

The chair creaked as Captain Carrot leaned forward. "No offense meant, Inspector Pessimal, but may I enquire as to what kind of issues of survival arise during double-entry bookkeeping?"

A. E. Pessimal sighed. "It can get pretty hazardous as the end of the fiscal year draws near, captain. However, I take your point and would like you to understand that I believe I have read every single memoir, manual, log, and message in a bottle—by which I mean, of course, message *taken* from a bottle—that is currently available, and I can assure you that you would be amazed at the terrible decisions that sometimes have to be made by a group of people so that *some*, if not all, may live. Classically we have the shipwrecked sailors adrift in an open boat far on the ocean with succor extremely unlikely. Generally, the procedure is to eat one another's legs, although sooner or later the supply of legs is going to run, if I may use the word, out; and then arises the question who will die so that some may live. Dreadful algebra, captain." Only then did

A. E. Pessimal blush. "I'm sorry. I know that I am a small, weak man, but I have amassed a large library; I dream of dangerous places."

"Perhaps you should walk through the Shades, inspector," said Carrot, "you wouldn't have to dream. Do carry on, Cheery."

Cheery Littlebottom shrugged. "But eating your own child, that's got to be wrong, yes?"

"Well, sergeant," said A. E. Pessimal, "I have read about such things and if you think of the outcomes, which are the death of both mother *and* child or the death of the child but the possible life of the mother, the conclusion must be that her decision is right. In his book *A Banquet of Worms* Colonel F. J. Massingham does mention this about the goblins and apparently, according to the goblins' world view, a consumed child, which clearly did emerge from the mother, has been returned whence it came and will, hopefully, be reborn anew at some future date when circumstances are more favorable with, therefore, no actual harm done. You may think that this view does not stand up to scrutiny, but when you're faced with the dreadful algebra, the world becomes quite a different place."

There was silence while they all contemplated this.

Carrot said, "You know how it is in a street fight, Cheery. Sometimes if things get hot and you know it's you or them—that's when you do the algebra."

"Fred doesn't seem to know where he is," said Cheery. "He wasn't running a temperature and his bedroom isn't particularly warm, but he acts as if he's very hot and he won't let go of that damn little pot. He shouts if anyone tries even to get near it. Actually, he screamed at me! And that's another thing, his voice has changed, he sounds like a man who's gargling rocks. I had a word with Ponder Stibbons at the university, but they don't appear to have anyone who knows anything much about goblins."

Captain Carrot raised his eyebrows. "Are you sure? I know for a fact that they have a Professor of Dust, Miscellaneous Particles and Filaments, and you tell me that there's no expert on an entire species of talking humanoids?"

"That's about right, sir. All we could turn up was stuff about what a bloody nuisance they are—you know the kind of thing."

"*Nobody* knows anything about goblins? I mean, stuff worth knowing?"

A. E. Pessimal actually saluted. "Harry King does, captain. There's quite a few of them downriver. They don't come into town much, though. You may remember that Lord Vetinari was gracious enough to ask for me to be seconded to the revenue in order that I might go through Mr. King's returns, given that all the other tax officers were frightened to set foot on his property. I myself, sir, was *not* frightened," said A. E. Pessimal proudly, "because I am protected by my badge and the majesty of the law. Harry King might throw a taxman out of the building, but he's clever enough not to try that with one of Commander Vimes's men, no indeed!" You could have lit the city with the proud glow from A. E. Pessimal's face as he tried to puff out a chest that mostly went in.

It became a little more swollen when Carrot said, "Very well done, inspector. You're a mean man with a smoking abacus indeed. I think I shall pay a visit to our old friend Harry first thing in the morning."

VIMES DID SOME THINKING about the problem of taking Young Sam to a crime scene, but frankly, the lad was showing himself to be up to just about any encounter. Besides, any lad wants to go and see where his dad works. He looked down at his son. "Would you be scared of a long walk in the dark, lad? With me and these ladies?"

Young Sam looked solemn for a moment and then said, "I think I'll let Mr. Whistle do the being scared and then it won't bother me."

The door to the secret tunnel, if indeed it was secret, was in Miss Beedle's cellar, which had quite a well-appointed wine rack and a general, not unpleasant smell of, well, a cellar. But once through the door there was a smell of distant goblins.

It *was* a long walk in the dark, especially when you were obliged to walk up quite a steep slope very nearly on hands and knees.

The smell of goblins grew stronger after a while, but during that while, you tended to get used to it. Here and there light shone into the gloom from holes to the outside world, which Vimes thought was sensible engineering until he realized that rabbits used this tunnel too, and had left plenty of droppings as evidence. He wondered whether he should pocket a few samples for Young Sam's collection and suggested this to Young Sam, toiling manfully behind him, who said, "No, Dad, got rabbits. Want elephant if we find one."

Rabbit poo, Vimes noticed, was about the size of a chocolate raisin, a thought which instantly dragged him back to his youth, when if by some means, never entirely legal, he had acquired some cash, he would spend it on a ticket to the fleapit music hall and buy a packet of chocolate raisins with the change. Nobody knew, or cared to guess, what the things were that scuttled and scratched down below the seats, but you soon learned a very important rule: if you dropped your chocolate raisins, it was vitally important not to pick them up!

Vimes stopped, causing Miss Beedle to walk into the sack of apples that she had asked him to carry, and got a grip on himself sufficiently to say, "I'd like a moment or two to catch my breath, Miss Beedle. Sorry, not as young as I was and all that. I'll catch you up. What are we carrying these bags for anyway?"

"Fruit and vegetables, commander."

"What? To goblins? I'd have thought they found their own food."

Miss Beedle inched her way around him and climbed on into the dark, saying, over her shoulder, "Yes, they do."

Vimes sat with Young Sam for a moment until he felt better and said, "How are you doing, lad?"

In the dark a small voice said, "I told Mr. Whistle not to worry, Dad, because he's a bit silly."

So is your father, thought Vimes, and is probably going to continue to be so. But he was on the chase. One way or another he was on the chase. Who you were chasing could wait. The chasing was the thing.

Anger helped Vimes up the last leg of the climb. Anger at himself and whoever it was who had punctured his holiday. But it was worrying: he had wanted something to happen and now it had. Somebody was dead. Sometimes you had to take a look at yourself and then look away.

He found Miss Beedle and Tears of the Mushroom waiting with a dozen or so other . . . ladies. It was a calculated guess, given that he had yet to find any reliable way of telling one goblin from another—except, of course, that Tears of the Mushroom was wearing her apron with pockets, which he hadn't seen before, and apparently neither had the other ladies, since Tears of the Mushroom was now the hit of the season as far as her sisters were concerned, given that they currently wore daring little outfits of old sacking, plaited grasses and rabbit skin. They gathered around her chorusing, presumably, the goblin equivalent of "Oh my dear, you look *fabulous*."*

★   However that might be rendered in a language that at its best sounded like a man jumping up and down on a very large packet of crisps.

Miss Beedle sidled up to Vimes and said, "I know what you're thinking, but it's a start. Carrying things, useful things, without having to use your hands—well, that's a step in the right direction." She pulled Vimes a little way from the newly formed goblin branch of the Women's Institute, who had by now attracted the attention of Young Sam, whose cheerful reluctance to be overawed by anything had clearly won over the girls, resulting in his being where he always felt he should be, the center of attention. It was a knack.

Miss Beedle went on, "If you want to change a whole people, then you start with the girls. It stands to reason: they learn faster, and they pass on what they learn to their children. I suppose you're wondering why we were trekking up here with all the sacks?"

Behind them, the apron was being tried on by one girl after another: this year's must-have item. Vimes turned back to the woman and said, "Well, this is just a guess, but I see a lot of rabbit bones around the place, and I have heard that you can die if you live only on rabbit, only I don't know why this is."

Miss Beedle lit up. "Well, Commander Vimes, you've certainly gone up in my estimation! Yes, rabbit has been the scourge of the goblin nation! I understand it depletes the body of some vital nutrient if you don't eat other things as well. Just about any green stuff will do, but the male goblins think a proper meal is a rabbit on a stick." She sighed. "Dwarfs know about this, and they're absolutely fanatical about good food, as you should be if you spend much of your time underground, but nobody cared to tell the goblins, as if they would listen anyway, and so bad health and premature death is their lot. Some survive, of course, mostly those who prefer rat or eat the *whole* rabbit, not just the more apparently edible bits, or they simply eat their vegetables."

She began to unfasten a sack of cabbages and continued, "I was well in with the wife of the head man here, because he got sick and I made certain he got a few good meals. Of course he swears it was because he did the magic, but his wife was remarkably sensible, and the other males don't worry about what the girls get up to, so they slip fruit and veg into their stews, saying they're magical, and so they have children who survive and thus we change the world one meal at a time. That is if the goblins get a chance to live at all." She looked sadly at the gossiping girls and said, "What they really need is a first-class theologian, because, you see, they agree with the rest of the world: *they* think they're rubbish! They think they did something very bad, a long time ago, and because of it they've lived like they do. They think they have it coming to them, as you might say."

Vimes frowned. He couldn't remember ever going into a church or temple or one of the numerous other places of more or less spirituality for any other reason than the occasional requirements of the job. These days he tended to go in for reasons of Sybil, i.e., his wife dragging him along so that he could be seen, and, if possible, seen remaining awake.

No, the world of next worlds, afterlives and purgatorial destinations simply did not fit into his head. Whether you wanted it or not, you were born, you did the best you could, and then, whether you really wanted to or not, you died. They were the only certainties, and so the best thing for a copper to do was to get on with the job. And it was about time that Sam Vimes got back to doing his.

Young Sam at this point had tired of petticoat company and had drifted over to an elderly goblin man who was working on a pot, and was watching with extreme fascination, to the apparent pleasure, as far as Vimes could tell, of the elderly goblin. That's a lesson to us . . . I don't know what kind of lesson, but it's a lesson, he thought.

Vimes waited until Miss Beedle returned from discussing the possible new fashion explosion with the girls, then politely asked her, "Did the victim have any unggue pots on her?"

"I would be amazed if she hadn't," said Miss Beedle. "One or two at the very least, but probably the quite small ones for use during the day."

"I see," said Vimes, "but were any found on her, er, afterward, I mean, if she was laid out?" He didn't know what the protocol was and continued, "Look, Miss Beedle, is it possible that she had an unggue pot on her that's now missing? I know they're valuable, of course—they're shiny."

"I don't know, but I'll go and ask the Cold Bone Wakes. He's the head goblin. He'll know."

That reminded Vimes. Feeling embarrassed, he delved into his pocket and took out a small package very, very carefully wrapped, and handed it to Miss Beedle with a pleading look. "I believe this belonged to the dead girl," he said. "A stone ring with a little blue bead in it? Can you see that it gets to someone here who'll value it?" All she had was a stone ring, he thought, and even that got taken away.

There were times when the world did not need policemen, because what it *really* did need was for somebody who knew what they were doing to shut it all down and start it all up again so that this time it could be done properly . . .

But before despair could entirely set in, Miss Beedle was back, and excited. "How apposite that you should ask that question, Commander! One of them *was* missing! Unggue cat!"

Vimes could register absolute flat-faced incomprehension as well as any copper born. It radiated a searchlight of ignorance, but that was fine because Miss Beedle was prepared to be a fountainhead of information. "I'm sure you know what everybody knows, commander, which is that goblins do, I might say religiously, store certain bodily secretions in pots, in the belief that these must be reunited with their corpse when they are buried. This obligation is called unggue. All goblins must, by custom, which is very strict among goblins, maintain the Unggue Had, the trinity of snot, nail clippings and earwax. The missing pot in this case is the pot of cat, which contains nail clippings. Don't get misled by the word 'cat.' Felines don't come into the picture . . . it's simply that there are only so many syllables in the world."

"And this is the first time you've heard that it's missing, Miss Beedle?"

"Well, this is my first time down here since yesterday, and it's a difficult time to talk to her family, as you may imagine . . ."

"I see," said Vimes, though he didn't, not very much—although he could sense a tiny bead of light growing in the darkness of his mind. He glanced again at Young Sam, who was studying the potmaker with every sign of forensic interest. That's my boy. He continued, "Did they look for the pot?"

"Looked everywhere, commander, even outside. And it'll be quite small. You see, every goblin makes a set of pots which are kept deep inside the cave. I don't know where they are, though in most other things they trust me. This is because humans steal pots. For this reason, most goblins make other comparatively small pots for daily use and for when they leave the cave, and decant them into the larger pots later, in secret." She tried to smile, and said, "I'm sure this seems quite outlandish to you, commander, but the making and maintaining of the pots is to them a religion in itself."

At this point Samuel Vimes was not keen to be heard giving his views about pots, so he contented himself with saying, "Is it possible that another goblin might have stolen the pot? Anyway, what size is 'quite small'?"

Miss Beedle gave him a surprised look. "If you trust me on any-thing, commander, trust me on this. No goblin would dream of steal-ing another goblin's pot. The concept of doing so would be totally alien to them, I assure you. The size? Oh, usually similar to a lady's compact or perhaps a snuffbox. They have a shine on them like opals."

"Yes," said Vimes, "I know," and he thought *bright colors in the dark*. He said, "I don't want to be difficult, but could I borrow another of the poor lady's pots? I might need one to show people what it is I'm looking for."

Miss Beedle looked surprised again. "That would be *impossible*, but I think that if I talk to Tears of the Mushroom she might, just might, loan you one of hers, in which case I may say you will be a very special person, commander. A pot usually changes hands only because of distress, but Tears of the Mushroom spends a lot of time with me and has learned, shall I say, the uses of flexible thinking and, if I may say so, she has taken a little bit of a shine to you."

She walked away, leaving the startled Vimes and Young Sam to their own devices. Here and there, goblins were doing whatever they did, tending small fires, sleeping, or in many cases fussing with their pots. And a few just sat there staring blankly at nothing at all, like a policeman wondering how you spell phantasmagorical.

And a new image dragged itself out of Vimes's memory. It was of a lot of little blue men shouting, "Crivens!" Ah yes, the Nac Mac Feegle! They lived in holes in the ground as well. Admittedly, these were said to be rather more salubrious than this midden-ridden cave system, but however you looked at it, they were in the same situation as the goblins. They lived on the edge too, but they—they *danced* on the edge, they jumped up and down on it, made faces at it, thumbed their snotty noses at it, refused to see the peril of their situation and, in general, seemed to have a huge appetite for life, alcohol, adventure and alcohol. As a copper, he shouldn't say it, because they could be a bloody nuisance, but there was something commendable about the cheerfully feisty way they faced, well, everything . . .

Somebody tugged at his sleeve. He looked down into the face of Tears of the Mushroom, with Miss Beedle standing over her like a chaperone. The other goblin girls stood behind the pair of them like an Ephebian chorus.

The solemn voice from the little face said, "Hearts must give, Mr. Po-leess-man."

With dreadfully bad timing, Miss Beedle broke in like an over-active schoolteacher, and Vimes was privately overjoyed to see a brief look of annoyance on Tears of the Mushroom's face.

"She means that if she is to trust you with a pot, then you must trust her with something equally valuable. I suppose you would call it a hostage situation."

No, I wouldn't, Vimes thought, looking into the dark eyes of the goblin girl. That was a strange thing: when he got past the features, which at best could be considered homely, depending on what kind of home you had in mind, the eyes were as human as you could imagine. They had a depth that not even the brightest animal could achieve. He reached for his wallet, and Miss Beedle said sharply, "Money won't do!"

He ignored her and finished pulling out the picture of Young Sam that he took everywhere and carefully passed it to Tears of the Mushroom, who took it as if holding a rare and delicate object—which, from the point of view of Vimes, it certainly was. She looked at it, then down at the boy himself, who gave her a cheery smile, and her eyes confirmed that the grimace on her face was in fact an answering smile. For Young Sam, the goblin cave was an interesting fairyland. You had to admire his ability not to be immediately frightened of anything.

Tears of the Mushroom looked back at the picture and then back at Young Sam and then at the face of Vimes. She tucked the picture carefully into her apron and pulled out her hand, holding a small, iridescent pot. She held it out to Vimes, her hand trembling slightly, and he found himself taking it gingerly in both hands. Then Tears of the Mushroom said in her strange voice, like a living filing cabinet, "Hearts have given." Which almost brought Vimes to his knees.

He thought: it could just as well have been her head grinning on the pub wall! *Someone* is going to burn!

In the back of his mind a cheerful voice said, "Well done, Commander Vimes, at last you are singing from my hymn sheet!"

He ignored it, feeling the little pot; it was as smooth as skin. Whatever it was made to contain, and he wasn't going to ask, the contents were masked by a carved latticework of flowers and mushrooms.

I N THE COOL DEPTHS of his cellar, Mr. Jiminy the publican was preparing for the evening rush when he heard a sound in the darkness among the barrels. He dismissed it as being yet another rat until a hand was clamped over his mouth.

"Excuse me, sir, I have reason to believe that you can help me with my inquiries." The man struggled, but Vimes knew every trick when it came to apprehending a suspect. He hissed, "You know who I am, sir, and I know what you are. We're both coppers and we've been around the houses. You said that the barman sees everything, hears everything and says nothing, and I'm a fair man, Mr. Jiminy, but I'm investigating a murder. A murder, sir, the capital crime, and maybe something much, much worse. So excuse me if I take the view that those who aren't behind me are standing in my way, with all that that entails."

Jiminy was running out of breath now, and squirming feebly. "Oh, too much of the booze and too little walking the beat, I fancy," said Vimes. "Now, I would not ask a man to break the barman's solemn oath, so when I take my hand away, we'll sit down peacefully and play a little game of charades. I'm letting go . . . now."

The barman wheezed a curse, and added, "You didn't need to do that, commander. I've got a bad chest, you know!"

"Not as bad as it might otherwise be, Mr. Jiminy. And now a word on the subject of being too clever."

The publican glared as Vimes went on, "I'm strictly a copper. I don't kill people unless they're trying to kill me. You may be aware of my batman, Mr. Willikins. You saw him the other day. Regrettably he's more direct, and also extremely loyal. A few years ago, to save my family, he killed an armed dwarf with a common ice knife. And he has other talents: among them, I have to say, is that he can iron a shirt as crisply as any man I know. And, as I say, very loyal indeed. C'mon, Jiminy. I'm a copper and you're a copper. You're still a copper whatever you say—the stain never leaves you. You know what I can do and I know what you can do and you're smart enough to choose the right side."

"All right, you don't need to rub it in," Jiminy grumbled. "We both know about the ins and outs." His voice was suddenly and almost theatrically helpful as he crooned, "How may I help you, officer, just like the good citizen that I am?"

Vimes carefully pulled out of his coat the little pot. It was indeed about the size of a snuffbox. The incongruity was not lost on Vimes: in one pocket he held the glorious gem, quite likely the repository of goblin snot, and in the other he had his own small snuffbox. How hilarious would it be if he'd mixed them up?

Jiminy certainly reacted when he saw it, although he probably thought he hadn't. There is a subtle difference between hiding your reaction and showing that you are hiding your reaction.

"All right, all right, Mr. Vimes, you're right. We don't have to play games, old coppers like us. I give in. I know what that is. Seen one like it recently, as a matter of fact."

"And?"

"I can give you a name, Mr. Vimes. 'Cos why? Cause he's a nut job, a toe rag, and he ain't from around here. Name of Stratford, or so they call him. A knife cove, the kind of bloke you never want to see walk through your pub door, I don't mind telling you. He isn't often here, thank goodness. The other day was the first time I've seen him in months. I don't know where he kips, but the snotty bugger he was hanging out with is called Ted Flutter, works for young Lord Rust up at Hangnail. His lordship is big in tobacco, so they tell me." Jiminy stopped.

Vimes interpreted this in exactly the way Jiminy wanted, he was sure. Lord Rust was up to something, Jiminy was insinuating, and throwing a bone to Vimes to get the man off his back. Some people would have thought this despicable, but the man was an ex-policeman, after all.

Jiminy gave a little cough as he endeavored to find another victim for Vimes to pursue. "But Flutter, well, you know, he's just a bloke. If someone needs help for something or other, he's the kind of bloke who'd be the lookout or be told to take away the bones. When not up to mischief I think he hangs wallpaper and runs a turkey farm up on the road toward Overhang. You can't miss it, it's a stinky ol' place and he doesn't take care of his birds. Not entirely all there, in my opinion."

Vimes seized his opening. "Tobacco, eh? Oh yes, Mr. Jiminy, I did think I smelled rather more tobacco down here than might otherwise be expected, and, of course, as a policeman, it's something that I'll have to look into, perhaps, when time allows." He winked, and Jiminy nodded knowingly.

With the atmosphere now tentatively upbeat, Jiminy said, "They brings a few barrels up here some nights and then picks it up again as and when. All right, I know it's the revenue and all that, but I don't see the harm. And since we understand one another so well, Mr. Vimes, I've been here for only three years. I know there was some stuff way back, maybe they did scrag a few goblins, I don't know, not my business. Don't know why, don't know who, if you get my meaning?" Jiminy was sweating like a pig, Vimes noticed.

There are times when reacting the way that simple, common decency requires fails to serve a higher purpose, and because of this Vimes merely gave the man a little smile and said, "One day, Mr. Jiminy, I'll bring a lady here. I think she'd be very interested to see your establishment."

Jiminy was puzzled but had the grace to say, "I'll look forward to it, commander."

"What I'm trying to say," said Vimes, "is that if this pub still has the head of a goblin hanging over the bar the next time I'm here there'll be a mysterious fire, do you understand? No doubt you want to keep in with young Lord Rust and his chums, because it always pays to keep in with the powerful. I know that well enough. You'll find me a good friend, Mr. Jiminy, and I'd like to suggest to you that it would not be in your interest to have Commander Vimes as your enemy. Just a word to the wise, you know, one copper to another."

With forced cheerfulness Jiminy said, in a voice that dripped butter and sugar, "No one ever said that Constable Jiminy didn't know how the wind was blowing, and since you've been so gracious as to visit my humble establishment I think I can take the view that the wind has begun to blow due Vimes."

Vimes lifted the cellar hatch to depart and said, "Oh, so do I, Mr. Jiminy, so do I, and if ever the weathercock decides to blow the other way, I'll bite its bloody head off."

Jiminy smiled uncertainly and said, "Do you have jurisdiction here, commander?"

And was dragged by the shirt to within an inch of Vimes's face, eyeball to eyeball, and Vimes said, "Try me."

F EELING RATHER CHIRPY AFTER this interlude, Vimes jogged to the lane that led to the hill and found Miss Beedle and Tears of the Mushroom at the door of the cottage. By the look of it they had been picking apples; several baskets of fruit had been piled up. He thought that Tears of the Mushroom smiled when she saw him, although how could you tell, really? Goblin faces were hard to read.

The pot was dutifully traded back for the picture, and Vimes couldn't help noticing, because he always made a point of noticing, that both he and the girl tried surreptitiously to examine their precious items without causing offense. He was sure he heard Miss Beedle stifle a sigh of relief. "Did you find the murderer?" she said, leaning forward anxiously. She turned to the girl. "Go inside, dear, while I talk to Commander Vimes, will you?"

"Yes, Miss Beedle, I will go inside as you request."

There it was again: a language of little boxes, opening and shutting as required. The girl disappeared into the house, and Vimes said, "I have information that two men were in the pub on the night of the murder, and one of them certainly had a pot. Neither of them, I've been led to believe, was a pillar of society."

Miss Beedle clapped her hands. "Well, that's good, isn't it? You have them bang to rights!"

It always embarrassed Samuel Vimes when civilians tried to speak to him in what they thought was "policeman." If it came to that, he hated thinking of them as civilians. What was a policeman, if not a civilian with a uniform and a badge? But they tended to use the term these days as a way of describing people who were not policemen. It was a dangerous habit: once policemen stopped being civilians the only other thing they could be was soldiers. He sighed. "As far as I know, miss, it is not illegal to have a goblin pot. Neither is it, strictly speaking, illegal to be described as not a pillar of society. Do goblins sign their pots in some way?"

"Oh yes, indeed, commander, goblin pots are always distinctive. Do these criminals have a *modus operandi*?"

Vimes's heart sank. "No, and I don't think they'd know one if they saw it." He tried to say this firmly, because Miss Beedle looked as if she would at any moment turn out with a magnifying glass and a bloodhound.

Then, falling across his world like a rainbow of sound, came music, drifting out of the open cottage window. He listened with his mouth open, entirely forgetting the conversation.

His Grace the Duke of Ankh, Commander Sir Samuel Vimes, was not a man who made a point of frequenting performances of classical music, or indeed any music that you couldn't whistle on the way home. But apparently being a nob carried with it a requirement to attend the opera, the ballet and as many musical events as Sybil could drag him to. Fortunately, they generally had a box, and Sybil, very wisely, having dragged him to the performance, did not subsequently drag him into consciousness. But some of it seeped through and it was enough for him to know that what he was hearing was the real, highbrow stuff: you couldn't hum it, and at no point did anybody shout "Whoops! Have a banana!" It was the pure quill of music, a sound that came close to making you want to fall on your knees and promise to be a better person. He turned wordlessly to Miss Beedle, who said, "She's very good, isn't she?"

"That's a harp, isn't it? A goblin playing a harp?"

Miss Beedle seemed embarrassed by the fuss. "Certainly, why shouldn't she? Strangely enough, her large hands are suited to the instrument. I don't think she understands the concept of reading music yet, and I have to help her tune it, but she does play very well. Heaven knows where she's getting the music from . . ."

"Heaven?" said Vimes, adding urgently, "How long will she be playing? Have I got time to bring Sybil over here?" He didn't wait for an answer but hurried off down the lane, clambered over a gate, caused a flock of sheep to explode in all directions, swore at a kissing gate, jumped over the ha-ha, completely ignored the he-he and totally avoided the ho-hum. He hurtled down the drive, scampered up the steps and, providentially, went through the front door at exactly the same time as a footman swung it open.

Sybil was taking tea with a group of ladies, which appeared to be obligatory procedure in the afternoons, but Vimes leaned against the wall and panted out, "You must come and listen to this music! Bring Young Sam! Bring these ladies if they want to come, but whatever you do, come on! I've never heard anything so good!"

Sybil looked around. "Well, we *were* just breaking up, Sam. You know, you look very flushed. Is anything the matter?" She looked imploringly at her friends, who were already rising in their seats, and said, "I do hope you'll forgive me, ladies. It's so very difficult being the wife of an important man." There was a slight barb to the last syllable. "I'm sure, Sam, that whatever it is can wait until I've said goodbye to my guests, yes?"

And so Sam Vimes shook hands, smiled, shook hands, smiled and fretted until the last twitterer had tweeted and the last lady had left.

Having seen the final carriage away, Lady Sybil came back in, flopped into a chair in front of Sam and listened to Vimes's garbled account.

"And this is that young goblin girl Miss Beedle has been teaching to talk?"

Vimes was almost frantic. "Yes! And she plays wonderful music! Wonderful!"

"Sam Vimes, when I take you to a concert you fall asleep in ten minutes. Do you know what? You've convinced me. Let's go, shall we?"

"Where?" said Vimes, in husbandly confusion.

Sybil affected surprise. "Why, to hear the young lady play the harp, of course. I thought that was what *you* wanted. I'll go and get my jacket while you find Young Sam, please? He's in the laboratory."

For Vimes, bewilderment was now accumulating. "The . . ."

"The laboratory, Sam! You know my family were famous meddlers, don't you? Willikins is in there with him, and I believe they're dissecting some, shall I say, excrement? Make certain they've both washed their hands—thoroughly," she added, on the way out of the room. "And tell them I was emphatic, and tell Young Sam what emphatic means!"

THE COACH STOOD EMPTY in the lane. They hadn't dared knock on the door, not while that heavenly music was drifting out of the cottage window. Sybil was in tears, but often she looked up, and said things like, "That shouldn't be possible on a harp!" Even Young Sam was transfixed, standing there with his little mouth open, while the music rushed in and, for a moment upon the world, lifted all hearts and forgave all sins—not having its work cut out in the case of Young Sam, a part of Vimes managed to reflect, but doing a sterling and heavyweight job on his father. And when the music stopped Young Sam said, "More!" and that went for his parents, too. They stood there, not looking at one another, and then the cottage door opened and Miss Beedle stepped out.

"I saw you out there, of course. Do come in, but quietly. I've made lemonade." She led them through the hall and turned into the living room.

Tears of the Mushroom must have been forewarned by Miss Beedle. She sat on a chair next to the harp with her oversized hands clasped demurely over her apron. Wordlessly, Young Sam walked over to her and cuddled her leg. The goblin girl looked panicky and Vimes said, "Don't worry, he just wants to show that he loves you." And he thought, I've just told a goblin not to be frightened of my son because he loves her and the world has turned upside-down and all sins are forgiven, except possibly mine.

A S THE COACH RATTLED gently back toward Ramkin Hall Lady Sybil said quietly to Vimes, "I understand that the young lady goblin who was . . . murdered could play the harp as well as Miss Mushroom."

Vimes stirred from his inner thoughts and said, "I didn't know that."

"Oh yes," said Sybil, in a curiously chatty voice. "Apparently Miss Beedle wants young goblin girls to have something to be proud of." She cleared her throat, and, after a pause, said, "Do you have any suspects, Sam?"

"Oh yes, two. I have the testimony of a reliable witness that they were in the area after the event, and I'm beginning to consider a chain of events that might lead me also to the whereabouts of Mr. Jefferson the smith. This is the countryside, after all. Everyone sees where you go and you never know who is behind a hedge. I believe they may have heard him invite me to Dead Man's Copse on what *The Times* would call 'that fateful night.'"

Sybil looked down at Young Sam, dozing between them, and said, "Do you know where they live?"

"Yes, one of them at least. I think the other one just hangs around, as they say." And now the rattle of gravel under wheel told them that they were going down the long drive.

Sybil cleared her throat again, and in a quiet voice said, "I fear you may have felt that I was being rather acerbic to you, Sam, on the subject of letting your professional concerns get in the way of our holiday. I may, at times, have been somewhat . . . blunt."

"Not at all, Sybil, I fully understood your concern."

It seemed that Lady Sybil really could have done with some cough drops, but she carried on carefully and said, "Sam, I'd be very grateful if you could see your way clear to perhaps taking Willikins with you to wherever it is that these scoundrels poison the world with their existence, and bring them to justice, if you would be so good."

He could feel her trembling with rage and said, "I was considering doing so as soon as possible, my dear, but I must tell you that things may not go entirely in accordance with the rulebook. After all, I'm out of my jurisdiction here."

But his wife said, "You're a stickler for the book, Sam, and I admire that, but the jurisdiction of a good man extends to the end of the world—though who will you take them to? Havelock would hang them, you know that. But he's a long way away. Nonetheless, Sam, I am certain of one thing and it's this: the worst thing you can do is nothing. Go to it, Sam."

"Actually, Sybil, I was considering delivering them to the local justices."

"What? They're a terrible bunch, apparently using what they

call the law here for their own ends! There'll be an enormous stink!"

Vimes smiled. "Oh dear, do you really think so?"

THERE WAS NO POINT going to bed, thought Vimes later that evening, and so he kissed his wife goodnight and went to the snooker room where Willikins was idly demonstrating one of the more socially acceptable skills he had learned during a misspent youth. The man straightened up when Vimes walked in and said, "Good evening, commander. Would you like a sustaining drink to be going on with?"

Vimes also indulged in a rare cigar because, well, what good is a snooker room without smoke twisting among the lights and turning the air a desolate blue, the color of dead hopes and lost chances?

Willikins, who knew the protocol, waited until Vimes had made his shot before coughing gently. "Oh, well done, sir, and I understand her ladyship is somewhat vexed about the goblin situation, sir. I believe this to be the case, sir, because I met her in the corridor earlier and she used language I haven't heard on the lips of a woman since my old mother passed away, gods bless her soul, if they can find it. But, well done again, sir."

Vimes laid his cue aside. "I want to get them all, Willikins. It's no good slamming up some local thug."

"Yes indeed, commander, it's all about potting the black."

Vimes looked up from his fiery drink. "I can see you must have played a lot in your time, Willikins. Did you ever see Pelvic Williams? Very religious man in his way, lived somewhere in Hen-and-Chickens Court with his sister, played like I've never seen anyone else play before or since. I swear he could make a ball jump the table, roll along the edge and drop back onto the cloth just where he wanted it, to drop neatly into the pocket." Vimes gave a grunt of satisfaction, and went on, "Of course, everyone used to say that was cheating, but he used to stand there, as meek as milk, just repeating 'The ball dropped.' Tell you the truth, the reason he never got beaten up was that it was an education watching the man. He once sank a ball by bouncing it off the lamp and a pint mug. But, like he said, the ball dropped." Vimes relaxed and said, "The trouble is, of course, that in real life rules are more stringent."

"Yes indeed, commander," said Willikins. "Where I used to play the only rule was that after you'd hit your opponent over the head with your cue you had to be able to run very fast. I understand from her ladyship that you might be requiring my assistance tonight?"

"Yes, please. We're going to the village of Hangnails. It's about twenty miles upriver."

Willikins nodded. "Yes indeed, sir, once the seat of the Hangnail family and most notably of Lord Justice Hangnail, who famously declared that he never took account of any plea of not guilty on the basis that 'criminals always lie' and was, by happy chance, the Worshipful Master of the Benevolent Company of Rope Makers and Braiders. With any luck, we'll not see his like again."

"Excellent, Willikins, and we'll stop en route to pick up our keen young local constable, who'll see fair play. I intend to make sure of that."

"Glad to hear it, sir," said Willikins, "but bear this in mind: what does it matter once the ball has dropped?"

I T WAS MRS. UPSHOT who opened the cottage door, gave a little scream, slammed the door, opened the door to apologize for slamming the door, and then shut the door carefully, leaving Vimes on the doorstep. Thirty seconds later Feeney opened the door, with his nightshirt tucked into his trousers. "Commander Vimes! Is something wrong?" he said, trying valiantly to tuck all the nightshirt inside.

Vimes rubbed his hands together briskly. "Yes, Chief Constable Upshot, almost everything is, but there is one part that can be made right with your help. Regarding the murder of the goblin girl, I have sufficient information to warrant apprehending two men for questioning. This is your manor, so professionally speaking I think it's only right and proper that you assist me with the arrests."

Vimes took a step into the room so that the face of Willikins was visible, and went on, "And I think you know Willikins, my manservant, who has volunteered to drive my coach and, of course, provide me with a clean white shirt should I need it."

"Yerrr," growled Willikins, turning to wink at Vimes.

"Chief Constable Upshot, I'd be obliged if you would arm yourself with whatever you think you might need and, since you don't have a pair of handcuffs worth a damn, oh I'm so sorry, then at least can you source some rope?"

The face of Feeney Upshot was a whole palette of conflicting emotions. I'll be working with the famous Commander Vimes—hooray! But this is big and serious—oh dear. But it'll be like being a real policeman—hooray! But there's already a hot water bottle in my bed—oh dear. On the other hand, if it all goes wrong, well, after all, the Duke of Ankh owns most of this place, so he'll have to take most of the blame—hooray! And maybe if I distinguish myself I can get a job in the city, so that my mum can live in a place where you don't lie awake at night listening to the mice fighting the cockroaches—hooray!*

---

* Regrettably, Constable Upshot was overly hopeful: in Ankh-Morpork the mice and the cockroaches had decided to forget their differences and gang up on the humans.

It was a treat for Vimes to watch the lad's face in the candle-light, especially as Feeney moved his lips as he thought. And so he said, "I'm sure, Chief Constable Upshot, that assistance in this matter will be very helpful to your future career."

This last comment caused Mrs. Upshot, peering over her son's shoulder, to flush with pride and say, "Hark at his grace, Feeney! You could make something of yourself, just like I'm always telling you! No arguing now, off you go, my lad."

This motherly advice was punctuated by Mrs. Upshot bobbing up and down so fast that she could have been harnessed to a sewing machine. Thank goodness for old mums, Vimes thought, as Feeney eventually got into the coach with a flask of hot tea, a spare pair of clean drawers and half an apple pie.

As the wheels started to turn, and after Feeney had finished waving to his old mum out of the window, Vimes, balancing care-fully against the rocking, lit the little spirit lamp that was all the coach had for illumination. He fell back into his seat again and said, "I'd be grateful, lad, if you would take some time to write down in your notebook everything I've said to you since I arrived this evening. It might be of assistance to both of us." Feeney practically saluted, and Vimes continued, "When we saw the dead goblin girl the other day, Mr. Feeney, did you make a note of that in your notebook?"

"Yes, sir!" Feeney nearly saluted again. "My granddad told me always to write everything down in my notebook!"

They bounced in their seats as the coach hit a stone and Vimes said quietly, "Did he ever tell you to accidentally sometimes turn over two pages at once so that you had the occasional blank page?"

"Oh, no, sir. Should I?"

The seat bounced them up and down again as Vimes said, "Strictly speaking, lad, the answer is no, especially if you never work with me. Now please write it all down, just as I asked. And since I am not as young as you, I'm going to try to get some rest."

"Yessir, I understand that, sir. Just one thing, sir? Mr. Stoner, the Clerk to the Magistrates, came to see me this afternoon, and had a chat and said not to bother about the goblin girl because goblins are officially vermin. He was very kind, and brought some brandy for my old mum, and he said that you were a fine gentleman but tended to get a bee in your bonnet, sir, what with being upper-class and out of touch, sir. Sir? Sir? Have you gone to sleep, sir?"

Vimes turned his head and in honeyed tones said, "Did you make a note of that in your notebook, lad?"

"Oh, yessir!"

"And you still got in this coach with me? Why did you do that, Mr. Feeney?"

Gravel rattled behind them and it seemed some time before Feeney Upshot had assembled his thoughts to his satisfaction. He said, "Well, Commander Vimes, I thought, well, that Mr. Stoner he's a nob more or less, and so is Commander Vimes, only he's a duke and is therefore a very big nob and if you're going to get caught between nobs, maybe you'd better pick the biggest one to be on the side of." He heard Vimes grunt, and continued, "And then, sir, I thought, well, I was up there, I saw that poor creature and what had been done to her, and I remembered that Stoner had tried to make a fool out of me by making me arrest your good self, sir, and I thought about the goblins and I thought, well, they're mucky and smelly and the old goblin was crying, and animals don't cry and goblins, well, they make stuff, beautiful stuff and as for pinching our pig swill and being generally mucky, we surely ain't short of humans around here who are pretty big in that respect, I could tell you some stories, and so I thought some more and I thought, well, that Mr. Stoner, I thought he must have got it wrong."

There was a rumbling as the coach went over a bridge and then the sound of wheels on packed flints was back. Feeney said anxiously, "Is that all right, sir?" He waited nervously. And then the voice of Vimes, and this time sounding rather far away said, "Do you know what that little speech you made was called, Mr. Feeney?"

"Don't know, sir, it's just what I think."

"It was called redemption, Mr. Feeney. Hold on to it."

V IMES WOKE FROM A doze in which he had dreamed about Young Sam playing a harp, and by the time he had understood that this was a dream the noise of the coach wheels had changed as they slowed down and stopped.

Willikins slid open the small slot that allowed discourse between passenger and coachman and said quietly, "Rise and shine, sir, we're about a quarter of a mile from Hangnails, population thirty-seven and still stupid. And you can smell turkey from here and wish you bloody well couldn't, excuse my Klatchian. I surmised that it might be a good idea to walk quietly the rest of the way, sir."

Vimes got down from the coach and stamped the cramp out of his limbs. The air stank with the curiously invasive smell of birds; not even goblins persecuted the sinuses one half so badly. But this was a tiny distraction compared with the thrill, yes, the thrill. How long was it since he had led a dawn raid? Far too long, that's how long, and now captains and senior sergeants got the job while he stayed in the office, *being* the Ankh-Morpork City Watch. Well, not today.

Whispering as they walked through the knee-high mist, he said, "You, Chief Constable Upshot, you will hammer on the front door when I give you the signal, and I will be stationed outside the back door in case the gentleman does a runner, okay?"

They were nearing the property now, yes, they would just need the two of them. The farmhouse looked barely big enough to have two doors, let alone three.

"What shall I say, commander?" hissed Feeney.

"Oh, blimey, you're the bloody son and grandson of coppers, my lad, what the hell do you think you should shout? Let me give you a clue. It does not include the word 'please.' I'll give you a whistle when I'm in position, got it? Good."

They walked with care across the stinking yard and Vimes took up station around the back, where an interesting thought occurred to him and he made a mental note. He then leaned against the dirty wall of the house a little bit away from the back door, took a pinch of snuff to clear the air of turkey and gave one faint whistle.

"Open up in the name of the law! You are surrounded! You have one minute to open the door! I mean it! Open the door! This is the police!"

Leaning cosily against the wall, Vimes grudgingly rated that as pretty good for a beginner, with one point taken off for adding "I mean it," then, as a man flew out of the back door, he stuck out his boot.

"Good morning, sir. My name is Commander Vimes! I hope you're in a position to remember yours!"

In the sheds the turkeys were going insane, causing a slight rise in the smell. The man struggled to his feet, looking around desperately.

"Oh, yes, you could run, yes, you could do that," said Vimes in a conversational tone of voice, "but it might be thought by others that this might indicate that you knew you had some reason to run. Now, personally, I would agree that anyone stopped by a copper should run like buggery, innocent or not, on first principles. Besides, we get so fat these days that we need the exercise. But do run if you want to, Mr. Flutter, because I can run too, and *very* fast."

By now Flutter was smiling the smile of a man who thinks that this copper is not very smart.

"I bet you don't have a magistrate's warrant, do ya'?"

"Well now, Mr. Flutter, why might you think that, eh? Perhaps you think the magistrates might not issue a warrant to arrest you, yes? By the way, thank you for showing me where the tobacco barrels are stored. Your cooperation will be taken into consideration."

Some days are bad days, like when you stare right down into the mangled corpse of a young woman, and then you get good days, when the suspect's darting eyes flashing across the yard show you exactly where the loot is hidden.

"I shall, of course, mention your cooperation to the authorities and, of course, in the local pub as well, ah, yes."

And now Mr. Flutter was relishing the thought of being seen as some kind of grass, so stupidly he went for, "I never told you anything about any tobacco, and you know it, copper!"

At this point Feeney stepped around the corner with his fearsome club raised and a look of almost comical aggression on his face. "You want me to give him the old one-two, commander, just say the word, guv!"

Vimes rolled his eyes in mock despair. "No need for that, Feeney, no need for that, just when Mr. Flutter here is so anxious to talk to us, understand?"

Flutter decided that the way forward was an appeal to Feeney. "Look, Feeney, you know me—"

He got that far and no further because Feeney said, "It's Constable Upshot to you, Flutter. My dad had you up before the beaks two dozen times, you know. He used to call you the bluebottle on account of whenever there was a load of shit going down he'd find you flapping about in it. And he told me to watch you, which is what I am doing right now, in fact." He glanced at Vimes, who gave him an encouraging nod and then said, "You see my problem, Mr. Flutter, we're not here to talk about contraband tobacco, okay? Now, I never saw myself as a revenuer, not a popular profession. I'm a copper pure and simple, right, and in my hand I have this man what is only doing a favor to his employer by storing a few barrels of tobacco in his shed, but on the *other* hand, well, if I found a murderer in the other hand, why, gods bless you, I might totally forget all about the first hand . . . Don't ask me to draw you a picture, Flutter, because my hands are full."

Flutter looked aghast. "This is about that goblin, right? Look, it wasn't me! Okay, I'm a bit of a naughty boy, I put my hand up to that, but I ain't like him! I'm a scallywag, not a damn murderer!"

Vimes looked at Feeney. Some people could be said to be as pleased as punch. Feeney could be said to look as pleased as Punch, Judy, the dog Toby, the crocodile and, above all, the policeman, all rolled in together. Vimes raised his eyebrows in new interrogation, and Feeney said, "I believe him, chief. He hasn't got it in him, I swear. The best he could manage would be knocking over an old lady for her purse, and even then she'd probably have to be blind too."

"There, you see!" said Flutter triumphantly. "I'm not really a *bad* person!"

"No," said Vimes, "you're a veritable choirboy, Mr. Flutter, I can see that, and I'm rather religious too, and I like chapter and verse, but are you willing to swear that the individual known as Stratford knifed a goblin girl to death on Hangman's Hill in the grounds of Ramkin Hall, three nights ago?"

Flutter raised a finger. "Can I say that I told him to stop, and he laughed, and I didn't know it was a girl neither—I mean, how can you tell?"

Vimes's face was deadpan. "Tell me, Ted, what would you have done if you *had* known? I'm intrigued."

Flutter looked down at his feet. "Well, I, well, well, I mean . . . not a girl, I mean . . . well, not a girl . . . I mean, that's not right, know what I mean?"

And you can find someone like this dangerous clown in nearly every neighborhood, Vimes thought. "Clearly chivalry is not dead, Mr. Flutter. Okay, Feeney, let's carry on. Mr. Flutter, why were you on Hangman's Hill on the aforesaid night?"

"We were just having a walk," said Flutter.

Vimes's face was again deadpan, so deadpan as to be mortified. "Of course you were, Mr. Flutter. Silly of me to ask the question, really. Constable Upshot, I can see Willikins over there having a smoke." He pushed at the open door and dragged Flutter inside. "Does this building have a cellar?"

Flutter was one step away from a toilet break, but nevertheless, being the kind of fool to dig himself in deeper, managed to sneer, "There might be. So what?"

"Mr. Flutter, I have already told you that I'm a religious man, and since you would test the patience of a saint I need to spend a moment in quiet contemplation, understand? I'm sure you know that there's always an easy way, and then again, there's always the hard way. Currently, this is the easy way, but the hard way is also quite easy, in a manner of speaking. Before talking to you again I want to be alone with my thoughts. And it occurs to me, Mr. Flutter, that you might have some thoughts about, as it were, legging it, and so my colleague, Chief Constable Upshot, will guard the door and I shall send in my batman, Mr. Willikins, to keep you company."

Before Vimes was even able to tap on the window, the door opened and Willikins, immaculate as ever, stepped into the grubby room, all smart and crisp with shiny shoes and a hint of pomade on his hair. The three men then watched Vimes heave at a likely ring on the floor, which pulled back to reveal the trap door to a dark cellar and a ladder going down.

Vimes said, "Constable Upshot, I need a little time to think in the darkness. I won't be long." He went down the ladder and pulled the trap door closed behind him.

The darkness said, "Ah, commander, at long last. I suspect that you're here to take a witness statement."

This is wrong, Vimes told himself. How can you take testimony from a demon, especially when it's one of no fixed abode? But on the other hand, who needs a witness statement if you've got a confession?

Up above, Ted Flutter's eyes rolled this way and that as he analyzed the situation. Let's see: we have one young twit who is playing at being a copper, and a snooty butler type, all pink and shiny. I reckon Mrs. Flutter's little boy is out of here. At this point, at this *very* point, Willikins, without looking at Flutter, reached into his jacket and there was a slap as he laid down on the table in front of him a steel comb. It gleamed. And it gleamed even stronger in Flutter's imagination. He took one look at Willikins' expression, and Mrs. Flutter's little boy decided he would sit very still until that nice Commander Vimes came back. Out of another pocket Willikins produced the sharpest-looking knife Flutter had ever seen and, without paying any attention whatsoever to Flutter, began to clean his fingernails.

In fact it was only a matter of seconds before the trap door was heaved back, and Vimes emerged, then nodded to Willikins, who secured the comb and walked out of the room without a word. Vimes regained the chair. "Mr. Flutter, I have a witness statement that puts you on Hangman's Hill on the night in question with another man, said man being known as Stratford. The witness tells me that you said to him that you could have got hold of some turkey blood, but he said that there were rabbits all over the place and he never missed with his slingshot. At this point the witness says a young goblin girl came out of the bushes and your companion struck at her as she was begging for her life—and furiously, to the extent that you yourself told him, in your words, to leave off, upon which he turned on you, still holding his knife, described to me as a machete, so swiftly that you urinated into your boots.

"No, don't speak, I haven't finished. Nevertheless, I am informed that you did say to your companion that you were supposed to leave just blood, and not, as you put it, 'guts all over the place,' whereupon he forced you to put them back into the cadaver and hide it further down the hill in some gorse bushes. No, I said don't talk! In your pocket you had a pork pie, which you'd brought from home, and three dollars in cash, which was your payment for this little errand.

"After that you and Stratford walked back some distance to your horses, which you had temporarily stabled in the tumbledown old barn on the other side of the village. The horses were a chestnut mare and a gray gelding, both of them broken down by ill use. In fact, the gelding threw a shoe as you were leaving, and you had to stop your companion from killing it there and then. Oh, and the witness told me that you were naked to the waist when you left, since your shirt was soaked with blood and you left it in the barn after an argument with Stratford. I'll recover it when we get back. Your friend told you to take your trousers off as well, but you declined; however, I noted splashes of blood on them earlier. I don't want to go to the expense of sending a rider back to the city, where my Igor will ascertain whether the blood is human, goblin or turkey. I said don't speak, didn't I? I haven't mentioned some of the other conversation between you and Mr. Stratford, because Feeney here is listening, and you should be relieved about that; gossip can be so cruel.

"And now Mr. Flutter, I'm going to stop talking and upon doing so I would like the first words you utter to be—pay attention—'I want to turn King's evidence.' Yes, I know we don't have kings anymore, but nobody has amended the law. You are a little shit, but I'm reluctantly persuaded that you were dragged into something beyond your control and worse than you could have imagined. The good news is that Lord Vetinari will almost certainly take my advice and you will live. Remember: 'I want to turn King's evidence,' that's what I want to hear, Mr. Flutter, otherwise I'll go for a walk and Mr. Willikins will comb his hair."

Flutter, who had listened to most of this with his eyes shut, blurted out the words so fast that Vimes had to ask him to repeat them more slowly. When he had finished he was allowed to go to the privy, with Willikins waiting outside, cleaning his nails with his knife, and Feeney was sent to feed the frantic turkeys.

For his part, Vimes entered one of the stinking sheds and prodded around in the dirty straw for what he knew would be there. He was not disappointed. Sufficiently close to, the smell of tobacco was just discernible above the stifling stink of turkey. He rolled a barrel out, found Feeney and said, "I think this is full of tobacco and so I'm intending to take it as evidence. Your job right now is to scout out a jemmy for me and somebody known to you as a decent upstanding citizen, insofar as there might be one around this place."

"Well, there's Dave who runs the Dog and Badger," Feeney volunteered.

"And he is an upstanding citizen?" said Vimes.

"I have seen him sitting down," said Feeney, "but he knows the score, if you get my meaning."

Vimes nodded and waited a few minutes before Feeney returned with a crowbar, a bandy-legged man and a small tail of people who, for the moment, until proved otherwise, had to be counted as "innocent bystanders."

They gathered around as Vimes prepared to open the barrel. He announced, "Pay attention, gentlemen. I believe this barrel contains contraband goods." He rolled up his sleeves—"You see that I have nothing up my sleeves, but a crowbar in my hand"—and with some effort on his part the lid of the barrel came off, and the smell of tobacco was overpowering. And some of the bystanders decided it was now time to take the wonderful opportunity for a quick nonchalant walk.

Vimes pulled out bale after bale of brown leaves bound with cotton. "Can't take too much on the coach," he said, "but if Mr. Dave here will, as an upstanding member of the community, sign to say that he saw me pull these from a sealed barrel, then you, Mr. Feeney, will take a brief statement and we can all go about our business."

Feeney beamed. "Oh, very well spotted, commander! I reckon you could hide anything in this stink, eh?" After a moment he looked at Vimes and said, "Commander?"

Vimes appeared to look through him and said, "You're going to go far, Chief Constable Upshot. Let's empty the whole barrel, shall we?"

He didn't know where the thought had come from. Maybe from first principles. If you were going to smuggle, where would you stop? What would your market be? How would you get the best price per pound of product carried? He pulled and pulled at the bundles, and one, almost at the bottom of the barrel, was noticeably heavier than the others. Trying to keep his expression unchanged, he handed the heavy bundle to Feeney and said, "I'd be grateful if you and Mr. Dave would open this bundle and tell me what you see inside." He sat down on the barrel and took a pinch of snuff while behind him he heard the rustling, and then Feeney said, "Well, commander, what this appears to be—"

Vimes held up a hand. "Does it look like stone dust to you, Feeney?"

"Yes, but—"

Vimes held up his hand again. "Does it appear to have little red and blue flecks in it when you hold it to the light?"

Sometimes the ancestral copper in Feeney picked up the vibration. "Yes, Commander Vimes!"

"Then it's a good job for you and your friend Dave"—Vimes glanced at the said Dave for the second time and decided to give him the benefit of the doubt—"that the two of you are not trolls, because if you were you'd be stone dead, as it were, right now. The stuff you are holding is *Crystal Slam*, I'd bet my badge on it. Troll kids use it as a drug, do you know that? They take a hit as small as your little pinky and think they can walk through walls, which they invariably do, too, and when they've done it a few times more they drop down dead. It's illegal everywhere in the world, and very difficult to make because the smell when they're boiling it up is unmistakable; you get a lot of sparks too. Selling it is a hanging offense in Ankh-Morpork, Uberwald and every troll city. Diamond King of Trolls gives a very handsome bounty to anyone who presents him with evidence of manufacture."

Vimes looked hopefully at the aforesaid Dave, just in case the man would take the bait. No, he thought, they wouldn't do it round here. All this tobacco must come from somewhere hot, and that means a long way away.

Gingerly, they broke open other barrels and found plenty of tobacco and several packs of very high-class cigars, one or two of which Vimes put in his breast pocket for detailed forensic examination later, and, somewhere at the bottom of every barrel, there were neat packets of Crystal Slam, Slunkie, Slab, Slice and Slap, all of them very nasty—although Slap was generally considered to be a recreational drug, at least if your idea of recreation was waking up in the gutter not knowing whose head you had on.

As many samples as possible were piled into the coach and Vimes only stopped when it started to creak. The other barrels were piled up and, at Vimes's instigation, a very proud Chief Constable Upshot set fire to them. When the controlled drugs caught alight there was a brief display of pyrotechnics and Vimes thought to himself that this was only the start of the fireworks.

As people came running out to see what was happening, Vimes reassured them of his bonafides and explained that Mr. Flutter would be away for a while, and could somebody please look after the birds. The responses he got made it clear that the neighborhood considered a world without Mr. Flutter and his stinking turkeys would be a much better world, so the last thing that Vimes did was to open the sheds and let the wretched creatures take their chances.

As a last little bright idea, Vimes beckoned to the nervous Dave and said, "Diamond King of Trolls will be very appreciative of this day's work. Of course, as serving officers we wouldn't be able to take any remuneration . . ."

"We wouldn't?" said Feeney hopelessly.

Vimes ignored this and continued, "I will, however, see to it that your help today is suitably rewarded." The publican's face lit up. Something about the words diamond and rewarded in the same sentence does that to a face.

THEY TRAVELED WITH THE creaking coach doors locked, but with a window slightly open because Mr. Flutter was currently not somebody you would wish to be in any confined space with: he appeared to be sweating turkeys.

King's evidence! That was a result! Flutter hadn't thought about arguing, and Vimes had seen his expression as the Summoning Dark's statement was presented to him. Vimes had noticed every wince and shiver of recollection that, taken together, added up to rights well banged. King's evidence! Any man would opt for that to save his skin, or maybe for a better class of cell. You took King's evidence to save your miserable hide and it might indeed do so, but at a price, and that price was death by hanging if you lied. It was one of the absolutes: lying when you had turned King's evidence was the lie of lies. You had lied to the judge, you had lied to the King, you had lied to society, you had lied to the world, and thus the cheerful Mr. Trooper would welcome you to the gallows, and shake your hand to show you there were no hard feelings, and shortly afterward would pull the lever that would drop you from the world you had betrayed, and stop . . . halfway down.

And then, of course, there were the troll drugs. The evidence of their existence worried Flutter so much that he invented new gods to swear to that he knew nothing about them. Vimes believed him. As far as Flutter was concerned, the barrels contained nothing more than tobacco. Good old tobacco, nothing harmful about tobacco, and smuggling it was, well, it really was like a game, everybody knew that. Nothing wrong with outsmarting the revenue, that was what the revenue was *for*! Vimes thought, isn't that how I've always said it worked? Little crimes breeding big crimes. You smile at little crimes and then big crimes blow your head off.

Flutter was sitting miserably on the opposite seat, possibly fearing being kicked to death by trolls, but then, as Vimes had noted, Flutter probably feared everybody. And so Vimes found it in his heart to offer him not so much a crumb as a bacon sandwich of good news. "You were in the company of a violent man, Ted. You thought you were just going to make life difficult for a copper, and suddenly you were an accessory of the first part to murder and, even if unwittingly, tangled up in extremely serious troll narcotics, the worst there is. But you've got into bad company, Ted, and I will say so in court."

Hope appeared in Flutter's red-rimmed eyes, and he said, "That's very kind of you, sir." That was it. No swagger, no whining, just gratitude for mercies received and fervently hoped for.

Vimes leaned forward and offered the bewildered man his snuffbox. Flutter took a large pinch and sniffed it up so hard that the inevitable sneeze tried to escape via his ears. Ignoring this, and the faint haze of brown in the air, Vimes leaned back and said cheerfully, "I'll have a word with the screws in the Tanty, they always owe me anyway . . ." Vimes looked at the hopeful face and thought, Blast it. I know they're pretty crowded right now. A squirt like him would be on a hiding to nothing, whatever I do. Oh well. He carried on, "No, Mr. Flutter, tell you what I'll do, at least we'll put you in a cell in Pseudopolis Yard. How about that? It can be lonely in a cell all by yourself, but some might consider that a blessing, especially after fifteen minutes in some parts of the Tanty and, besides, my lads are fairly chatty when there's not much happening. We also have a better class of rat, the straw is fresh and we don't gob in your stirabout, and if you're helpful and don't keep people awake at night, then you'll be as right as rain."

"You won't have any trouble from me, commander!" The words came tumbling, frantic to be heard and terrified that they might not.

"Glad to hear it, Ted," said Vimes jovially. "I like a man who makes the right choices! Incidentally, Ted, who suggested you play the little trick on the hill?"

"Honestly, sir, it *was* Stratford, sir. He said it would be a little joke. And I know what you're going to ask me next, sir, and I asked him who was behind all this, because it worried me a bit, seeing as I mostly just breed turkeys and roll barrels around, you understand?" Flutter assumed the expression of a simple, honest working man. "He said that if he told me he'd have to kill me, and I said to him, I said, 'Thank you all the same, Mr. Stratford, but I won't put you to the trouble' and kept my mouth shut, 'cos he had a funny look in his eye." Flutter seemed to think for a moment and added, "He *always* has a funny look in his eye."

Vimes tried to pretend that this was of little interest. Like a man with a butterfly net, a killing jar and a passion to pin to a cork board the last of the very rare Lancre blue butterflies, that has just taken its repose on a thistle nearby, he tried to do nothing to make his quarry take flight.

In an offhand way he said, "But you do know, don't you, Ted? I mean, you're smart, Ted, underneath it all. A lot of people would say that two planks are smarter than you, but frankly you can't make a success of things in this old world without keeping your eyes open and your ears too, right?"

But of course, who would tell anything important to a twerp like Flutter? He wasn't even a henchman—you needed a certain amount of tactical thinking before you could properly hench—but henchmen hang about, and when they're with someone as thick as Flutter they don't always guard their tongues.

Aloud he said, "It's a shame really, Ted, you being the only one to get banged up for all this, seeing that all you really did was help out a mate for a couple of dollars and a pint, don't you think?

Terrible, ain't it, that decent folk have to take the rap, yes? Especially when it's a big rap." He stopped talking and watched Flutter's face.

"Weeeell," said Flutter, "one day when he was a bit excited he did say to me that Lord Rust depended on him, took him into his confidence and everything and made sure his pockets always jingled, but I reckoned that was nothing but boasting."

Vimes was impressed at his own patience and said, "Look, Ted, did you ever hear either of them talk about the goblin girl?"

A horrible grin suffused the man's face. "I could if you want me to, commander!"

Vimes stared at Flutter for a moment and said, "Ted, I want to know things that you have either seen or heard. Not things you may have imagined and, and this is the important bit, Ted, not things made up to please me, right? Otherwise I won't any longer be your friend . . ." Vimes stopped to think for a moment. "Did you ever hear Lord Rust or Stratford say anything about the blacksmith?"

It was an education watching the prisoner rack his brains. He looked like a big dog chewing a toffee. Apparently he found something because his next words were, "The blacksmith? I didn't know that it was about the blacksmith. Yeah, when we were stacking in the yard young Lord Rust came up to Stratford and said something like, 'Any news about our friend?' and, well, Stratford said, 'Don't you worry sir, he's going to see the Queen,' and they both laughed, sir." In the silence he said, "Are you all right, sir?"

Vimes ignored this and said, "Have you any idea what he meant?"

"Nosir," said Flutter.

"Is there anything called the Queen around here? Maybe a public house, perhaps? Maybe a riverboat?" Vimes thought, Yes, they all have strange names, there has to be a Queen among them.

Once again the dog chewed the toffee. "Sorry, commander, I don't really know anything about that. No boat on the river called the Queen."

Vimes left it at that. It was a result. Not the best result. Nothing that would satisfy Vetinari, but a hint at least of a minor conspiracy to send Jethro to somewhere he did not want to be. Vimes at least had to be satisfied.

Vimes realized that Flutter was holding up his hand cautiously, like a child half-fearful of a reprimand from the teacher.

"Yes, Ted?" he said wearily.

The man lowered his hand. "Will I be able to find a god, sir?"

"What? Find what god?"

Flutter looked embarrassed but recovered manfully. "Well, sir, I'm hearing about people who go into prison and find a god, sir, and if you find a god then you get better treatment and maybe you get let out sooner, on account of praying, and I was wondering if I was in the Watch House that there might be more or less chance of god availability, if you get my drift. I don't want to be a trouble, of course."

"Well, Ted, if there was any justice in the universe I think there would be quite a few gods in the Tanty, but if I were you and faced a choice between the possibility of heavenly intervention, and a definite three meals a day that haven't been spat on and no big blokes snoring in your ear all night and the certain knowledge that if you have to go down on your knees then it will only be to pray, then I would say heaven can wait."

The sun was already well up now and Willikins was keeping them moving at a good pace. Vimes took notice of that fact. The Street was talking to him even if it was in fact nothing more than a wide lane. He nudged Feeney awake. "Soon be home now, lad, and I think Mr. Flutter can be housed in your lovely lockup, don't you?"

Flutter looked puzzled, and Vimes said, "Good grief, man. Surely you didn't think I could rush you all the way to Ankh-Morpork in one go? As it is I'll have to send someone to get some-one else to come all the way down here with the hurry-up wagon! Don't worry, the lockup is strong and cozy and made of stone, plus—and I'm led to believe that this is indeed a big plus, this—Mrs. Upshot will probably make you a delicious Bang Suck Muck Muck Dog, with carrots and garden peas. Speciality de Maison-ette."

RANK HAS ITS PRIVILEGES, Vimes thought, when he alighted near the old lockup a little later. "Chief Constable Upshot, please settle our prisoner down, see that he gets fed and watered and so on and so forth, okay, and, obviously, do the paperwork."

"The what, sir?"

Vimes blinked. "Is it possible, Mr. Feeney, that you don't know what paperwork is?"

Feeney was perplexed. "Well, yes, sir, of course, but gener-ally I just jot down the name in my notebook, sir. I mean, I know who he is, and I know where he is and what he's done. Oh, yes, and since the trouble we had with old Mr. Parsley, after he had a skinful, I also make certain to check if the prisoner is allergic to anything in Bhangbhangduc cuisine. It took me all day to clean out the place, on account of there'd been a tiny bit of winky." Seeing Vimes's expression, he went on, "Very popular herb, sir."

"*Habeas corpus*, lad! You want to be the copper here, right? Then Mr. Flutter is *your* prisoner! You are responsible for him. If he gets ill, then he is *your* problem, if he dies then he is *your* corpse, and if he gets out and away then you would find yourself in a situ-ation so problematical that the word 'problem' just would not fit the situation. I'm trying to be helpful, honestly, but I could just as easily take him up to the Hall. We've got loads of cellars and we could easily bed him down in one of them, no problem. But then if I have to do that, what good are you?"

Feeney looked shocked. He pulled himself upright. "I wouldn't hear of that, sir, and neither would my ancestors, sir. After all, we've never had anyone who has even been near a murder."

"Very well, then, give me a receipt for the prisoner, which is a very important thing, and I'll go back to the Hall to have a nap."

Vimes stepped back as a riverboat came into view and a very small tidal wave of muddy water splashed gently on the little quayside. The boat was another one with paddle wheels; Sybil had explained all about them. An ox patiently trod its way around a treadmill in the bilges and wonderful gearing caused the paddle wheels to turn.

The pilot of this one waved at him. As it went past he saw a woman in the stern, hanging out clothing, watched by a cat. A good life, at the speed of an ox, he thought, where probably no one is ever going to try to kill you. And, just for a moment, he felt jealous, while a line of barges followed the boat past a flotilla of ducklings. Vimes sighed, got back in the coach, was driven to the Hall by Willikins and, after a very brief shower, sank into the pillows and descended into darkness.

P EOPLE SAID THAT THESE days Ankh-Morpork was moving. Others said that while this might be true, so was a sufficiently aged cheese. And, like the hypothetical cheese, it was bursting out of its mold, in this case the outermost walls, which were, in the words of Lord Vetinari, "a corset that should be unlaced." One of the first to let themselves spread had been Harry King, now,

of course, known as Sir Harold King. He was a scallywag, a chan-
cer, a ruthless fighter and a dangerous driver of bargains over the
speed limit. Since all this was a bit of a mouthful, he was referred
to as a successful businessman, since that more or less amounted
to the same thing. And he had the knack of turning rubbish into
money. As Captains Carrot and Angua walked along the tow path
toward the reedy swamps downriver, Harry King's flame burned
ahead of them. All was grist to the mills of the King of Muck. His
armies of workers swept the streets, emptied the cesspits, cleaned
the chimneys, scoured the middens of the slaughterhouse district
and carried away from those selfsame houses all those bits of previ-
ously living matter that could not, for the love of decency, be put
in a sausage. They said that Harry King would suck the smoke out
of the air if he thought he could get a good price for it. And if you
wanted a job, Harry King would give you one, at a wage not very
much less than you might get elsewhere in the city, and if you stole
from Harry King you would get what you deserved. The mills
of Harry King stank, of course, but now the city itself did not, at
least not as badly as it used to, and some people were complaining
about the loss of the famous Ankh-Morpork smell, rumored to be
so strong that it kept away illnesses and ailments of all sorts and,
moreover, put hairs on your chest and did you good.

Ankh-Morpork being what it was, there was already a Smell
Preservation Society.

The two watchmen began to breathe less deeply as they approached the smoke and fumes. A small city surrounded the workings, a shanty town knocked together with Harry's blessing by the
workers themselves because, after all, that meant they wouldn't be
late for work.

The security officer at the gate opened it instantly as they
approached. Harry was probably not honest, but if there was

dishonesty it happened at times and places that did not concern the Watch, and faded from the memory of all concerned just as soon as the ripples of the splash had died away and the tide had gone out.

Also going out as Carrot and Angua climbed the outside steps to the large office where Harry presided over his kingdom was a man, moving horizontally at speed, with Harry King's big hands grasping him by his collar and the seat of his pants and finally throwing him down the steps, accompanied by a shout, "You're fired!" The watchmen stood aside as the man rolled down from step to step. "And if I see you again, the dogs is always hungry! Oh, hello, Captain Carrot," said Harry, his voice suddenly all matey, "and the charming Miss Angua too. My word, what a lovely surprise, do come in, always a pleasure to be of assistance to the Watch!"

"Sir Harry, you really shouldn't throw people down the steps like that," said Carrot.

Harry King looked innocent and spread his huge hands widely, and said, "What? Are those bloody steps still there? I gave orders to have them taken away! Thank you for the advice, captain, but the way I see it is that I caught him trying to steal my money and so if he's still alive then on the whole I reckon we're square. Coffee? Tea? Something stronger? No, I thought not, but take a seat, no harm in that, at least."

They sat down and Carrot said, "We need to talk about goblins."

Harry King looked blank, but said, "Got a few of them working for me, if that's any help. Decent workers, you might be surprised to know. A bit weird in their ways, not the fastest, but once they've got the hang of what you want them to do you can just leave them to it until you tell them to stop. I pay them half what I pay humans and I reckon they do twice as much work, and do it better. Be happy to hire another hundred if they turned up."

"But you pay them far less than humans?" said Angua.

Harry gave her a pitying look. "And who else would pay them anything at all, love? Well, business is business. It's not like I chain them down. Okay, not many people would want to employ goblins on account of the stink, but I know by the wrinkling of your pretty nose, captain, that I stink too. It goes with the job. Besides, I let them stay on my land and they make those weird little pots in their spare time, and I see to it they don't have much of that, and when they have enough money for whatever they want, they bugger off back to where they came from. Young Slick and his granny are the only ones that's ever stayed. Gonna make a name for himself, that one."

"We'd like to talk to some of the goblins about the pots you mentioned, if that's okay by you, Harry?" said Carrot.

Harry King smiled and waggled a finger at him. "Now, I'll take that from you two, because we've all seen a bit of the world and know what's what, but outside this office it's *Sir* Harry, okay? Personally, I ain't all that bothered, but her ladyship is a stickler, oh my word, yes! Nose so high in the air it brings down sparrows, I'm telling you! Still, I can't say it does any harm." Harry King, or possibly Sir Harold King, thought for a moment. "Out of interest, why do you want to talk about goblin pots?"

Angua hesitated, but Carrot said, "We are both very interested in goblin folklore, Sir Harry."

Harry King chuckled. "You know, I never could read your face, Captain Carrot. I'd hate to play poker with you! Okay, it's not my business, I'll take you at your word. Just you go down the steps and make your way to the sorting belts and find Billy Slick, and tell him that Harry King would deem it a favor if he would be so good as to take you to see his old granny, okay? No need to thank me, I suspect old Vimes put in a good word about me to Vetinari when the medals was being given out, if you know what I mean. They say one hand washes the other, but I bet that when it came to old Harry King it had to scrub."

T HEY FOUND BILLY SLICK stacking old copies of the *Ankh-Morpork Times* onto a truck. You could always recognize a goblin, although this one, in his grubby overall, looked like any other working man in the place. The only difference was that he was a *goblin* working man.

Carrot tapped him gently on the shoulder and Billy looked round. "Oh, coppers."

"We've come from Harry King, Billy," said Carrot, adding quickly, "You've done nothing wrong. We just want to learn about unggue pots."

"*You* want to learn about unggue?" Billy stared at Carrot. "I know I ain't done nothing wrong, guv, and I don't need you to do the telling of me and I wouldn't touch any of those bloody pots to save my life. I'm working my way up, I am. Can't be bothered with fairy stories."

Angua stepped forward and said, "Mr. Slick, this is quite important. We need to find someone who can tell us about unggue pots. Do you know anyone who can help?"

Billy looked her up and down superciliously. "You're a werewolf, ain't ya? Can smell you a mile off. And what would you do if I said I didn't know anybody?"

"Then," said Carrot, "we would regrettably have to go about our business."

Billy looked sideways at him. "Would that be the business of giving me a good kicking?"

The morning sun shone on Carrot's enthusiastically polished breastplate. "No, Mr. Slick, it would not."

Billy looked him up and down. "Well, there's my granny. Maybe she'll talk to you, maybe she won't. I'm only telling you that much because of Mr. King. She's right careful about who she talks to, you may bet your helmet on that. What do you want to talk about pots for, anyway? She hardly gets out of bed these days. Can't see her doing a robbery!"

"Nor do we, Billy, we just want some information about the pots."

"Well, you've come to the right lady, she's an expert, so I reckon, always fussing about the bloody things. Got a bottle of brandy on you? She's not one for strangers, my granny, but I reckon that anyone with a bottle of brandy is no stranger to Granny as long as the drink holds out."

Angua whispered to Carrot, "Harry's got a huge drinks cabinet in his office, and it's not like this is bribery. Worth a try?"

She waited with Billy Slick while Carrot went on the errand, and for something to say, she said, "Billy Slick doesn't sound much like a goblin name?"

Billy made a face. "Too right! Granny calls me Of the Wind Regretfully Blown. What kind of name is that, I ask you? Who's going to take you seriously with a name like that? This is modern times, right?" He looked at her defiantly, and she thought: and so one at a time we all become human—human werewolves, human dwarfs, human trolls . . . the melting pot melts in one direction only, and so we make progress. Aloud, she said, "Aren't you proud of your goblin name?"

He looked at her with his mouth open, showing his pointy teeth. "What? Proud? Why the fruckle should *anyone* be *proud* of being a *goblin*? Except my granny, of course. Come along inside, and I surely hope that the brandy arrives quickly. She can be fretful without the brandy."

Billy Slick and his granny lived in a building of sorts in the shanty town. Willow and other saplings had been liberated from the damp swamps and used to make a reasonably large hemisphere, the size of a small cottage. It seemed to Angua that some skill and thought had gone into the construction: smaller twigs and branches had been interwoven with the structure and some had, as is the way with willow, rooted themselves and sprouted, and then somebody, presumably Billy Slick, had further interwoven the new growth so that, in the summertime at least, it was a pretty good gaff, especially since somebody had meticulously filled most of the gaps with smaller weaves. Inside, it was a smoky cave, but the dark-accustomed eye of the werewolf saw that the inner walls had been lined very carefully with old tarpaulin and any other rubbish that could be persuaded to bend, to keep away drafts. Okay, it had probably taken less than two days to build and cost nothing, but the city was full of people who would have been overjoyed to live there.

"Sorry about this," said Billy. "I can't say that Harry is a big payer, but he turns a blind eye to us snaffling the occasional bits and pieces if we don't get cheeky about it."

"But you've even got a stove pipe!" said Angua, astonished.

Billy looked down. "Leaks a bit; waiting for me to solder a few patches on, that's all. Wait here, I'll just make sure she's ready for you. I know she'll be ready for the brandy."

There was a polite knock on the door which turned out to be courtesy of Captain Carrot who was on his way back with the brandy. He carefully opened the battered and many-times-painted outside door and let in some light. Then he looked around and said, "*Very* cozy!"

Angua tapped her foot. "Look, he's even jigsawed broken bits of roof tile together to make a decent floor cover. There's some thoughtful construction going on here." She lowered her voice and whispered, "And he's a goblin. It's not what I'd expected—"

"Got bloody good hearing as well, miss," said Billy, re-entering the room. "Amazing, innit, what tricks us goblins can learn. Cor, you'd almost think we were people!" He pointed toward a hanging of some sort of felt that obscured the other end of the room. "Got the brandy wine? Off we go, then. Hold the bottle out in front of you, that usually does the trick. Officers, the lady ain't my granny as such, she's my great-granny, but that was too much of a mouthful for me when I was a little kid, so Granny she became. Let me do the talking, 'cos unless you are a bloody genius, you won't understand a blind word she says! Come on in, quickly, I've got to go and make her lunch in half an hour, and, like I said, you've probably got until the drink runs out."

"I can't see a thing," said Carrot, as the felt somberly swung back behind them, and Angua said, carefully, "I can. Would you be so good as to introduce us to your great-grandmother, Billy?"

Carrot still fought for any kind of vision but heard what he thought was the goblin boy speaking, although it sounded as if he was chewing gravel at the same time. Then, after a sense of movement in the darkness, another voice, cracking like ice, answered him. Then Billy quite clearly said, "Regret of the Falling Leaf welcomes you, watchmen, and bids you give her the bloody brandy right now."

Carrot held the bottle out in the direction of Billy's voice, and it was swiftly passed on to the shape beginning to form in front of him as sight trickled back. The shape apparently said, according to Billy, "Why you come to me, po-leess-man? Why you need help from dying lady? What is unggue to you, Mr. Po-leess-man?

Unggue is ours, ours! No good for you here, big Mr. po-leess-man!"

"What is unggue, madam?" said Carrot.

"No religion, no ringing bellsey, no knees all bendey, no chorus, no hallelujah, no by your leave, just unggue, *pure* unggue! Just unggue, who come when need. Little unggue! When gods wash hands and turn away there is unggue who roll up the sleeves! Unggue strikes in the dark. If unggue don't come himself, he send. Unggue is everywhere!"

Carrot cleared his throat. "Regret of the Falling Leaf, we have a man, a policeman, a good man, who is dying of unggue. We don't understand; please help us understand. In his hand he is holding an unggue pot."

The screech must have echoed around the works; it certainly made the little shack rock. "Unggue thief! Pot stealer! Not fit to live!" Billy translated with every sign of embarrassment. The old goblin woman tried to stand up and sank back into her cushions, muttering.

Angua tried: "You are wrong, old lady. This pot came to him by chance. He found it, it is the pot called soul of tears."

Regret of the Falling Leaf had filled the world with noise. Now she appeared to empty it with silence. She said, bitterly and come to that, curiously, considering the fact that her great grandson said she didn't know much Ankh-Morporkian, "Found in goblin cave, oh yes! Found on end of shovel, oh yes! Bad cess to him!"

"No!" Suddenly Carrot was face to face with the goblin woman. "It came to him by accident, like a curse. He never wanted it and he didn't know what it was. He found it in a cigar."

There was a pause in which, presumably, the old woman was doing some complex thinking, because she said, "Would you pay me my price, Mr. Po-leess-man?"

"We gave you the brandy," said Angua.

"Indeedy, wolf whelp, but that was for consultation only. Now it's price for diagnosis and cure, which will be from the snuff mill, two pounds of sweet raspberry, one pound of angler's chum, and one pound of Dr. Varies' *medicated* upright mixture, just the job on a winter's day." Something like a laugh escaped from the old goblin woman's mouth. "Glad of the fresh air," she added. "My lad he gets around and about and says you are trustworthy, but goblins have learned not to rely on word, so we will seal the bargain the old way, which we have all understood since time was time."

The bewildered Billy stood back as a long hand with longer fingernails extended toward Carrot, who spat on his own hand and slapped it, with no thought of health and safety, on to the palm of Regret of the Fallen Leaf who cackled again. "That can't be broke, that, it can't be broke. *Never.*" After a moment's hesitation she said in an offhand voice, "Wash hand after using."

There was a glug from the brandy bottle, and Billy Slick's old granny went on, "A pot of tears, you say?" Angua nodded. "If so, only one meaning. A poor goblin woman, a *starving* woman, had to eat her newborn baby, because she could not feed it. I hear you stop breathing for a moment. That such things happen? Is awful truth, oh yes. Is often awful truth in bad country when times are hard and food is nothing. And so, weeping, she carved a little unggue pot for soul of her baby and cried life into it and sent it away until better times when baby will come back."

Quietly, Carrot said, "Could you tell us anything more, madam?"

The old goblin was silent for a moment and then said, "Inside cigar, wrapped in tobacco? Ask the man who sell tobacco!"

Billy turned his granny's brandy bottle upside down and not a drop came out.

"One last thing, please, madam: how can we help our friend? By the sound of it he's dreaming that he's a goblin!"

Little black eyes shone as the goblin said, "I trusting you for tobacco. Now trusting you for another bottle of brandy. Find goblin cave! Find goblin maiden! Only such a one will be able to grasp the pot, in hope one day of having child! So it goes, no other way. And big problem for you, Mr. Po-leess-man, is that goblin girl these days are hard to find. None here. Maybe none anywhere. We shrivel and shrink like old leaves. Goodbye until more brandy. No! Make that Cognac from Quirm. Special reserve. Sixty dollars if bought from Horrids on Broadway or two for one deal at Twister Boote's bottle shop in the Shades. Slight taste of anchovy, but no questions asked and none answered."

The old voice went silent, and gently the watchmen came back to the stuff of reality around them, troubling images fading into recent memory.

Carrot managed to say, "I'm so sorry to have to ask, but will this harm my sergeant? He seems to be having continuous nightmares and we can't get the pot out of his hand!"

"Three bottle of brandy, Mr. Po-leess-man?" translated Billy.

Carrot nodded. "Okay."

"How long pot had him?"

Carrot looked at Angua. "About two days, madam."

"Then get your man to a goblin cave as quick as you can, Mr. Po-leess-man. He may live. He may die. Either way, three bottle of brandy, Mr. Po-leess-man." Small black eyes twinkled at Carrot. "So nice to meet a real gentleman. Hurry *up*, Mr. Po-leess-man."

The old lady slumped back into her mound of pillows and rugs. The audience was over, just like the brandy.

"Granny *likes* you," said Billy, his voice full of awe as he ushered them out. "I can tell. She never threw anything at you. Better get her the snuff and the brandy pretty soon, however, otherwise she might get a bit stroppy in an occult sort of way, if you hear what I'm saying, or rather, of course, what I ain't saying. Nice to meet you folks, but old man King doesn't like to see people not working."

"Excuse me, Billy," said Carrot, grabbing him by his skinny arm. "Are there any goblin caves anywhere around here?"

"You got what you wanted, officer. There ain't none, as far as I know. I don't care. You could try up-country, that's my advice, but I really don't care. If you find a goblin cave on a map you can bet your teeth there won't be any goblins there anymore, not live ones, at least."

"Thank you very much for your assistance, Mr. Slick, and may I congratulate you on having a grandmother with such good grasp of contemporary vocabulary?" said Carrot.

There was a delighted shriek from the direction of the dome, the walls of which were very thin.

"Damn right! Granny Slick ain't so thick!"

"Well, perhaps we have a result," said Carrot as they headed back into the city, "but, well, I know Ankh-Morpork is a melting pot of a city, but don't you think it's rather sad when people come here and forget their ancestry?"

"Yes," said Angua, not looking at him. "It is."

When they were back in Pseudopolis Yard, Carrot filled in Cheery with as much information as he could. "I'd like you to go and see the tobacconist. Ask him where his tobacco comes from. We know there's lots of smuggling going on anyway, so he'll be worried. It might be a nice idea to take along an officer whose mere presence will worry him a little more. Wee Mad Arthur is back from leave."

Cheery grinned. "In that case, I'll take him. He worries *every-body*."

M R. BEWILDERFORCE GUMPTION WAS having a good day so far. He had been to the bank to deposit the takings and had bought two tickets to the opera. Mrs. Gumption would be very pleased about that and certainly more pleased than she was to be called a Gumption. She was always urging him into high society or, at least, high*er* society, but in some ways the name Gumption always held you back. And now he held open the door to his emporium and saw the policeman sitting patiently in the chair.

Cheery Littlebottom stood up. "Mr. Bewilderforce Gumption?"

He tried to smile. "I generally see Fred Colon, officer."

"Yes. And it's Sergeant Littlebottom. But strangely enough it's about Sergeant Colon that I'm visiting you today. Do you remember giving him a cigar?"

Mr. Gumption was suffering from the illusion that many people have that policemen don't see people lying all the time, so he said, "Not as I recall," to which Cheery replied, "Mr. Gumption, it is a well-known fact that Sergeant Colon buys or otherwise procures his tobacco requirements from your noble establishment."

Once again Bewilderforce led off on the wrong note. "I want to see my lawyer!"

"I'd like to see your lawyer as well, Mr. Gumption. Perhaps you'd send someone to collect him while I and my colleague wait here?"

Bewilderforce looked around bewildered. "What colleague?"

"Oh, aye, that'll be me well enough," said the constable known, sometimes briefly, as Wee Mad Arthur, who had been lurking behind a packet of cigarettes.

Two police officers are far more than doubly worse than one, and Cheery Littlebottom took advantage of the sudden panic to say, carefully, "It's a very simple question, Mr. Gumption. Where did that cigar come from?"

Cheery was aware that Commander Vimes didn't like the phrase "The innocent have nothing to fear," believing the innocent had everything to fear, mostly from the guilty but in the longer term even more from those who say things like "The innocent have nothing to fear"; but Bewilderforce was fearful—she could see him sweating.

"We know you're a smuggler, Mr. Gumption, or perhaps I should say that you take advantage of very good deals when they are, ahem, presented to you. Right now, however, all I need from you is to tell me where that cigar came from. Once you've been so kind as to tell me that, we'll walk out of this building in a happy and cooperative frame of mind."

Bewilderforce brightened up. Cheery continued, "Of course, other departments of the Watch might wish to visit you in due course. At the moment, sir, you just have to deal with me. Do you know where that batch of cigars came from?"

Valiantly Bewilderforce tried it on. "I buy from dealers all the time," he said. "It'd take me ages to go through the records!"

Cheery kept smiling. "No problem there, Mr. Gumption, I'll call for my expert colleague Mr. A. E. Pessimal, right now. I don't know if you know of him? It's amazing how quickly he can work through paperwork and I'm sure he'll find time in his busy schedule to help you out at no cost whatsoever."

Five minutes later a gray-faced and breathless Bewilderforce handed Cheery a small scrap of paper.

Cheery looked up at him. "Howondaland? I thought that tobacco mostly came from Klatch?"

Bewilderforce shrugged. "Well, they've been starting up plantations in Howondaland now. Good stuff, too." Feeling a little bit bolder, Bewilderforce went on. "All properly paid for, I can tell you. Yes, I know there's smuggling going on, but we don't have any truck with that. No need to when you can get a pretty good deal by buying in bulk. It's all in my ledgers. Every invoice. Every payment. All set down properly."

Cheery relented. A. E. Pessimal could probably find something to excite him *somewhere* in the Gumption ledgers. After all, business was business. But there was business and there was bad business. It didn't do to get complicated. She stood up. "Thank you very much for your assistance, Mr. Gumption. We'll trouble you no further."

Bewilderforce hesitated and said, "What's up with Fred Colon? He's a bit of a scrounger, I don't mind saying, but I would hate anything to have happened to him. It wasn't . . . poison or anything, was it?"

"No, Mr. Gumption. His cigar started singing to him."

"They don't usually do that," said Bewilderforce nervously. "I'll have to check my stock."

"Please do that, sir. And while you're doing so perhaps you'll look out for this little list of snuff products?"

The tobacconist took it from her carefully. His lips moved and he said, "That's quite a lot of snuff, you know."

"Yes, sir," said Cheery. "I'm authorized to pay cash down."

Bewilderforce looked extremely bewildered. "What? Policemen pay?"

W ALKING THE STREETS IN the company of Wee Mad Arthur presented a difficulty even for a dwarf like Cheery Littlebottom. He was around six inches high, so if you spoke to him while you walked you sounded like a madman. On the other hand, he heartily disliked being picked up. You just had to put up with it. Most people made a slight detour if they saw Wee Mad Arthur in any case.

They arrived back at the Watch House and reported to Carrot and the first thing he said to Cheery was, "Do you know where there are any goblin caves, Cheery?"

"No, sir. Why do you ask?"

"I'll explain later," said Carrot. "It's fairly unbelievable. Did you find out anything from old Gumption?"

Cheery nodded. "Yes, sir. Sergeant Colon's haunted cigar came from Howondaland, no doubt about it."

Carrot stared at her. "I didn't think there were goblins in Howondaland? All Jolson's family come from there." He snapped his fingers. "Hang on one moment." He ran down the corridor to the canteen and came back followed by Constable Precious Jolson, a lady for whom the word large simply would not do. Everything about her was, as it were, family-sized, including her good nature. Everybody liked Precious. She seemed to be a fountainhead of jolliness with always a cheerful word for anybody, even when she was picking up a brace of drunks and throwing them into the hurry-up wagon.

After brief questioning Precious said, "Dad sent me over there last year, remember, wanted me to find my roots. Can't say I took to it, really. Nice weather. Not much to do. Not very exciting really, unless you try to stroke one of the cats, they get kind of stroppy. Never heard of goblins there, not the sort of place for them, I suspect. Excuse me, captain, can I get back to my tea now?"

The silence that followed was broken by Carrot, who said, "Howondaland is months away by boat, and broomsticks don't work very well over water, even if we could persuade the wizards to lend us one. Any ideas?"

"Crivens!" said Wee Mad Arthur. "No problemo! I reckon I could get there in less than a day, ye ken."

They stared at him. Wee Mad Arthur was small enough to ride on the back of any bird larger than a medium-sized hawk—his aerial broadcasts from the sky concerning traffic hold-ups in the city* were a regular feature of Ankh-Morpork street life—but all the way to another continent?

He grinned. "As ye ken, I was away for a wee while lately, making the acquaintance o' my brothers, the Nac mac Feegle? Weel, they fly the birds a lot, and there's a thing they have called the craw step, ye ken? And I reckon I'm canny enough to use it, ye ken."

"That's three kens in one speech, Wee Mad Arthur," said Angua, to laughter from the rest of the watchmen. "You really got into the Feegle thing, didn't you!"

"Oh, ye may scoff, but I'm the only one of ye scunners who knows why we get so many big birds flying over the city at this time o' year. Ankh-Morpork is hot! See the big plume of smoke and fumes? That's all heat. It lifts ye up, a free ride that puts the wind under your wings. Have ye heard of the surreptitious albatross? No, because only me and the Professor of Ornithology at the university know about it, and he only knows because I told the scunner. Outside the mating season it never touches ground. That's not the only thing that's odd. It's an eagle masquerading as a type of albatross. Ye could call it a shark o' the sky, and I reckon one of them will do me nicely. They like the city. They hover up where you'll never see them unless you really know how to look. There's always one about, and I could leave today. What you say?"

"But, constable," said Carrot, "you'll freeze that high up in the sky, won't you?"

---

* Which were, in fact, a permanency in any case.

"Oh aye, I ken my thermal drawers may not be sufficient, which is why the word 'brandy' is about to enter this conversation. Trust me on this, captain. I reckon I can be back within twa days."

"How many is that?" said Angua.

Wee Mad Arthur rolled his eyes. "*Two*, captain, for the likes o' you."

I N FACT IT TOOK Wee Mad Arthur only an hour to identify the peaceful-looking bird drifting happily high above the city with the meal it had just had courtesy of a seagull, the feathers of which were even now drifting gently toward the cityscape below. The surreptitious albatross had no enemies that it couldn't easily digest, and paid little attention to the nondescript and relatively harmless hawk soaring toward it, right up until it found Wee Mad Arthur landing on its back. It struggled but was unable to reach the Feegle, because he was sitting comfortably and had his hands around its neck; Wee Mad Arthur tended toward the swift methods of domesticating wildlife.

The surreptitious albatross fought for yet more height by constantly spiraling up on the huge wide pillar of free lift—as Ankh-Morpork was known and understood by the avian com-munity—and Wee Mad Arthur passed the time by memorizing a tiny penciled map of the world. Really, it wasn't difficult. On the whole, continents aren't hard to find, and neither are the edges of continents, where by general consensus, you tended to find ships moored. Wee Mad Arthur was the world expert at looking for things from above, which amused him, given that most people who wanted to see Wee Mad Arthur had to look down.

Oh well, he thought, let's go!

It was called the craw step, and the Nac mac Feegle of the chalk country had carefully shown their brother how it works when you are sitting on top of a large bird.

People in Ankh-Morpork looked up at the *bang* high above and then, given that the sky was still clear, lost interest. Meanwhile, on one astonished surreptitious albatross sat one hugely satisfied Feegle, who settled down in the feathers and began to eat a piece of the single hardboiled egg and two-inch slice of bread that were his rations for the trip,* while the universe rushed past them making a noise like *weeeeeeeeeeeeeeeeee.*

D ARKNESS HAD LASTED ABOUT four hours when Vimes was woken by a small boy bouncing up and down on the bed, and therefore on Sam Vimes, and saying, "Willikins has found a bird that just died. Dad! Mum says I can di . . . ssect it if you say it's all right, Dad!"

Vimes managed a mumbled, "Yes, all right, if your mother says so," before slipping back into the black. And the black spread around him. He heard himself thinking: the Summoning Dark could tell me everything I need to know, and that is the truth. But would the truth that it told me be *the* truth, and how would I know that? If I rely on it then in some way I become its creature. Or perhaps it becomes mine? Perhaps we have an accord and it helped me under Koom Valley and because of that the world is a better place? Surely the darkness has no reason to lie? I've always liked the night, the dead of night, those nights that are sheer blackness, making dogs nervous and causing sheep to leap their hurdles out of

---

* Wee Mad Arthur was, as a Feegle, a very economical watchman to have, given that, size for size, he ate in a year what human watchmen ate in a week, although it had to be admitted he could drink, size for size, more alcohol in a week than any human watchman could drink in a year.

terror. Darkness has always been my friend, but I cannot let it be my master, though sooner or later I will have to take an oath, and if I lie, me, the chief policeman, then what am I? How could I ever again rebuke a copper for looking the other way?

He turned over among the pillows. And yet the cause is good. It is a good cause! The man Stratford did kill the goblin girl, I have the evidence of his associate and the word of a being whose assistance has been of material use to society. Admittedly, I have put a man in fear, but then, people like Flutter are *always* in fear, and better that he fears me than Stratford, because I at least know when to stop. He's just another red ball on the baize, and for that matter, I suppose, so is Stratford. He'll have a boss. They always have a nobby boss because nearly everybody around here is either a worker or nobby, and as far as I know practically everybody doesn't have a good word to say for goblins. It's a target-rich environment, and the trouble with a target-rich environment is that it is useless if you don't know which target you have to aim at.

Vimes dropped back into deep sleep, and was almost instantly shaken awake by the best efforts of his son, industriously pounding on the heap that was Vimes in slumber. "Mum says to come, Dad. She says there's a man."

Vimes wasn't a dressing-gown type of person, so he struggled back into his clothing and made himself as presentable as a man could who needed a shave and didn't appear to have the time to get one.

There was a man sitting in the lounge, wearing a fantailer hat, jodhpurs and a nervous smile, three things that mildly annoyed Vimes. A nervous smile generally meant that somebody was after something they shouldn't have; he personally thought a fantailer looked silly; and as for the jodhpurs, no man should meet a copper if he is wearing trousers that make his legs look as though he has just burgled a house full of silverware and shoved it hastily down his trousers. In fact, Vimes thought he could see the outline of a teapot, but possibly that was his eyes playing mischievous tricks on him.

The wearer of this presumably self-inflicted triple misfortune stood up as Vimes entered. "Your grace?"

"Sometimes," said Vimes. "What can I do for you?"

The man looked apprehensively at Lady Sybil, who was sitting comfortably in the corner with a little smile on her face, and said, "Your grace, I'm afraid I must serve you with this Cease and Desist order, on behalf of the board of magistrates for this county. I am very sorry about this, your grace, and I hope you will understand that it does go against the grain to have to do this to a gentleman, but no one is above the law and the law must be obeyed. I myself am William Stoner, clerk to said justices—" Mr. Stoner hesitated because Vimes had strolled over to the door.

"Just making sure you don't leave in a hurry," said Vimes, as he locked the door. "Do sit down, Mr. Stoner, because you're just the man I want to talk to."

The clerk sat down carefully, clearly not wanting to be that man. He held in front of him a scroll with a red wax seal affixed, the kind of thing believed to make a document official—or at least expensive and difficult to understand, which, in fact, amounts to the same thing.

Suddenly, Vimes realized that all those years being confronted by Lord Vetinari had in fact been a masterclass, had he but known. Well, it was time for the examination. He went back to his chair, sat back comfortably, steepled his fingers together and frowned at the clerk over the top of them for ten whole seconds, a length of time that used to unnerve him every time it happened, and so should surely work on this little tit.

Then he cracked the silence with, "Mr. Stoner, several nights ago murder was committed on my land. Landownership means something around here, doesn't it, Mr. Stoner? It appears that this was done to implicate me in the disappearance of one Jethro Jefferson, a blacksmith. You may consider me somewhat offended, but that was nothing like the amount of offense I experienced when I met Constable Feeney Upshot, our local copper, a decent lad, kind to his old mum, who nevertheless seemed to feel that he answered to a mysterious board of magistrates, rather than to the law. The magistrates? Who are the magistrates? Some kind of local body? There appears to be no oversight on these people, no circuit judge and— I haven't finished talking yet!"

Mr. Stoner, his face gray, sank back into his seat. So did Vimes, trying not to catch Sybil's eye in case she laughed. He made his face a mask of calm again and continued, "And it appears, Mr. Stoner, that officially, in this parish, goblins are vermin. Rats are vermin, so are mice, and I believe that pigeons and crows may be also. But they don't play the harp, Mr. Stoner, they don't make exquisitely configured pots, and, Mr. Stoner, they do not beg for mercy, although I must say I've seen the occasional mouse attempt it by wriggling its nose winsomely, which did indeed lead me to put the hammer down. But I digress. Goblins may be wretched, unhygienic and badly fed, and in that they are pretty much like the commonality of most of mankind. Where will your magistrates put the ruler, Mr. Stoner? Then again we don't use a ruler in Ankh-Morpork, because once the goblins are vermin, then the poor are vermin, and the dwarfs are vermin, and the trolls are vermin. She wasn't vermin and she pleaded not to die."

He leaned back and waited for Mr. Stoner to realize that he did in fact have the power of speech. When he did so, the clerk dealt with his situation in true clerkly fashion, by ignoring it. "Nevertheless, Mr. Vimes, you are out of your jurisdiction and, I may say, encouraging Constable Upshot in ways of thinking and, I might say, behavior that will bode ill for him in his career—"

The clerk got no further than that because Vimes interrupted with, "What career? He has no career! He's a copper all by himself, except maybe for some pigs. He's a good lad at heart, doesn't scare easy, and he writes with a clear, round hand and can spell, too, which in my book makes him automatically sergeant material. As for bloody jurisdiction, murder is the crime of crimes. According to the Omnians it was the third crime ever committed!* I know of no society anywhere in the world that doesn't consider it a crime to be pursued with vigor, understand? And as for the law, don't try to talk to me about the law. I am not above the law, but I stand right underneath it, and I hold it up! And currently I work with Mr. Feeney, and we have an accessory to murder in his cell, and justice, not convenience, will be served."

"Well done, Sam," said Sybil loyally, giving the small but distinctive clap that people give when they want other people to join in.

Mr. Stoner, on the other hand, simply said, "Well done, sir, but nevertheless my instructions are to arrest you. The magistrates have sworn me in as a policeman, you see, and young Upshot has been relieved of his duties." He winced, because of the sudden freeze.

Vimes stood up and said, "I don't think I'm going to allow you to arrest me today, Mr. Stoner! I dare say Sybil will allow you a cup of tea, should you want it, but I'm going to see Chief Constable Upshot." And he stood up, unlocked the door and walked out of the room, out of the Hall and, at a reasonable speed, headed down to the lockup.

---

* The first two being common theft and public indecency.

Halfway down, Willikins overtook him, saying, "I couldn't help hearing all that garbage, commander, on account of how I was listening at the door as per section five of the gentleman's gentleman's code. What a nerve! You'll need me to watch your back!"

Vimes shook his head. "I don't think a civilian should get involved, Willikins."

Willikins had to run faster, because Vimes was speeding up, but he managed to gasp out, "That is a hell of a thing for you to say to me, commander." And hurried on regardless.

S OMETHING WAS GOING ON at the lockup—it looked to Vimes as though it might be a domestic disturbance, a ruckus, possibly a fracas or even a free-for-all, in which case it was definitely unlucky for some. A happy thought occurred: yes, maybe it was an affray, always a useful word because nobody is quite certain what it means, but it sounds dangerous.

Vimes burst out laughing as soon as he saw what was going on. Feeney was standing in front of the lockup, his face beetroot red and his ancestral truncheon in his hands. Quite possibly it had already been used on the small mob trying to assault the lockup, because there was a man lying on the floor clutching his groin and groaning. However, Vimes's lengthy experience told him that the man's carefully targeted misfortune had a lot to do with Mrs. Upshot, who was in a semicircle of men, all of them ready to jump back as soon as she waved her broomstick at them. "Don't you dare say my lad Feeney ain't a copper! He *is* a copper, and so was his dad, and his granddad and his great-granddad before him." She paused for a moment and went on, grudgingly, "Pardon me, I tell a lie, *he* was a criminal, but anyway that's *nearly* like being a copper!"

The broomstick made a whooshing sound as she swung it backward and forward. "I know you lot! Some of you is gamekeepers, and some of you is smugglers, and a few of you is bastards, excuse my Klatchian!" By now she had caught sight of Vimes, and pausing only to bring her broomstick down like a mallet on the foot of a man who made a step in the wrong direction, she pointed her finger at Vimes and yelled, "See him? Now he is a gentleman, and also a great copper! You can tell a real copper, like my Henry, gods bless his soul, and Commander Vimes too, 'cos they've got proper badges what have been used to open thousands of beer bottles, I dare say, and believe me one of them would hurt you if they tried to stick it up your nose. The flimsy bits of cardboard you boys is waving makes me laugh! Come any further, Davey Hackett," she said to the nearest man, "and I will shove this broomstick in your ear, trust me, I will!"

Vimes scanned the mob, trying to sort out the vile and dangerous from the innocent and stupid, and was about to brush off a fly from his head when he heard the gasp from the crowd, and saw the arrow on the cobbles and Mrs. Upshot looking at her broom falling into two pieces.

In theory, Mrs. Upshot should have screamed, but she had been around coppers for a long time, and so, face red, she pointed at the broken broom and said, as only an old mum could say, "That cost half a dollar! They don't grow on trees, you know! It wants paying for!"

Instantly there was the jingle of frantic hands in pockets. One man with great presence of mind removed his hat and coins showered into it. Since many of these coins were dollars and half-dollars snatched in haste, Mrs. Upshot would clearly be self-sufficient in broomsticks for life.

But Feeney, who had been simmering, smacked the hat to the ground just as it was proffered. "No! That's like a bribe, Ma! Someone shot at you. I saw the arrow, it came straight out of this lot, right out the middle! Now I want you to go inside, Ma, 'cos I'm not going to lose you as well as Dad, understand? Damn well get inside the house, Ma, the reason being, the moment you shut the door I intend to show these gentlemen their manners!"

Feeney was on fire. If a chestnut had fallen on his head it would have exploded, and his rage, pure righteous rage—the kind of rage in which a man might find the idea and the inclination and, above all, the stamina to beat to death everyone around him—was a pant-wetting concern to the befuddled citizens quite outweighing the secondary one, which was that there was at least six dollars of any-body's money lying there on the cobbles, and how much of it could they get away with reclaiming?

Vimes did not say a word. There was no room to say a word. A word might dislodge the brake that held retribution in check. Fee-ney's ancestral club over his shoulder looked like a warning from the gods. In his hands it would be sudden death. No one dared run; of a certainty, to run would be to make yourself a candidate for whistling oaken crushing.

Now, perhaps, was the time. "Chief Constable Upshot, may I have a word, as one policeman to another?"

Feeney turned on Vimes a bleary look, like a man trying to focus from the other end of the universe. One of the outlying men took this as a cue to leg it, and behind the crowd there was a thump and the voice of Willikins, saying, "Oh, I do beg your pardon, your grace, but this gentleman stumbled over my feet. Regrettably, I have very large feet." And, to accompany the apology, Willikins held up a man whose nose would probably look a lot better by the end of next week.

All eyes turned to Willikins, except those of Vimes—because there in the shadows, keeping his distance from the mob, was that bloody lawyer again. Not with the mob, obviously, a respectable lawyer could not be part of a mob, oh no, he was just there *watching*.

Feeney glared at the rest of the men, because tripping can come so easily to a man. "I appreciate your man's assistance, commander, but this is my manor, if you know what I mean, and I will have my say."

Feeney was panting heavily, but his gaze swept backward and forward to find the first man to move or even look like someone about to move some time in the future. "I am a policeman! Not always a good one or a clever one, but I am a policeman and the man in my lockup is my prisoner, and I'll defend him to the death, and if it's the death of some bastards who stood in front of my old mum with crossbows they didn't know how to use, well, so be it!" He lowered his voice to less than a scream. "Now, I know you, just like my father did, and granddad too—well some of you at least—and I know you ain't as bad as all that—"

He stopped for a moment, staring. "What are you doing here, Mr. Stoner? Standing there next to a mob? Have you been making a few pockets jingle?"

"That statement is actionable, young man," said Stoner.

Vimes carefully made his way to Stoner and whispered, "I won't say you're pushing your luck, Mr. Stoner, because your luck ran out the moment you set eyes on me." He tapped the side of his nose. "A word to the wise: I've got big feet too."

Oblivious to this, Feeney went on, "What I want you all to know is that a few nights ago a goblin girl up on the hill was chopped up while she was pleading for her life. That's bad. *Very* bad! And one reason is that a man who can chop up a goblin girl will chop up your sister one day. But I will help my . . ." Feeney hesitated and then said, "colleague, Commander Vimes, and will bring those responsible to justice. And that ain't all, oh dear me not by a long chalk, because you see I know, just like you do, that three years ago a load of goblins were grabbed in the night and rounded up to be sent down the river. My poor old dad did what he was told and turned a blind eye, but I ain't doing the same thing. I don't know if any of you helped, and right now that don't concern me overmuch, 'cos folks around here tend to do what they're told, although maybe some like doing what they're told more than others."

Feeney turned around, making certain that all knew they were included. "And I know something else! I know that late yesterday, when we were actually on the way to Hangnails, a bunch of goblins from Overhang were grabbed and put on an ox boat down the river to—"

"What! Why haven't you told me all this before?" Vimes shouted.

Feeney didn't look in his direction, keeping his gaze on the mob. "What before? Sorry, commander, but it's been all go and I only found out just before this bunch arrived, since when it's all got busy. The boat probably came past here while we were still opening barrels in Hangnails. This lot wanted me to hand over my— your—*our* prisoner, and then of course my old mum got involved, as it were, and you know it's always difficult when it involves an old mum. *I never told anyone to move, did I?!*"

This was to a man in some distress who was almost bent double with his hands on his groin.

"I'm very sorry, er, Feeney, er, Constable, er, Chief Constable Upshot, but I really need the privy, if it's all the same to you, please, thanking you very much?"

Vimes looked down at the crouching man and said, "Oh, dear me, it's you, Mr. Stoner! Willikins! Do take him somewhere where he can go about his business, will you? But be sure to bring him back here. And if it turns out that he didn't really need to do any business, do him the courtesy of making sure that he does." He wanted to say a great deal more at this time, but this was, after all, Feeney's patch and the lad was surprisingly good at it, when it came to pushing people who pushed old mums.

And the boy hadn't finished yet; his mood had simply moved from molten steel to cold, hard iron. "Before I tell you what happens next, gentlemen, I'd like to draw your attention to the goblin sitting up there in the tree, watching you all. All you who are locals know Stinky, and you know sometimes you give him a kick, or sometimes he blags a cigarette off you, and sometimes he runs you a little errand, yes?"

There was a sense of sweating relief among the crowd that the worst appeared to be over now. In fact it had only just begun. "Commander Vimes would like you to know, and so indeed would I, that the law applies to everybody, and that means it applies to goblins as well."

There was a certain amount of nodding at that and Feeney continued, "But if the law applies to goblins then goblins have rights and if goblins have rights then it would be right to have a goblin policeman attached to the Shire force."

Vimes looked at Feeney with amazement and a not inconsiderable amount of admiration. That had got them: they had all been nodding and he had led them by the nod and before they knew it they were nodding at a goblin officer.

"Well, gentlemen, I am intending to make Stinky a probationary special constable, just so he can keep me up to date with what's happening up on the hill. He'll have a badge, and anyone giving him a kick from now on will be assaulting a police officer in the course of his duty. I think the penalty for doing that is not just being hanged, but also to let you bounce up and down for a bit afterward. This is an internal force decision, which does not require the authority of any magistrate. Is that not so, Commander Vimes?"

Vimes was amazed at how his mouth responded without any reference to his brain. "Yes, Chief Constable Upshot, as per section 12, part 3 of the Laws and Ordinances of Ankh-Morpork, generally considered a model for police procedure," he added confidently, knowing that no one present would have ever clapped eyes on them and would quite likely not be able to read them even if they had.

Inside Vimes winced. He'd got away with having dwarfs, trolls and finally even werewolves and vampires in the Watch, albeit on certain obvious conditions, but that had been the result of leverage over the years. Vetinari always said, "What is normal? Normal is yesterday and last week and last month taken together." And, Vimes supposed, they had slipped things in one at a time to allow normal to gradually evolve—although Mr. Stinky, or rather Probationary Special Constable Stinky, had *really* better confine his policing activities to the cave. Yes, not such a bad idea at that, indeed if only he could get them to leave chickens alone maybe normal would have a chance. After all, people seemed quite easy about having their rights and liberties taken away by those they looked up to, but somehow a space on the perch was a slap in the face, and treated as such.

And now Feeney, getting out of breath, was nearly talked out. "I can't force any of you to tell me anything, but is there any one of you anxious to help me with my inquiries?"

Vimes tried not to let anyone see his expression, least of all Feeney. Of course, Captain Carrot had once been like that and—was it possible?—maybe even young Sam Vimes had been like that too, but surely anyone could see that you never expect people who are part of a crowd to put up their hand and pipe up, "Yes, constable!

I'd be very happy to tell you everything I know, and I'd like these fine gentlemen here to be my witnesses."

What you *did* do after a performance like that was just wait, wait until somebody sidles up and whispers something when you are alone, or just tilts his head in the right direction, or, and this had happened to Vimes, writes three initials in the spilled beer on a bar top and industriously wipes it clean within two seconds. Some bright spark would think: you never know your luck; after all, Feeney could be a coming man, right? And a happy relationship might come in handy, one day.

Vimes blew away the pink cloud of embarrassment. "Well, gentlemen, speaking as commander of the Ankh-Morpork City Watch, it seems to me that your senior police officer is being considerably lenient with you. I would not be, so be grateful for him. How many of these . . ." and here Vimes inserted a sneer, *"gentlemen* do you really know, Chief Constable Upshot?"

"Oh, about half of them, commander, that's to say their names, families, home addresses and similar. The rest of them are from other places. I can't say that they're all angels, but they're mostly not too bad."

This sensible little speech in the circumstances earned Feeney a few smirks and a certain relieved look all round, and, happily, an opening for Vimes, who said, "So which one of them had an arrow ready in his crossbow, do you think, Mr. Feeney?"

But before Feeney had time to open his mouth Vimes had spun round to confront the returning Mr. Stoner, whose digestion had let him down. Willikins, whose instincts seldom failed, was still keeping an eye on him. Loudly and cheerfully Vimes said, "I see that my good friend Mr. Stoner is back, and he's a lawyer and I'm a policeman and we know how to talk to one another. Do come this way, Mr. Stoner."

He grabbed the unwilling lawyer gently but firmly by the arm and led him some way from the crowd, who watched, Vimes was pleased to see, with immediate deep suspicion.

"You *are* a lawyer, are you not, Mr. Stoner? Not a criminal lawyer by any chance?"

"No, your grace, I specialize mostly in land and property matters."

"Ah, far less dangerous," said Vimes, "and I suppose you're a member of the Ankh-Morpork bar, presided over by my old chum Mr. Slant?" He had said it convivially, but Vimes knew that the name of the old zombie would strike terror into any lawyer's heart—although whether Mr. Slant still had one of his own was questionable. And now Mr. Stoner must be thinking quite quickly. If he had any sense, and read his *Law Journal* between the lines, he would be aware that while Mr. Slant would bow (rather stiffly) to the rich and influential, he did not like mistakes, and he did not like seeing the law being brought into disrepute by inept lawyers and laymen, believing that this particular duty should be left to senior lawyers, such as Mr. Slant, who could do it with care and panache and AM$300 an hour. And Mr. Stoner should be thinking that, since it appeared that landowners around here had made up the law to suit themselves, which was the prerogative of the legal profession as a whole, Mr. Slant would not be a happy zombie; and, as custom and practice now dictated that he should no longer walk around groaning with his hands held out directly in front of him (one of them perhaps holding a severed head for effect), he was known to vent his still considerable spleen on snotty young lawyers with ideas above their station by talking to them for some time in a calm, low voice, causing them to say afterward that the severed head was, by contrast, the vegetarian option.

Vimes watched the young man's face as he considered his meager options and found that there was no plural.

"I did endeavor to properly advise the justices as to their situation, of course," he said, like a man rehearsing a plea, "but I'm sorry to say that they took the view that since they own the land hereabouts, then they decide the law of said land. I have to say that they are, in themselves, quite decent people."

Vimes was surprised at how well his temper was keeping these days. He said, "Land, I quite like land, it's one of my favorite things for standing on. But land, and landlord, and law, well . . . A man might get quite confused, yes? Especially in the presence of a pretty good fee? And it's quite easy for people to be jolly decent people when they can afford to hire thoroughly un-decent people, people that don't even need orders, just a nod and a wink."

At this point there was a roll of thunder, not really appropriate to the last comment, and therefore without occult significance. Nevertheless, it was a giant roll that trundled around the sky, dropping blocks of sound. Vimes looked up and saw a horizon the colors of a bruise, while all round him the air was calm and warm and insects and other creatures that he couldn't guess at were buzzing in the undergrowth. Satisfied that he need not look for cover yet, he turned his attention back to the squirming lawyer.

"May I suggest, Mr. Stoner, that you suddenly develop a pressing reason to go to the city and possibly talk to some of the senior lawyers there? I suggest that you describe yourself as foolish, and when they see your damp trousers, that will act as corroboration, believe me. If necessary, I might find it in my heart to make a statement on your behalf, to the effect that I think you were silly and badly led rather than criminal."

The look of gratitude read well, and so Vimes added, "Why don't you try criminal law? It's mostly grievous bodily harm and murderers these days. You could call it ointment for the soul. Just a couple of things, though: what do you know about goblins being

sent downriver? And what do you know about the disappearance
of Jefferson the blacksmith?"

It's never nice to face a difficult question when you're thinking
about getting on a horse and travelling long distances at speed. "I
can assure you, your grace," replied the man, "that I know nothing
about the disappearance of the smith, if indeed he hasn't simply gone
to work elsewhere. And goblins? Yes, I know that some were sent
away some years ago, but I took up this post two years back and I
cannot comment on those circumstances." He added primly, "I have
no knowledge whatsoever of any goblins being dispossessed of their
accommodation lately, as the chief constable appears to believe."

Turning his back so the craning crowd could not easily see what was
happening, Vimes glared at him. "I congratulate you on your careful
ignorance, Mr. Stoner." He then grabbed the prim lawyer by the neck
and said, "Listen to me, you little shit. What you tell me may strictly
speaking be true, but you are a bloody stupid lawyer if you haven't realized that a bunch of landowners cannot decide all by themselves that
anything they want to do is the law. If you want to keep in with both
sides, Mr. Stoner, and I imagine that you do, then you might find a
moment in your busy schedule to tell your *former* employers that Commander Vimes knows all about them and Commander Vimes knows
what to do about them. I know who they are, Mr. Stoner, because Chief
Constable Upshot has given me a list of names."

Vimes gently released the pressure and said quietly, "Very soon
this will be an unfortunate place for you, Mr. Stoner." Then, turning, so that the crowd could see, he took the bewildered lawyer's
hand, shook it lavishly and said loudly, "Thank you very much
for such valuable information, sir. It'll make my investigations a
whole lot simpler, I can tell you! And I'm sure that Chief Constable
Upshot will feel exactly the same way. It would be a much easier
life for all of us if other upstanding folk were so quick to assist the

police with their inquiries." He looked at the stricken lawyer and said more quietly, "I am no judge, but some of those men have a certain look about them. I know the sort, probably got more teeth than brain cells, and now, Mr. Lawyer, they're wondering how much you know and how much you've told me. I wouldn't stop to pack if I was you, and I hope you've got a fast horse."

The lawyer left at speed and, at a meaningful nod from Feeney, so did the mob, more or less evaporating into the scenery; and Vimes thought, another one snookered. Get the reds, get the colors, but sooner or later you're after the black.

And now he was left with the company of only Willikins and the chief constable, who looked around like someone realizing that he might not only have bitten off more than he could chew, but also more than he could lift. He straightened up when he saw Vimes looking at him. It was time for a little reinforcement, so Vimes walked over and slapped the lad on the back. "Well, I don't know, I'm sure! Well done, Chief Constable Upshot, and this time I'm not laughing at you, Feeney, I'm not making fun, I'm not talking you down, and I cannot believe that you are the lad I met only a few days ago! You stood up to them, right enough! A bunch of dangerous idiots! With a lawyer!"

"They shot an arrow at my old mum! Oh, they said they didn't, 'cos they was hoping to frighten us off! They said they had no arrows! So I said, quick as a wink, well, you wouldn't have any arrows now if you'd shot them at my old mum, would you? So that proves it, I told them, I said, that's logic, and they didn't know what to say!"

"Well, I'm at a loss for words myself, Feeney, because it seems to me that I heard you say some more goblins were sent downriver yesterday. How did you find that out?"

Feeney waved a thumb in the direction of the lockup and grinned. "Here's the key, sir, just you go and talk to our prisoner.

You'll love it, sir, he was beside himself when he knew they were coming for him and he sang like a nightingale, didn't he just!"

"Generally, we say that they sing like a canary," said Vimes, turning toward the stubby little building.

"Yes, sir, but this is a rural police station, sir, and I know my birds, sir, and he sang like a nightingale, right enough! A beautiful watery cadence, sir, second only to the trill of the robin in my opinion, possibly occasioned by his being really, really scared, sir. I'll have to slosh a bucket in there in a minute."

"Well done again, Feeney! Might I suggest at this time that you go in and see to your old mum? She'll be worried about you. Old mums do worry, you know."

WEE MAD ARTHUR WAS impressed. Why hadn't anybody told him about the craw step before? Well, it was only recently that he had learned that he was, by birth, a Nac mac Feegle instead of, as he had been given to understand, the child of peaceful, shoe-making gnomes. Feegles did not wear shoes and neither were they peaceful. Like many people before and after, Wee Mad Arthur had always thought that he was in the wrong life.

When the truth had fortuitously been uncovered, it all seemed to make sense. He could be proud of being a Nac mac Feegle, albeit one who enjoyed the occasional visit to the ballet and could read a menu in Quirmian and, for that matter, read at all.

He cruised above the warm blue skies of Howondaland in great circles and enjoying himself no end. The whole continent! There were people on it, so he understood, but mostly what he was seeing from the air was either desert, mountain or, most of all, green jungle. He allowed the albatross to drift on the thermals as his keen eyes searched for what he suspected might be there. It was, in fact, not a thing, as such, but a concept: rectangular. People who planted things *liked* rectangular. It was orderly. It made things easy.

And there it was! Right down there on the coast. Definitely rectangular and quite a lot of it. After a brief meal of hardboiled egg he persuaded the bird to perch in a treetop. Jumping to the ground was no fearsome undertaking for one of Feegle stock.

As evening began to fall, Wee Mad Arthur walked through line after line of fragrant tobacco plants. But also noticeably rectangular, in this land where geometry was rare, were the sheds, visible not far away.

He moved stealthily to begin with and increasingly more stealthily when he saw the pile, white and complex in the gloaming. The whiteness consisted of bones. Small bones, not Feegle but far too small for human; and then, when he investigated further, he saw the corpses. One of them was still moving, more or less.

Wee Mad Arthur recognized a goblin when he saw one. There were enough people who did not like Feegles for Feegles not to be too snotty on the subject of goblins. They were a damn nuisance, but even Feegles would be happy to agree that so were they themselves. And being a nuisance is not something you should die of. In short, Wee Mad Arthur recognized this situation as very bad.

He took a look at the one who was moving. There were wounds all over it. One leg was twisted back on itself and suppurating scars covered its body. Wee Mad Arthur knew death when he saw it and that was in the air right now. He looked at the pleading in the goblin's one remaining eye, took out his knife and ended its suffering.

While he was staring at this, a voice behind him said, "And where the hell did you escape from?"

Wee Mad Arthur pointed to his badge, which to him was the size of a shield, and said, "Ankh-Morpork City Watch, ye ken?"

The burly human stared at him and said, "There ain't no law here, whatever you are, you little squirt."

As Commander Vimes always said in his occasional rousing speeches to his men, it was the mark of a good officer if he or she is able to improvise in unfamiliar circumstances. Wee Mad Arthur recalled the words very clearly. "Nobody expects you to be a first-class lawyer," Vimes had said, "but if you have evidence that suggests that your proposed action is, on the face of it, justified, then you should take it."

And then Wee Mad Arthur, ticking off points in his head, thought: slavery is illegal. I know it used to be done, but I don't know anywhere it's done anymore. The dwarfs don't do it and neither do the trolls and I know that Lord Vetinari is dead against it. He checked all this again to make certain that he had got it right, and then looked up at the scowling human and said, "Excuse me, sir? What was that you just said to me?"

The man smiled horribly, grasping the handle of his whip. "I said, there ain't no law here, you rabid little skunk."

There was a pause and Wee Mad Arthur glanced down at the dead goblin on the stinking bone-filled midden. "Guess again," he said.

As battles go, it was one of the most one sided, because that side belonged to Wee Mad Arthur. There were only a dozen or so guards on the plantation, because starving creatures in chains do not, as a rule, fight back. And they never knew who they were fighting. It was some kind of force that sped backward and forward across the ground and then up your trouser leg, leaving you in no heart whatsoever for fighting or, for that matter, anything else.

Punches came out of nowhere. Those who ran were tripped. Those who didn't were left unconscious. It was, of course, an unfair fight. It generally is if you are fighting even one Nac mac Feegle, even if you are a platoon.

Afterward, Wee Mad Arthur found chains in some of the huts and carefully chained every recumbent guard. Only then did he open the other huts.

T HE IRON DOOR OF the lockup slammed against the stone as Vimes entered; nevertheless he was taking care where he placed his feet.

And Mr. Flutter sang, he certainly sang. Vimes was in no ornithological position to judge the singing in terms of nightingale or robin equivalent, but even if he had sung like a frog it would not have mattered, because he sang about a moocher called Benny No-Nose, who hung about as such men do in the hope of picking up unconsidered trifles and had traded a pair of boots—"I don't know where they came from, and no more do you, okay?"—for a turkey the very evening before the nightmare began for Ted.

"Well, sir," Flutter told him. "You asked me about what happened years ago, see, and what with one thing and another, what might have happened yesterday didn't cross my mind, if you see what I mean? It was all so sudden like. Anyway, yeah, he said they'd coupled a tender behind a two-oxen riverboat that very afternoon, and it smelled to him like goblins, him living near their cave in Overhang, and you never forget that smell, or so he said to the dockmaster, a man known to one and all as Wobbly No-Name, on account of him often walking funny when the drink is on him, and was told, 'Yeah, they're sending them down while the going is good, and you never saw them, and neither did I, understand?' Someone must think it very important 'cos Stratford is on the boat. Someone must have stamped their foot about that because Stratford, well, he don't like boats. Don't like water, come to that. Won't travel on a boat at all if he can help it."

Vimes didn't whoop. He didn't even smile, he hoped—you made sure you didn't if you could help it—but he gave himself a point for being civil to Flutter. You couldn't get off Feegle free after a charge of accessory to murder, but there were ways and ways of doing time, and if this all worked out as he hoped it would, Flutter might find that time would pass comfortably, and even, perhaps, faster than usual.

He said, "Well, thank you, Ted, I'll look into it. In the meantime, I'll leave you in the capable hands of Chief Constable Upshot, to whom a prisoner is as sacred as his dear old mum, trust me." He pulled out the key to let himself out, and then paused as if an important point had just aimlessly struck him. "A two-oxen boat? Does that go twice as fast?"

And now Flutter was a riverboat expert. "Not really, but you can pull more load, even through the night, see? Now, your one-ox boat has to stop overnight at a cattle landing, so as the beast can have its rations and a jolly good chew and some shut-eye before dawn and there's a cost in time and money, right there."

Prisoner or not, Ted was now a self-styled lecturer to the unfortunately ignorant. "But with two oxen, well, one can be taking a bit of a rest while the other is keeping the boat moving. I reckon there were three barges behind that one, not too much for one ox downstream at this time of year." He sniffed. "I wanted to be an ox boat pilot, but of course, the bloody Zoons* had got it sewn up. I did do a season on one, mucking out and feeding, but I prefer turkeys."

---

* A race of freshwater mariners found everywhere in and around the Sto Plains. They are said to be incapable of lying, although this piece of information has been provided by the Zoons themselves, causing, as it were, a philosophical conundrum. Certainly it is maintained that they find the concept of a lie so difficult to understand that the few among them who have mastered the technique are venerated and given high office in Zoon society.

"And the name of the boat?" said Vimes carefully.

"Oh, everybody knows it! It's the biggest on the river. Everybody knows the *Wonderful Fanny*!"

Internal monologues can play themselves out quite fast, and Vimes's went: Let me think. Ah yes, almost certainly there was a captain who had a wife who was probably named Francesca at birth, but that's too much of a mouthful, and he named his boat after her because he loved her very much. And there you have it. There is no need to dwell on the subject, because there are only so many words, letters and syllables available to the tongue, and if you can't come to terms with that then you might as well never get out of bed. And so, having got his brain sorted out, he released the clamps on his silly-embarrassed-face reflex and said, "Thank you for your cooperation, Ted, but if you had told us earlier we might have been able to catch the damn boat!"

Flutter looked at him in astonishment. "Catch the *Fanny*? Bless you, sir, a man with one leg could do that! She's a bulk carrier, not a streaker! Even going all night she won't have got much past Fender's Bend by now. There are bends all the way, you see? I reckon you never get more than half a mile without a bend! And it's full of rocks, too. Seriously, you have to zigzag so much on Old Treachery that you're often crossing your own wake."

Vimes nodded at this. "One last thing, Ted. Remind me again . . . What exactly does Mr. Stratford look like?"

"Oh, you know the type, sir, sort of average. Dunno how old he is. Maybe twenty-five. Maybe twenty. Sort of mousy hair. No scars that show, amazingly." Ted looked embarrassed at this paucity of information and shrugged. "Sort of average height, sir." He scrabbled for details and gave up. "To tell you the truth, he sort of looks like everyone else, sir, that is until he gets angry"—Ted's face lit up—"and *that*, sir, is when he looks like Stratford."

WILLIKINS WAS SITTING ON the bench under the chestnut tree with his hands resting peacefully on his knees.
He was good at it. He had a talent for resting that had escaped
Vimes. It must be a servant thing, Vimes thought: if you don't
have anything to do, don't do anything. And right now *he* could
do with a rest. Maybe evidence was going downstream even as he
stood there, but by the sound of it at a speed that could almost be
overtaken on foot. Regrettably Sybil was right. At his age you had
to be sensible. You sometimes had to catch your breath, while you
still had some. He sat down beside the man, and said, "An interesting day, Willikins."

"Indeed, yes, commander, and may I say that young Constable
Upshot handled his responsibilities with great aplomb. You have a
talent for inspiring people, sir, if I may say so."

There was silence for a while, and then Vimes said, "Well, of
course, we were helped by the fact that some bloody fool actually let
an arrow go! You could see them thinking about what might happen
if you're one of the gang that killed a dear old lady. That's a kind of
trouble you don't get out of easily. That opened them up! And it was
obviously a real stroke of luck for us," Vimes added, without turning his head. He let the silence continue as the storm raged in the
distance, while, nearby, whatever it was that was chirruping in the
bushes carried on doing so in the warm, sultry afternoon.

"It puzzles me, though," he went on, as if a thought had only
just crossed his mind. "If it was someone in the front of the crowd
who had loosed his crossbow then surely I would have seen it, and
if it was one toward the back then he would have to have been
clever and skilful enough to sight through maybe a very narrow
space. That would be *very* clever shooting, Willikins."

Willikins was still staring placidly ahead. Vimes's sideways glance spotted no hint of moisture on his brow. Then the gentleman's gentleman said, "I expect these country lads excel at trick shooting, commander."

Vimes slapped him on the back and laughed. "Well, that's the funny thing, don't you think? I mean, did you see their gear? It was low-grade stuff, in my opinion, not well maintained, the kind of stuff that granddad brought back from some war, whereas that arrow, I recognized that evil little package as a custom-made bolt for the Burleigh and Stronginthearm Piecemaker Mark IX, you remember?"

"I am afraid you will have to refresh my memory, commander."

Vimes was beginning to enjoy himself and said, "Oh, you must! Only three of them were made, and two of them are still under wizard-assisted lock and key in the company vaults and the other—surely you remember this?—is locked safely in that little vault that we made in the cellar in Scoone Avenue last year? You and I poured concrete while Sybil and the lad were out, and rubbed dirt all over the floor so that you had to know it was there in order to find it. It's a hanging matter for anyone to be found with one of them, according to Vetinari, and the Assassins' Guild told the *Times* that hanging would be a picnic compared with what would happen to anyone they found in possession of one of those. I mean, think about it: can't hardly tell it's a crossbow. Silent, folds up and fits in a pocket in an instant, easily concealed and deadly in the hands of a skilled man, such as you or I." Vimes laughed again. "Don't be surprised, Willikins, I recall your prowess with even a standard military bow during the war. Heavens know what someone like you could manage with the damn Piecemaker. I just wonder how one turned up out here in the country. After all, Feeney confiscated all the weapons he found, but maybe one of those chaps had hidden it in his boot. What do you think?"

Willikins cleared his throat. "Well, commander, if I may speak freely, I might surmise that there are many workers at Burleigh and Strongintharm, which is one factor, and, of course, the directors of the most famous weapons producer on the Plains might also have decided to hide away a few souvenirs before the range was banned, and who knows where they might have got to. I can think of no other explanation."

"Well, of course you may be right," said Vimes. "And while it's a terrifying thought that one of these things might be out on the streets somewhere, I must admit that the idiot who used it really helped us out of a difficult situation." He paused for a while and then said, "Have you had a pay rise lately, Willikins?"

"I am entirely satisfied with my remuneration, commander."

"It is entirely deserved, but to be on the safe side, I'd like you, as soon as we are back home, to check in the cellar just in case, will you? Because obviously, if there are more of those bloody things out there, I want to make certain that I've still got one too." And as Willikins turned away Vimes continued, "Oh, and Willikins, it's a damn good job for you that Feeney cannot put two and two together."

Was that the faintest sigh of relief? Surely not. "I will expedite that as soon as we enter the building, commander, and I am certain that should you yourself want to go down there some time later to make a personal check, you will find it resting where it has always been."

"I'm sure I shall, Willikins; but I wonder if you could solve a problem for me? I have to catch the *Wonderful Fanny*."

He added hurriedly, "Which is a boat, of course."

"Yes, sir, I am aware of the vessel in question. Remember that I'd already been here for some time before you and her ladyship arrived, and I happened to be near the river when she went upstream.

I recall the people pointed her out to me. I was given to understand that she was going up to Overhang to load up, probably with iron ore brought down from the dwarf mine, which rather surprised me, given that normally they smelt directly at their mines and export the bar-stock, this being a more economical method, sir."

"Fascinating," said Vimes, "but I think that however slow it goes, I ought to get after her."

Feeney was just emerging from the cottage.

"I've heard about the . . . the boat, lad. We should get going while it's still light."

Feeney actually saluted. "Yes, I have that in hand, sir, but what about my prisoner? I mean, my old mum could give him his meals and empty his bucket for him, won't be the first time she's had to do that sort of thing, but I don't like leaving her by herself, right now, if you get my thinking?"

Vimes nodded. Back home he only had to snap his fingers for a watchman to become immediately available, but now . . . Well, he had no choice. "Willikins!"

"Yes, commander?"

"Willikins, against my better judgement and I dare say yours, I hereby appoint you to the rank of Special Constable and I command you to take the prisoner back to the Hall and keep him under lock and key there. Even a bloody army would be mad to attack the Hall with Sybil in it. But just in case, Willikins, I can think of no man better suited to guard my family."

Willikins beamed and saluted. "Yes, sir, orders received and understood, sir. You can depend on me, sir, only . . . er, well, when we get back to the city could you, er, please not let anyone know that I was a copper for a while? I have friends, sir, dear friends who have known me for a long time and they would cut my ears off if they heard I was a copper."

"Well, far be it from me to whiten a man's name against his will," said Vimes. "Do we have an understanding? I'd be grateful if you could refrain from too much adventureishness. Just guard the prisoner and ensure that no harm comes to him. If this means a little judicious harm has to come to someone else, I will regretfully accept the fact."

Willikins looked solemn. "Yes, sir, fully understood, sir. My comb will not leave my pocket."

Vimes sighed. "You have a great many things in your pockets, Willikins. Ration their usage, man. And by the way, please tell Sybil and Young Sam that Daddy is chasing the bad men and will see them again soon."

Feeney looked from Vimes to Willikins. "Glad that's sorted out, gentlemen," he said, and smiled nervously. "Now, if you're ready, commander, we'll just go along to the livery stable and pick up a couple of horses." With that he began to walk smartly down to the village, leaving Sam Vimes no alternative but to follow.

Vimes said, "Horses?"

"Absolutely, commander. From what I hear we should catch up with the *Fanny* in an hour. To tell you the truth, we could probably outrun it, but it's best to be on the safe side, don't you think?"

Feeney looked sheepish for a moment and then added, "I don't usually ride much, sir, but I'll try not to disgrace myself in front of you."

Vimes opened his mouth. Then Vimes shut his mouth, trapping the words: *Lad, I'd rather ride a pig than horse, if it's all the same to you? I mean, pigs just run along, but horses? Most of the time I've got nothing against horses, and then I come down very firmly against horses, and then I'm shot up in the air again so that once more I have nothing against horses, but I know that in half a second the whole damn thing starts again, and yes before you come out with the whole business of "It's all right if you rise up when they go down" let me say that has never ever worked for me, because then I'm either above and a little behind the horse or against the horse so firmly that I'm really glad that Sybil and I have decided to have only one child . . .*

Feeney was, however, in keen and chattering form. "I expect there were a lot of horses at Koom Valley, eh, sir?"

And Vimes was stuck. "Actually, lad, the trolls have no use for them and the dwarfs are said to eat them, on the quiet."

"Gosh, that must've been a blow to a fighting man like yourself, commander?"

Fighting man? Maybe, Vimes thought, at least when no alternative presents itself, but how in the seven hells did you get the idea that I'm comfortable even looking at horses? And why are we still walking toward some barn that is going to be full of the wretched things, stamping and snorting and dribbling and rolling their eyes backward like they do? Well, I'll tell you why. It's because I'm too damn scared to tell Feeney that I'm too damn scared. Hah, the story of my life, too much of a damn coward to be a coward!

Now Feeney pushed aside a heavy wooden gate, which, to Vimes's susceptible ear, creaked like a fresh gallows, and he groaned as they stepped through. Yes, it was a livery stable, and it made Vimes liverish. And there they were, the inevitable hangers-on: bandy-legged, no more than one button on their coats, and a certain suggestion of rat about the nose and wishbone about the legs. You could have played crockett with them. Every one of them would have a straw in his mouth, presumably because that's what they lived on. And, helplessly, Vimes was introduced to men who knew they had heard of him, very big policeman certainly, while Feeney painted a picture of him as just the sort of man who would insist on riding the swiftest beast that they had installed in the stalls.

Two evil-looking mounts were led out, and Feeney generously

brought the larger over to Vimes. "There you go, sir. Back in the saddle again, eh?" he said, and handed the reins to Vimes.

While Feeney was negotiating the hire, Vimes felt something tug at his leg and he looked down into the grinning face of Special Constable Stinky, who hissed, "Big trouble, fellow po-leess-maan colleague? Big trouble for a man scared of horses. Damn right!? Hate horse, can smell fear. You take me, po-leess-maan. I fix. No worry. You need Stinky anyway, yes? You find frightened goblin? Panic panic panic! But Stinky say shut gob goblins, this man despite appearances not too much of an arsehole, yes indeed!"

The wretched little goblin lowered his cracked voice still further, and added, so that Vimes could barely hear it, "And Stinky never ever said anything about po-leess-maan's shirt-washing man and very cross bow, hey? Mr. Vimes? *There is no race so wretched that there is not something out there that cares for them, Mr. Vimes.*"

The words hit Vimes like a slap in the face. Had the little bugger said that? Had Vimes really heard it? The words had dropped into the conversation as if from somewhere else, somewhere *very* elsewhere. He stared at Stinky, who rattled his teeth at him cheerfully and swung himself dreadfully under the horse just as, on the other side of the yard, the brains trust of debating equestrian experts settled the negotiations with Feeney. The apparent boss spat on his hand and Feeney, against all public safety procedures, spat on *his* hand and then shook hands and then money changed hands, and Vimes hoped that it washed its hands.

Then, in front of Vimes, possibly to its own amazement, the horse knelt down. Vimes had only seen that in a circus, and everyone else acted as if they'd never seen it at all.

Stinky had miraculously disappeared, but when incredulous eyes are watching, as the venerable philosopher Ly Tin Weedle says, you have to do something or be considered, in the great scheme of things, a tit. And so Vimes went bowlegged and shuffled along the horse as nonchalantly as he could, and made the strange clicking noise that he'd heard ostlers use for every command, and the horse got to its hooves, raising Vimes as gently as a cradle to the astonishment and subsequent wild applause of the bandy-legged throng, who clapped and said things like, bless you, sir, you ought to get a job in a circus! And at the same time Feeney was all admiration, unfortunately.

The wind was blowing up, but there was still some daylight left, and Vimes let the constable lead the way at a gentle trot, which indeed turned out to be gentle.

"Looks like rain coming in, commander, so I reckon we'll take it a little gently until we get down past Piper's Holding, and then round by the shallows at Johnson's Neck, where we can canter around the melon plantation, and by then we should be able to see the *Fanny*. Is that all right by you, sir?"

Sam Vimes solemnly waited for a few seconds to give the impression that he had the faintest idea about the local landscape, and then said, "Well, yes, I think that should be about right, Feeney."

Stinky dragged himself up the horse's mane, grinning again, and held up a large thumb, fortunately his own.

Feeney gathered up the reins. "Good, sir, then I think we'd better bustle!"

It took Vimes a little while to fully understand what was going on. There was Feeney, on his horse, there was the statutory clicking noise, and then no Feeney, no horse, but quite a lot of dust in the distance and the cracked voice of Stinky saying, "Hold on tight, Mr. Po-leess-maan!" And then the horizon jumped toward him. Galloping was somehow not as bad as trotting, and he managed to more or less lie on the horse and hope that somebody knew what was going on. Stinky appeared to be in charge.

The track was quite wide and they thundered along it, trailing white dust; and then suddenly they were heading downward while the land on Vimes's right was going up and the river was appearing behind some trees. He knew already that it was a river that saw no point in hurrying. After all, it was made up of water, and it is generally agreed that water has memory. It knew the score: you evaporated, you floated around in a cloud until somebody organized everybody, and then you all fell down as rain. It happened all the time. There was no point in hurrying. After your first splash, you'd seen it all before.

And so the river meandered. Even the Ankh was faster—and while the Ankh stank like a drain, it didn't wobble slowly backward and forward, from one bank to the other, as Old Treachery did, as if uncertain about the whole water cycle business. And as the river wiggled like a snake, so did the banks, which, in accordance with the general placid and unhurried landscape, were overgrown and thick with vegetation.

Nevertheless, Feeney kept up the pace, and Vimes simply clung on, on the basis that horses probably didn't willfully try falling into water of their own accord. He remained lying flat because the increasingly low branches and tangled foliage otherwise threatened to smite him off his mount like a fly.

Ah yes, the flies. The riverside bred them by the million. He could feel them crawling over his hair until some leaf or twig swatted them off. The likelihood of spotting the *Wonderful*— boat without having one's head smacked off seemed extremely little.

And yet here, suddenly, was a respite for Vimes's aching backside, the sand bar with a few logs marooned on it, and Feeney just reining his horse to a stop. Vimes managed to get upright again, just in time, and both men slid to the ground.

"Very well done, commander! You were born in the saddle, obviously! Good news! Can you smell that?"

Vimes sniffed, giving himself a noseful of flies and a very heavy stink of cattle dung. "Hangs in the air, don't it?" said Feeney. "That's the smell of a two-oxen boat, right enough! They muck out as they go, you know."

Vimes looked at the turgid water. "I'm not surprised." Perhaps, he thought, this might be the time to have a little discussion with the kid. He cleared his throat and looked blankly at the mud as he got his thoughts in order; a little trickle of water dribbled over the bar, and the horses shifted uneasily.

"Feeney, I don't know what we'll be getting into when we catch up with the boat, understand? I don't know if we can turn it round, or get the goblins out and then get them home overland, or if we'll even have to ride it down all the way to the coast, but I'm in charge, do you understand? I'm in charge because I am very used to people not wanting to see me in front of them, or even alive."

"Yessir," Feeney began, "but I think—"

Vimes plowed on. "I don't know what we're going to find, but I suspect that people who try to take over boats, even a floating dung machine like the *Fanny*, probably get treated by the crew as pirates immediately, and so *I'm* going to give the orders and I want you to do exactly what I tell you, okay?"

For a while it looked as though Feeney was going to object, and then he simply nodded, patted his mount and waited, while another tiny wave splashed beside the horses. The sudden silence of someone normally so talkative disconcerted Vimes, and he said, "Are you waiting for something, Feeney?"

Feeney nodded and said, "I didn't wish to interrupt you, commander, and as you say, you are in charge, but I was waiting until you said something I wanted to hear."

"Oh yes? Such as?"

"Well, sir, to begin with I'd like to hear you say that it's time to mount up and get out of here really fast because the water is rising and soon the alligators will wake up."

Vimes looked around. One of the logs, which he had so carelessly dismissed, was extending legs. He landed on the back of his horse with the reins in his hand in little more than a second.

"I'll take that order as a given, then, shall I?" shouted Feeney as he sped after Vimes.

Vimes did not attempt to slow down until he judged them high enough up the bank not to be of interest to anything that lived in water, and then waited for Feeney to catch up.

"All right, Chief Constable Upshot, I'm still in charge, but I agree to respect your local knowledge. Will that satisfy you? Where *is* the water coming from?"

It certainly was rising: when they had started out you would have needed a ruler to be certain that it was flowing at all, but now little waves were dancing after one another and a light rain was starting to fall.

"It's that storm coming up behind us," said Feeney, "but don't worry, sir, all that means is that the *Fanny* will tie up if it gets too strong. Then we can just climb on board."

The rain was falling faster now and Vimes said, "What happens if it decides to carry on? It's not too far off sundown, surely?"

"That won't be a problem, commander, don't you worry!" shouted Feeney with infuriating cheeriness. "We'll stay on the trails. No water ever gets up that far. Besides, wherever she is, the *Fanny* will have running lights on, red ones, oil lamps as a matter of fact. So don't worry," Feeney finished. "If she's still on the river we'll find her, sir, one way or the other, and may I ask, sir, what your intentions are then?"

Vimes wasn't certain, but no officer ever likes to say that, so instead he parried with a question himself. "Mr. Feeney, you make this river sound like a picnic! Look over there!" He pointed across the river to a spot where the water spun and gurgled and was almost visibly rising as they stared at it.

"Oh," said Feeney, "you always get debris coming down Old Treachery. The only time to worry is if you get a damn slam.* They only happen very rarely when circumstances are right, sir, and you can be sure the captain will have the *Fanny* well out of any danger if one of those should happen. Besides, he can't possibly navigate the river in bad weather at night; Old Treachery is full of snags and sand bars. It would be suicidal, even for a pilot as good as Mr. Sillitoe!"

They rode on in silence, except for the terrible swirling and gurgling of dark waters down in the torrent below the bank. Only a little daylight remained now and it was a dirty orange, helped out occasionally by flashes of lightning, followed by stone-cracking thunder. In the woods on either side of the river trees lit and occasionally burned, which was, Vimes thought, at least a help to navigation. The rain was soaking his clothing now, and so he shouted in a voice which betrayed his belief that he would not like the answer to what he was about to ask, "Apropos of nothing, and just to pass the time, lad, would you tell me what *exactly* a damn slam is?"

Feeney's voice was initially drowned by a thunder-roll behind them, but on the next go he managed, "It's an occasional phenomenon caused by a storm getting stuck in the valley and the debris of the storm getting piled up in a certain way, sir . . ."

Stinky scrambled up from who would dare to speculate where and up onto the horse's head. He glowed with a faint blue corpse

---

* Technically, the violent surge of water on Old Treachery was written down in technical manuals as a Dam Slam, but anyone who has experienced one learns to swear, hence the subtle change of name.

light. Vimes reached out a finger to touch him and a tiny blue flame danced across his hand. He knew it. "St. Ungulant's fire," he said aloud, and wished that he was in a position to use it to light his last cigar, even if it was an exhalation of the corpses of the drowned. Sometimes you just *needed* a little tobacco.

Feeney was staring at the blue light with an expression of such horror that Vimes hardly dared to disturb him. But he said, "Then what happens, lad?"

Lightning, with a sense for the dramatic moment, illuminated Feeney's face as he turned. "Well, commander, the debris will build up and up and tangle until it's one mass, and the river is building up so much behind it that sooner or later it'll overcome the strength of the natural dam, which will plow down the river, mercilessly sweeping up or capsizing everything in its path, all the way to the sea, sir. That's why this river is called 'Old Treachery'!"

"Well, of course," said Vimes. "I'm a simple man from the city who doesn't know very much about these things, but I take it that a build-up of debris which plows its way downriver sweeping up or capsizing everything in its path all the way down to the sea is generally considered to be a bad thing?"

There was a long-drawn-out creak behind them as another tree was hit by a flash. "Yes, sir. You left out the word 'mercilessly,' sir," said Feeney, carefully. "I think we really *should* try to catch up with the *Fanny* as quickly as possible."

"I think you're right, lad, and right now I suggest—"

Whatever it was that Stinky was doing, and whatever it was that Stinky actually was, the horses were already becoming skittish to the point of bolting. There was so much water in the air and so little light left that the difference between the river and the shore could only be judged by seeing which one you fell into.

And there was solid rain now, rain that blew from every

direction, including upward, and the symphony of dark destruction was punctuated by the sound of banks slipping inexorably into the churning water. The horses were now frantic and direction had no meaning, and nor did warmth and the world was nothing but darkness, water, cold despair and two red eyes.

Feeney saw them first and then Vimes picked up the smell. It was the rich, desperate smell of oxen getting *really* worried and was thick enough to stink its way out of the turmoil. Amazingly, the boat was still churning the water, making progress of sorts despite the fact that its trailing flotilla of barges was jack-knifing, tangling and generally swishing across the river like the tail of an angry cat.

"Why didn't she tie up somewhere?" shouted Feeney to the storm. It sounded like despair, but Vimes dismounted, grabbed the sticky shape of Stinky and slapped his horse on the rump. It certainly stood a better chance by itself now than it did with him, after all.

And then for a moment his inner eyes looked at Koom Valley. He had nearly died that day as water poured off the valley walls and thundered through the endless caves in the limestone, smacking him against the walls, banging him on the floors and ceilings and finally dropping him on a tiny beach of sand, in utter darkness. And the darkness had been his friend, and Vimes had floated on the face of the darkness, and there he had found enlightenment growing, and understood that fear and rage could be hammered into a sword, and the desire to once again read a book to a child could be forged into a shield and armor for a ragged dying castaway, who thereafter shook hands with kings.

After that, what could be frightening about rescuing goblins and who knew how many other people from a floundering boat on a black and treacherous river in thundering, steaming darkness?

He was running now along the squelching bank, water pouring down his neck. But running wasn't enough. You had to think. You thought that the pilot of the boat knew the river and knew the boat. He could have moored at any time, couldn't he? And he hadn't done so, but he clearly wasn't a fool, because even having known the river for only a few hours, Vimes could see that no fool would survive on it for more than a few journeys. It was built to be a trap for the stupid.

On the other hand, if you were not stupid then being an ox-boat pilot was a pretty good gig: you'd have prestige, respect, responsibility and a steady wage for a steady job, in addition to the envy of all the little boys on every landing stage. Sybil had told him all about them, with some enthusiasm, one evening. So why, in such a decent position, would a man pilot such a valuable boat with a valuable cargo down a river on an evening that promised annihilation around every snake-like bend when no blame would attach to mooring up for a while?

Money? No, Vimes thought. They call this river Old Treachery, and surely money wasn't any good to you when you were sinking dreadfully in its muddy embrace. Besides, Vimes knew men like that, and they tended to be proud, self-reliant and impossible to bribe. He probably wouldn't jeopardize the boat, even if you held a knife to his throat— But traditionally the family comes too; the pilot was always working from home, wasn't he?

And what would a desperate pilot do then? What would he do if a knife was held to the throat of a wife, or a child? What else could he do but sail on, trusting a lifetime of experience to see them all to safety? And it wouldn't be one unwelcome guest, no, because then you would try to run the boat heavily aground while you, muscles tensed, would rely on the confusion to leap at the fallen man and strangle him with your bare hands, but that would only work if he hadn't brought along an ally. And so then you stayed at the wheel, hoping and praying, and expecting, at any moment, the rumble of the damn slam.

Feeney was sprinting along the bank after him now, and managed to pant, "What are we going to do, sir? Seriously, what are we going to do!"

Vimes ignored Feeney for a moment. Rain, boiling surf and fallen logs were enough to contend with, but he kept his eye on the line of barges. Right now there was a rhythm as they snaked back and forth, but it was constantly interrupted by bits of driftwood and whatever attempt at steering was happening along there in the wheelhouse. Every time the rearmost barge hit the bank there was a moment, one precious little moment, when a man might jump aboard, if that man were foolish.

So he jumped, and realized that a jump would have to beget another jump and failure to keep the rhythm would mean falling back into the torrent, but jumping on to the next barge, which was swinging and bucking in the swell, you just hoped that you didn't get a foot stuck between the two of them, because two twenty-five-foot barges colliding as a sandwich with your foot in the middle would do more than just leave a bruise. But Stinky ran and jumped and pirouetted just ahead of him and Vimes was quick enough to get the message, landing squarely on the next barge, and so, surprisingly, did Feeney, who actually laughed, although you had to be within a foot of him to hear that.

"Well done, sir! We did this when I was a lad . . . every boy did . . . the big ones were best . . ."

Vimes had got his breath back after the first two jumps. According to what Feeney had told him, the *Wonderful Fanny* was a bulk carrier, big and slow, but it could take any load. There could be anything in these barges, he thought, but there was no smell of goblins yet and there were two barges still to go and weather that was trying to get even worse.

With that thought, there was Stinky again, who apparently could come and go without ever being seen either coming or going. And he still glowed faintly. Vimes had to crouch to speak to him. "Where are they, Stinky?"

The goblin farted, quite probably as a clown does, more for entertainment than relief. Clearly happy at the response, he cracked, "Number one barge! Easy to get to! Easy to feed!"

Vimes eyed the distance to the barge immediately behind the *Fanny*. Surely there had to be some kind of walkway? Some means of getting into the barges so that the crew could access the cargo? He turned again to Feeney, dripping with rain and illumined by another flash of lightning. "How many crew, do you think?"

Even this close, Feeney had to shout. "Probably two men, or a man and boy, down below in what they call the cowshed! Along with the engineer, and generally a loadmaster or cargo captain! Sometimes a cook, if the captain's wife doesn't want to do the job, although mostly they do, and then one or two lads learning the business and acting as general lookouts and wharf rats!"

"Is that all? No guards?"

"No, sir, this ain't the high seas!"

Two barges crashed together, sending up a plume of water that succeeded in at last filling Vimes's boots right to the top. There was no point in emptying them, but he managed to growl through the storm, "I've got news for you, lad. The water's getting higher."

He steeled himself for the jump on to the next erratic barge and wondered: Even so, where are the people? Surely they don't all want to die? He waited and jumped again as the barge presented itself, and landed heavily just in time to see his sword cartwheeling roguishly into the stormy water. Cursing, and struggling to keep his balance, he awaited the next opportunity to narrowly survive and this time succeed. He leapt again and almost fell backward between the crashing timbers but, balancing perilously, fell forward instead and fell in and right through a tarpaulin, into an indistinct face which cried, "Please! Please don't kill me! I'm just a complicated chicken farmer! I'm not carrying any weapons! I don't even like killing chickens!"

Vimes had managed to land with his arms around a plump man who would have screamed again had Vimes not clamped a hand over his mouth and hissed, "This is the police, sir. Sorry for the inconvenience, sir, but who the hell are you and what is going on? Come on, there's no time to waste." He pushed the man further into the barge and a soggy darkness and a recognizable smell told Sam Vimes that whether the frantic speaker was complicated or not he wasn't lying about the chickens. From the clucking, feathery gloom in the wire baskets beyond, there emanated yet another smell, announcing that a large number of chickens, never the most stoical creatures at the best of times, were now *very* frightened.

A vague silhouette demanded, "The police? Here? Pull the other leg, mate! Who do you think you are? Bloody Commander Vimes?"

The barge bucked again and an errant egg spun out of the darkness and smacked into Vimes's face. He wiped it off, or at least spread it around a bit and said, "Well, well, sir, are you always this lucky?"

HIS NAME WAS FALSE; in full it was Praise and Salvation False, and inevitably, when you have a false name you will insist on explaining why, even when imminent watery death is not only staring you in the eye but also everywhere else, possibly including both your trouser legs. "You see, sir, my family originally came from Klatch, and our name was Thalassa but, of course, over a period of time people tend to mispronounce the way they—"

Vimes interrupted him, because that was a more acceptable alternative to throttling him. "Please, Mr. False, can you tell me what's been happening on the *Fanny*?"

"Oh dear, it was terrible, it really was extremely terrible! There was shouting and yelling and I'm sure I heard a woman screaming! And now we keep hitting the bank, or at least that's what it sounds like! And the storm, sir, it'll have us under in two shakes of a lamb's tail, I'm certain of it!"

"And you didn't go forward to see, Mr. False?" said Vimes.

The man looked startled. "Commander, I breed complicated chickens, sir, extremely complicated chickens. I don't know anything about fighting! Chickens never get all that aggressive! I'm really sorry, sir, but I didn't go to see in case I saw, sir, see? And if I saw, sir, then I'm sure people would see me, sir, and since I reasoned that they would be people who were alive after other people might possibly be dead, sir, and maybe had a responsibility for said deaths, sir, I made certain that they didn't see me, sir, if you see what I mean? Besides, I have no weapons, weak lungs and a wooden toe. And I'm alive, at the moment."

In truth, Vimes thought there was an inescapable logic to all this, so he said, "Don't worry about it, Mr. False, I bet you've got enough to do with your complicated chickens. So, no weapons at all, then?"

"I'm very sorry to disappoint you, commander, but I'm not a strong man. It was all I could do to drag my toolbox on board!"

Vimes's face stayed blank. "Toolbox? You have a toolbox?"

Mr. False clutched the wall again as the barge bounced off something it shouldn't have, and said, "Well, yes, of course. If we manage to get off at Quirm I've got a site that I must make ready for a hundred chicken houses, and if you want a job done properly these days then you have to do it yourself, right?"

"You're telling an expert," said Vimes as another crash sent them both staggering. "I wonder if I could take a look at this tool-box of yours?"

There are times in the symphony of the world, when its aural kaleidoscope of crashes, thunderbolts, screams and storms suddenly merges into one great hallelujah! And the contents of the chicken farmer's innocent toolbox, which contained nothing not made of ordinary iron and steel and wood, nevertheless gleamed in the eyes of Commander Sam Vimes like the hosts of heaven. Mallets, hammers, saws, oh my! There was even a large spiral awl! What could Willikins have managed with a toy like *that*? Hal-le-lu-jah! Oh, and here was a crowbar! Vimes balanced it in his hand, and felt the Street rise until it touched his feet. The complicated chicken man had heard a woman screaming . . .

Vimes spun around as the tarpaulin was pushed aside and Feeney dropped into the barge in a flurry of spray. "I know you didn't give me the signal, commander, but I thought I'd better tell you the water is going down."

Vimes saw Mr. False close his eyes and groan, but turned back to Feeney and said, "Well, that's a good thing, isn't it? The water? Going down?"

"No, it isn't, sir!" yelled Feeney. "It's still raining hard and the water level is going *down*, and that means that upstream of us enough broken trees and bushes and mud and other junk are piling up to make a dam which is getting bigger and bigger and growing out sideways as the water builds up behind it, sir. Can you see what I mean?"

Vimes did. "Damn slam?"

Feeney nodded. "Damn right! We have two choices: would you rather die on the river or under it? What are your orders, please, sir?"

Another collision shook the barge, and Vimes stared at darkness. In this terrible twilight somebody was managing to stop this boat from foundering. A woman had screamed and Vimes had a crowbar. Almost absent-mindedly he reached down into the open toolbox and picked up a sledgehammer, handing it to Feeney. "There you go, lad. I know you've got your official firewood, but things might get up close and personal. Chalk it up to the dreadful algebra of necessity, but try not to hit me with it."

He heard the voice of Feeney saying, more frantically this time, "What are we going to do, commander?!"

And Vimes blinked and said, *"Everything!"*

T HE WIND CAUGHT THE tarpaulin as Vimes pulled it open, and it flapped off across the river, leaving the complicated chicken farmer living in hope and broken eggs. They pulled themselves out into the darkness, their shadows dancing to the rhythm of the lightning. How the hell was the pilot navigating in all this? Lamps up front? Surely they could do nothing on a night like this except show up the darkness. But although there was a suspicion, at every bang and bounce, that the *Fanny* was in real trouble, Vimes could hear now the splashing of the paddle wheels like one solid dependable theme in the cacophony, a regular, reassuring sound. It was making way. There was some order in the world, but how could the pilot manage the chaos? How could you steer when you couldn't see?

Feeney had explained in a hurry and Vimes had expressed utter disbelief even faster. "It's true, sir! He knows every bend in the river, he knows the wind, he knows how fast we're going and has a stopwatch and an hourglass in reserve. He takes a turn when it's time to take it. Okay, he's shaving the banks a bit with the old *Fanny*, but she's pretty tough."

They jumped together on to the last barge and found a hatch that was locked. However, a crowbar is a universal pass key. And there, under the hatch, were goblins, tied hand and foot, every one, and they had been stacked like cabbages. There were hundreds of them. Overwhelmed, Vimes looked around for Stinky, who turned out to be behind him.

"Okay, my friend, over to you. We'll cut them loose, certainly, but I wouldn't mind a bit of reassurance that I won't suddenly have a load of angry goblins twisting my head backward and forward to see which way would take it off, understand?"

Stinky, already as skinny as a skeleton, looked even thinner when he shrugged. He pointed at the groaning heaps. "Too sore, too stiff, too hungry, too . . ." Stinky looked closely at a goblin at the bottom of a pile and touched a flaccid hand, "too dead to chase anyone, Mr. Po-leess-maan. Hah! But later, give food, give water and they chase. Oh, they chase like the buggery, you bet! Once I talk to them, oh you bet! But I will say to them, po-leess-maan, him big arsehole, okay, but kind arsehole. I will say to them, you whack him, I whack you on account that I po-leess-maan now. Special Po-leess-maan Stinky!"

Vimes considered that was the best valedictory he could expect in the circumstances. Just then Feeney managed to lever the lid off a large drum, one of several rolling around on the deck. Immediately the terrible stench in the barge doubled in intensity, and he backed away with his hands over his mouth. Stinky, on the other hand, sniffed approvingly. "Hot damn! Turkey gizzards! Food of the gods! Bastard murder voyage, but okay catering."

Vimes stared at him. Well, okay, he thought, he hangs around near humans so he picks up a vocabulary, maybe that is suspiciously clever. Perhaps Miss Beedle gave him language lessons? Or maybe he's just some occult adventurer from hell knows where having fun at the expense of a hardworking copper. Not for the first time.

Feeney was already cutting ropes, and Vimes tried to resurrect as many goblins as he could in a hurry. It was no errand for anyone with a concern for hygiene or even a notion of what the word meant—though after an hour in a storm on Old Treachery, it had no meaning anyway. They staggered up, and fell down again, found their way to the upended barrel of dead turkey bits and stumbled over slippery decks to a sloshing and now half-empty water trough that Feeney had found and was filling by the simple expedient of sticking a bucket over the side. They were coming back to life; *mostly* they were coming back to life.

The barge bounced off a bank again, and amid tumbling goblins Vimes grabbed for a handhold. Half the entire barge was full of barrels which, if you sniffed anywhere near them, were certainly not full of sweet roses. He braved the rocking deck again and said, "I don't think all this is for a little voyage to the seaside, do you? There's more barrels of stinking turkey entrails than this lot of poor devils could possibly get through in a week! Someone was expecting a long journey! Good grief!"

The barge had smacked into something and, by the sound of breaking glass, that something had been smashed. Feeney stood up, holding on to a rope, and, wiping turkey gizzard off his coat, said, "Voyage, sir. Not journey, sir. You wouldn't need all this stuff if you're traveling on land. I reckon they're bound for somewhere a long way away."

"Do you think it'll be a holiday of sun, sea, surf and fun?" said Vimes.

"No, sir," said Feeney, "and they wouldn't like it if it was, would they? Goblins like the dark."

Vimes slapped him on the shoulder. "Okay, Chief Constable

Upshot, don't hit somebody who surrenders and, if a man drops his weapon, be a little bit wary of him until you're certain he hasn't got another one tucked away somewhere, right? If in doubt, knock 'em out. And you know how to do that: use the old Bang Suck Cling Buck on them, eh?!"

"Yes, sir, that's a recipe for shoe polish, sir, but I'll bear it in mind."

Vimes turned to Stinky, who already looked slightly fatter than usual. "Stinky, I don't have the faintest idea what is going to happen next. I can see your chums are starting to look alive, and so you've got the chance that we all get, sink or swim, and I can't say better than that. Come on, let's go, Feeney."

This close, the *Wonderful Fanny* was now a rolling, creaking mess, half-covered by flying weeds and sticks. Apart from the storm and the clanging and creaking of the mechanisms, it was silent.

"Okay," said Feeney quietly, "we'd better go in by the cattle door at the stern, sir, or as you would say, 'the back.' It won't be a difficult jump, there's lots of handholds because the loadmaster has to come out here to see to the barges. Can you see that double door and the little wicket gate? We go in that way. There'll likely be more cargo along the cattle ramp, because a loadmaster never wastes floor space, and then we go midships . . ."

"That is to say 'the middle of the ship'?" said Vimes.

Feeney smiled. "Yes, sir, and watch out because it's a mass of machinery. You'll see what I mean, because you're smart. Take the wrong step and you could fall into a gear or on top of an ox, never a happy occasion. It's noisy, smelly and dangerous, so if there are many bandits on this boat I wouldn't expect to find them there."

I would, Vimes thought; our Mr. Stratford is the kind of maniac who would want to keep going in suicidal circumstances. Why? So that the cargo is a long way away before anyone knows about it? And Stratford works for Lord Rust and the Rusts believe the world belongs to them. We're taking goblins somewhere, but they want to keep them alive—why?

The shock of another collision brought him back to the dreadful here and now, and he said, "I'd expect to find any crew here being watched like hawks in case they put a spanner in the works."

"Oh, very smart, sir, very smart indeed. There has to be some light in there for safety's sake, but not much and all behind glass 'cos of . . ."

Feeney hesitated, so Vimes suggested, "Fire, perhaps? I've never known an engineer who doesn't shove grease wherever he can."

"Oh, it's not exactly the grease, sir, it's the beasts. The gas does build up, so it does! And if the glass breaks, well, it's regrettably spectacular. Two years ago the *Glorious Peggy* was blown out of the water for just such a reason!"

"Do they eat the Hang Suck Butt Dog with turnips around here?"

"No, sir, not as far as I know, but Bhangbhangduc fusion cookery is very popular on the boats, it's true. Anyway, further on you'll find the pilot's cabin, the sleeping quarters and then the wheelhouse, which has very wide windows, which is another good reason to attack from behind."

Refreshingly, it was a short leap with a good handhold at the end of it. Vimes had no worries about being heard. The deck creaked under his feet as he crept inside the *Wonderful Fanny* and sidled toward the middle of the ship, or whatever the hell the real term for it was, but then she creaked everywhere, and all the time, and groaned, too. The boat was so noisy that a sudden patch of silence might have drawn attention to itself. And I'm looking for somebody who looks like everybody else, he thought, right up until he looks like the vicious killer he is. Well, that seems straightforward.

Vimes was vaguely aware of huge wheels spinning frantically off to either side and chains traveling overhead and now, here, at the top of the flight of stairs, was somebody who clearly wasn't where they should have been . . .

It was a woman, with a small girl clinging to her dress. They had been loosely tied to a creaking beam, and a small oil lamp overhead held them in the center of its circle of light. And this was probably because there was a man sitting a little way away from them on a stool, with a crossbow lying on his lap.

And here was a puzzle because a length of string had been tied to each of his legs. One length of string ran across the floor and disappeared downward into what was, to judge by the heat, the farmyard stink and the occasional bellow of troubled ungulate, the cowshed that Vimes had just passed. The other string disappeared forward toward the wheelhouse.

The woman spotted him and immediately clasped the child to her chest and very slowly put a finger to her lips. He had to hope that the man hadn't noticed, and did *not* have to hope that the woman realized that he was there to rescue her, not to add to her troubles. That wasn't necessary, but he did feel better that she was a lady fast on the uptake. He held up a hand in front of Feeney, but the lad was definitely future captain material; he hadn't moved at all. Like Vimes, he had become an observer. And Vimes observed, and let the dark rise up to assess the situation in its own inimitable way. This wasn't the Summoning Dark, or at least he fervently hoped not. It was just his own human darkness and internal enemy, which knew his every thought, which knew that every time Commander Vimes dragged some vicious and inventive murderer to such mercy or justice as the law in its erratic wisdom determined, there was another Vimes, a ghost Vimes, whose urge to chop that creature into pieces on the spot had to be chained. This, regrettably, was harder every time, and he wondered if one day that darkness would break out and claim its heritage, and he wouldn't know . . . the brakes and chains and doors and locks in his head would have vanished and he wouldn't know.

Right now, as he looked at the frightened child, he feared that moment was coming closer. Possibly only the presence of Feeney was holding the darkness at bay, the dreadful urge to do the hangman out of his entitlement of a dollar for the drop, thruppence for the rope and sixpence for his beer. How easy it is to kill, yes, but not when a smart young copper who thinks you are a good guy is looking to you. At home, the Watch and his family surrounded Vimes like a wall. Here the good guy was the good guy because he didn't want anyone to see him being bad. He did not want to be ashamed. He did not want to be the darkness.

The bow was pointed at the two hostages and its holder had surely been told to fire if a leg pull sounded the alarm. Would he do it? You needed to age a bit for the dark to start trickling in, although there were always one or two who were born as darkness on legs, who would kill for a pastime. Was he one? Even if he wasn't, would he panic? How light was the trigger? Could a sudden jerk set it off?

Outside, the storm raged. Whether the water was going down or not didn't seem all that important, given there was so much of the damn stuff around already. The woman was watching him out of the corner of her eye. Oh well, every moment counted . . .

Timing his steps carefully, as if a footstep would be heard in all the thunder and creaking, Vimes crept up to the unsuspecting guard, clamped both hands around his neck and jerked upward. The arrow thudded into the ceiling.

"I don't want anybody to get hurt." Vimes tried to say it in a friendly way, but went on, "If you think you can pull strings, kid, then let me tell you that you'll run out of gasp before I run out of squeeze. Chief Constable Upshot, grab that weapon and tie up this gentleman's legs. You may keep his weapon. I know you like them."

He must have inadvertently decreased the pressure, for his captive said hoarsely, "I don't want to kill anybody, sir, please! They gave me the bow and told me I was to fire if the boat stopped or I got a pull on the ropes! Do you think I'd do that, sir? Do you really think I'd do that? I was only sitting here in case one of them came in! Please, sir, I never came along for anything like this! It's Stratford, sir, he's a total nutjob, sir, a bloody killer, he is!"

There was a crash and the whole boat shook. Maybe the pilot's stopwatch had let him down. "What's your name, mister?"

"Eddie, sir, Eddie Brassbound. I'm just a water rat, sir!" The man was trembling. Vimes could see his hand shaking. He turned to the woman with the child, who was being supported now by Feeney, touched his forelock and flashed his carefully secreted badge. "Madam, I'm Commander Vimes of the Ankh-Morpork City Watch. Has this man mishandled you or the little girl in any way?"

The woman had barely moved. She reminded him of the younger Sybil, calm and collected and much more likely to fight than scream, but she wouldn't fight until she was ready. "It was done pretty slick, commander, just when I was putting Grace to bed. The bastards came on as owners of some cargo and acted like decent boys until my husband said he reckoned the weather was going to get really bad. I was in the galley, I heard a lot of yelling and then we were put down here. Personally, sir, I would deem it a favor if you killed every man jack of them, but life can't be all fun. As far as this one is concerned, well, he could have been less gentlemanly, so although I'd like you to throw him into the river I wouldn't object if you refused to tie a heavy weight to his leg."

Feeney laughed. "Wouldn't need weights, ma'am! The river is having a party and we're all guests! I'm a pretty good swimmer, and I wouldn't dare jump into what's out there."

Vimes grabbed Brassbound and stared into his eyes. After a moment he said, "No, I know a killer's eyes when I see them. That doesn't mean you ain't a pirate, though, so we're going to keep an eye on you, okay, so don't try anything. I'm trusting you. Heavens help you if I'm wrong."

Brassbound opened his mouth to speak, but Vimes added quickly, "You could make your life a little easier and possibly longer, Mr. Brassbound, if you were to tell me how many of your jolly parcel of rogues there are on the *Fanny*."

"Don't know, sir. Don't know who's still alive, see?"

Vimes looked at the woman as the boat gave a lurch. It was a strange sensation—for a moment Vimes felt almost weightless— and there was a commotion behind them in the cowshed among the great spinning wheels. When he got his balance he managed to say, "I take it that you *are* Mrs. Sillitoe, madam?"

She nodded. "Yes, I am, commander," she said as the little girl clung more tightly to her. "I know my husband is still alive, because so are we . . . at the moment." She stopped as another surge lifted the entire boat, then the *Fanny* came down with a splash and a spine-numbing thump, followed by the long-drawn-out bellow of a bullock who had had enough, *and* the start of a scream.

Vimes, Feeney and Brassbound picked themselves up off the floor. Mrs. Sillitoe and her daughter were, amazingly, still vertical and Mrs. Sillitoe wore a grim smile. "That sound you heard was one of the pirates dying, I'm extremely pleased to say! That means everyone else in the cowshed is alive. Shall I tell you why? He almost certainly didn't hop! Those lifts and drops are little slams to me: somewhere behind us a damn slam is getting so big that bits of it are calving off and coming down all the way to us at speed, you see, raising the water level and dropping it again like a stone as they go past—and that's when you have to know enough to dance to the rhythm! Because if you don't dance to the rhythm of the slam you'll dance with the Devil soon enough! A man went down there with a crossbow when the fighting started. By the sound of it he wasn't familiar with the dance. I expect it was Ten Gallon Charlie who got him when he was on the ground, poor lamb. Charlie is the Bullock Wrangler. If he hits a man once, no one will ever have to hit him again." Mrs. Sillitoe said that in a matter-of-fact, satisfied voice. "If you want to try to steal from our riverboat you have to be prepared for some considerable inconvenience."

And I thought the *city* was on the tough side, Vimes thought. He noticed that a prudent Feeney had rearmed the confiscated crossbow and said, "I'm going below to make certain. Mrs. Sillitoe, how many other pirates do you think there are?"

"There were four that came aboard as owners of the cargo." She began to tick them off on her fingers. "Mr. Harrison the load-master got one of them, but another one stabbed him, the devil. I know only one of them went down to the cowshed, and another one helped this simpering little bastard rig up the ropes so that if anybody was left to try any funny business we were hostage, and then that other man went up to the wheelhouse. I was told that we would be all right, provided my husband gets the cargo to Quirm." The little girl clung to her dress as the woman continued, her face wooden. "Personally, I don't believe it, but he hasn't harmed my husband yet. He's counting, all the time he's counting. My husband is listening to Old Treachery and remembering! Trying to out-think sixty miles of murderous water! And if he dies, it wins, wherever you are . . ."

"Feeney, keep your crossbow pointing at this gentleman, will you?" said Vimes. "And if he makes any movement whatsoever, up to and including trying to blow his nose, you have my full authority to shoot him somewhere where it will be seriously inconvenient."

Vimes headed to the steps and nodded to Feeney and Mrs. Sillitoe, raised a finger and said, "Be with you in just one minute!" And hurried down into the hot and noisome heart of the *Wonderful Fanny*. Snooker, Vimes thought. Knocking the balls until you have the right one right on cue.

He felt pressure on his feet surge as the vessel lifted, and instantly jumped into the air, landing neatly as the *Fanny* slapped back down into the water.

He was confronted by a man who would surely make even Willikins think twice. "You'd be Ten Gallons? Mrs. Sillitoe sent me down here. I'm Commander Vimes, Ankh-Morpork City Watch!"

And the man with a face like a troll and a body to match said, "Heard about you. Thought you were dead!"

"I generally look like this at the end of boat trips, Mr. Gallons," said Vimes. Then, pointing to an apparent corpse on the floor between them, "What happened to him?"

"I fink *he* is dead," Ten Gallons leered. "I've never seen a man suffocated by his own nose before."

It was hard to hear anything down in the cowshed given the complaining of the oxen and the ominous whirring of overstressed gears, but Vimes shouted, "Did he have a crossbow?"

Ten Gallons nodded and fingers thicker than Vimes's wrist unhooked said weapon off a nail on the wall. "Would come with you, mister, but it's all the three of us can do to hold things together down here!" He spat. "Ain't really any hope anyway, the damn slam is right behind us! See you on the other side, copper!"

Vimes nodded at him, examined the crossbow for a moment, made a little adjustment and, satisfied, climbed up the steps.

Vimes looked at the few people left on the *Wonderful Fanny* who weren't pouring water on the backs of steaming oxen or trying to hold the boat in one piece and above water. The shocks were indeed getting closer together, he was sure of it, and surely, once there was a big enough hole, the whole damn dam would give way.

All the occupants of the cabin except Brassbound, who fell over, jumped together as yet another surge raised the boat.

There was a sharp intake of breath from Feeney as Vimes went over to the trembling Brassbound, who had clearly realized that he was likely to be the unlucky winner of the first-over-the-side contest. And Feeney actually groaned when Vimes handed the man the recovered crossbow saying, "I told you, Chief Constable, I know a killer when I see one and I need back-up and I'm sure that our Mr. Brassbound is very eager to get himself promptly on to the good side of the law right now, a decision that might well make him look better in court. Am I not right, Mr. Brassbound?"

The young man nodded fervently.

Vimes added, "I'd rather have you down here, Feeney. Until I know exactly who is still on this tub, I'd like you to look after the ladies. Right now I'm not sure I know who's alive and who's dead."

"The *Fanny* is not a tub, commander," said Mrs. Sillitoe sharply, "but I'll forgive you this one time."

Vimes gave her a little salute as all but Brassbound jumped and once again the idiot floundered.

Vimes turned toward the stairs. "It's going to be Stratford up there with the pilot, isn't it, Mr. Brassbound?"

Another, bigger surge this time, and Brassbound landed heavily. He managed to get out, "And he's heard about you, you know how it is, and he's determined to get down to the sea before you catch up with him. He's a killer, sir, a stone killer! Don't give him a chance, sir, I beg you for all our sakes, and do it quickly for yours!" The air was electric, truly electric. Everything metal shook and jangled. "They say the dam is going to break pretty soon," said Brassbound.

"Thank you for that, Mr. Brassbound. You sound like a sensible young man to me and I'll say so to the authorities."

The worried young man's face was wreathed in smiles as he said, "And you're the famous Commander Vimes, sir! I'm glad to be at your back."

There were a lot of steps up to the wheelhouse. The pilot was king and rode high over the river, monarch of all he surveyed even if, as now, rain hammered at the expensive glass windows as if it found such solid slabs of sky offensive. Vimes stepped inside quickly. It was hardly worth shouting, given that the storm drowned out everything, but you had to be able to say that you'd said it: "Commander Vimes, Ankh-Morpork City Watch! Statute of necessary action!" Which didn't exist, but he swore to himself that he would damn well get it enacted as soon as he got back, even if he had to call in favors from all over the world. A lawman faced with a dreadful emergency should at least have some kind of figleaf to shove down the throats of the lawyers!

He could see the back of Mr. Sillitoe's head with his pilot's cap. The pilot paid Vimes no attention, but a young man was standing looking at Vimes in knock-kneed, pants-wetting horror. The sword he had been carrying landed heavily on the deck.

Brassbound was hopping from one foot to the other. "You'd better take care of him right now, commander, he'll have a trick or two up his sleeve and no mistake!"

Vimes ignored this and carefully patted the young man down, freeing up one short knife, the sort a river rat might carry. He used it to cut a length of rope and tied the man's hands together behind him. "Okay, Mr. Stratford, we're going downstairs. Though if you'd like to dive into the water first I won't stop you."

And then the man spoke for the first time. "I ain't Stratford, sir," he said, pleading. "I'm Squeezy McIntyre. That's Stratford behind you with the crossbow pointing at you, sir."

The man formerly known as Brassbound gave a chuckle as Vimes turned. "Oh my, oh my, the great Commander Vimes! I'll be damned if you ain't as dumb as a pile of horseshit! You know the eyes of a killer when you see them, do you? Well, I reckon I've killed maybe sixteen people, not including goblins, of course, they don't count."

Stratford sighted on Vimes and grinned. "Maybe it's my boyish features, would you say? What kind of bloody fool cares about the goblins, eh? Oh, they say they can talk, but you know how those little buggers can lie!" The tip of the crossbow drifted back and forward hypnotically in Stratford's hands. "I'm curious, though. I mean, I don't like you, and sure as salvation I'm going to shoot you, but do me a favor and tell me what you saw in my eyes, okay?"

Squeezy took the opportunity to hop desperately down the steps just as Vimes said, with a shrug, "I saw a goblin girl being murdered. What lies did *she* tell you? I know the eyes of a murderer, Mr. Stratford, oh I surely do, because I've looked into eyes like that many times. And if I need reminding, I look into my shaving mirror. Oh, yes, I recognize your eyes and I'm interested to see what you're going to do next, Mr. Stratford. Though now I come to think about it, maybe it wasn't sensible of me to give you that crossbow. Maybe I really *am* stupid, because I'm offering you the opportunity to surrender to me here and now and I'm doing it only once."

Stratford stared with his mouth open and then said, "Hell, commander, I've got the drop on you, and *you* want *me* to surrender to *you*? Sorry, commander, but I'll see you again in hell!"

There was a space in the world for the crossbow to sing when the grinning Stratford pulled the trigger. Unfortunately, the sound that it made approximated to the word *thunk*. He stared at it.

"I took the safety pin out and stamped it into the dung," said Vimes. "You can't fire it without the pin! Now, I expect you have a couple of knives about your person, and so if you fancy cutting your way out past me, then I'd be happy to accommodate you, although I'll tell you that firstly you won't succeed, and secondly, if you manage to get past a boy who grew up on the streets of Ankh-Morpork there's a man down there with a punch that can fell an elephant, and if you knife him you'll just make him more annoyed—"

The surge this time was bigger than ever, and Vimes banged his head on the cabin's roof before coming down again in front of Stratford and kicking him smartly in the official police officer method and also the groin.

"Oh, come on, Mr. Stratford, don't you have a reputation to keep up? Feared killer? You should spend some time in the city, my lad, and I'll make certain you do." Stratford fell backward and Vimes continued, "And then you'll hang, as is right and proper, but don't worry—Mr. Trooper does a nifty noose and they say it hardly hurts at all. Tell you what, just to get the adrenaline pumping, Mr. Stratford, imagine I'm the goblin girl. She begged for her life, Mr. Stratford, remember that? I do! And so do you. You fell down at the first surge, Mr. Stratford. River rats know what to do. You didn't, although I must say you've covered it very well. Whoops!"

This was because Stratford had indeed tried his hand with a knife. Vimes twisted his wrist and flung the blade down the stairs just as the glass in the wheelhouse smashed and a branch longer than Vimes plowed across the room, shedding leaves and dragging torrential rain and darkness behind it.

Both the lamps had gone out and, as it turned out, so had

Stratford, hopefully through a shattered window, possibly to his death, but Vimes wasn't sure. He would have preferred *definitely*. But there was no time to fret about him, because now came another surge, and water poured in through the glassless windows.

Vimes jerked open the little gate to the pilot's deck and found Mr. Sillitoe struggling up out of the pile of storm-washed debris. He was moaning, "I've lost count, I've lost count!"

Vimes pulled him upward and helped him into his big chair, where he banged on the arms in frustration. "And now I can't see a damned thing in all this murk! Can't count, can't see, can't steer! Won't survive!"

"I can see, Mr. Sillitoe," said Vimes. "What do you want me to do?"

"You can?"

Vimes stared out at the homicidal river. "There's a thundering great rock coming up on the left-hand side. Should it be doing that? Looks like there's a busted landing stage there."

"Ye gods! That's Baker's Knob! Here, let me at the wheel! How close is it now?"

"Maybe fifty yards?"

"And you can see it in all this? Damn me, mister, you must have been born in a cave! That means we ain't that far from Quirm now, a touch under nineteen miles. You think you could stand lookout? Is my family okay? That little snot threatened to harm them if I didn't keep the *Fanny* on schedule!" Something big and heavy bounced off the roof and spun away into the night, and the pilot went on, "Gastric Sillitoe, delighted to make your acquaintance, sir." He stared ahead. "I've heard of you. Koom Valley, right? Happy to have you aboard."

"Er, Gastric? Whole tree spinning in current near left-hand shore, ten yards ahead! Nothing much to see on right."

The wheel spun frantically again. "Obliged to you, sir, and I surely hope you won't take it amiss if I say that we generally talk about port and starboard?"

"Wouldn't know about that, Gastric, never drank starboard. Mass of what looks like smashed logs ahead, forty yards, looks like small stuff, and I see a faint light high up on our right, can't tell how far away." Vimes ducked and a jagged log bounced off the back of the wheelhouse. Beside him the pilot sounded as if he had got a grip on things now.

"Okay, commander, that would be Jackson's Light, very welcome sight! Now I've found my bearings and an hourglass that ain't busted, I'd be further in your debt if you'd go below and tell Ten Gallons to cut loose the barges? There's a chicken farmer on one of them! Best to get him on board before the dam breaks."

"And hundreds of goblins, Gastric."

"Pay them no mind, sir. Goblins is just goblins."

For a moment Vimes stared into the darkness, and the darkness *within* the darkness, and it said to him, "You're having fun, aren't you, commander! This is Sam Vimes being Sam Vimes in the dark and the rain and the danger and because you're a copper you're not going to believe that Stratford is dead until you see the corpse. You know it. Some people take a devil of a lot of killing. You know you saw him go out of the cabin, but there's all kinds of ropes and handholds on the boat, and the bugger was wiry and limber, and you know, just as day follows night, that he'll be back. Double jeopardy, Commander Vimes, all the pieces on the board, goblins to save, a murderer to catch—and all the time, when you remember, there is a wife and a little boy waiting for you to come back."

"I always remember!"

"Of course you do, Commander Vimes," the voice continued, "of course you do. But I know you, and sometimes a shadow passes every sun. Nevertheless, the darkness will always be yours, my tenacious friend."

And then reality either came back or went away and Vimes was saying, "We bring the goblins aboard, Gastric, because they . . . Yes, *they* are evidence in an important police investigation!"

There was a further surge, and this time Vimes landed up on the deck, which was a little bit softer now because of the ragged carpet of leaves and branches. As he got up Mr. Sillitoe said, "Police investigation, you say? Well, the *Fanny* has always been a friend of the law but, well, sir, they stink like the pits of hell, and that's the truth of it! They'll frighten the oxen something terrible!"

"Do you think they aren't frightened already?" said Vimes. "Er, small logjam ahead on the right. All clear on the left." Vimes sniffed. "Trust me, sir, by the smell of it they're pretty nervous as it is. Can't you just stop and tie us up to the bank?"

Sillitoe's laugh was brittle. "Sir, there are no banks now, none that I'd try to get to. I know this river and it's angry and there's a damn slam coming. Can't stop it any more than I could stop the storm. You signed up for the long haul, commander: either we race the river or we fold our hands, pray to the gods and die right now." He saluted. "Nevertheless, I can see you're a man, sir, who does what he sees needs doing, and, by hokey, I can't argue with that! You've done a man's job as it is, Commander Vimes, and may the gods go with you. May they go with all of us."

Vimes ran down the steps and grabbed Feeney in passing as he danced over the heaving floor to the cowshed. "Come on, lad, it's time to ditch the barges. There's too much of a drag. Mr. Ten Gallons? Let's get those doors open, shall we? Mr. Sillitoe has put me in charge down here. If you want to argue, feel free!"

The huge man didn't even attempt an argument, and punched the doors open.

Vimes swore. Mr. Sillitoe had been right. There was roaring not far behind them and a river of lightning and blue fire was sweeping down the valley like a tide. For a moment he was hypnotized, and then got a grip. "Okay, Feeney, you start getting the goblins on board and I'll fetch our chicken farmer! The bloody iron ore can sink for all I care."

In the glaring light of the damn slam Vimes jumped twice to land on the barge from which was already coming the squawking of terrified birds. Water poured off him as he dragged open the hatch and shouted, "Mr. False! No, don't start grabbing the chickens! Better off farmer with no chickens than a load of chickens with no farmer! Anyway, they'll probably float, or fly, or something!"

He coaxed the frightened man on to the next barge to find that it was still full of bewildered goblins. Feeney was looking out from the open door at the rear of the *Fanny*, and above the roar and hissing Vimes heard him shout, "It's Mr. Ten Gallons, sir! He says no goblins!"

Vimes glanced behind them, and then turned back to Feeney. "Very well, Mr. Feeney, keep an eye on the goblins' barge while I discuss matters with Mr. Ten Gallons, understand?"

He flung Mr. False on to the deck of the *Fanny* and looked around for Ten Gallons. He shook his head. What a copper that man would make if properly led by human beings. He sighed. "Mr. Ten Gallons? I told you, Mr. Sillitoe has given me carte blanche. Can we discuss the matter of the goblins?"

The giant growled, "I ain't got no cart and I don't know no Blanche, and I ain't having no goblins on my deck, okay?"

Vimes nodded, poker-faced, and looked exhaustedly at the deck. "Is that your last word, Mr. Ten Gallons?"

"It damn well is!"

"Okay, this is mine."

Ten Gallons went over backward like a tree and began to sleep like a log.

The street never leaves you . . .

And what the University of the Street told you was that fighting was a science, the science of getting the opponent out of your face and facedown on the ground with the maximum amount of speed and the minimum of effort. After that, of course, you had a range of delightful possibilities and the leisure in which to consider them. But if you wanted to fight fair, or at least more fair than most of the other street options, then you had to know how to punch, and what to punch and from precisely which angle to punch it. Of course, his treasured brass knuckles were an optional but helpful extra but, Vimes thought as he tried to wring some blood back into his fingers, probably any court, after sight of Ten Gallons, would have forgiven Vimes, even if he used a sledgehammer.

He looked at the brass knuckles. They hadn't even bent: good old Ankh-Morpork know-how. The country may have the muscle but the city has got the technology, he thought, as he slipped them back in his pocket.

"Okay, Mr. Feeney, let's get them in, shall we? Find Stinky, he's the brains of the outfit."

POSSIBLY STINKY *was* THE brains of the outfit. Even at the end Vimes was never certain just what Stinky was. But the goblins, spurred by his crunchy chattering, ran and leapt like ugly gazelles past Vimes and into the boat. He took one look at the growling death behind them, made the last jump into the boat and helped Feeney shut and bolt the doors. And that meant that now, with the ventilation gone, the bulls in the basement were getting nostrils full of goblin. It wasn't, Vimes thought, all that bad when you got used to it—more alchemical than midden—but down below there was a lot of shouting and a jerk as the beasts tried to stampede inside their treadmill.

Vimes ignored it, despite the shuddering of the boat, and shouted, "Let go of the barges, chief constable! I hope you really do know how!"

Feeney nodded and opened the hatch in the floor. Spray blew in and stopped when he knelt down and stuck his hand into the hole.

"Takes quite a few turns before they drop, commander. If I was you I'd be holding on to something when the iron ore goes!"

Vimes elbowed his way through the terrified goblins, pulled himself with care up into the wheelhouse again, and tapped Gastric on the shoulder. "We're dropping the barges any minute!" The pilot, still clinging to the wheel and squinting into the dark, gave a brief nod; nothing less than a scream would be heard in the wheelhouse now. The wind and debris had smashed every window.

Vimes looked out of the rear window and saw the great, floating, flying desolation of lightning-laced wood, mud and tumbling rock closing in. For a moment he thought he saw a naked marble lady tumbling with the debris and clutching her marble shift as if defending the remains of her modesty from the deluge. He blinked and she was gone . . . Perhaps he'd imagined it . . . He shouted, "I hope you can swim, sir?" just as the damn slam caught up and the apparition called Stratford dived through the window and was fielded neatly by Vimes, to Stratford's great surprise.

"Do you think I'm a baby, Mr. Stratford? Do you think that *I* don't think?"

Stratford squirmed out of Vimes's grip, spun neatly and threw a punch which Vimes very nearly dodged. It was harder than he had expected, and, to give a devil his due, Stratford knew how to defend and, perish the thought, was younger than Vimes, much younger. Yes, you could tell the eyes of a murderer, at least after they had done more than three or so and got away with it. Their eyes held the expression some gods probably had. But a killer in the process of trying to kill was always absorbed, constantly calculating, drawing upon some hideous strength. If you cut their leg off they wouldn't notice until they fell over. Tricks didn't work, and the floor was slippery with the debris of half a forest. As they kicked and punched their way back and forth across the wheelhouse deck, Stratford was winning. When had Vimes last eaten, or had a decent drink of water, or slept properly?

And then from below was the cry "Barges away!" And the *Wonderful Fanny* bucked like a thoroughbred, throwing both of the fighters to the floor, where Vimes barely had room to kick and fend off blows. Water poured over them, filling the cabin to waist level, reducing Vimes's stamina to almost nothing. Stratford had his hands around his throat, and Vimes's world turned dark blue and full of chuckling water, banging against his ears. He tried to think of Young Sam and Sybil, but the water kept washing them away . . . except that the pressure was suddenly gone, and his body, deciding that his brain had at last gone on holiday, flailed upward.

And there was Stratford, kneeling in water that was falling away very fast, a matter probably of no concern to him now since he was holding his head and screaming, owing to the fact that suddenly there was Stinky, spreadeagled on Stratford's head, reaching down and kicking and scratching anything that could be kicked off, scratched or, to one lengthy scream, pulled.

His Grace the Duke of Ankh, assisted by Sir Samuel Vimes, with the help of Commander Vimes, got to his feet, with the last-minute assistance of Blackboard Monitor Vimes, and all of them coalesced into one man as he leapt across the shaking deck just too late to stop Stratford pulling Stinky—and a certain amount of hair—off his head, and throwing him to the streaming deck and stamping on him heavily. There was no mistaking it. He'd heard the crack of bones even while airborne, and so what hit Stratford was the full force of the law, and its rage.

The street is old and cunning; but the street is always willing to learn and that is why Vimes, in mid air, felt his legs unfold and the full majesty of the law hit Stratford with the traditionally unstoppable One Man He Up Down Very Sorry. Even Vimes was surprised and wondered if he would be able to do it again.

"We're on the wave!" Gastric shouted. "We're on it, not under it! We're surfing all the way to Quirm, commander! There's light ahead! Glory be!"

Vimes grunted as he wrapped the last of the rope from his pocket around the stunned Stratford, tying him tightly to a stanchion. "Sink or swim, you're going to pay, Mr. Stratford, from heaven, hell or high water, I don't care which."

And then there was a creaking and a bellowing as the frantic oxen redoubled their attempts to escape the stench of the goblins immediately behind them, a surge skyward and while it would be most poetic to say that the waters were on the face of the earth, in truth they were mostly on the face of Samuel Vimes.

V IMES WOKE IN DAMP and utter darkness with sand under his cheek. Some parts of his body reported for duty, others protested that they had a note from their mother. After a while little insistent clues evolved: there was the sound of surf, the chatter of people and, for some reason, what sounded like the trumpeting of an elephant.

At this point something stuck a finger in one of his nostrils and pulled hard. "Upsee-daisy, Mr. Po-leess-maan, otherwise you biggest pancake I ever seen! Upsee-daisy! Save Goblins! Big hero! Hurrah! Everybody get clap!"

It was a familiar voice, but it couldn't have been Stinky, because Vimes had seen the little goblin completely crushed. But Vimes tried to pull himself up anyway and this was almost impossible because of the stinking fishy-smelling debris that covered him like a shroud. He couldn't bring his arm around to swat whatever blasted thing it was that was still tugging at his nostril, but he did manage to at least raise himself enough to realize that there was a *lot* of debris on top of him.

He could make out what seemed like the thump of an elephant's footfall, and in his state of comfortable hallucination wondered idly what an elephant was doing at the seaside, and how much care said elephant would take to avoid just another load of flotsam. This thought crystallized just as the tugging at his nose stopped and the cracked voice shouted, "Rise and shine, Mr. Vimes, 'cos here come Jumbo!"

Vimes managed the champion press-up of all time and sprang clear, dripping driftwood and barnacles, just as a foot the size of a dustbin thumped down where his head had been.

"Hooray, no flattery for Mr. Vimes!"

Vimes looked down and saw, about half an inch from the family-sized toenail of the elephant, who incidentally now wore an expression of some embarrassment, the figure of Stinky bouncing up and down excitedly on the tip of its trunk. Other people had spotted Vimes too, and were hurrying toward him, and it was with a terrifying relief that he spotted the distinctive helmets of the Quirm City Watch, which he had always thought were far too fussy and militaristic for proper coppers, but now viewed as shining beacons of sanity.

An officer with a captain's helmet said, "Commander? Are you all right? Everyone thought you'd been washed away!"

Vimes tried to brush mud and sand off his torn shirt and managed to say, "Well, the lads back in Ankh-Morpork gave me a bucket and spade for my holiday, so I thought I ought to try it out. Never mind about me, what about the *Fanny*? What about the *people*?"

"All fine, sir, as far as we can tell. A few bangs and bruises, of course. It was amazing, sir, the men who look after the elephants at Quirm Zoo saw it happen! They take the creatures down to the surf in the morning to have a wash and a bit of a play before the crowds come along, and one said he saw the *Fanny* go right over the top of the dock on the crest of the wave, sir, and it sort of settled down on the beach. I had a look inside, and I'd say she'll need a month or so in the boat yard, and the paddle wheels are smashed to blazes, but it'll be the talk of the river for years!"

By now an apologetic zookeeper was steering his charge away from Vimes, allowing him to see a beach covered in damp rubbish and, he was surprisingly pleased to note, quite a large number of chickens, scratching busily for worms. One of them, totally oblivious to Vimes, scratched at some seaweed for a moment, hunkered down with a cross-eyed expression, gurgled once or twice and then stood up, looking rather relieved. He saw that it had left an egg on the sand. At least he supposed it to be an egg. It was square. He picked it up and looked down at the chickens, and in his half-hallucinating state said, "Well, that definitely looks complicated to me."

Out on the surf the two oxen were standing nearly neck deep in the water, and perhaps it was only his imagination that led Vimes to believe that the water around them was steaming.

And now more people were running and chickens were running away, and there was even Ten Gallons, and Mrs. Sillitoe with her daughter, looking damp, and with blankets around them, but most importantly not looking dead. Vimes, who had been holding his breath for too long, breathed out. He breathed out even further when Ten Gallons slapped him on the back, and Mrs. Sillitoe gave him a kiss. "What about Gastric?" he said, "And where's Feeney?"

Mrs. Sillitoe smiled. "They're fine, Commander Vimes, as far we can tell. They're a bit battered, but sleeping it off. No long-term problems according to the medic. I'm sure they'll be fine, thanks to you!"

She stood back as a Quirmian officer handed Vimes a mug of coffee. It had sand in it, but never had sandy coffee tasted better. "All sorted out very well, you might say, sir. We even made sure those damn goblins caught their boat!"

Never in the field of coffee-making had so much of the stuff been sprayed so far and over so many. Vimes stared beyond the surf where, in the distance, a ship had left the port and was making good sail. He said, "Fetch me Acting Captain Haddock right now!"

Acting Captain Haddock arrived at a run six minutes later and Vimes couldn't help noticing that he had a bit of breakfast around the edge of his mouth. "Our relationship with Commandant Fournier is cordial at the moment, is it not?" said Vimes.

Haddock grinned widely. "Commander, when he gets down here you may have to try hard to stop him kissing you on both cheeks. Mrs. Sillitoe is his daughter."

"Was happy to be of assistance," said Vimes, looking around absently, "and so would you tell these gentlemen that I want a fast boat, one fast enough to catch that ship, and a decent squad of men to crew it, and I want them now, and while I'm waiting I'd like someone to get me a clean shirt and a bacon sandwich . . . without avec."

"They have a pretty swift cutter, commander, for chasing smugglers!"

"Good, and get me a cutlass. I've always wanted to try one."
Vimes thought for a moment and added, "And make that another
two bacon sandwiches. And a lot more coffee. And make that one
more bacon sandwich. And, Haddock, if you can scavenge a bottle of
Merkel and Stingbat's very famous old brown sauce, I swear I'll make
you a full sergeant when your term here is up, 'cos any man who
can find a proper down-and-dirty Ankh-Morpork sauce in Quirm,
home of five hundred bloody types of mayonnaise, without getting
his eye full of spit *deserves* to be a sergeant in anybody's force!"

And then, as whatever had been holding Sam Vimes up drained
away, he fell gently backward, dreaming of bacon sandwiches and
brown sauce.

Even Constable Haddock or, as he was now, Acting Captain
Haddock, would agree that he was not the sharpest knife in the
box, but it was amazing, the things you could open with a blunt
instrument. As he hurried away on this prestigious errand he was
stopped by one of the Quirm officers, who said, "Hareng!* Have
you heard of a watchman called Petit Fou Artour?"

"Wee Mad Arthur? Yes, he's one of our lads!"

"Well, you had better come quickly, my friend, because he is in
our Watch House. Strong little fellow, isn't he? A few of the other
officers had laughed at him, he said, but I believe that they have
learned the error of their ways—the hard way, as it happened. Apparently he has been sent to find Commandant Vimes."

S AM VIMES AWOKE FROM a pig's nightmare to find himself
lying on a pile of sacks in a godown in the docks. He was

---

* Constable Haddock's immediate nickname when he joined the force was
Kipper, because policemen's minds worked that way.

carefully lifted to his feet by Acting Constable Haddock and led unsteadily to a crude table behind which was a chef presiding over the sizzling makings of a bacon sandwich, or rather several bacon sandwiches. "He screamed a bit," said Haddock, "when I insisted on no mayonnaise, but right now you can do no wrong here, commander. And I have one unopened bottle of Merkel and Stingbat's finest, sir, the only one in the city. I'm afraid, however, that you'll have to eat on the go, but the chef is packing the sandwiches in a hamper, with hot charcoal to keep them warm. No time to hang about, sir. The cutter will leave the dock in ten minutes."

A notebook was pushed under Vimes's nose. "What's this?"

"Your signature to my promotion to full sergeant, commander," said Haddock carefully. "I hope you don't mind, but you did promise."

"Good man," said Vimes. "Always write things down."

Haddock looked proud. "I've also arranged to have on board a selection of cutlasses for your perusal, commander."

Vimes struggled into his new shirt, and as his head appeared he said, "I want you to come too, Kipper. You know your way around here better than me. By the way, what did you do with the prisoner?"

Haddock said, "What prisoner would that be, commander?"

And for a moment Vimes's blood froze. "You didn't find a man tied up anywhere on the *Fanny*?"

Now Haddock looked worried. "No, sir, no one by the time we got there. The place was a mess, sir. Sorry, sir, we didn't know!"

"No reason why you should've done. Sorry to shout, but if the Quirm police think the sun is shining out of my arse then tell them they should be looking for a youngish-looking individual known as Stratford. He's a double murderer, at least . . . vicious and by now certainly armed. Tell them they'll be doing everybody a favor if they keep guard on the boat, on the walking wounded and all the lads in your infirmary, and also they should send a clacks to Pseudopolis Yard right now to say that Commander Vimes requires that two members of the Watch should hasten via golem horse to Ramkin Hall to keep guard over Lady Sybil and Young Sam. I don't want them to hang about: I know those things are bad news to ride, but Stratford is a nut job—they *must* hurry!"

"Excuse me, commander," said one of the Quirm officers, "we all speak pretty good Morporkian here. *Everybody* here speaks Morporkian. If you hear us speaking Quirmian it's because we want to talk about you behind your back. We salute you, Commander Vimes, we will send your clacks and search everywhere for your murderer and take great care of the wounded. Now, please hurry down to the dock. The *Queen of Quirm* is pretty ancient, only one step away from being a hulk. Our cutter should catch up with it in a few hours. Shall we go?"

COME ON, SIR," SAID Haddock, "and Wee Mad Arthur will brief you on the way."

"Wee Mad Arthur!"

"Yes, commander. Apparently he got sent to foreign parts to do with this goblin business, flew back to Ankh-Morpork and then got sent straight here to you. He's got a story to tell you and no mistake."

"Where is he?" said Vimes.

"They should be releasing him from custody right now, sir. A laughable misunderstanding, no real harm done, all will be forgiven and all will probably heal, I'm sure."

Vimes was wise enough to leave it at that.

O F COURSE, THE SEASICKNESS didn't help, but that didn't begin to cut in until afterward, when Wee Mad Arthur had finished his breathless account. "And what did you find in the huts?" said Vimes.

"More goblins, sir, all shapes and sizes, little ones too. Most of them dead, the rest in a very bad way, in my opinion. I did what I could for them, such as it was. To tell ye the truth, sir, I think they were bewildered about everything, the poor wee devils, but there's grub and water there of a sort and I don't reckon those guards are going to move in a hurry, ye ken." He made a face and added, "Really weird, those goblins. I let them out and they just milled around, not knowing what the hell to do. I mean, crivens, if it were me I'd be out of there like a shot and give those scunners a right good kicking in the fork while they was lying down. As for the men, well, I kenned this was urgent and I could always fly back tomorrow and pour some water on them at least, but I thought the Watch should know and so made haste back to Ankh-Morpork and they told me where you'd gone on holiday, and Lady Sybil said you'd gone down that mucky old river, so all I had to do was fly down until I got to Quirm and when I found a big awful terrible mess I kenned that was something to do with you, commander."

Wee Mad Arthur hesitated. He was never quite sure what Vimes thought of him, given that the man considered Feegles in general a nuisance. When Vimes was slow to reply, he asked, "I hope I did what ye would have done, commander?"

Vimes looked at Wee Mad Arthur as if he was seeing him for the first time. "No, constable, you did not do what I would have done, which is fortunate, because if you had, then you would be in front of me on a charge for using brutally excessive force in the execution of your duties. However, *you* will get a medal and an official commendation for this, constable. Right now we're chasing another ship that's taking more goblins to that wretched place. And although I imagine you must be very tired, I expect you'd like to come along for the ride? Incidentally, may I congratulate you personally, constable: for someone raised as a gnome you really have got the hang of the whole Feegle business, haven't you? You beat up a dozen armed men single-handed?"

"Oh aye, sir," said Wee Mad Arthur slyly, "but it was nae fair, I had them outnumbered. Och, and by the way in some of them sheds there was all kinds of like alchemy stuff. Didn't ken what it was, but ye might find it o' interest."

"Well spotted," said Vimes. "Why don't you go down below and get a rest?"

"Aye, I will sir, but as soon as I can I have to run an errand regarding Sergeant Colon, who is in a verra bad way indeed." He looked at Vimes's blank expression and continued. "Did ye nae know? He got some goblin geegaw given tae him and it's put some kind of fluence on him quite cruel, and he's a-screaming and a-shouting and making oot like a goblin all day long according to Sergeant Littlebottom. She's moved him into the sanatorium."

"Sergeant Colon!"

"Aye, sir. And according to Captain Angua we have to find a goblin cave to break the fluence, ye ken? Sounds a wee bitty weird to me, but half the Watch is oot searching the place for goblins and they cannae find even one o' the poor wee beings, being as the wee beasties is hardly going tae advertise these days, if you are getting my meaning." Once again Wee Mad Arthur looked at Vimes.

"Sergeant Colon!"

"That's what I told you, sir."

The blood came back to Vimes's face as rational thought came back to his brain. "Can he travel?" Wee Mad Arthur shrugged. Ahead of them the *Queen of Quirm* seemed a little closer. "Then if you please, constable, can you go back to the clacks at the Quirm Watch House and tell them to put Fred on a coach to Ramkin Hall as soon as possible, okay?" Vimes added, "Best if Cheery comes with him, I should think." And in his head he added, *Fred Colon! He hates anything non-human, on the quiet.* And for now he left it at that, given what lay ahead, but thought, Fred Colon! I wonder what kind of pots *he* would make.

Behind him, Wee Mad Arthur whistled a strange note and a seagull trailing the cutter in the vague hope of a free meal of fish entrails found a weight on its back and a voice in its ear saying, "Hello, beastie, my name is Wee Mad Arthur."

Vimes liked to have his feet on something solid, such as his boots, and he liked his boots to do likewise. The sail of the *Queen of Quirm* now clearly visible, the cutter left the safety of the harbor and hit what is generally known as a moderate swell. And Commander Vimes, the Duke of Ankh-Morpork, Sir Samuel Vimes and, not least, Blackboard Monitor Vimes, was *definitely* going to eat his bacon sandwiches and not throw up in front of other watchmen.

And he didn't, and didn't know how, although he did at one point think he detected, high in the rigging, the shape of a small goblin grinning down at him. He put it down to the bacon sandwiches, which were valiantly trying to come back up, just as he valiantly kept them down.

Stratford would have got onto that damn hulk, he was sure of it. Damn sure of it. He would want paying, for one thing, and he wouldn't want hanging. Vimes hesitated. How sure of it should Vimes be? How much was he prepared to gamble on a hunch? It was Stratford after all. He was smart and nasty, so you covered every angle, even though you knew that a smart man in a hurry could find a new angle for himself.

And so all the people who made up Sam Vimes walked backward and forward across the poop deck, or the scuppers or the starboard or whatever the damn slippery rocking wood he was standing on was called, veering between hope, nausea, despair, self-doubt, nausea and the thrill of the chase and nausea, while the cutter seemed to hit the hard bits of every wave as it plunged onward after the *Queen of Quirm* and justice.

The lieutenant came up to him and saluted, quite smartly, and said, "Commander, you have asked us to pursue the ship because it is carrying goblins, but I know of no law against taking goblins *anywhere.*"

"There ought to be a law, because there certainly is a crime, do you understand?" said Vimes. He patted the lieutenant on the shoulder and continued, "Congratulations! This cutter of yours is actually traveling faster than the law. Lieutenant, the law *will* catch up. Goblins can speak, they have a society and I've heard one of them play music that would make a bronze statue burst into tears. The process of modern policing is such that I'm certain that these have been taken from their home, and the ship that we're following is taking them somewhere where they don't want to go. Look, if you're queasy about it, just help me get on that ship and I'll sort things out by myself, okay? And, besides, I believe our murderer could be on the boat as well. But, it's up to you, lieutenant."

Vimes nodded toward the prow and added, "We're so close I can see the faces of their crew. Maybe you should tell me your intentions, lieutenant?"

Vimes felt a little sorry for the lad, but not too much. He had taken the job, he had accepted the promotion and the money that went with it, hadn't he? Any copper worth his truncheon would at least take a look at the *Queen* now they'd come this far, wouldn't they?

"Very well, commander," said the lieutenant. "I'm not sure of my bearings, but we will hail the *Queen* and ask permission to come aboard."

"No! You don't *ask*! You tell them to stand by to be inspected by the police! And if you're not concerned about the goblins, then it is a fact that I am in pursuit of a murderer," Vimes added. "The capital crime—one that we can't ignore!"

In fact, he could see the *Queen* was already heaving two.* It was even hoisting a white flag, much to his surprise.

And her captain was waiting for them as the cutter drew alongside. He had a look of resignation on his face, and said, "We won't make any trouble, officers. I know it was a bloody stupid thing to do. We've got the man you're looking for, and we're bringing him up now. It's not like we're pirates, after all. Good morning, Lieutenant Perdix, sorry to put you to any trouble."

Vimes turned to the lieutenant. "You know the captain?"

"Oh yes, commander, Captain Murderer is well respected on this coast," said the lieutenant as the cutter gently kissed the *Queen*. "Smuggles, of course, they all do it. It's a sort of game."

"But Captain . . . *Murderer*?" said Vimes.

The lieutenant scrambled on to the *Queen*'s deck with ease and gave Vimes a hand up, saying, "The Murderers are a highly respected family in these parts. To tell you the truth, commander, I think they rather like the name. They'd object more to Smuggler, I suspect."

"We're bringing the bloke up right now, lieutenant," said the captain, "and he ain't very happy."

---

* Or three or four, as far as Vimes the landlubber was concerned.

Vimes looked him up and down and said, "I'm Commander Vimes, Ankh-Morpork City Watch, currently investigating at least two murders."

Captain Murderer's eyes shut, and he put a hand over his mouth for a moment before saying, in a voice weeping with forlorn hope, "That wouldn't be *that* Commander Vimes, would it?"

"Captain . . . Murderer . . . produce for me the man I'm after, then I'm sure you'll find me on a friendly footing. Do you get my meaning?"

There was some shouting and thumping down below and several suggestions that somebody was getting kicked very hard. Eventually a man with a cloth tied round his face as a blindfold was half pushed and half dragged up onto the deck. "To tell you the truth, I'll be glad to see the back of him," said the captain, turning away.

Vimes made sure the man was held fast by the sailors, and pulled down the mask. He looked into bloodshot eyes for a moment and then, very calmly, said, "Lieutenant, will you please impound the *Queen of Quirm* and arrest the captain and first mate on a charge of kidnapping and possibly abduction of a number of persons, specifically Mr. Jethro Jefferson, also goblins to the number of fifty or more. There may be other charges.

"You can't abduct goblins," said Captain Murderer. "Goblins is cargo!"

Vimes let this one pass for the moment. Captain Murderer would be orientated to the world as seen by Commander Vimes at Commander Vimes's leisure. For now he said to the lieutenant, "I also suggest that you lock up the captain and first mate in the brig, if that is what it's called, because when Mr. Jefferson here has got his hands free I think he's going to try to punch somebody's lights out. I'm sure this can all be sorted out, but someone's going to suffer for this and it's just a matter of deciding who it's going to be."

He thought for a moment and then countermanded, "No, I think that first I'll talk to the captain, in the captain's quarters. Kipper, I'd like you to come and take notes. *Lots* of notes. Good to see you, Mr. Jefferson. Lieutenant, to the best of my knowledge Mr. Jefferson is guilty of no crime other than being in possession of a hot temper. But although he's a man I'm very glad to find, he's not the bastard I'm currently looking for."

IT WAS, ACTING CAPTAIN Haddock thought, a good thing that he had a decent amount of room in his notebook . . .

"Captain Murderer, let me recap," said Sam Vimes after a while, idly swiveling in the captain's chair; it squeaked. "Some men unknown to you, but whom you decided to treat with respect because they had the right password, which is to say the password you used in your dealings with *smugglers*, with whom you have developed what I might call an understanding, delivered to you a man, bound and gagged, and told you to take said man to Howondaland to, and I quote 'cool his heels for a little while'; and you have also told me that these men said to you that this was okay by the law."

The swivel chair under Vimes squeaked once or twice as he twisted for dramatic effect, and he went on, "Captain Murderer, I represent the law in Ankh-Morpork, and you may be aware that a number of influential politicians throughout the world trust my judgment, and, Captain Murderer, I know of no law that makes kidnapping legal, but I'll ask my colleague and an expert on Quirmian law whether he knows of any local edict that makes it legal to tie up somebody who has committed no crime and drag him onto a boat and send him to a questionable distant location against his will."

The swivel chair only had one chance to squeak again before

Lieutenant Perdix said, ponderously, "Commander Vimes, I know of no such change in the law, and therefore, Captain Murderer, I arrest you," and here the lieutenant placed a hand on the stricken captain's shoulder, "on a charge of kidnapping, aiding and abetting kidnapping, actual and possibly grievous bodily harm, and other charges that may arise in the course of our continued investigations. In the meantime, upon its return to port, the *Queen of Quirm* is impounded and will, you may be sure, be inspected down to its gunwales."

Vimes swiveled the chair again until his face was not visible to the downcast captain but could be clearly seen by the lieutenant, then winked at him and got a little nod in response. He rotated the chair again and said, "Depriving an innocent man of his liberty even for a week, captain, is a very serious crime. However, the lieutenant has told me that you are well thought of on this coast and in general are considered to be a model citizen. Personally, I don't like a world in which small men who act out of fear, or even out of a misguided deference, get thrown into prison while big men, the instigators if not the perpetrators of crime, get off totally free. I expect you don't like that world either, eh?"

Captain Murderer stared down at his sea boots as if he was expecting them to explode or perhaps break into song. He managed to mutter, "You're right there, commander!"

"Thank you, captain! You're a man of the world. Right now you need a friend, and I need names. I need the names of the people who got you into this mess. Now, Mr. Jefferson the blacksmith has told me that in all conscience he cannot say that he was particularly badly treated once he was in your *illegal* hospitality. Apparently he was reasonably well fed, given beer and a daily tot of rum and even provided with a number of back issues of the magazine *Girls, Giggles and Garters* to while away his time. *He* also wants names,

Captain Murderer, and it may just be that if we had those names, all put down legally in an affidavit, he might just be persuaded to forget his imprisonment in exchange for a certain sum of money, to be negotiated, and a chance to go hand to hand, fair and square, no holds barred, with your first mate, who he describes as a 'bag of shite,' a nautical term which I don't pretend to understand. Apparently said man took pleasure in thumping him when he objected to his imprisonment, and Mr. Jefferson would like, as it were, to settle the score."

Vimes stood up and stretched his arms as if taking the cramp out of them. "Of course, captain, this is all very irregular, especially since we have here our lieutenant, a decent, clean and upstanding young officer, but I suspect that if he brought the *Queen* into dock and you in front of the authorities on a smuggling charge he might consider honor to be satisfied. It would be a bit of a knock for you, but not one half as bad as being an accessory to kidnapping. Don't you agree?" Vimes went on, cheerfully, "The lieutenant here will have got a feather in his chapeau and may put in a *bon mot* on your behalf, I suspect, what with you being an otherwise upstanding and, above all, *helpful* citizen."

Vimes winked at Lieutenant Perdix. "I'm teaching this young man bad habits, captain, and so I suggest that *you* treat him as a friend, especially if at any time in the future he asks you any innocent questions to do with shipping movements and merchandise and other such concerns. It's up to you, Captain Murderer. I think you know names, the names at least of the men you deal with, and also the name of their employer? You want to tell me anything?"

The boots shuffled. "Look, commander, I don't want to become enemies with powerful men, if you know what I mean?"

Vimes nodded, and leaned forward so that he could look the man in the eyes. "Of course, I quite understand that captain," he said quietly, "and that is why you should give me the names. *The names*, captain. *The names*. Because, Captain Murderer, I understand you do not wish to upset influential men, and right now I have half a mind to have your ship impounded and destroyed because you were trafficking in living, breathing, intelligent, creative if somewhat grubby sapient creatures. Strictly speaking, I would get into trouble for authorizing this, but who knows? The world can change quite quickly, and it's changing quickly for you." He slapped the captain on the back. "Captain Murderer, here and now I'd like you to think of me as a friend."

And Vimes listened and the red balls bounced across the baize, cannoning off the colored balls, and the law was being broken wholesale for the purpose of upholding the law. How could you explain that to a layman? How could you explain it to a lawyer? How could he explain it to himself? But it was all happening fast and you got on top of it or perished. So you did your best and faced such music as anyone cared to play.

T HE *Queen of Quirm* docked that day, two and a half months earlier than expected, to the dismay, distress or possibly even delight of the wives of the crew. The harbormaster made a note of this, and also was intrigued by the fact that most of the crew after disembarkation immediately wandered along past the other ships in port to a quiet area of beach close to the repair yard where the somewhat battered *Wonderful Fanny* was already being pulled up the slipway.

Walking alongside his boat, like a mother hen with one enormous chick, was Captain Sillitoe, nursing a plaster cast on his arm; he brightened up when he saw Vimes. "Well, sir, I have to hand it to you, by my halibut, so I must! You played a man's job in getting us safely home, sir! I won't forget it, and nor will my wife and daughter!"

Vimes looked up at the boat and hoped for the best. "She looks extremely battered to me, captain—I mean the boat, not your wife, of course."

But it appeared that the captain was determined on optimism. "We lost much of the gearing for the paddle wheels, but truth to tell she was long overdue for refit in any case. But, my dear commander, we rode a damn slam, with all souls safe! And, moreover—What the seven hells are *they* doing?"

Vimes had already heard the shrill notes of a flute, but he had to look down to see, marching resolutely across the beach, a large number of goblins. At their head, and for a moment appearing bright blue, was Stinky, playing an old and empty crab leg. As he passed Vimes he stopped playing long enough to say, "No seaside rock for goblins! Hooray! Home again, home again, as fast as they can! And them above as watches, they applaud! And them what tries to stop, oh yes, Constable Stinky and his little chums, he find Stinky will be worst nightmare."

Vimes laughed. "What? What do you mean? A goblin with a badge?" He had to walk fast as he said that, because Stinky was understandably dead set on getting the goblins out of there as soon as possible.

"Stinky don't need no badges, fellow po-leess-maan! Stinky worst nightmare all by himself! Remember a little boy? Little boy open book? And he see evil goblin, and I see nasty little boy! Good for us, little boy, that we were *both* right!"

Vimes watched them march away, speeding up until they reached the undergrowth at the edge of the dockyard, where they disappeared, and for a moment it occurred to Vimes that even if he rushed forward and fished around for any trace of goblin he would not find one. He was bewildered. This didn't matter very much; bewilderment was often a copper's lot. His job was to make sense of the world, and there were times when he wished that the world would meet him halfway.

"Are you feeling all right, commander?"

Vimes turned and looked at the serious face of Lieutenant Perdix. "Well, I'm not certain when I last slept properly, but at least I can stay standing up! And I have all the names and descriptions." Three names, and one, oh, what a name that was, that is if you trusted the word of someone happy to be called Captain Murderer. Well, the man was in his fifties, not a good age to have to run and hide. No, Murderer was not going to be a problem. Nor was Jefferson, idiot firebrand though he was. What Jefferson had suspected, Captain Murderer *knew*. But Vimes, on the other hand, hadn't demanded the chance to take a crack at the *Queen*'s first mate, admittedly an unpleasant-looking cove with a chin like a butcher's boot. He was swaggering toward them now, with the apprehensive Captain Murderer fussing along behind him.

Vimes strolled up to the blacksmith, who seemed no worse for his impromptu voyage. "Come on, sir, Murderer will pay you whatever it takes to keep the lieutenant happy, and keep his own boat. Chalk it up to experience, eh?"

"There's still that bloody first mate," said the blacksmith. "The rest of the crew were civil enough but he's a bullying bastard!"

"Well," said Vimes, "here he is and so are you, it's man-to-man, and I'll stay here to see fair play. It's an interesting day here. We're trying a different kind of law, one that's quick and doesn't have to trouble any lawyers. So go on, he knows what you want, and so do you, Mr. Jefferson."

Other crewmen were congregating at this end of the beach. Vimes looked from face to face, all showing the working man's intuition that a good bit of healthy violence might cheerfully be expected, and read the unspoken language. The first mate did look like a man who made a lot of use of his fists and his temper, and so, Vimes thought, there *would* probably be many among the crew who would like to see him given a little lesson—or even a great big one. He beckoned both the men toward him.

"Gentlemen, this is a grudge match; you both know the score. If I see a knife may the gods help him who holds it. There is to be no murder here, saving you of course, captain, and in front of you all I give my word that I'll stop the fight when I deem that one man has definitely had enough. Gentlemen, over to you." And with this he stood back smartly.

Neither man moved, but Jefferson said, "Do you know the Marquis of Fantailer Rules devised for the proper conduct for a bout of fisticuffs?"

The first mate's smile was evil. He said, "Yus, I do!"

Vimes didn't see, not actually *see* with his own eyes, what happened next, surely no one could, but it was agreed later that Jefferson had spun around in a blur and laid the sailor flat. The sound of his heavy body thumping down on the sand was all that broke the silence.

After one second, Jefferson, massaging some blood back into his fist, looked down at the fallen giant and said, "I don't." He turned and looked at Vimes. "You know? He deliberately pissed on the goblins in the hold. Bastard."

Vimes tensed in case the fallen man had chums without a sense of humor, but in fact there was laughter. After all, a big man had gone down heavy right enough, bang to rights, and that was a definite result in anybody's money. "Well done, Mr. Jefferson, a fair fight if ever I saw one. Perhaps these gentlemen will take the first mate back to his ship for a lie-down."

Vimes delivered this as an instruction, which was instantly obeyed as one, but he added, "If that's all right by you, Captain Murderer? Good. And now I think that you and I'll go, in an entirely friendly way, along with the lieutenant here, to the Quirm Watch headquarters, where there will be a little matter of affidavits to sign."

"I expect you will want to be leaving with some haste, commander," said the lieutenant as they strolled along the Rue de Wakening.

"Well, yes," said Vimes. "I'm supposed to be on holiday. I'll pick up young Feeney from the infirmary and find some way of getting back to the Hall."

The lieutenant looked surprised. "And you don't want to get back on the heels of the murderer as soon as possible, sir?"

"Him? I'll see him soon enough, I have no doubt about that, but, you see, even he is not exactly the end of things. Do you play snooker down here?"

"Well, I haven't learned to play, but I understand the game, if that's what you're asking."

"Then you'll know that the ultimate aim of the game is to sink the black, although you'll hit all the other colors during the course of a frame, and you'll bash the red ones again and again, sometimes making use of them to further your strategy. Well, I know where to find the black, and black can't run. The others? The captain has helpfully given us names and descriptions. If you wish to arrest them yourselves, for aiding and abetting the practice of trafficking sapient creatures for profit, then I leave that honor to the Quirm constabulary."

Vimes grinned. "As for me, after I have the affidavits I intend to go straight back to see my wife and little boy, who I have shamefully, no, desperately neglected over the past few days, and do you know what? Just as soon as I've got there, I'm going to bring them back down here! My wife will enjoy the fresh air, and Young Sam will just *love* the elephants, oh, won't he just!"

The lieutenant brightened up. "May I suggest, then, that after dinner you take the overnight boat? It will be the *Black-Eyed Susan*, quite speedy, like her namesake, according to popular legend. She's due to go upriver in, let me see, three quarters of an hour. She's very fast, doesn't take much in the way of cargo so they gear her up high. You'll be home in the morning, how about that? Just time to get yourself smartened up, and if you like the idea then I will get one of the men to go and find the *Susan*'s captain and make certain she doesn't leave without you."

Vimes smiled. "What's the weather forecast?"

"Clear skies, commander, and Old Treachery is as flat as a mill pond, scoured of every snag and boulder for the rest of the season. It's plain sailing from now on."

"Good evening, your grace!" The voice was somewhat familiar and Vimes saw, sauntering down the boulevard, what at first seemed liked a man wearing a huge cummerbund until further swift forensic inspection showed that it was the hermit from the Hall. His beard was remarkably clean and wrapped around his body, as were two young ladies of the giggling persuasion.

Vimes peered at him. "Stump? What are you doing down here?"

This caused further giggling.

"I'm on holiday, commander! Yes, indeed! Every man should have a holiday, sir!"

Vimes didn't know what to say and so patted the man on the shoulder and said, "Knock yourself out, Mr. Stump, and don't forget the nourishing herbs."

"I think I'm going to need them, commander . . ."

S AY WHAT YOU LIKE, the food in the Quirm Watch House canteen was pretty damn good, even if they did use a shade too much avec, thought Vimes; avec on *everything*.

Vimes, well fed and cleaned up and with some *very* important paperwork stuffed down the inside of his freshly laundered and immaculately ironed shirt, walked with Chief Constable Upshot down the quayside toward the *Black-Eyed Susan*. The lieutenant and two of the guards accompanied him to his cabin, where the dwarf butler demonstrated to him the cleanliness of the bed and the crispness of the sheets.

"Honored to have you sleeping in them, commander. You will find that the *Susan* gives a very smooth ride, although she can sometimes bounce around a little, very much like her namesake, but least said, soonest mended. And, of course, there is a berth next door for officer Feeney. You gentlemen might like to see the *Susan* get under way, perhaps?"

They did. The *Susan* had two oxen, just like the *Wonderful Fanny*, but with no heavy cargo and only about ten passengers she was the express of Old Treachery. Her paddle wheels, highly geared indeed, left a line of white water all down the valley behind her.

"What happens now, commander?" said Feeney, leaning on the rail as they watched Quirm disappearing in the wake behind them. "I mean, what are we going to do next?"

Vimes was smoking a cigar with great pleasure. Somehow this seemed the time and the place. Snuff was all very well, but a good cigar had time and wisdom and personality. He would be unhappy to see this one go.

"I don't need to do anything now," he said, turning to look at the sunset. And I don't often see sunsets these days either, he thought. Mostly I see midnights; and I don't need to chase Stratford, either. I know him like I know myself. He mentally paused, momentarily shocked at the implication.

Aloud he continued, "You saw those two Quirmian officers get on the boat, didn't you? I arranged that. They will, of course, make certain that we have an undisturbed voyage. The crew have also been told that there may be some attempt by a murderer to board the boat. According to the lieutenant, Captain Harbinger can vouch for all of his crew as having sailed with him loyally for many years. Personally, of course, I'll make certain the door to my berth is locked, and I'd suggest you do the same thing, Feeney.

"Greed is at the center of this, greed and hellish poisons. They're both killers and greed is the worst, by a long way. You know, usually when I'm talking to young officers such as yourself I say that in a certain type of case, you should always follow the money, you should ask 'Who stands to lose? Who stands to gain?'" Vimes regretfully tossed the butt of his cigar into the water. "But sometimes you should follow the arrogance . . . You should look for those who can't believe that the law would ever catch them, who believe that they act out of a right that the rest of us do not have. The job of the officer of the law is to let them know that they are wrong!"

The sun was setting. "I do believe, Commander Vimes, that you have something in you that would turn the wheels of this boat all by itself if a man could but harness it!" said Feeney admiringly. "And I remember reading somewhere that you would arrest the gods for doing it wrong."

Vimes shook his head. "I'm sure I never said anything of the sort! But law is order and order is law and it must be the highest thing. The world runs on it, the heavens run on it and without order, lad, one second cannot follow another."

He could feel himself swaying. Lack of sleep can poison the

mind, drive it in strange directions. Vimes felt Feeney's hand on his shoulder. "I'll help you along to your cabin, commander. It's been a *very* long day."

V IMES DIDN'T REMEMBER GETTING undressed and into bed, or rather into bunk, but he clearly had done so and, according to the little bits of white foam on the cabin's tiny washbasin, he had cleaned his teeth as well. He had slept the sleep of the dead except for the bit where bits fall off and you crumble into dust, and all he could recall was cool blackness and, rising now to the surface, a certainty, as if a message had been left in the blackness to await the return of thought. *He is after you, Blackboard Monitor Vimes. You know this because you recognize what was in his eyes. You know that type. They want to die from the day they are born, but something twists and so they kill instead. He will find you, and so will I. I hope the three of us meet in darkness.*

As the message drained away Vimes stared at the opposite wall, in which the door now opened, after a cursory knock, to reveal the steward bearing that which is guaranteed to frighten away all nightmares, to wit, a cup of hot tea.*

"No need to get up, commander," came the cheerful greeting of the steward, as he carefully placed the cup of tea in a little indentation that some foresighted person had designed into the tiny cabin so that said teacup would not slide around. "The captain would like to inform you that we'll be docking in about twenty minutes, although of course you'll be welcome to stay aboard and finish your breakfast while we clean the scuppers and take on fresh

---

* The sound of the gentle rattle of china cup on china saucer drives away all demons, a little-known fact.

oxen and, of course, pick up mail and fodder and a few more passengers. In the galley, I have today . . ." and here the steward enthusiastically rattled off a menu of belly-stuffing proportions, concluding triumphantly with, "a bacon sandwich!"

Vimes cleared his throat and said gloomily, "I don't suppose you have any muesli, do you?" After all, Sybil was only twenty minutes away.

The steward looked puzzled. "Well, yes, we would have the ingredients, of course, but I didn't peg you as a *rabbit food* man?"

Vimes thought about Sybil again. "Well, perhaps today my little nose is twitching."

Luxurious though the cabin was, roomy it was not. Vimes managed to shave with a razor donated by the steward, "with the compliments of the captain, commander," and a thoughtfully placed basin, soap, flannel and minute towel, which at least helped him to deal with the form of ablution his old mother had called "washing the bits that showed." He paid attention to them, nevertheless, taking some pains in the knowledge that this little wooden world would evaporate very soon and he would be back in the world of Sam Vimes, husband and father. Periodically, however, as he made himself respectable, he turned back to himself in the shaving mirror and said, "Fred Colon!"

The luxury cabin had turned out to be wonderful to sleep in, although so small that in reality it would only be suitable for a fastidious corpse. But eventually, when every part of Vimes he could reach had been decently, if erratically, scrubbed and the steward had brought him a hermit-sized portion of fruits and nuts and grains, he looked around to see what he might have left behind and saw a face in the shaving mirror. It was his own, although it must be said the phenomenon is not unusual in shaving mirrors. The Vimes in the mirror said, *You know he doesn't just want to kill you.*

That wouldn't be good enough for a bastard like that, not by a long way. He wants to destroy you and will try everything until he does.

"I know," said Vimes, and added, "You're not a demon, are you?"

"Absolutely not," said his mirror image. "I *might* be made up of your subconscious mind and a momentary case of muesli poisoning occasioned by a fermenting raisin. Watch where you walk, commander. Watch everywhere." And then it was gone.

Vimes stepped away from the mirror and turned around slowly. It *must* have been my face, he said to himself, otherwise it would have been the other way round, wouldn't it?

He walked down the gangway into reality and what turned out to be Corporal Nobby Nobbs, beyond whom reality does not get much more real.

"Good to see you, Mr. Vimes! My word, you're looking fit! Your holiday must be doing you a lot of good. Got any bags?" This was asked in the absolute certainty that Vimes would have *no* bags, but a show of willing is always worth a try.

"Is everything all right?" said Vimes, ignoring this.

Nobby scratched his nose and a bit fell off. Oh yes, thought Vimes, I'm back, all right!

"Well, the usual stuff that happens is happening, but we're on top of it. Could I draw your attention to the hill over there? They were very careful not to harm the trees, and Lady Sybil herself promised a lingering death to anyone who upset the goblins."

Mystified, Vimes scanned the skyline and saw Hangman's Hill. "Hells bells! It's a clacks tower, it's a bloody *clacks* tower! Sybil will go totally librarian about it!"

"As a matter of fact, Mr. Vimes, Lady Sybil was all for it by the time she'd read all of Captain Carrot's note. He said this was no time for you to be out of touch. You know that, sir, very persuasive officer, which is how come he got the clacks company to rush up here toot sweet with a temporary tower. Worked all night, so they did, and got it lined up on the Grand Trunk sweet as a nut!"

This time Nobby picked his nose, briefly inspected the contents for interest or value, then flicked them away and went on, "Only one thing, sir, the *Ankh-Morpork Times* wants to interview you about how you are a great hero what saved someone's wonderful fanny—"

There was a pause while they waited for Feeney to stop choking with laughter and get his breath back and then Vimes said, "Corporal Nobby Nobbs, this here is Chief Constable Upshot. I call him chief constable because he's the only law in these parts, that is until now. This is *his* patch, and so you will respect it, okay? Who else came with you from the Smoke?"

"Sergeant Detritus, Mr. Vimes, but he's up at the Hall, guarding her ladyship and Young Sam with delicate surreption."

A part of Vimes had unknowingly been holding its breath. Detritus and Willikins? Together they could face an army. He shook himself. "But not Fred Colon?"

"No, Mr. Vimes, as I understand it we were on our way when the second clacks came through, but I reckon that he'll be here pretty soon."

"Gentlemen, I'm going home," said Vimes, "but, Mr. Feeney, how soon will another boat go down to Quirm?"

Feeney beamed. "You're in luck, commander. The Roberta E. Biscuit will be going tomorrow morning! Just the job for what I think you might want. Big and slow, but you won't mind that, because there's gambling and entertainment. Lots of tourists on it, but don't you worry, sir, your name is big on the river already. Trust me! Say the word and the captain of the *Biscuit* will make certain that there's a king-size, I mean, sorry, commander-size stateroom for you, how about that?"

Vimes opened his mouth to ask, is it expensive? And shut it again with the embarrassed realization that the Ramkin fortune could almost certainly buy every vessel on Old Treachery.

Feeney, like the good copper he was becoming, noticed that slight moment of hesitation and said, "Your money won't be good on the river, commander, believe me. The savior of the *Fanny* won't have to buy his own cigars or a stateroom anywhere along Old Treachery!"

Nobby Nobbs was almost bent double with laughter and managed to choke out, "The *Fanny*!"

Vimes sighed. "Nobby, her name was Francesca, Fanny for short. Understand?" It didn't work with some people; it only just did with Vimes. "And, Nobby, I want you to wait here, and as soon as Fred's coach arrives you're in charge of getting him up to the goblin cave on the hill, okay?"

"Yes, Mr. Vimes," said Nobby, looking at his boots.

"And, Nobby, if you see a goblin who stinks like a latrine and glows slightly blue, well, that's a fellow copper and don't you forget it."

S YBIL WAS HALFWAY DOWN the lane as Vimes quickly walked up it, and Young Sam was running ahead and cannoned into his father's legs, throwing his arms around them as best he could.

"Dad! I know how to milk a goat, Dad! You have to pull its tits, Dad, they're all wiggly!" Vimes's expression did not change as Young Sam went on. "And I'm learning to make cheese! And I have some badger poo now, and some weasel poo, too!"

"My word, you have been busy," said Vimes. "Who told you the word 'tits,' lad?"

Young Sam beamed. "That was Willy the cowherd, Dad."

Vimes nodded. "I'll have a little talk to you about that later, Sam, but first I think I'll have a word with Willy the cowherd." He lifted up Young Sam, ignoring a twinge in his back. "I hope that washing your hands played a part in these adventures?"

"I take care of that," said Lady Sybil, catching up. "Honestly, Sam, I let you out of my sight for hardly any time at all and here you are a hero, *again*! Really! Honestly, the whole river is talking about it! Fights on a riverboat? Maritime chases? Oh dear me, I don't know where to put my face, so if you would be so kind as to let our child down carefully I'll press said face mightily to yours!"

When Vimes surfaced for breath he growled, "It is a *real* bloody clacks tower, isn't it, yes? And now *The Times* have got hold of all this they'll make out I'm some kind of hero, the damn fools!"

With the suction released, Lady Sybil said, "No, Sam—well maybe a little of that, but you would be amazed at how fast news travels along the river. Apparently you were standing on the wheelhouse roof of the *Wonderful Fanny* fighting with a murderer, and he shot a crossbow at you and it bounced off! I'm told there's going to be a large artist's impression in tomorrow's paper! Once again, I won't know where to put my face!" And then Sybil couldn't contain herself anymore and burst out laughing. "Frankly, Sam, you may have *anything* you want for dinner tonight."

Vimes leaned over and whispered, causing his wife to slap his hand and say, "Later, perhaps!"

At this point, somewhat emboldened, Vimes said, "I couldn't help noticing that the bridge is severely damaged?"

Sybil nodded. "Oh, yes dear, a terrible storm, wasn't it? It took away the entire central arch and all of the three disgraces.* "I

---

* The Three Disgraces were apparently the daughters of Blind Io (but you know how people talk); they were Nudicia, Pulchritudia and Voluptia.

remember them from my childhood. My mother used to put her hand over my eyes when we crossed the bridge and so I took a keen interest in them, especially as one was scratching her bottom." Her smile brightened. "But don't worry, Sam, naked ladies are not difficult to come by."

Vimes took comfort from her smile, and a tiny treacherous suspicion bubbled up once more. He thought he had stamped it down, but the damn thing kept coming back. And so he cleared his throat and said, "Sybil, you did discuss plans for my holiday with Vetinari, didn't you?"

Sybil looked surprised. "Why yes, dear, of course. After all, he is technically your superior. Only technically, of course. I had a word with him on the subject at some charity do or other. I can't remember which right now as there're always so many. But there wasn't any difficulty. He said that it was high time you took a decent rest from your valiant activities!"

Vimes was wise enough not to utter the words that entered his mouth, and instead said, carefully, "Er, so he didn't actually suggest that you came down to the Shires?"

"To be honest, Sam, it was quite some time ago, but we both have your best interests at heart, as you surely know. We generally discussed the matter and that's it, really."

Vimes left it at that. He would never know for sure. And anyway, the ball had dropped.

LATER, SAMUEL VIMES, ALL of him, had a bath in the huge bathroom with his nose only just above the surface and came out feeling exactly the same man as before but at least a lot cleaner. The affidavits were in the strongroom, and when the Ramkins design a strongroom, it's not a room that you'll get into in a hurry:

first you needed a combination, which opened a smaller but nevertheless dangerously efficient safe, simply to remove a key which then had to be inserted in locks hidden in three separate clocks in the Hall and each key triggered a clockwork timing mechanism. Sybil told him that she had fond memories of her grandfather running split-arse, as the old man called it, down the main hall to get the key into the last lock before the clock controlling the first lock had run down and certainly before the guillotines dropped. *What we have we keep*, Vimes had thought as he tried it out. Well, they definitely meant it. Now, he dressed in clothes that didn't smell of fish. What next?

I T WAS NICE TO have a walk with Young Sam again. Dad self-consciously out for a walk with his lad, yes? That was the picture. Regrettably, *this* picture included a distant prospect of Sergeant Detritus, who was merging with the landscape, a feat that a troll officer can achieve by simply removing his armor and sticking a geranium behind his ear, whereupon he becomes, being of a rocky and stony persuasion, pretty much part of the landscape without even trying. Usually the troll officers wore super-sized versions of the standard-issue armor, because a lot of the power of a copper consists in *looking* like a copper.* Safety considerations didn't matter; there were plenty of weapons which, if handled with skill, could go through steel armor, but all they would do to a naked troll was make him angry.

Right now Detritus was failing to maintain a low profile. He

---

* That is to say, something bigger than he in fact is, which will turn very nasty if you think you can give this copper in front of you now a seeing-to because you are afloat to the tonsils on beer.

was a bodyguard, that was the truth of it, and he was also carrying his Peacemaker which could, as it were, do what it said on the box. Some weapons are called a Saturday Night Special; Detritus's multi-arrow crossbow would last you all week. And somewhere, where Vimes couldn't see him, which meant that nobody else could either, there was Willikins. *There* was your picture: Dad taking his lad for a walk in the presence of enough firepower to kill a platoon. Sybil had insisted, and that was that. Vimes himself being in danger was one thing, and Sybil had accepted that right from the start, but Young Sam? Never!

As they strolled up Hangman's Hill to see the new clacks tower, Vimes told himself that Stratford would not use a bow. A bow was for expediency, but a killer . . . now a killer would want to be up close, where he could see. Stratford had killed the goblin girl and had gone on killing her long after she was dead. He was a boy who liked his fun. He would want Vimes to know who was killing him. Vimes, Vimes realized, knew killers too well for his own peace of mind.

As they arrived on the hill they were met by a grinning Nobby, who saluted with a variation on the theme of smartness, but with some embarrassment, because he was not alone. A young goblin woman was sitting next to him. Nobby hastily tried to shoo her away and she, apparently with reluctance, retired to a minimum safe distance, still looking adoringly at the corporal.

Despite everything, Vimes tried to suppress the urge to smile, and managed to turn it into a stiff look.

"Fraternizing with the natives, are you, Nobby?"

Young Sam wandered over to the goblin girl and took hold of her hand, which was something he tended to do to any female that he met for the first time, a habit which his father considered would quite possibly open doors for him in later life. The girl tried gently to pull her hand away, but Young Sam was a ferocious holder.

Nobby looked embarrassed. "I ain't fraternizing with her, Mr. Vimes, she wants to fraternize with me! She come out with the straw basket of little mushrooms and gives them to me, honestly!"

"Are you sure they aren't poisonous?"

Nobby looked blank. "Don't know, Mr. Vimes. I ate them anyway, very nice, very crunchy, slightly nutty you might say, and Fred's here now, sir. This young lady"—and to Vimes's surprise and approval Nobby did not put inverted commas around the word lady—"walked right up to him, took this weird shiny pot thing out of his hand, which was amazing because no one else could get it off of him, and there he was! Just like normal! Although I think we're going to have to remind him about washing, and crapping only in the privy and so on."

Vimes gave up. It was true that every organization had to have its backbone, and therefore it stood to reason that there also would have to be some person who equated to the bits usually destined for dog food. But Nobby was loyal and lucky, and if there is anything that a policeman really needs, it's luck. Maybe Nobby had got lucky.

"What are you doing up here, Nobby?" he said. Nobby looked at Vimes as if he were mad, and pointed to the wobbling temporary clacks tower. "Have to check the clacks messages, Mr. Vimes. Actually, young Tony, who is the only one manning it, *he* sort of types them, and wraps them around a stone and they drops down, which is—" There was a rattle on Nobby's helmet and he deftly caught a stone wrapped in a strip of paper before it hit the ground. "Which is why I stand just here, Mr. Vimes." Nobby unrolled the paper and announced, "One double stateroom and one single on the *Roberta E. Biscuit*, departing at 9 p.m. tomorrow! Lucky you, Mr. Vimes. Clacks! What would we do without it, eh?"

There was a shout from above: "Stand back, man coming

down!" and Vimes saw the whole structure of the clacks tower tremble as the young man carefully lowered himself from one spar to another, testing every one before putting his weight on it. He dropped the last few feet and held out his hand to Vimes. "Pleased to meet you, Sir Samuel! Sorry it's shaky, but we were still working on it last night. A real rush job! Needs must when Lord Vetinari drives, you might say. We'll do it properly later if that's okay by you? I've got it lined up on a Grand Trunk tower, and they'll bounce it to anywhere you want, plus a feed down to a clacks on your house, too. Of course you'll have to have somebody manning this one to maintain the link, but from what I see that won't be a problem." The young man saluted Vimes and added, "Best of luck to you, sir, and now I'm off to have my meal and a wash."

There was another clang on the helmet of Nobby Nobbs, and a wad of paper wrapped around a pebble fell at his feet.

The young clacksman picked it up proprietorially and read the message. "Oh, it's just an acknowledgment of service closure, confirming that I am standing down for a break. My assistant typed it. He didn't really need to pass it on, but he is a conscientious little bugger and I have never seen such a quick study. Show him how to do something once and that's enough! Reliable little devil as well. And with those big hands he has no problem with the keyboard."

As the man strode off whistling down the hill, Vimes jumped to a conclusion like a grasshopper. "Stinky! Just you come down here, you little perisher!" he yelled.

"Right here, commander!" The little goblin was already standing almost between Vimes's boots.

"You? You! *You* operating a *clacks*? Can you read?"

Stinky held out both large hands. "No, but can look, but can remember! Green man say 'Stinky, this pointy thing it called A' and Stinky don't need telling twice, and he say 'This one, look like bum, he called B.' Good fun!" The cracked voice wheedled, but in a way that seemed to Vimes to be full of cynical knowingness. "The goblin is useful, goblin is trustworthy, goblin is helpful? *Goblin isn't dead!*"

And it seemed to Vimes that he was the only one hearing these words. Young Sam had shuffled up to hold Stinky's hand, but had thought better of it. Under his breath, Sam Vimes said, "What *are* you, Stinky?"

"What are *you*, Sam Vimes?" Stinky grinned. "Hang, Sam Vimes. Hang together or hang separately. Above all, hang on. Hang, Mr. Vimes."

Vimes sighed. "I think it's quite likely that I might, " he said gloomily. He looked around to find himself pinned in the gazes of Young Sam, Nobby Nobbs and the goblin girl who had been looking at Nobby as if the little corporal was an Adonis. Embarrassed, he shrugged and said, "Just a passing thought."

H OWEVER YOU PUT IT, Fred Colon was one of Vimes's oldest friends—and it was sobering to think that so was Nobby Nobbs. Vimes found the sergeant halfway down the goblin cave looking strangely pink, bemused, but nevertheless quite cheerful, possibly because he was eating a roasted rabbit like there was no tomorrow—which clearly had been the case for the rabbit. Cheery was watching him with some care from a distance, and when she saw Vimes gave him a smile and a thumbs-up sign, which was reassuring.

Fred Colon tried to salute, but had to think about it for a moment. "Sorry about this, Mr. Vimes, had some kind of nasty turn. All a bit vague, really, and suddenly here I am among these people."

Vimes held his breath and Colon continued, "Very nice, very

helpful, very generous, too. They've been giving me all kinds of mushrooms, extremely tasty. Not very well versed in the trouser department, but I speak as I find. Makes a man think; I ain't sure what, but it does." He looked around with a strange fluorescence in his eyes. "Nice in here, isn't it? Nice and calm away from the maddening crowd. Wouldn't mind staying here for a bit . . . Nice."

Sergeant Colon stopped, flung the rabbit bones over his shoulder and reached down quickly into the mess of stones beside him. He picked one up. Was it Vimes's imagination or did it twinkle for a moment as it once again turned into just a stone.

"Stay as long as you like, Fred," said Vimes. "I've got to go, but Nobby'll be around, and just about everybody else from the Watch or so it seems. Stay as long as you like"—he glanced at Cheery Littlebottom—"but perhaps not *too* long."

More thoughts passed as Young Sam's daily stroll progressed back down the hill and through the village, and when Jiminy appeared at the doorway of the pub and gave Vimes a little nod that spoke volumes, Vimes's passing thought was that an astute publican knows which way the wind is blowing and adjusts his sails accordingly. No one knew better than he that no one knows where rumors come from and how they are spread, but the little convoy, even though it included Nobby Nobbs and the goblin girl, got smiles and nods where a week ago there would have been blank stares. Because the dreadful truth is that nobody wants to support the losing side.

When they reached Ramkin Hall again Vimes found Sybil in the rose garden, apparently deadheading, something that had to be done because it was on the list of things you had to do in the country whether you liked to do it or not. She glanced up at her husband and then got on with what she was doing, and said quietly, "You've been worrying people, haven't you, Sam? Lady Rust popped in unexpectedly for a social visit, right after you left." *Snip! Snip!* went the pruning shears, furiously.

"Did you let her in?"

Snip! Snip! "Of course! Of course!"

There was another *Snip! Snip!* "And I gave her tea and chocolate macaroons, too. She may be an ignorant whey-faced bitch who gives herself a title that is not rightfully hers, but there is such a thing as manners, when all is said and done." *Snip! Snip! Snap!* "I only did that because that one rather spoils the symmetry, honestly. Anyway, I had a lecture about maintaining standards, and banding together in defense of our culture, you know the sort of thing, it's always just a code."

Lady Sybil leaned back with her shears poised, and regarded the rosebushes like a bloody-handed revolutionary looking for his next aristocrat. "Do you know what the bitch said? She said, 'My dear, who cares what happens to a few trolls! Let them take drugs if they want to, that's what I say.'" Eyes ablaze, Sybil continued, "And so I thought about Sergeant Detritus and how often he's saved your life, and then there was young Brick, that troll lad he adopted. And it made me so angry that I nearly said something unrepeatable! They think that I'm like them! I hate that! They just don't get it! They've got on well for years without ever having to think differently, and now they don't know how!" *Snip! Snip! Crack!*

"You've just killed a rosebush, dear," said Vimes, impressed. It took a pretty good grip to push those blades through an inch of what looked like a small tree.

"It was a brier, Sam, wouldn't ever do any good."

"You could have given it a chance, perhaps?"

"Sam Vimes, you treasure your ignorance of gardening, so

don't start weaving a social hypothesis in front of an angry woman holding a blade! There *is* a difference between plants and people!"

"Do you think her husband sent her?" Vimes said, standing back a little. "He is in the frame, you know, and I expect by the end of the day to be able to link him to smuggling, trafficking in goblins and certainly in attempting to send Jethro Jefferson abroad to get him out of the way. I know what happens to the goblins taken to Howondaland and it's not good for their health. Jefferson told me that Rust was behind the eviction of the local goblins three years ago. I'm hoping to get confirmation of this very shortly. All in all, it'll wipe the smile off his aristocratic face, at least."

The birds were singing and roses were pumping perfume into the air and Lady Sybil dropped the shears into her apron pocket.

"It will shame *old* Lord Rust, you know."

"Don't think I don't know that," said Vimes. "The old boy tried to warn me off when we first got here, which just about shows his talent as a tactician. But I'll say this for the old bastard: he is honorable, honest and straightforward. It's a shame that he is also pigheaded, stupid, and incompetent. But you're right, it'll hurt him, although he must have killed so many soldiers by his own incompetence that shame should by now be second nature to him, an old friend as it were." He sighed. "Sybil, every time I have to arrest some twit who thought he could get away with swindling or extortion or blackmail, well, I know that there is probably going to be a family in difficulties, you understand? I think about it. It preys on my mind. The trouble is, the idiots commit the crimes! As it is, I'm trying to spare some of the hangers-on in this case, provided their gratitude results in testimony. I can stretch the law for the greater good, but that's the end of it."

Sybil nodded sadly, and then sniffed and said, "Can you smell smoke?"

Willikins, who had been standing patiently, said, "Corporal Nobbs and his, ahem, young . . . lady wandered off into the shrubbery with Young Sam, your ladyship. Sergeant Detritus accompanied them with what I now believe to be called . . ." Willikins savored the word like a toffee, "surreption."

This last fact was testified to by the shrubbery itself, because no shrubbery, however large, could hide the fact that a troll had just walked through it.

T HERE WAS A SMALL, neat fire burning in the shrubbery, watched passively by Detritus and Young Sam, and nervously by Corporal Nobbs, who was watching his new young lady cooking something on a spit.

"Oh, she's cooking snails," said Sybil, with every sign of approval. "What a provident young lady."

"Snails?" said Vimes, shocked.

"Quite traditional in these parts, as a matter of fact," said Sybil. "My father and his chums used to cook them up sometimes after a drinking session. Very wholesome, and full of vitamins and minerals, or so I understand. Apparently if you feed them on garlic they taste of garlic."

Vimes shrugged. "I suppose that has to be better than them tasting of snails."

Sybil pulled Sam off to one side and said quietly, "I think the goblin girl is the one that they call Shine of the Rainbow. Felicity says she's very smart."

"Well, I don't think she'll get anywhere with Nobby," said Vimes. "He's carrying a torch for Verity Pushpram. You know, the fishmonger?"

Sybil whispered, "She got engaged last month, Sam. To a lad

who's building up his own fishing fleet." They stared through the leaves and tiptoed away.

"But she's a goblin!" said Vimes, out of his depth.

"And he is Nobby Nobbs, Sam. And she is quite attractive in a goblin sort of way, don't you think? And to be honest, I'm not sure that even Nobby's old mother knows what species her son is. Frankly, Sam, it's not our business."

"But what if Young Sam eats snails?"

"Sam, given what he's already eaten in his short life I wouldn't worry, if I was you. I expect the girl knows what she's doing, they generally do, Sam, believe me. Besides, this is limestone country and there's nothing poisonous for the snails to eat. Don't worry, Sam!"

"Yes, but how will—"

"Don't worry, Sam!"

"Yes, but I mean—"

"Don't worry, Sam! There's a troll and a dwarf in Lobbin Clout that have set up home together, so I've heard. Good for them, I say, it's their business and definitely not ours."

"Yes, but—"

"*Sam!*"

DURING THE AFTERNOON SAM Vimes worried. He wrote dispatches and walked up to the new tower to send them. Goblins were sitting around the tower now, staring at it. He tapped one of them on the shoulder, handed it the messages and watched it climb the tower as if it were horizontal. A couple of minutes later it came down with a smudged confirmation-of-sending slip, which it handed to him along with several other messages before sitting down to stare at the tower again.

He thought: you have lived your life in and around a cave in a hill and now here is this magical thing that sends words, right on your doorstep. That's got to command respect! Then he opened the two messages that had arrived for him, carefully folded up the paper and walked back down the hill, breathing carefully and taking care not to punch the air and whoop.

When Vimes reached the cottage of the woman who, to Young Sam, would forever be the poo lady, he stopped to hear the music. It came and went, there were false starts, and then the world revolved as liquid sound called out of the window. Only then did he dare to knock at the door.

Half an hour later, walking with the measured gait of the career copper, he proceeded to the lockup. Jethro Jefferson was sitting on a stool outside. He was wearing a badge. Feeney was learning fast. The constabulary of the Waterside owned precisely one badge, made of pot metal, and so, pinned to the shirt of the blacksmith was a carefully cut-out cardboard circle with, inscribed in painstaking handwriting, the words "Constable Jefferson works for me. Be told! Signed: Chief Constable Upshot."

There was a second, empty stool by the blacksmith, reflecting the doubling of the staff. Vimes sat down with a grunt. "How do you like being a copper, Mr. Jefferson?"

"If you're looking for Feeney, commander, he's on his lunch break. And since you ask, I can't say coppering sits very well with me, but maybe it's the kind of thing that grows on you. Besides, the smithy is a bit quiet right now, and so's the crime." The blacksmith grinned. "No one wants *me* chasing them. I hear things are happening, right?"

Vimes nodded. "When you see Feeney, tell him that the Quirm constabulary has picked up two men who apparently volunteered the information that they had shanghaied you, amongst other misdemeanors, and it seems they have a whole lot of other information that they are desperate to tell us in exchange for a certain amount of clemency."

Jefferson growled. "Give me five minutes with 'em and I'll show 'em what clemency is."

"You're a copper now, Jethro, so you don't have to think like that," said Vimes cheerfully. "Besides, the balls are all lining up."

Jefferson gave a hollow laugh, laden with malice, "I'd line their balls up for them . . . and just you see how far apart. I was a kid when the first lot were taken and that bloody Rust kid was there all right, yes indeed, urging everybody on and laughing at them poor goblins. And when I ran out into the road to try and stop it, some of his chums gave me a right seeing to. That was just after my dad died. I was a bit innocent in those days, thought that some people were better than me, tipped me hat to gentry and so on, and then I took over the forge and if that don't kill you it makes you strong."

And he winked, and Vimes thought, you'll do. You'll probably do. You've got the fire.

Vimes patted his shirt pocket and heard the reassuring rustle of paper. He was rather proud of the note at the end of the clacks message, which was a personal one from the Commandant in Quirm. It read, "When they heard that you were on the case, Sam, they were so chatty that we used up two pencils!"

And then Sam Vimes went to the pub just as the men were coming in and sat in the corner nursing a pint of the beetroot juice with a touch of chilli, to help down a snack consisting of one pick-led egg and one pickled onion nestling in a packet of crisps. Vimes did not know very much about gastronomy, but he knew what he liked. And, as he sat there, he saw people talking to one another and looking at him, and then one of them walked slowly over, holding his hat in front of him in both hands as if in penitence. "Name of Hasty, sir, William Hasty. Thatcher by trade, sir."

Vimes moved his legs to make room and said, "Pleased to make your acquaintance, Mr. Hasty. What can I do for you?"

Mr. Hasty looked around at his fellows, and got that mixed assortment of waves and hoarse whispers that adds up to "Get on with it!" Reluctantly he turned back to Vimes, cleared his throat, and said, "Well, sir, yes, of course we knew about the goblins and no one liked it much. I mean they're a bloody nuisance if you forget to lock your chicken coop and suchlike, but we didn't like what was done, because it wasn't . . . I mean, wasn't *right*, not done like that, and some of us said we would suffer for it, come the finish, because if they could do that to goblins then what might they think they could do to real people, and some said real or not, it wasn't right! We're just ordinary people, sir, tenants and similar, not big, not strong, not important, so who would listen to the likes of us? I mean, what could we have *done*?"

Heads leaned a little forward, breaths were held, and Vimes chewed the very last vinegary piece of crisp. Then he said, directing his gaze to the ceiling, "You've all got weapons. Every man jack of you. Huge, dangerous, deadly weapons. You could have done *something*. You could have done *anything*. You could have done everything. But you didn't, and I'm not sure but that in your shoes I might not have done anything, either. Yes?"

Hasty had held up a hand. "I'm sure we're sorry, sir, but we don't have weapons."

"Oh, dear me. Look around. One of the things that you could have done was think. It's been a long day, gentlemen, it's been a long week. Just remember, that's all. Remember for next time."

In silence, Vimes walked across to Jiminy at the bar, noticing above the man a patch on the wall showing gleaming paint on the plaster. For a moment Vimes's memory filled that space with a goblin's head. Another little triumph.

"Jiminy, these gentlemen are drinking at my expense for the rest of the evening. See they get home okay even if wheelbarrows have to be deployed. I'll send Willikins down to settle with you in the morning."

Only the sound of his boots broke the silence as he walked to the pub door and closed it gently behind him. Fifty yards up the road he smiled when he heard the cheering start.

T HE *Roberta E. Biscuit* was, unlike the *Wonderful Fanny*, a boat that strutted its stuff. It looked like a Hogswatch decoration, and on one deck a small band was trying to play as hard as a large band. Waiting on the quayside, though, was a man wearing a hat that the captain of any fleet would desire. "Welcome aboard, your grace, and of course your ladyship. I'm Captain O'Farrell, master of the *Roberta*." Then he looked down at Young Sam and said, "Want to take a turn at the wheel, young shaver? That shall be arranged! And I bet your daddy would like a turn, too." The captain shook Vimes's hand industriously, saying, "Captain Sillitoe had nothing but good things to say about you, sir, nothing but good things indeed! And he hopes to see you again some day. But in the meantime, it's my duty, sir, to make you King!"

The thoughts of Sam Vimes collided in their rush to get through first. Something about the word "king" was getting in the way.

Still smiling, the captain said, "That is to say King of the River, sir, a little honor that we bestow on those heroes who have taken on Old Treachery and bested him! Allow me to present you with this gold-ish medal, sir. It's a small token, but show it to any captain on the river and you'll be carried for free, sir, from the mountains to the sea if you so desire!"

Whipped to a frenzy by the oration, the crowd burst into loud applause and the band struck up with the old classic "Surprised, Aren't You?" and bouquets of flowers were hurled into the air, and then picked up again carefully, because waste not, want not. And the band played and the wheels turned and the water was whisked into a foam as the Vimes family went down the river for a wonderful holiday.

Young Sam was allowed to stay up to see the dancing girls, although he didn't see the point. Vimes, however, did. And there was a conjuror and all the other entertainment people subject themselves to in the name of fun, although he did laugh a bit when the conjuror picked his pocket in order to put in the ace of spades and found himself holding the knife that Sam had brought along just in case. When you aren't expecting it, that's when you should expect it!

And the conjuror had *not* expected it and looked goggle-eyed at Vimes until he said, "Oh my, you're *him*, aren't you? Commander Vimes himself!" And to Vimes's horror, he turned to the crowd with, "A big hand, please, ladies and gentlemen, for the hero of the *Wonderful Fanny!*"

In the end Vimes had to take a bow, which meant obviously that Young Sam took a bow next to him, causing much moistening of female eyes throughout the restaurant. And then the barman, who apparently didn't know the score, created on the spot the "Sam Vimes," which Sam later pretended to be embarrassed about when it became part of the repertoire in every drinking establishment on the Plains, apart from, of course, those where the clientele tended to open their bottles with their teeth.* In fact, he was so overcome by the honor that he actually drank one of the cocktails and another afterward as well, on the basis that Sybil couldn't really

---

* Or, perhaps, somebody else's.

object in the circumstances. Then he sat signing beer mats and pieces of paper and chatting to people rather more loudly than he normally chatted until even the barman decided to call it a day and Sybil towed her tipsy husband to bed.

And on the way to their suite he distinctly overheard one lady say to another in passing, "Who's the new barman? Never seen him on this run before . . ."

THE *Roberta E. Biscuit* plowed on into the night, the water leaving a temporary white trail behind her ample stern. One ox had been led into the stable in the scuppers, leaving the other one to maintain some sensible headway while the pleasure cruise paddled toward the morning. Everyone except the pilot and the lookout was sleeping, drunk or otherwise prone. The barman was nowhere to be seen; barmen come and go, after all—whoever notices the barman? And in the corridor of staterooms a figure waited in the shadows, listening. It listened for whispers, creaks and snores building up.

There was a snore, oh yes! The shadow drifted along the dark corridor, the occasional betraying creak lost among the symphony of sounds made by any wooden boat under way. There was a door. There was a lock. There was a gentle exploration; being the kind that *portrays* cunning and strength rather than actually having them. There was a lockpick, a delicate movement of hinges, and the same movement again as the door was gently pushed shut from the inside. There was a smile so unpleasant that it could almost be seen in the dark, especially by the dark-assisted eye, and so there was a scream, instantly cut short—

"Let me tell you how this is going to be," said Sam Vimes, as urgent sounds suddenly filled the corridor. He leaned over the body spreadeagled on the floor. "You will be humanely handcuffed for the rest of this voyage, and you will be watched carefully by my valet Willikins, who, apart from making a really good cocktail, is also not burdened by being a policeman." He squeezed a little harder and went on in a conversational tone, "Every now and again I have to sack a decent copper for police brutality, and I *do* sack them, you may be sure of that, for doing what the average member of the public might do if they were brave enough and if they had seen the dying child, or the remains of the old woman. They would do it to restore in their mind the balance of terror." Vimes squeezed again. "Often the law treats *them* gently, if it worries about them at all, but a copper, now, he's a lawman—certainly if he works for me—and that means his job stops at the arrest, Mr. Stratford. So what's stopping me from squeezing the life out of a murderer who has broken into the room he thought would hold my little boy, with, oh dear me, such a lot of little knives? Why will I squeeze him only to unconsciousness, while despising myself for every fragment of breath I begrudge him? I'll tell you, mister, that what stands between you and sudden death right now is the law you don't acknowledge. And now I'm going to let you go, just in case you die on me, and I couldn't have that. However, I suggest you don't try and make a run for it, because Willikins is not bound by the same covenant as I am, and he is also quite merciless and very fond of Young Sam, who's sleeping with his mother, I'm glad to say. Understand? You picked the single room, didn't you, where the little boy would be. It's lucky for you that I'm a bastard, Mr. Stratford, because if you'd broken into the stateroom, where my wife, although I never dare tell her so, is snoring at least as loud as any man, you would have found that she has at her command a considerable amount of weaponry and, knowing the temper of the Ramkins, she would have quite probably done things to you that would make Willikins say 'Whoa, that's going a bit too far.' What they have they keep, Mr. Stratford."

Vimes momentarily changed his grip. "And you must think I'm a bloody fool. Some bloke they reckoned was a great thinker once said, 'Know yourself.' Well, I know myself, Mr. Stratford, I'm ashamed to say, right down to the depths, and because of that I know *you*, like I know my own face in the shaving mirror. You're just a bully who found it easier and easier and decided that everybody else wasn't really a real person, not like you, and when you know that, there's no crime too big, is there? No crime you won't do. You might reflect that, while you're going to hang, I'm quite certain that Lord Rust, your boss, will in all probability walk free. Did you really think he'd protect you?"

The prostrate Stratford mumbled something.

"Sorry, sir, didn't quite catch that?"

"King's evidence!" Stratford blurted out.

Vimes shook his head, even if Stratford couldn't see it. "Mr. Stratford, you're going to hang, whatever you say. I'm not going to bargain with you. You must surely realize that you have nothing to bargain with. It's that simple."

On the floor Stratford growled, "Damn him! I'll tell you anyway! I hate the smarmy bugger! What do you want me to say?"

It was a good job that he couldn't see Vimes's face, and Vimes merely said, "However, I'm sure that Lord Vetinari will be very happy to hear anything that you have to say, *sir*. He's of a mercurial nature and I'm sure there is hanging or *hanging*."

Slumped on the floor and wheezing, Stratford said, "Everyone had that bloody cocktail, I saw them! You had three, and everybody says you're a lush!"

There was laughter as the door came open, letting in a little light. "His grace had what you might call the Virgin Sam Vimes," said Willikins, "no offense meant to the commander: ginger and chilli, a dash of cucumber juice and a lot of coconut milk."

"And very tasty," said Vimes. "Take him away, Willikins, will you, and if he tries anything you know what to do . . . you were born knowing what to do."

For a moment Willikins touched his forelock and then said, "Thank you, commander, I appreciate the compliment."

AND SAM VIMES FINISHED his holiday. Of course it couldn't be entirely fun, not with the clacks, not with people sending messages like, "I don't want to bother you, but this will only take a moment of your time . . ."

A great many people didn't want to bother Sam Vimes, but with a great effort of will they somehow managed to overcome their distaste and do so nevertheless. One of them, and this message did not contain an apology of any sort, came from Havelock, Lord Vetinari, and read, "We will talk about this."

That morning Vimes hired a small boat with its captain and spent a happy time with Young Sam picking periwinkles off the rocks on one of the many small islands off the Quirm coast, and then they gathered driftwood, made a fire, and boiled them and ate them with the help of a pin, racing to be the first to get one wiggly morsel out of its shell, and of course there was brown bread and butter and finally plenty of salt and vinegar, so that the periwinkles tasted of salt and vinegar rather than of periwinkles, which would be a disaster.*

With the boys out of the way, Sybil changed the world in her own quiet way, by sitting at the table in their apartment and

---

* For those unfamiliar with them, periwinkles, like cockles and whelks, might be considered the snot of the sea.

writing, in the neat cursive script that she had been taught as a girl, a large number of clacks messages. One of them was to the Director of the Royal Opera House of which her ladyship was a major patron, another was to Lord Vetinari, and three more went to the secretary of the Low King of the dwarfs, the secretary of Diamond King of Trolls and the secretary of Lady Margolotta of Uberwald, ruler of all that country that was above ground.

But it didn't stop there. No sooner had the maid come back from carrying the first batch to the top of the hill than she was sent spinning up there again with all the rest. Lady Sybil was a ferocious writer of letters, and if there was any person of substance on the Plains and beyond who didn't get a letter from Sybil that day, it was because their name had fallen out of her beautifully bound and obsessively updated little black book, which was, in fact, a delicate pink with tiny embroidered flowers on it, and a small phial of perfume. Nevertheless the only comparable weapon in the entire history of persuasion was probably the ballista.

In the afternoon Lady Sybil took tea with some of her girl-friends, all old girls from the Quirm College for Young Ladies, and had a very satisfactory time talking about other people's children while silently, driven by messages sleeting across the land with a precision and speed that no wizard would have contemplated, the world began to change its mind.

CONCURRENTLY, VIMES TOOK YOUNG Sam to the zoo, where he met the keepers, nearly all of whom had known somebody on the *Wonderful Fanny* and who opened every door to them, and nearly every cage. The curator himself came along to witness this cheerful six-year-old who was methodically weighing giraffe poo on a pair of ancient snuff scales, dissecting it with a couple of old kitchen knives, and making notes in a notebook with a picture of a goblin on the front. But for Sam Vimes a highlight was the elephant's delivery that Young Sam had been looking forward to—just as the Vimes party approached, Jumbo obliged and his son was, almost literally, in a hog heaven. Not even the philatelist finding a rare reversed-head blue triangle stamp in an unregarded secondhand stamp collection could have been happier than Young Sam toddling away with his steaming bucket. Young Sam had seen the elephant.

And so had Sam Vimes. The curator had said that Young Sam was incredibly gifted, and seemed to have a natural grasp of the disciplines of natural philosophy, a comment that caused Sam's father to nod wisely and hope for the best.

They rounded off the day with a visit to the funfair, where Vimes gave the man a dollar for the ride on the upsy-daisy machine and was given change for a quarter-dollar. When he objected the man swore at Vimes, lashed out and was surprised to be caught in a grip of steel, marched through a cheering crowd and handed over to the nearest Quirm copper, who saluted and asked if Vimes could sign his helmet. That was a small thing, but, as Vimes always said, behind small things you often find big things. He also won a coconut, a definite result, and Young Sam got a stick of rock candy with "Quirm" all the way through, which stuck his teeth together, another memorable occasion.

I N THE MIDDLE OF the night Vimes, who had been listening to the pounding of the surf for some time, said, "Are you awake, dear?" And then, because this is how these things are done, raised his voice a little when he got no answer and repeated, *"Are you awake, dear?"*

"Yes, Sam. I am now."

Vimes stared at the ceiling. "I wonder if it's all going to work."

"Of course it will! People are very enthusiastic about it, you know; they're intrigued. And I've pulled more strings than an elephant's corset. It will work. What about you?"

There was a gecko on the ceiling; you didn't get them in Ankh-Morpork. It looked at Vimes with jeweled eyes. He said, "Well, it'll be more or less a standard procedure." He shifted uneasily, and the gecko retreated to the corner of the room. "I'm a bit worried, though, some things I've done come within the law and one or two others are rather *ad hoc*, as it were."

"You were just opening a way for the law to flow in, Sam. The end justifies the means."

"I'm afraid a lot of bad men have used that to justify bad things, dear."

Under the covers Sybil's hand reached out to touch his. "That's no reason why one good man shouldn't use it to justify a good thing. Don't *worry*, Sam!"

Woman's logic, Sam thought: everything is going to be all right because it *ought* to be all right. The trouble is, reality is never as simple as that and doesn't allow for paperwork.

Vimes dozed comfortably for a while and then heard Sybil say, in a whisper, "He's not going to escape, is he, Sam? You said he's good with locks."

"Well, they have damn good locks on the cells here in Quirm, there's a guard watching him at all times and he's going to be taken up to Ankh-Morpork on their hurry-up wagon under armed escort. I can't imagine the circumstances that would allow him to escape. After all, the Quirm lads want to do this one by the numbers. I bet they'll have shined up their armor until it looks like silver. They'll want to impress me, you see? Don't worry, I'm certain nothing will go wrong."

They lay there, comfortable, and then Vimes said, "The curator of the zoo was very complimentary about Young Sam."

Sleepily, Sybil murmured, "Perhaps he'll be another Woolsthorpe, but maybe this time with the missing ingredient of common sense."

"Well, I don't know what he's going to be," said Sam Vimes, "but I do know he'll be good at it."

"Then he'll be Sam Vimes," said Sybil. "Let's get some sleep."

NEXT DAY THE FAMILY went home, which is to say that Sybil and Young Sam went home to Ankh-Morpork on a fast coach, after a small hiatus which led to Young Sam's growing collection being removed from inside the coach and strapped to the roof, while Sam Vimes took the *Black-Eyed Susan* back to the Hall, because there was still a matter of business to be concluded. Since he was a King of the River the pilot let him steer for part of the way, admittedly staring obsessively over his shoulder, just in case. And Vimes had fun, an infrequent event. It is a strange thing to find yourself doing something you have apparently always wanted to do, when in fact up until that moment you had never known that you had always wanted to do it, or even what it was, but Sam Vimes, for a moment upon the world, was a riverboat pilot and was as happy as a cat full of sixpences.

That night he lay alone in the vastness of Ramkin Hall—except, of course, for the hundred or so servants—turning the events of the previous week over and over in his head, and especially his own actions during them. Time and again he cross-examined himself mercilessly. Had he cheated? Not exactly. Had he misled? Not exactly. Had he acted as a policeman should? Well, now, that *was* the question, wasn't it?

In the morning two young maids brought him his breakfast and Vimes was amused to see that they were accompanied by a footman as a chaperone. In a way he found that rather flattering. Then he went for a walk through the lovely countryside, listening to the liquid notes of the robin et cetera (he couldn't remember the names of the others, but they were jolly good singers all the same).

And as he walked he was aware of eyes upon him from every cottage and field. One or two people came up to him, shook him frantically by the hand and ran away just as quickly, and it seemed to Vimes that the world was dragging around after him. Nervousness was so saturating the atmosphere that he felt that any time soon he should shout "BOO!" at the top of his voice.

But Vimes was merely waiting . . . Waiting for the evening.

THE COACHES STARTED TO arrive at Ankh-Morpork's Opera House very early. This was going to be an important occasion: it was said that not only the Patrician would be there, but that he would be accompanied by Lady Margolotta, ruler of all Uberwald, plus the dwarf ambassador, and the black ruby viceroy of Diamond King of Trolls, who arrived in the city with almost as many courtiers, secretaries, bodyguards, chefs and advisors as had been brought by the ambassador from the dwarfs.

In an unsophisticated way, the people of Ankh-Morpork were very sophisticated and the streets buzzed more busily than usual. Something like this was important. Great matters of state would be settled over the canapés. The fate of millions and suchlike would be most likely decided by a quiet word in a corner somewhere and thereafter the world would be a slightly different place, you see if it isn't.

Unless you had a gold-edged invitation to the Opera House

that evening this was no occasion to be fashionably late, in case you were left fashionably standing fashionable at the back, craning unfashionably to see over the heads of other people.

T OWARD SUNSET VIMES LOUNGED outside the lockup, happy to acknowledge the fraternal salute of the pilot of a small boat that sailed past. Then he strolled along the lane until he reached the pub and took a seat on the bench outside. He took out his snuffbox, looked at it for a moment and decided that on an occasion like this Sybil would have probably allowed him a cigar.

Through the smoke of the first luxurious pull he stared at the village green and most especially at that pillar of what seemed to be broken wickerwork. Somehow, soundlessly, it was speaking to him, calling to him, just as it had when he had first seen it. After a few more thoughtful puffs he wandered toward the pub door. Jiminy beamed at him from under the freshly painted sign of the Commander's Arms, where he was enjoying the pint that the parsimonious publican drinks every day when cleaning the pipes. It's old beer, obviously, but what's beer but liquid bread, eh? And bread can't do you no harm.

"You look a bit preoccupied, commander," said the publican. "A mite pensive, as it were?"

Vimes nodded toward the tottering spire. "How important is that, my friend?"

The barman glanced at the stack as if he couldn't care less. "Well, you know, it's just a load of old wicker hurdles, that's all. They just stack them there after the annual sheep fair so they don't get in the way. A bit of a landmark, you might say, but not that much."

"Oh," said Vimes. He stared at the tower. Nothing really, then, but nevertheless it spoke to him.

Vimes stared at the heap for a while and then followed Jiminy into the bar.

"How much brandy do you have in here?"

"Not much call for it, but I'd say five or six bottles and a small barrel." Jiminy stared intently at Vimes. Vimes knew Jiminy for what he was: nothing else but a man who knew enough to always be on the winning side.

Vimes puffed his cigar again. "Put two of them aside for me, will you? And you'd better make sure you've got good beer on tap, because pretty soon you're going to have a lot of customers."

He left the barman bustling as he went back outside and he continued to stare, his mind elsewhere, and in many places. Of course it'll work, he told himself. They've all got watches and I know they'll have synchronized them, even if they don't know how to spell synchronize. It's a shout like any other, and I've trained most of them and I reckon that they know that if somebody says to them, "Do you know who I am?" they know enough to say, "Yes, you're nicked!" and he smiled inwardly when he thought that among the officers drafted in from the city were two trolls, two vampires, a werewolf and a dwarf. That's what they probably call symbolic, he thought. He pulled out his own watch again, just as the early seekers of an evening pint began to appear. Right about . . . now.

T HERE WAS A HUGE jamming of coaches around the Opera House as would-be patrons, high or low, forsook their carriages and took to their feet, fighting their way through the throng that was seeking admission. Of course, it helped if you had a squad of trolls or dwarfs with you.

Ankh-Morpork liked surprises, provided they didn't involve the revenue. The curtain was not due to go up for another hour, but that didn't matter, because the important thing was to be there and even more importantly to be seen to be there, especially by the people *you* wanted to see. Whatever it was going to be it was going to be an occasion, and you would have been there and people would have seen you there and it was important and, therefore, *so were you*.

It would be a night to remember, even if the mysterious performance was an act to forget. The really rich often put on these things out of vanity, but this one looked particularly mysterious and possibly a jolly good laugh if it fell on its face.

Day was turning into night. The pub was filling up, as were the drinkers, who had been told by Jiminy that they were drinking courtesy of Commander Vimes, again. And Jiminy watched him carefully from the doorway as the shadows lengthened and Vimes stood there, motionless, occasionally looking at his watch.

At last the lad everybody knew as young Feeney turned up, with his arm still in its cast but, nevertheless, the old boys agreed amongst themselves, looking rather more grown-up than they'd ever seen him before. He was accompanied by Jefferson the blacksmith, whom they regarded as a ticking bomb at the best of times, and he had a badge, just like Feeney. People overflowed from the pub as the two of them went up to Vimes, and there was an unheard conversation. They'd wondered why the blacksmith was carrying a megaphone, but now they watched him hand it to Vimes, and Feeney and the blacksmith walked back toward the pub and people parted like a wave to let them through.

Vimes looked at his watch again. More people were hurrying toward the green. People with an instinct for the dramatic had run home to say that something was up and you'd better come and look. And country people liked a spectacle, or even a serious death, just like city people. They too liked to say, "I was there," even if it came out as "I was there, ooh-arr."

Vimes put his watch in his pocket for the last time, and raised the megaphone to his lips.

"LADIES AND GENTLEMEN!" The blacksmith had hammered out a pretty good loud-hailer and the voice echoed across the green. "I have heard it said, ladies and gentlemen, that in the end all sins are forgiven." Out of the corner of his mouth he said, so that only Feeney and the blacksmith could hear, "We shall see." And then he continued. "Bad things have been done. Bad things have been ordered. Bad orders have been obeyed. But they never will be again . . . will they, ladies and gentlemen? Because there needs to be a law, but before there is a law, there has to be a crime!"

There was absolute silence in the gloom as he walked over the green to the tower and broke the two bottles of brandy on its woodwork, stepped back a little way and threw the glowing end of his cigar after them.

I N THE OPERA HOUSE the gossip faded and died as Lady Sybil stepped through the curtains and onto the stage. She was a woman of, as they say, ample proportions, although she felt that some of them were more than ample. However, she could afford the very best dressmakers and did indeed have the manner and poise that were the symbol of her class, or at least the class she had been born into, and so she stepped out in front of the curtain and applause broke out and grew. When she judged that it had gone on long enough she made a little gesture which magically silenced the auditorium.

Lady Sybil had exactly the right voice for these occasions. Somehow she could make everybody think she was talking just to them. She said, "My Lord Patrician, Lady Margolotta, your grace the viceroy, ambassadors, ladies and gentlemen, I am so touched you have all decided to come along to my little twilight soirée, especially since I have been rather naughty and have been very sparing of information." Lady Sybil took a deep breath, which caused several elderly gentlemen near the front of the audience to very nearly burst into tears.*

"I have been privileged recently to find a musician beyond compare, and without more ado I will let you into this wonderful secret. Can we have the house lights down, Jeffrey? Good. Ladies and gentlemen, I am honored to be able to present to you tonight Tears of the Mushroom playing her own composition, *The Twilight Serenade*. I hope you will like it, and, in fact, I know that you will."

Lady Sybil stepped back as the curtains dragged themselves aside, and took a chair next to Tears of the Mushroom, who was seated obediently at her concert harp.

Beneath the seemingly impregnable composure, Sybil's heart was bouncing like a flamenco dancer. A low light—that had been the thing. The girl shouldn't be able to see the thousands out there. Sybil had taken her in hand, fearful that sudden exposure to the massed gaze of Ankh-Morpork, far from her home, would

---

* It had been said by someone years before that to see Sybil Ramkin's upholstered bosom rise and fall was to understand the history of empires.

have some terrible effect, but in fact it wasn't working like that. The girl had a curious tranquillity, as if she hadn't realized that she should be in awe. She smiled at Sybil in her strange way and waited, with fingers poised, over the strings. There was no sound but the susurration of people asking one another what the intense little figure they were seeing really was. Lady Sybil smiled to herself. By the time they realized, it would be too late. She looked at her watch.

THE FLAMES WERE SO high over the Ramkin Estate that the blaze could surely be seen all the way to Ankh-Morpork (bet you a gallon of brandy and a brace of turbot). There was barely any wind and it stood there like a beacon.

Vimes announced to the gathered throng, "Ladies and gentlemen, the area known as the Shires is under the rule of law tonight, and by that I mean the proper law, the law that is written down for everybody to see, and even to be changed if enough people agree. Chief Constable Upshot and Constable Jefferson are currently acting with the backing of their colleagues in the Ankh-Morpork City Watch, who would like to be assured that their colleagues receive the respect that is due. At this moment, a number of people from the Shires are being courteously brought here, although possibly to their dismay. Some of them will be the people who call themselves your magistrates and they will be taken away and asked to explain to a lawyer by what right they have assumed that position. If any one of you wants to argue with me, please come on and do so. The law is there for the people, rather than the other way round. When it is the other way round don't hesitate to grab your weapons, understand? The bar is still free, BUT BEFORE YOU STAMPEDE, THERE IS ONE MORE THING!"

Vimes had to put the megaphone back to his mouth because the mention of "bar" and "free" in one breath has an invigorating effect on people. "Right now, ladies and gentlemen, the goblins on Hangman's Hill, and indeed all other goblins in this area, are under my protection and the protection of the law. They are also subject to it, and I'll see to it that they have their own police force. It appears that they make natural clacks operators, so if they wish they can derive a revenue from so doing. I'm paying to have that clacks tower made permanent. You will benefit from it and so will they! They won't need to steal your chickens because they'll buy them from you, and if they *do* pinch them, then that's a crime and will be treated as such. One law, ladies and gentlemen . . . One size fits all!"

There was a cheer at this, as loud as any cheer in the vicinity of the prospect of a free bar can be. Of course, some of it might have been cheer at the fact that there was now some justice in the world, but on the whole it was quite likely that the bar won the day. You didn't have to be a cynic, you just had to understand people.

Vimes walked slowly toward the brightly lit pub, although the chances of getting inside were small. On the other hand, the chances of being given a hug by Miss Felicity Beedle were exactly one hundred per cent, because that was what she was doing, while being watched sheepishly by the blacksmith.

Vimes let go of her hand as she said, "You are a great man, commander, and I hope they put up a statue to you!"

"Oh dear, I hope not! You only get a statue when you're dead!"

She laughed, but Vimes said, "Listen, Miss Beedle, right now I don't know if I'm facing a statue or the sack. Some of the ways I've acted have been quite lawful, and others have been somewhat . . . debatable. I have an officer who can do with numbers what Sergeant Detritus can do with a hammer and he's going through the records of the son of one of the most influential people in Ankh-Morpork. And at the same time experienced police officers have visited the home of every member on the list of local magistrates. They are presenting them with a document, under my seal, informing them that they are no longer members of the self-elected board of magistrates of the Shires and reiterating that there may be formal charges to be made. My justification for this *ought* to work, but now? It's probably going to be a case of who has the best lawyers.

"The future, Miss Beedle, is somewhat uncertain, but I have to tell you that Young Sam, thanks to you, is probably going to be the world expert on poo. I must tell you that his mother and I are very pleased and only hope he aspires to higher things."

There was already the rattle of wagons and coaches in the distance; the sound of pigeons coming home to roost. "I think I'll soon have people to talk to, Miss Beedle, although I suspect that they'd rather not talk to me."

"Of course, commander. Can I say that the goblins seem very attached to your Corporal Nobbs? They treat him as one of their own, in fact, and he seems to be very fond of Shine of the Rainbow, as she is of him. You may be interested to know that the goblin name for him is Breaking Wind?"

She did not appear to smile and Vimes said, "Yes, very apt. I've always thought of Nobby as a draft-extruder. In fact, at my wife's *express* suggestion I have breveted him to the rank of sergeant for his stay here, and I hope that he'll assist the goblins to understand the benefits of the law—although, of course, the fusion might simply mean that people's chickens will be more expertly stolen from now on."

"Oh, you are a joker, commander!"

Vimes's expression had not changed and did not change now. "Yes, aren't I?"

He turned to Jefferson. "You know, things would have been a lot easier if you'd trusted me at the start."

The blacksmith shrugged. "Why should I have trusted you? You're a nob."

"Do you trust me now?"

The blacksmith's gaze remained steady for longer than Vimes could be happy with, but at last the man smiled and said, "Yeah, for now."

There was only one reply that Vimes could conceivably deliver. He smiled back and said, "A policeman's answer if ever I heard one."

As the couple strolled away there was a polite cough behind Vimes. He turned around and recognized the worried face of the colonel. "Do you have a minute, commander?"

Oh dear, thought Vimes.

"May I first say, commander, that I firmly agree with what you are doing and heavens know it needed doing." The colonel coughed again and said, "You will not have any disagreement with me on that point." Vimes waited and he continued, "My wife is a rather foolish woman who does appear to worship things like titles and, if I may say so, gives herself airs. Her father was a fisherman, an extremely good one, but do you know what? I think she would rather die than have anyone know."

There was another pause, and in the red light Vimes could see the shine on the old man's face. "What is going to happen to her, commander? At the moment, two polite young ladies in Ankh-Morpork City Watch uniform are standing guard over her in our house. I don't know if this helps very much, but the first thing she did when the arresting officers arrived was make them tea. There is such a thing as good manners, you see. Is she going to prison?"

Vimes felt the urge to say, "Would you like her to?" but he choked it back, because of the tears. "It's Charles, isn't it?"

The colonel looked surprised. "As a matter of fact, commander, it's Chas to my friends."

"Am I one of them?" And Vimes went on, "Other people will decide what has to be done here. I've merely made certain that nobody can inadvertently leave before I've had a chance to talk to them all, do you understand? I'm not the judge and nor would I be allowed to sit on a jury. Coppers aren't. And right now I'm not even certain what the penalty is for being stupid, vain and unthinking, although it does occur to me that if I was to put in prison every person guilty of these crimes we'd have to build about five hundred more.

"Speaking for myself," Vimes continued, "I'd like to see that murderers, if such I might find, are seen and dealt with as murderers, and the frightened and unthinking obedient also treated as they deserve. And right now, sir, I'd just like to not be living in a world of bloody fools. Personally, I have no particular interest in seeing your wife in prison, although I have a suspicion that if she was put in the women's wing of the Tanty her horizon would be usefully expanded and I expect she'd be so bossy that she'd be running the place after a couple of weeks."

"I do love her, you know," said the colonel. "We've been married for fifty-five years. I'm very sorry you've been troubled and, as I've said, I envy you your job."

"I think, perhaps, I should envy her her husband," said Vimes. "You know, colonel, I'll be happy just for the truth to come out, preferably on page one of the *Ankh-Morpork Times*, if you understand me."

"Absolutely, commander."

Vimes looked down at the man, who now looked rather relieved, and added, "For what it's worth, I suspect Lord Vetinari will make certain of his backing and possibly there will be some token punishments. Too many skeletons, you see, too many cupboards. Too many things around the world that maybe happened too long ago. What in the world can you do if some copper is going to go around digging them up? That's called realpolitik, sir, and so I suspect that the world will go on and you will not be very long without the company of your wife, which should, if I'm any judge, mean that you can have more or less anything for dinner that you want for the next week."

The idea seemed to uplift the colonel's spirits. The old man smiled. "Do you know, commander, I'm sure that, if treated with respect, potted shrimps might turn out to be my bosom chums."

The colonel held out his hand and Vimes took it, shook it and said, "Bon appétit."

AFTERWARD, THERE WERE SEVERAL explanations about why the Quirm wagon containing a very important prisoner overturned in the middle of the night and rolled down a very steep hill, coming to bits as it did so. You could blame the dark, you could blame the fog, you could blame its speed and above all you could blame the express mail coach from Ankh-Morpork that ran straight into it on the corner.

By the time the wounded were in any state to comprehend what had happened they were minus one prisoner, who appeared to have picked the lock of his shackles, and plus one guard whose throat had been cut.

It was dark, it was cold, it was foggy and, hunched together, the survivors waited until dawn. After all, how could you find a man in darkness?

STRATFORD WAS GOOD AT speed. Speed was always useful, and he stayed on the road that was just visible in the murk.

It didn't really matter where he went; after all, he knew no one had ever given a description of him that helped. It was a gift to be indescribable.

After a while, however, he was surprised and delighted to hear a horse trotting along the road behind him. Some brave traveler, he thought, and smiled in the fog and waited. To his further surprise, the horse was reined to a halt a little way from him and the rider slid off. Stratford could barely make out a shape in the shimmering, water-laden air.

"My word! The famous Mr. Stratford," said a voice cheerfully, as the stranger strolled toward him. "And let me tell you right now, if you make any kind of move you'll be so dead that the graveyards would have to run backward."

"I know you! Vimes sent *you*, after *me*?"

"Oh, dear me no, sir," said Willikins. "The commander doesn't know I'm here at all, sir, and nor will he ever. That is a certainty. No, sir, I'm here, as it might be, out of a matter of professional pride. By the way, sir, if you're thinking of killing me and taking my horse I'd be most grateful if you'd try that right now."

Stratford hesitated. There was something about the voice that induced hesitation. It was calm, friendly, and . . . worrying.

Willikins strolled a little closer and there was a chuckle in his voice. "My word, sir, I'm a bit of a fighter myself, and when I heard about you chopping up that girl and that, I thought, goodness me, I thought. And so the other day, when I had my day off in lieu—very important your day off in lieu, if you're a working man—I took a trip up to Overhang and learned a few things about you, and, my word, did I learn a few things. You *really* scare people, eh?"

Stratford still hesitated. This didn't sound right. The man had a straightforward and cheerful voice, like a man you didn't know very well having a companionable chat in the pub, and Stratford was used to people being very nervous when they spoke to him.

"Now, me," said Willikins, "I was raised by the street as a fighter and I fight dirty, you can depend on that, and I'll fight anybody, but I never punched a girl . . . oh, except Kinky Elsie, who was always game for that sort of thing and had me by the I'm-not-going-to-mentions at the time and my hands were tied, in more ways than one, as it were, and so I had to give her a sharp nudge with my foot. Happy days. But you? You're just a killer. Worthless. A bully. I fight because I might get killed and the other bloke might win, or maybe we'd both end up in the gutter, too weak to throw another punch, when, quite likely, we'd prop each other up and go to the pub for a drink and a wash."

He took another step closer. Stratford took a step back. "And you, Mr. Stratford, set out to kill Commander Vimes's little lad, or worse. And do you know what is even worser? I reckon that if you'd done so, the commander would have arrested you and dragged you to the nearest police station. But inside he'd be cutting himself up with razorblades from top to bottom. And he'd be doing that because the poor bugger is scared that he could be as bad as you." Willikins laughed. "Truth is, Mr. Stratford, from where I sits he's a choirboy, he really is, but there has to be some justice in the world, you see, not necessarily law justice, but *justice* justice, and that's why I am going to kill you. Although, because I'm a fair man I'm going to give you a chance to kill me first. That means one or other of us will die, so whatever happens the world is going to be a better place, eh? Call it . . . cleaning up. I know you have a weapon because you'd have run if you didn't, and so I reckon you have a blade from one of those poor buggers from Quirm and I warrant that in all the confusion you probably stabbed him with it."

"I did, too," said Stratford. "And he was a copper and you're just a butler."

"Very true," said Willikins, "and much older than you and heavier than you and slower than you, but still a bit spry. What've you got to lose?"

Only the horse, steaming patiently in the mist, saw what happened next, and being a horse was in no position to articulate its thoughts on the matter. Had it been able to do so it would have given as its opinion that one human ran toward another human carrying a huge metal stick while the other human quite calmly put his hand into his breast pocket. This was followed by a terrible scream, a gurgling noise and then silence.

Willikins staggered to the side of the road and sat down on a stone, panting a little. Stratford certainly had been fast, no doubt about that. He wiped his forehead with his sleeve, pulled out a packet of cigarettes and lit one, staring at nothing but the fog. Then he stood up, looked down at the shadow on the ground and said, *"But not fast enough."* Then, like a good citizen, Willikins went back to see he if he could help the unlucky gentlemen of the law, who appeared to be in difficulties. You should always help the gentlemen of the law. Where would we be without them?

T HE CHIEF SUB-EDITOR OF the *Ankh-Morpork Times* really hated poetry. He was a plain man and had devoted a large part of his career to keeping it out of his paper. But they were a cunning bunch, poets, and could sneak it up on you when your back was turned. And tonight, with the paper already so late that the lads downstairs were into overtime, he stared at the report just delivered by hand from Knatchbull Harrington, the paper's music critic. A man of whom he was deeply suspicious. He turned to his deputy and waved the page angrily. "'Whence came it, that ethereal music?' See what I mean? What's wrong with 'Where did that music come from'? Bloody stupid introductory sentence in any case. And what does ethereal mean, anyway?"

The deputy sub hesitated. "I think it means runny. Could be wrong."

The chief sub-editor stood in misery. "Definitely poetry!"

Somebody had played some music that was very good. Apparently it made everybody amazed. Why didn't that twit in his rather feminine purple silk shirts just write something like that? After all, it said everything that you needed to know, didn't it? He took out his red pencil, and just as he was applying it to the wretched manuscript there was a sound on the metal staircase and Mr. de Worde, the editor, staggered into the office, looking as if he had seen a ghost or, perhaps, a ghost had seen him.

He looked groggily at the two puzzled men and managed to say, "Did Harrington send in his stuff?"

The chief sub held out the offending stuff in front of him. "Yes, guv, a load of rubbish in my opinion."

De Worde grabbed it, read it with his lips moving and thrust it back at the man. "Don't you dare change a single word. Front page, Bugsy, and I hope to hell that Otto got an iconograph."

"Yessir, but, sir—"

"And don't bloody argue!" screamed De Worde. "And now, if you'll excuse me, I'll be in my office."

He clattered on up the stairs while the sub-editor and his deputy stood gloomily reading Knatchbull Harrington's copy again. It began:

W hence came it, that ethereal music, from what hidden grot or secret cell? From what dark cave? From what window into par-

adise? We watched the tiny figure under the spotlight and the music poured over us, sometimes soothing, sometimes blessing, sometimes accusing. Every one of us confronting ghosts, demons and old memories. The recital by Tears of the Mushroom, a young lady of the goblin persuasion, took but half an hour or, perhaps, it took a lifetime, and then it was over, to a silence which spread and grew and expanded until at last it exploded. Every single patron standing and clapping their hands raw, tears running down our faces. We had been taken somewhere and brought back and we were different people, longing for another journey into paradise, no matter what hell we had to atone for on the way.

T HE CHIEF SUB AND his deputy looked at each other with what Knatchbull would certainly have called a "wild surmise." At last, the deputy sub-editor ventured, "I think he liked it."

T HREE DAYS PASSED. THEY were busy days for Vimes. He had to get back into the swing again, although, to tell the truth, it was a case of getting out of one swing and into another one, while they were both swinging. So much paperwork to read! So much paperwork to push away! So much paperwork to delegate! So much paperwork to pretend he hadn't received and that might have been eaten by the gargoyles.

But today, in the Oblong Office, Lord Vetinari was close to ranting. Admittedly you needed to know him very well to realize this. He drummed his fingers on the table. "Snarkenfaugister? I'm sure she makes these things up!"

Drumknott carefully put a cup of coffee on his master's desk. "Alas, sir, there really is such a word. In Nothingfjord it means a maker of small but necessary items such as, for example, spills and very small clothes pegs for indoor use and half-sized cocktail sticks for people who don't drink long drinks. The term could be considered of historical interest, because my research this morning turned up the fact that the last known snarkenfaugister died twenty-seven years ago in a freak pencil-sharpener accident. As a matter of fact, I gather that your crossword adversary herself does actually come from Nothingfjord."

"Ah! There you have it! All those long winters sitting around the stove! Such terrible patience! But she runs the pet shop in Pellicool Steps! Dog collars! Cat biscuits! Mealworms! Such deviousness! Such subterfuge! Such a vocabulary! Snarkenfaugister!"

"Well, sir, she is now the chief crossword compiler for the *Times*, and I suppose those things go with the territory."

Lord Vetinari calmed down. "One down, one across. She has won and I am cross. And, as you know, I am very rarely cross, Drumknott. A calm if cynical detachment is generally my forte. I can change the fate of nations but am thwarted at every turn by an apparently blameless lady who compiles crosswords!"

Drumknott nodded. "Indeed, sir, but on that note, if you will permit me to extend that note a little, may I remind you that Commander Vimes is waiting in the other room."

"Indeed? Show him in, by all means."

Vimes marched in, saluted very *nearly* smartly, and stood to attention.

"Ah, your grace, it is good to see you back at last. How went your holidays, apart from lawless actions, ad hoc activities, fights, chases on both land and sea and indeed freshwater, unauthorized expenditure and, of course, farting in the halls of the mighty?"

Vimes's gaze was steady and just above the Patrician's eye line. "Point of detail, my lord: didn't fart, may have picked nose inadvertently."

"The exigencies of the service, I assume?" said Lord Vetinari wryly. "Vimes, you have caused a considerable amount of paperwork to cross my desk in the last few days. In some cases the writers wanted your head on a plate, others were more circumspect because the writers were in mortal dread of a prison cell. Can I make one thing perfectly clear, your grace, the law cannot operate retrospectively. If it did, none of us would be safe.

"Lord Rust junior may have done, indeed *has* done many bad things, but making slaves of goblins under current law cannot be one of them. However, as I suspect, the recent revelations about his additional activities have done his reputation a considerable amount of no good. You might not know this, Vimes, but in society this sort of thing can be worse than a prison sentence, possibly worse than a death. Young Gravid is a man with not many friends right now. I hope that will give you some pleasure."

Vimes said nothing, but he thought, *the ball dropped*.

Vetinari glared at him and said, "I have here an eloquent missive from Lord Rust senior, pleading for the life of, if not the freedom of, his son, who he fully admits has trodden the family honor into the mud." Lord Vetinari held up a hand. "His Lordship is an old man and so, Vimes, if your next remark was going to be something on the lines of *'even further'* then I suggest you deploy a little charity. His lordship is anxious to avoid a scandal. Apart from that, may I have *your* views?"

"Yes. The scandal has already taken place, sir, more than once," said Vimes coldly. "He trafficked in living, breathing and thinking people. Many of them died!"

"Once again, Vimes, I have to tell you that laws cannot be made retrospectively."

"That may be so," said Vimes, "but what about the troll kids, who took that damn rubbish? Are you going to ask the Diamond King if *they* should be retrospective?"

"I can assure you, Vimes, that the laws will be upheld, and since you ask, right now I am having to negotiate with the King who is demanding, *demanding* of me—me, Vimes—that young Lord Rust be handed over for questioning regarding the manufacture and distribution of absolutely deadly troll narcotics. Of course, under troll law the wretched man would be put to death, and I am saddened to say that at this moment in the complex world of human, troll and dwarven politics, I feel that that might have some long-term repercussions, making it an unfortunate option for this city. I have to negotiate this problem, and, believe me, it's going to take a lot of quid for the pro quo. And it's only nine thirty in the morning!"

Vimes's knuckles reddened. "They are living creatures who can talk and think and have songs and names, and he treated them like some kind of disposable tools."

"Indeed, Vimes, but, as I have indicated, goblins have always been considered a kind of vermin. However, Ankh-Morpork, the kingdom of the Low King and also that of the Diamond King, Uberwald, Lancre and all the independent cities of the plain are passing a law to the effect that goblins will henceforth be considered as sapient beings, equal to, if not the same as, trolls and dwarfs and humans and werewolves, et cetera et cetera, answerable to what we have agreed to call 'the common law' and also protected by it. That means killing one would be a capital crime. You have won, commander, you have won. Because of a song, commander. Oh, and of course other efforts, but it was your wife who got most of the ambassadors to her little amusement which, I may say, Vimes, was eloquence personified. Though frankly, Vimes, I find myself shamed. One spends one's life scheming, negotiating, giving and taking and greasing such wheels as squeak, and in general doing one's best to stop this battered old world from exploding into pieces. And now, because of a piece of music, Vimes, a *piece of music*, some very powerful states have agreed to work together to heal the problems of another autonomous state and, almost as collateral, turn some animals into people at a stroke. Can you imagine that, Vimes? In what world could that possibly happen? All because of a song at twilight, Vimes. *All because of a song.* It was a thing of strangely tinkling tones and unbelievable cadences which somehow found its way into our souls, reminding some of us that we have some. Lady Sybil is worth a dozen diplomats. You are a lucky man, commander."

Vimes opened his mouth to speak, but Vetinari interrupted. "And also a bloody fool, a bloody, headstrong fool. The law must start with a crime? I understand, but don't condone." Vetinari picked the letter off his desk. "Lord Rust asks that his son be given a moderately short sentence, subsequent to which he be allowed to emigrate to Fourecks, to start a new life. Since the man was deeply involved in smuggling the fine will be harsh."

He held up a hand. "No, hear me out; after all, I am the tyrant in this vicinity." Vetinari slumped into his chair, wiped his brow and said, "And I have already lost my temper with an otherwise inoffensive sweet lady who compiles crossword puzzles for the *Times*. However, Vimes, Lord Rust refers to you as a man of honor and probity and astonishing integrity and vigilance. Moreover, he is disinheriting his son, which means upon his death his title will devolve to his daughter Regina, a ferocious woman, very difficult and hot-headed. And that, Vimes, creates another problem for me. His lordship is extremely frail and, frankly, I was looking forward to dealing with the son, who is an ignorant, arrogant, pompous idiot, but his sister? She is smart!" and then, almost to himself, Lord Vetinari added, "But at least she doesn't compile crosswords . . . Now you can speak, commander."

"There was a murder," said Vimes sullenly.

Vetinari sighed hugely. "No, Vimes! There was a slaughter! Do you not understand? At that point goblins were vermin and no, do not shout at me! At this very moment in palaces and chancelleries all over the world goblins are becoming as human as you or I, but that was then. I would like you to be fully aware that the reason that Stratford would have gone to the tender mercies of Mr. Trooper is that he and his ruffians boarded the *Enormous Fanny*—Yes, what is it?"

Vetinari looked around as Drumknott tapped him on the shoulder. There was a muffled whispering before Vetinari cleared his throat and said, "Of course, I meant the *Wonderful Fanny*," and he did not exactly meet Vimes's gaze as he continued. "That was an act of piracy and the good people of Quirm, where the . . . boat in question was registered, are all in favor of the death penalty for that kind of thing. I am aware of his manifold other crimes but, alas, you can only hang a man once . . . Although, as it turned out, apparently Mr. Stratford was mortally wounded in a collision three nights ago, being thrown some distance from the wreckage with a surgically cut throat. Convenient, don't you think?"

"Don't you dare look at me like that, *sir.*"

"Heavens, I wouldn't accuse you, commander, I was just wondering if you knew of any other person with a grudge against the corpse?"

"Nossir," said Vimes, pulling himself to attention.

"You know, Vimes, some times your expression becomes so wooden that I think I could make a table out of it. Just tell me this: did you give any instructions?"

How does he do it? thought Vimes. How? Out loud he said, "I don't know what you are talking about, sir, but if what I suspect to be true is so, then the answer is no. If there was any foul play that night it wasn't by my order. I wanted to see Stratford on the gallows. That's *legal*." And he thought, I am never going to broach the subject with Willikins.

Vetinari's eyebrows rose as Vimes went on, "But his lordship's wretched son is being allowed to go on a long holiday full of sun, sea, surf and sand and economically priced wines!" He slammed his fist on the desk and Vetinari looked pointedly at it until Vimes took it away. "Are you going to leave it at that?"

"It has been known, as people put it, for the leopard to change its shorts. All of us hope for a little redemption, whether if we deserve it or not. We will keep an eye on the young fool, you can be certain of that."

"Oh, you're sending the Dark Clerks after him?"

"Vimes, the Dark Clerks are a myth, as everybody knows. To tell you the truth, some flunkey from our embassy down there will pay attention to his progress. And now the world is a better place, commander. You have no understanding, Vimes, no understanding at all of the deals, stratagems and unseen expedients by which some of us make shift to see that it remains that way. Do not seek perfection. None exists. All we can do is strive. Understand this, commander, because from where I sit you have no alternative. And remember, for this week's work *you* will be remembered. Lord Rust may not like it but news travels fast. The truth will be known and written down in the history books." Vetinari gave a wan smile. "It will, I shall see to it. And, slightly better than before, the world will continue to turn."

Vetinari picked up yet another piece of paper, appearing to glance at it, and said, "You may go, commander, in the knowledge that I, for so many reasons, envy you. My regards to your good lady."

Vimes looked at Drumknott. The man's face so assiduously betrayed nothing that it betrayed everything.

Vetinari pulled a file toward him and picked up his pen. "Don't let me detain you, commander."

A N HOUR LATER LORD Vetinari was sitting at his desk with his fingers steepled, apparently lost in thought, staring at the ceiling, and, to Drumknott's surprise, occasionally waving his hand as if conducting some hidden music. Drumknott knew enough not to disturb him, but at last he dared to say, "It was a most memorable recital, wasn't it, sir?"

Vetinari ceased being the invisible conductor and said, brightly, "Yes, it was, wasn't it? They say that the eyes of some paintings can follow you around the room, a fact that I doubt, but I am wondering whether some music can follow you for ever." He appeared to pull himself together and continued, "On the whole, the Rust dynasty, though not exactly empowered with brains, tends to be an honorable and patriotic bunch, by and large, am I not right, Drumknott?"

Drumknott meticulously and unnecessarily tidied some paperwork and said, "It is indeed so. Young Gravid is a regrettable exception."

"Do you think him beyond redemption?" said Vetinari.

"Quite likely not," said Drumknott, carefully folding a pen wiper. "However, Arachne is working in Fourecks at the moment as a filing clerk in our embassy. She pleaded for the position because she's particularly attracted by venomous spiders."

"Well, I suppose every girl should have a hobby," said Vetinari. "And are there a lot of them in Fourecks?"

"The place is positively overwhelmed, I am given to understand, sir, and apparently Arachne already has a large selection of them."

Vetinari said nothing, but remained sitting with eyes closed.

Drumknott cleared his throat. "They do say, sir, that in the end all sins are forgiven?"

Reluctantly, Havelock, Lord Vetinari tore his recollection away from the wondrous music that he longed to hear again. "Not all, Drumknott, not all."

I N BED THAT NIGHT in Scoone Avenue, listening to the absence of owls and nightjars, Vimes said, "You know, dear, I'll have to go back to the Shires soon. Feeney is a good lad but they need a proper headquarters and the right kind of guidance and that doesn't mean just Nobby Nobbs and Fred Colon."

Sybil turned over. "Oh, I don't know, Sam. Fred and Nobby aren't as bad as all that and might be all that's needed right now. I mean, they're coppers, but they amble about extremely slowly and on the whole it's good to see them around. Right now you've got two young men full of vim and vigor and if you don't want to upset things it might just be that, in this bewildered place, they should be backed up by slow and steady, don't you think?"

"You are, as always, right, my dear."

"Besides, I've seen Fred, and having to rethink his world view has clearly shaken him a little."

"He'll get over it," said Vimes. "Once you get past the stupid Fred there is, against all expectations, a decent man there."

Sybil sighed. "Yes, Sam, but that decent man needs a holiday out in the sunshine away from the smoke and the grime and the terrible spells."

"But they're the best bits!" said Vimes, laughing.

"No, he needs a holiday. Everybody needs a holiday, Sam, even you."

"I've just had one, dear, thank you."

"No, you had a few days interspersed with fighting and floods and murders and I don't know what else. Look at your desk, make certain everybody is on their toes, and then we'll go down there for another week, do you hear me, Sam Vimes?"

EPILOGUE

AND THREE MONTHS LATER Sam Vimes went on holiday again, and this time he was allowed to steer the *Black-Eyed Susan* all the way to Quirm without hardly hitting anything important, and was so happy that they had to find another cat full of sixpences for him to be as happy as.

He was amazed at how much fun a holiday could be, but not so amazed as he was eight months after that when he and Sybil were invited to be guests at the wedding of Ms. Emily Gordon to the eldest son of Sir Abuthknott Makewar, owner of the famous Makewar pottery manufactory and incidentally the inventor of Makewar's Crispy Nuts, the breakfast cereal of champions, without whose nourishing roughage the bowels of Ankh-Morpork would be more congested than was good for them. The wedding present from Vimes and Sybil was a silver egg coddler, Sybil being of the view that you can't go wrong with a coddled egg.

And Vimes was gratified when he noticed at the ceremony that one of the daughters was wearing a spanking new nurse's uniform and three of the others were sporting some quite fabulous and also, according to Sybil with great glee, quite scandalous bonnets from the new Gordon Bonnets range.

There was an apology from the ax-wielding Hermione, but according to her mother she was detained in the woods dealing with a very large and troublesome *Pinus*, which caused Vimes's face to go blank until Sybil nudged him and pointed out that the pinus strobus was the official name for the white pine.

But most of all, later that year, Vimes was totally amazed to find that the bestselling novel taking the Ankh-Morpork literary world by storm was dedicated to Commander Samuel Vimes.

The title of the book was *Pride and Extreme Prejudice*.

ABOUT THE AUTHOR

Terry Pratchett's novels have sold more than 75 million copies (give or take a few million) worldwide. He lives in England.